VILLAIN COMPLEX

Rory North

I love you the way the sky loves a storm.

Content information available at
rorynorth.com/content-warnings

Cover created by Rory North,
featuring photo by Artyom Korshunov; sourced from Unsplash

CHAPTER ONE

Supervillains weren't supposed to pay for coffee. In fact, Julian Godfrey had come into this very cafe last week—in full costume—to politely demand a free latte on his way home from holding a CEO hostage upstate. He'd already forgotten the man's name, but the ransom money was going to fund some extravagant kitchen upgrades in his apartment.

But today, Julian wasn't here for a drink. He was here to sit in the corner of the cafe and send emails and read and, of course, finalize his plan to take an entire city block hostage. Rather than a villainous costume, he was dressed in the clothes he wore to his day job at the library: black pants, a dark purple button-up, and a black blazer.

He did still want his coffee, though.

Julian contemplated tonight's plan as he stood in line. This would be the biggest demonstration of his power yet. He'd been preparing for months, and it had taken a lot of training to ensure he'd be able to pull it off.

Most importantly, he'd be doing it alone. He had to. If he succeeded, the city would be forced to realize him as a true threat. More than just the lackey of a bigger villain. He was already feared, to a degree, but maybe the people of New Atlas would finally regard him with the same awe as they did Blazar.

Julian planned to relinquish control of the apartment block in exchange for a considerable sum of cash. Not the most original idea, but money wasn't his real goal, anyway. He was going to lure in the city's biggest hero and completely destroy him. Or at least, kick his ass hard enough to keep him out of commission for a few months.

One of the cashiers waved Julian over. "Next, please!"

"Macchiato. Sixteen-ounce," he told her as he reached the register.

"That'll be five ninety-eight."

Julian opened his wallet and pulled out a single five-dollar bill. Damn. He'd thought he had more cash. "Hold on, let me find my card—"

"You're a dollar short?" came a voice from his right.

Julian glanced up. The woman who'd spoken removed a dollar from her own wallet and held it out to him, despite his fingers already starting to tug his credit card free. He briefly considered turning it down. He had plenty of money to burn, after all.

But why say no to convenience?

"Thank you," Julian said, looking her over as he accepted the dollar. She was nearly a foot shorter than him, probably around five-three. She wore a white flannel over an oversized teal New Atlas University tee, her skin was light brown, and—

"Your hair's blue," he noted, lifting an eyebrow. Her curly hair, pulled back into a ponytail, was dark for only a few inches at the roots. The rest was a faded turquoise.

She laughed. "Yeah, I get that a lot. And it's no trouble, really."

Julian watched her walk away while the cashier finished the transaction.

"Here's your change. We'll have that out in a minute." The cashier dropped a couple of pennies into his hand. "Next!"

Julian moved to the edge of the crowd waiting for drinks. Surprise lingered with him. Yes, sure, plenty of people were nice enough to offer a complete stranger a dollar without being threatened, but he'd already been reaching for his credit card. He hadn't *needed* the money.

He was intrigued enough to consider approaching the woman and starting a conversation, but she grabbed her coffee and left before he could settle on what to say. An employee called out his order a moment later. He took his macchiato and made his way to a table in a far corner of the cafe, one of the few that hadn't been taken over by college students or employees just getting off work.

You don't take a free drink from a restaurant because you can't afford it, Blazar had told him once. *If you're after money, you rob a bank. You take the drink to remind people you could be anywhere, at any time. You take the drink to remind people that they're never really safe.*

Julian sipped his coffee. His free hand closed into a fist, and a single stone formed in his grasp. The pebble rested on his palm when he opened it.

That was all he'd been able to do as a child. It took a lot of energy to form matter, after all. But even before he'd fully developed his geogenesis powers, he was at least able to manipulate his creations. Thank god for that. Blazar probably wouldn't have kept him around if all he could do was make tiny rocks.

Another sip. The block Julian would be attacking in a few hours was a short walk from here. He'd pass it on his way to the Complex. The area had become familiar—over the course of the past month, he had spent countless hours generating stone beneath the streets—but it would be nice to take one last look before he made his move tonight. He had a lot of asphalt to break through.

He took out his phone and responded to a few scheduling emails from other library employees. Checked the time. Skimmed the news. Checked the time again.

It was nearly five-thirty when he finished his coffee. He ran a hand through his dark hair as he rose to his feet, his anticipation growing. He hadn't been this excited about a fight in a long time.

During his walk to the Complex, Julian assessed the sidewalk beneath him, searching for the largest cracks, the weak spots where he could focus his efforts. Storm Warning would have no choice but to show up. This would be the biggest threat the city had ever seen—save for a few of Blazar's stunts, of course. It was hard to compete with some of the fires that man had started.

Around him, New Atlas basked in warm evening light and the atmosphere of spring. There was the incessant drone of traffic, sure, but there was also the chatter of birds and buzz of insects lured by the trees that city planners had crammed in wherever they could.

Fifteen minutes of walking brought Julian to the alley that hid the Complex's entrance. The elevator he took could only be accessed with a key, and the only floor it went to was the top.

The elevator was halfway up the building when a text came in from Blazar. *When are you returning to the COVE?*

About to walk in, Julian replied, unable to help a small sigh. He'd never dare say it to Blazar's face, but he hated calling their base the COVE. It wasn't the word itself that irritated him, but the absurd acronym Blazar had come up with to fit it: Complex Of Villainous Entities.

Well, the name didn't matter much anymore. There were only four of them left. Blazar was still a force to be reckoned with, but the days of an actual league of villains patrolling New Atlas were long gone.

The elevator door opened, allowing Julian to step directly into the open living area. At the opposite end of the space were the double doors to the balcony and a hallway leading to the bedrooms. To the left was a kitchen furnished with shiny high-tech appliances, and to the right were the couches and a massive monitor that Damselfly was currently using to watch reality TV.

"Hey, Julian." Damselfly looked up from where she was draped across the couch. Her long insect-like wings fluttered as she twisted herself around to watch Julian enter, glittering vibrant blue in the light from the kitchen. "How are your books?"

She didn't really care. The others took any opportunity they had to make a jab at Julian's day job. "Library's doing great," he told her. "Is Blazar in?"

"Nope."

"What about Lord Saturn?"

"Haven't seen her, either." Damselfly's head tipped to the side. Her chin-length waves of black hair moved with her, brushing against the pale skin of her face. "What are you up to?"

"I'm getting into a fight tonight," Julian told her.

"Ooh, Storm Warning?"

"Hopefully."

The strongest hero in the city. The most charismatic. And the most fun to fight. The other New Atlas heroes who popped up enough to be household names hardly did anything more than fight common criminals in back alleys. The minor villains they used to battle had been driven out of the city years ago. Or killed.

Julian ran into the smaller heroes from time to time, as did Damselfly and Lord Saturn. But Storm Warning was the only one who ever dared to confront Blazar.

"Well, if you're looking for the mask that only covers the top half of your face, it's in the sink," Damselfly said.

"Why is it in the sink?" Julian asked. He frowned. "And how did you know I was looking for that one?"

"You use the full mask for missions. Half mask is for big public shows. Like fighting Storm Warning." Damselfly shrugged. "And we were out of dishes, and I needed something to put my nachos on."

Julian sighed as he entered the kitchen and picked his mask out of the sink. "Did the other two say when they'd be back?"

"Nope." Damselfly folded her arms over the top of the couch and rested her chin on them. Her dark eyes settled on the mask in Julian's hands. "Why, you looking for backup tonight?"

"I don't need backup." The sink turned on with a hiss. Julian squirted soap onto the mask's metal surface and watched it foam up. Thankfully, the cheese stains vanished quickly.

"All right, well, I'm here if you change your mind." Damselfly thought for a moment. Her wings twitched. "On second thought, there's a new episode of Haunted Weddings tonight, so I probably won't come out."

"Glad I can count on you." Julian rinsed off his mask and wiped it dry with a towel. He'd been the youngest villain at the Complex until Damselfly showed up. While Blazar had succeeded at hammering responsibility into Julian, Damselfly hadn't been so keen on establishing herself. She preferred to tag along on whatever plans the others came up with.

"I don't get why this girl is having her wedding at her university," Damselfly said, her attention back on the TV. She tossed a piece of popcorn into her mouth and continued speaking as she chewed. "I mean, I get there was a murder, but these buildings are so ugly."

Julian considered asking what exactly the point of the show was, but he didn't have time to listen to another one of Damselfly's spiels.

"You gonna go to college, Julian?" she asked.

He'd considered it before, but Blazar had turned him off the idea. *You don't need it. You're powerful. You can take whatever you want.* He'd tried to dissuade Julian from getting a job, too, but he and Saturn had day jobs. And Julian wanted something to occupy his time, even if he didn't need the money.

"I don't know," Julian finally answered. "I'm already twenty-four."

"That's young!"

Bold words, coming from a sixteen-year-old. "I guess," Julian replied. His mind jumped to the New Atlas University shirt that woman at the cafe had been wearing. He'd spent a fair amount of time looking at their website. Was she a student? Or did she just know someone at the school?

Julian shook off the thought. The sun would be setting soon. It was time to get ready.

His costume waited for him in his room. The pants and shirt were a deep shade of purple and, like any decent suit, made of a material sturdy enough to protect him from minor blows and small blades. Then there were the white gloves, the white boots, and the collared golden-yellow cape that fastened at the neck. Julian liked it, despite Blazar's occasional jab—*Still haven't gotten rid of the cape yet?*—but he wasn't stupid. The fastener was easy to undo, so he could pull it off before any fight really got going.

The final piece was the bronze mask with rectangular slits for his green eyes to peer through. It was the most iconic part, too. The thing people thought of when they heard his name. There were five points at the top—the peak in the middle being the largest—that gave it a faint resemblance to a crown.

As Damselfly had noted, he had two masks: one that covered his entire face, and the one he'd be wearing tonight that left the bottom half exposed. It made conversation easier. And threatening heroes. A small device embedded in the bottom edge of the mask—designed by Lord Saturn—altered the sound waves of his voice as he spoke, deepening it enough that only people who knew him well would be able to recognize it.

Julian left his room and returned to the Complex's entrance.

"I'll watch you on the news!" Damselfly called as he reached the door. "Well, when my show's on commercial."

Julian paused in front of the elevator. "Don't we have every streaming service?"

"I don't think you know how TV works." Damselfly waved her tablet. "Besides, if I don't watch it live, I can't follow what people are saying on social media."

"Blazar might want to use the monitor to watch me."

"I don't think he's coming by tonight."

"We'll see." Julian could worry about Blazar later. It was time to focus.

Right now, he was Citadel.

CHAPTER TWO

It would be nice to be able to fly. Storm Warning could. But Julian had to work with the gifts he'd been given.

A pillar of stone broke through the concrete beneath him and lifted him into the air. By the time he was stepping onto the roof of a building at the center of his target block, civilians had taken notice. Some ran for cover. Others began recording on their phones. As stupid as it sounded, it wasn't necessarily a bad idea. The quicker a villain's appearance took over social media, the quicker the heroes learned what was going on. Plus, good videos made money.

Julian strolled to the middle of the roof and planted his feet. He could sense the earth moving far below him, and all the energy around him ready to be shaped into stone. The ground trembled. He found his perimeter.

Sidewalks crumbled and broke open to make way for the rising walls of stone.

It wasn't an easy thing to practice without being noticed. After training for months to build up his endurance, Julian had taken a short trip to a remote part of New York's mountains and practiced constructing walls like these. Days of building them up and pushing them around and tearing them back down made him confident he could pull off the plan. It also left him drained for weeks. Whether or not this worked, he wouldn't be pulling any more big stunts for a while.

The stone walls continued to rise, cutting off the block from the rest of the city. Once Julian was satisfied with their height, he hopped onto one and crossed to the opposite edge.

People gathered below. The closest news station already had reporters on the scene. Perfect.

"I'll keep it simple," Julian shouted. "One million dollars to stop the walls from closing in and destroying these buildings. I estimate you have half an hour. Max."

Short but sweet. His announcement finished, Julian turned away from the people and strolled to the other side of the stone wall. There, he waited, cape billowing with the occasional gust of wind.

It wasn't long before company showed up.

The sky, already darkening with the sunset, went black as heavy clouds formed directly above the city block. A flash of lightning illuminated the silhouette of an approaching figure. Thunder followed, and Julian grinned.

Storm Warning landed on the wall with a resounding thud, sinking to one knee. In the next flash of lightning, he rose to his feet and surveyed Julian's work. One of his eyebrows lifted. "This is new."

The rising wind whipped the hero's half-length white cape around. The cape was fastened at his right shoulder with a small gold lightning bolt. It matched his short white boots and gloves, while his dark blue supersuit matched the mask that covered the upper half of his face. Above the mask was a head of short, fluffy blonde hair, and behind it were blue eyes with unfathomable depths.

"I've been working on it for a long time," Julian told him, his gaze still flitting over Storm Warning's tall stature and thick muscles. He'd seen the man up close before more than a handful of times, but that didn't make him any less intimidating.

"Looks exhausting," Storm Warning replied.

"I'm managing." Julian pushed against the wall beneath them with his power, upping the speed at which it crawled toward the nearest building. "I don't suppose you have my money?"

Storm Warning strolled toward him. "Doesn't really seem your style, Citadel," he said coolly. "And I'm not convinced these walls are going to hold up as long as you say."

"You want to find out?" Julian was walking forward now, too. "I do enjoy a good demonstration."

"As do I. But I think you need better lighting."

The clouds above lit up. There was a flash, and then pain shooting through every inch of Julian's body. His walls jerked to a halt, the grinding of stone on sidewalk ceasing. Julian stumbled forward and barely managed to avoid tumbling off the wall.

"Sorry, did I say lighting?" Storm Warning asked. "I meant lightning."

"Aw, Storm. You should know I can take a hit from you by now." Julian rose to his full height and lifted his hands. A massive piece of stone broke free from the wall and shot through the air toward Storm Warning. The hero dove off the wall to avoid being crushed.

A moment later, he rose into the air above Julian. "Just getting warmed up."

He swooped down and grabbed Julian. The two flew through the air for a brief but disorienting moment before colliding with a rooftop. Julian couldn't help but wince when his back hit the concrete. He could take a lot, but this was pushing it.

Storm Warning, who'd landed on top of Julian, pushed himself up and lifted a hand. Electricity jumped from his palm to Julian's chest, sending another jolt of pain through him.

Julian's jaw clenched. He focused on the air above Storm Warning and generated a large boulder. Storm Warning moved to the left to dodge. Julian rolled to the right. The boulder hit the roof hard enough to send thin cracks running in every direction.

As Julian rose to his feet, he unfastened his cape and let it fall to the roof.

"Running out of energy yet?" Storm Warning asked.

"Let's find out." Julian extended his hand. A piece of concrete—the material typically had just enough real stone in it for him to manipulate—

ripped itself from the building and flew into his grasp, twisting into a staff. He charged and swung at Storm Warning. The first swing missed. The second struck the hero square in the chest.

Storm Warning stumbled back, but he didn't look too bothered by the blow. "You really think it's going to end differently this time?"

"I do." Julian smirked. Disks of stone peeled away from the outer layer of the wall and spun through the air around Storm Warning. "Like I said. I've been planning."

Something flashed across Storm Warning's expression. Was he actually nervous? Julian pressed forward. He was going to win this. The disks' orbits tightened, bringing them closer to Storm Warning. "Aren't you tired of fighting, Storm?" Julian asked.

"Aren't you?"

Julian's eyes narrowed. He was the one starting fights. All Storm Warning did was stop him.

Storm Warning glanced to the right. "Your walls have stopped moving," he noted.

"The buildings aren't what you should be worried about," Julian told him. "You're the one in danger now." He flung one of the disks at Storm Warning. The circle of stone crashed into him and knocked him to the ground.

"I'd do the typical spiel where I invite you to join me," Julian continued, starting toward him. "But I know you'd never even consider it."

There was a grunt of pain, and then a response. "Of course I've considered it."

Julian paused. "What?"

Storm Warning pushed himself off the ground and met Julian's gaze. "This isn't easy. Taking what I want—I could do that. I could be like you. I make the choice every day not to."

Julian rolled his eyes. "And you're getting nothing out of it but some broken ribs." He closed the gap between them, dropped to one knee, and brought his face close to Storm Warning's. "There are more villains than heroes around here, and I don't see that changing anytime soon."

Storm Warning's steady gaze didn't waver. In fact, he lifted his chin in defiance. "You know, I've met a lot of villains who don't think they're villains," he said. "I'll admit, it's refreshing that you aren't delusional."

"Thank you, I appreciate that."

Storm Warning grabbed the front of Julian's suit and yanked him to the ground. The hero was back on his feet in a heartbeat. He pulled back a fist. Julian quickly pushed up a section of stone beneath Storm Warning, launching him backward through the air.

A drop of rain bounced off Julian's nose as he stood up. "Nice try, but a little rain's not going to hurt me."

Storm Warning, who had managed a graceful landing about twenty feet away, chuckled. "I'm still warming up. Try this on for size."

A torrent of water poured down on Julian, knocking him back to the ground. Once the blast subsided, he pushed himself up, coughing up water. The disks he'd been spinning in the air clattered to the ground around him and Storm Warning.

Storm Warning followed the downpour with another painful strike of lightning. Spots danced in Julian's vision. This was usually the part of the fight where he started to lose.

But he had his new weapon. The wall. A towering mass of his creation, crafted from his element. A tool he could tear apart and manipulate with perfect precision.

"Rain's nice, Storm!" Julian staggered as he rose to his feet. He coughed again. "But I'll do you one better."

The disks returned to the air and drifted toward each other. With a terrible grinding sound, they merged together into one massive slab of stone.

"I learned this trick last week," Julian said. It was a trick that took a lot of concentration. Hopefully, he'd be able to pull it off here. It would be *incredibly* embarrassing if he screwed this up.

Storm Warning's expression darkened. He backed toward the edge of the roof. The slab followed, its shadow staying on him. Julian's fists tightened, and the slab split into dozens of dagger-sharp shards.

He brought them down on Storm Warning. Storm Warning jumped off the roof.

Julian raced to the roof's edge. As he reached it, Storm Warning shot up past him, rising above the nearby wall. Julian jumped. A platform of concrete rose to meet him and launched him into the air. He landed on the wall and continued his sprint toward Storm Warning.

The stone shards moved with Julian. He slid to a halt on the slick stone and flung out his arms, sending the shards flying at Storm Warning again. While Storm Warning moved higher to dodge them, Julian sent another blade of stone spinning through the air.

The distraction worked. The blade sliced across Storm Warning's chest and left a deep gash.

Storm Warning dropped onto the wall, a hand pressed to the wound, face twisted in pain. Blood dripped onto stone. Julian summoned the shards back to his hand and shaped them into a staff. He raced toward Storm Warning.

Despite the injury that was starting to look worse than Julian had anticipated, Storm Warning straightened up and drifted back into the air. Away from the wall. Julian jumped and swung.

All his strength, all his inner rage, his ever-burning need for his mentor's respect and the city's fear…it all went into the blow. The staff struck the side of the hero's head.

Storm Warning fell from the sky.

One last flash of lightning cut through the sky above, momentarily blinding Julian. The rain slowed, then stopped entirely. The last red rays of the sun pierced the fading storm. Julian's feet thudded against the stone wall. His landing sent a jolt through him, but the pain retreated quickly.

And then he was staring down at the street, empty except for the figure of Storm Warning far below.

"Come on, Storm, I'm not falling for that one." Julian's voice echoed off the nearby buildings. There was an odd tightness in his chest. He split the section of stone he stood on from the rest of the wall and pushed it down into the earth, bringing himself to the ground. He moved with caution, bracing himself for a sudden attack. "I've still got my walls."

Did he dare to hope that Storm Warning was dead? Storm Warning could take a beating, but the head was a tricky place. His advanced healing didn't make him invincible.

If the hero was really gone, Julian and the other villains could demand whatever the hell they wanted from the city. Well, as long as they didn't push things so far that heroes from New York intervened.

People were emerging from nearby buildings, but no one dared to approach the body.

"Storm Warning!" Julian's voice rose. He took a few slow steps toward the fallen hero. Nothing.

And yet, there was a weight in Julian's chest. No, Storm Warning wasn't the type to trick him like this. If he was alive, why not just blast Julian with lightning again?

Julian closed the gap between them. Knelt down. Swept his gaze across Storm Warning's still chest. After a moment's hesitation, he reached out to touch the side of his face.

Just flesh and blood. A man who could be killed.

A man who was dead.

"Well, then," Julian murmured. He rose and turned around. The pockets of people gathered around building entrances pushed themselves back, away from him. He laughed. The cold sound that came out didn't feel like *his* voice. There was an odd disconnect in his mind, a part of him that refused to believe he'd truly succeeded. But he had.

A stone pillar erupted from the ground beneath Julian, carrying him into the sky.

CHAPTER THREE

Charlotte Hathaway saw Storm Warning fall from the sky.

Maybe it had been stupid to walk toward the giant stone walls instead of away from them, but they were blocking the route back to her apartment. Her only options were to take a much longer way home, or to wait for Storm Warning to finish fighting Citadel.

She watched the fight from the sidewalk, ignoring the people who pushed past her on their way seek refuge in the shops. The wind picked up, pulling stray curls of blue hair free from her ponytail and whipping around the flannel she'd tied at her waist.

It was hard to follow the battle when the two were inside Citadel's walls. But once they returned to the top of the wall towering over the street, Charlotte couldn't tear her eyes away.

And then Citadel delivered that final blow.

By the time Charlotte's mind caught up with her legs, she was already racing to the end of the street, toward the intersection where Storm Warning had fallen. She was nearly there when someone else on the sidewalk grabbed her arm.

"What are you doing?" the woman asked, eyes wide.

Charlotte glanced at her. "Storm Warning—"

"Citadel is still out there!"

Charlotte turned her head in time to see Citadel step off a pillar and disappear over the other side of the wall. She yanked her arm free from the woman's grasp and kept running. If Storm Warning was still alive, someone needed to get him help.

He had to be alive, right?

A puddle of rainwater had formed beneath the hero's body. Some of it was probably blood, too. As Charlotte dropped to her knees next to him, she could hardly believe her eyes. Here she was, only feet away from the city's greatest hero. And she was alone.

There was a massive wound across Storm Warning's chest, spilling blood that darkened the front of his suit and stained his cape red.

"Storm Warning?" Charlotte tried. "Can you hear me?" Her eyes stung. The lights of nearby buildings blurred. "Hello?" She dared to rest a hand on his chest. No movement. No breathing.

Charlotte sniffed and dropped her head, resisting the urge to break down entirely but unable to find the strength to stand. What was she doing out here? Storm Warning was beyond saving now. They all were. She needed to get away before Citadel did something worse.

A white glow emanated from the wound in Storm Warning's chest. Charlotte wiped her arm across her face and sniffed again. "Storm—?"

Dark, metallic liquid emerged from the wound and floated up into the air. The liquid formed a solid sphere a couple of feet above Storm Warning's chest. Frowning, Charlotte reached out to touch it.

It shocked her. She flinched and yanked her hand back. The sphere melted back into liquid and followed her finger. Heart skipping in her chest, she rose to her feet and took a step back from the body. The liquid moved faster now, following until it found the skin of her arm. She gasped at its freezing touch.

Metal sliced through her skin and liquified again as it sank under the surface. Charlotte yelped in pain. Clutched her arm.

A shadow passed over her. There was movement on top of Citadel's wall. In a panic, Charlotte swung her head, located the closest alley, and ran.

"Is someone down there?" a voice called. *Citadel.*

Charlotte forced her legs to move faster and held her throbbing arm close to her chest. She couldn't feel any blood, but she was too scared to check. The shadows of the alleyway swallowed her.

A thud echoed overhead. Citadel had landed on the roof of the building to Charlotte's left. "I saw you by his body," he said. "Come out!"

Charlotte slammed into a door and tried the handle. Locked. She banged a fist against it. "Hello? Anyone in there?" she hissed as loud as she dared. Nothing.

She tipped her head back and shouted in frustration. "What do you want, Citadel? Haven't you done enough already?"

"Did you know him?" Citadel asked. His figure appeared at the edge of the roof overhead, looking down at her. He clutched his cape in one hand. "Storm Warning?"

Charlotte's eyes narrowed. "I didn't have to. He was a hero."

She was ready to try running again when the door in front of her swung open. A man wearing a restaurant uniform gestured for her to enter. Charlotte stumbled in, and the door slammed shut behind her.

The man twisted the lock. "What were you doing out there?" he asked.

Charlotte ignored the question. "Thank you!" she exclaimed as she rushed past him, already scanning for another door she could exit through.

"Wait, you can't go back out there," the man said, following her through the restaurant's kitchen.

"There has to be a way. I need to get to Bergamot Street." Charlotte's arm still throbbed with pain, and she still couldn't bring herself to look at it. Avoiding eye contact with the skin, she grabbed the flannel from around her waist and shrugged it on.

The man hesitated. "You could take our west exit and cut through the plaza, but it'd be safest to wait until—"

"The plaza!" There were enough trees there to give her cover. "Thank you again! Stay safe!"

When Charlotte reentered the night, the city was eerily quiet. Sure, there were distant sirens and an occasional shout, but there wasn't a soul in her field of vision. No sign of Citadel, either. Even the hum of traffic had quieted to an unsettling level.

The burst of adrenaline that had kept her going earlier faded quickly. Her pace slowed as she neared Bergamot Street, and before long she had tears streaming down her face. She choked back her sobs, desperately trying to hold them in until she could get to safety.

Her apartment building came into view, but Charlotte didn't feel much relief at the sight. Every step hurt. Her body begged her to sit down and rest for a minute. *Come on.* She gritted her teeth. *You're almost there.* She really wished she'd kept up with her running routine.

Finally, she stumbled into her apartment and flipped the kitchen light on.

Spencer Higgs—her cousin and roommate—sat on the couch in the living area watching TV. He rested an arm on the couch's back and turned to watch Charlotte enter. It only took him a moment to realize something was wrong. "Charlie? You okay?"

"Storm Warning's dead." Charlotte barely got the words out.

Spencer was on his feet in an instant. He rushed to Charlotte's side. "How? Was it Blazar?"

Charlotte shook her head. "Citadel."

Spencer returned to the couch, picked up the remote, and switched to a local news station. His eyes widened as a reporter spoke over a still image of Storm Warning falling from the sky. He ran a hand through his chest-length blonde hair. "Shit."

Blinking away fresh tears, Charlotte asked, "What do you think will happen to the city?"

"I don't know." There was a faraway look in Spencer's gaze. His pale face looked cold in the light of the TV.

"The other heroes will do something, right?"

"Hopefully."

A fresh wave of stinging pain reminded Charlotte that she had a bigger problem right now than the fate of New Atlas. She pulled up the sleeve of her flannel and felt a jolt of alarm. A silver scar ran across her arm where the strange liquid had touched her skin.

Charlotte swallowed. "Um, something happened to me out there."

Spencer looked over. When his eyes settled on the scar, the concern in his expression grew. He muted the TV. "What the hell happened to you?"

"I went up to Storm Warning's body. This...orb came out of his chest and it turned into liquid and I think it's in me, now."

"You touched a weird floating orb?"

"It touched me first!"

Spencer pinched the bridge of his nose. "Okay, okay. Uh, does it hurt?"

"Yeah." Charlotte winced. "Should I call a doctor?"

"A doctor? We should be thinking about going to the hospital. They might be able to remove it surgically."

Charlotte shook her head. The world spun around her. But despite the pain and slight nausea, the thought of removing the thing made her hesitate. "I mean, it was inside Storm Warning. Maybe it's not a bad thing."

"Yeah, or maybe you could die!" Spencer was pacing back and forth now, which made Charlotte even dizzier. "We don't know anything about him. Just because he could survive having that in him, doesn't mean you can."

Charlotte stumbled past Spencer, toward the hallway. "I'm exhausted. I can't deal with this right now."

"Charlie!" Spencer called after her. "You can't just go to bed!"

"I'll be fine," Charlotte insisted. "The pain's starting to fade, I think." She reached her bedroom door and grabbed the handle.

Spencer caught up to her and grabbed her shoulder. "Oh, for the love of—look, could you at least leave your door open so I can check on you?"

Charlotte didn't have a chance of breaking out of his firm grip. Spencer was tall and lithe—with delicate features that often got him called "pretty"—and didn't look particularly strong. But all you had to do was watch him move furniture around to know he spent a fair amount of time at the gym. Charlotte *really* needed to start tagging along with him.

"Sure," she conceded. "But I don't think I'm gonna get much sleep if you're coming in every five minutes."

Spencer rolled his eyes. "Better tired than dead."

"All right, all right." Charlotte made her way to her bed and collapsed onto her back. She probably should have changed out of her damp clothes, but she was already slipping out of consciousness.

And then the morning sun was streaming through her window, and birds were chirping, and Charlotte was very much Not Dead. At least, she hoped she wasn't dead. Groaning, she rolled out of bed. Her feet thudded against the ground.

Something was different.

Charlotte rose to her full height, caught a glimpse of herself in her full-length mirror, and clapped a hand over her mouth.

For starters, "full height" was a good five inches higher than it used to be. The too-large university tee she'd fallen asleep in was almost a perfect fit now. A little tight, even. Charlotte examined her right arm. The silver scar had faded to the point that if she hadn't known it was there, she probably wouldn't have noticed it.

That wasn't the only change. Charlotte looked like the more muscular girls at the campus gym she'd always wished she had the willpower to keep up with. Buffer, even. She laughed.

"Charlotte?" Spencer called from the other side of the apartment. "You awake?"

"Sure am!" Charlotte pulled herself away from the mirror and strolled out of her room.

Spencer choked on his water as Charlotte entered the kitchen. "Uh, did you get taller?" he asked from where he sat at the table.

Charlotte grinned. "Cool, right?"

"That's one way of putting it." Spencer lifted an eyebrow. Even after just waking up, his hair was stupidly voluminous, as usual. No matter how much Charlotte pestered him, he insisted he wasn't using any products. *Unfair.* Still, Charlotte was too excited about her new height and muscle to be jealous for more than a few seconds.

"How are you going to explain this to people?" Spencer asked.

That was enough to wipe away Charlotte's excitement. "Good point," she groaned. "Oh, god. What am I going to tell my parents next time they visit?"

"Tell them you're going to the gym now," Spencer suggested. "Maybe it'll be believable by then."

"Lifting weights doesn't make you grow five inches!"

"Tell them you did steroids."

Charlotte barely heard the comment. "I'm going to need new clothes! Most of my stuff won't fit anymore!"

"Yeah," Spencer said. "And you're probably going to want something nice, if you want to go to the funeral."

"Storm Warning's funeral?" Charlotte walked to the table and slid into the chair across from Spencer. "When is it?"

"Tonight."

That was fast. "Are they revealing his identity?" Sometimes heroes had a will that allowed their identities to be announced to the public after death, while others chose to be anonymous forever.

"Nope." Spencer took another sip of his water. "A few heroes flew in from New York to handle the whole thing. Old friends of his, I guess."

Charlotte assumed Spencer meant that the heroes literally flew in, seeing as how New York was only a couple of hours away by car. "Think they'll stick around to fight Citadel?"

Spencer sighed. "That would be nice. But New York has its own problems. I doubt they'll stay long."

"Hm." Charlotte ran a hand along her new muscles. "Well, maybe a smaller hero will have to start doing a little more work around here." There weren't many. Wrecking Ball, Jackrabbit, Collider, Airborne…none of them were known for fighting big villains.

That didn't seem to reassure Spencer. His expression darkened. "The funeral's at seven. You wanna go?"

Charlotte nodded.

Concern still lingering on his face, Spencer added, "I'm going to go visit my parents after the funeral, and I might stay the night at their place. Are you sure you're going to be okay?"

Charlotte didn't know Spencer's parents that well, despite their mothers being sisters. She and Spencer hadn't even been particularly close until she'd decided to attend New Atlas University, and he'd offered the room in his apartment vacated by a graduating senior.

"Pretty sure I can handle anything at this point," Charlotte said. Okay, maybe she had a little too much confidence. She was probably stronger than she had been yesterday, but that didn't mean she was invincible.

Storm Warning hadn't been, after all.

"Okay." Spencer was quiet for a moment. "So, do you think you have his powers?"

"Hm." Charlotte stared at her hand and tried to make something happen. Anything. She imagined electricity running through her fingers.

"What are you doing?" Spencer asked. "Trying to electrocute us?"

"I don't know. I can't feel anything." Charlotte closed her fist. "I guess we'll see."

CHAPTER FOUR

Julian felt unstoppable when he returned to the Complex.

It was the morning after the fight when he walked in. He'd wanted to deal with his injuries on his own back at his apartment and take a few hours alone to relish his victory. The downside was that hadn't slept much, unable to stop his racing mind from wondering what Blazar's reaction to the news had been. What he would say when he saw Julian.

"Julian!" Blazar was waiting when Julian entered, leaning against the wall by the elevator with his arms folded. "You actually did it. I must admit, I'm—"

"Impressed?" Julian tried.

"Surprised."

Julian frowned. "What, you didn't think I could beat him?"

"Not by yourself." Blazar shrugged. "Don't take it personally. Storm Warning's been around for a long time. I was starting to think he'd never go down."

Blazar's strawberry blonde hair was long, for him—a couple of inches. It must have been a few days since he last shaved it for his villain persona. Most days he was Blake Sullivan, and his odd ability to manipulate his super speed into accelerating his hair growth provided a convenient addition to his civilian disguise. The nice suit also suggested he'd been at his day job recently.

He was a formidable man as a civilian, but when his head was shaved and he wore his villain suit, it really emphasized the militaristic look he gave off. Blazar had never actually been in the military, but he'd acted enough like a drill sergeant when training Julian to give the impression, anyway. The muscles and strong, wide jaw helped.

"Well, he's down now," Julian said. The last of his stress faded away, the tension in his shoulders easing. Things were finally going his way.

Blazar stepped away from the wall and straightened up, reminding Julian that even with his above-average height, the older man towered over him. "I assume you found the stormoid?"

Julian frowned. "The what?"

The shift in Blazar's expression made Julian tense.

"The source of Storm Warning's power," Blazar said, his voice tinged with annoyance. "We don't know exactly what it is—yet—but we know it was inside of him. It usually showed up as a sphere in his chest on Saturn's scans. Sometimes it took on a liquid form in his blood, mainly when he was healing from bad injuries."

"No one told me any of that!" Julian forced himself to pause a moment and get his tone under control. Blazar didn't take kindly to being yelled at, even if he was the one in the wrong. "How long have you known?"

"Hm. Not sure. A couple years?" Blazar rubbed his chin. "I really thought we mentioned it to you."

"You didn't."

Footsteps sounded from the hallway. Lord Saturn and Damselfly emerged together and entered the living room.

"Well, that's unfortunate," Blazar said, not acknowledging their arrival. "We need the stormoid."

"What for?" Julian asked.

"To train a new villain, of course!" Blazar laughed. "Can you imagine if we had someone with Storm Warning's power on our side? We'd be unstoppable."

Of course it hadn't been enough to defeat the seemingly invincible hero. *Of course* Blazar would find some way to be disappointed in Julian's success.

Julian shook his head as if to shed his growing dismay. "Well, it must still be in his body, right?" he asked. "I can...retrieve it."

"You'd better hope you can," Blazar said. "We need to scare off any heroes who think they can take his place."

"I'll get it," Julian promised. After a moment's hesitation, he asked, "Where do you plan to find someone else to train?"

"Don't worry about that. I'll find us some candidates," Blazar replied. "Now, I'm off to work. You get this taken care of."

Julian stepped aside so Blazar could pass him and leave the Complex. While the elevator door slid shut behind him, he turned his attention to Lord Saturn and Damselfly.

Out of costume, Lord Saturn—or Sophia Novak, as she was known at the car manufacturer where she worked as an engineer—was a woman in her mid-thirties with light skin and dark red-orange hair kept up in a bun. It was as striking as natural red hair could get. "I'm surprised Blazar wasn't more pissed," she said. Her arms folded, rustling the fabric of her dark red button-up. "He's wanted to get his hands on the stormoid since we figured out it existed."

Julian crossed the living room to stand in front of her and Damselfly. "No one ever mentioned it to me."

Saturn shrugged. "I picked it up after I started taking full-body scans of heroes in fights. Blazar said he'd mention it to you." Over the years, she'd been able to implement tech into her helmet to run x-rays, thermal scans, and night vision. There was probably more, but Julian had a hard time following her when she explained her inventions. Still, he was fairly certain she'd been taking those full body scans for a few years now.

"Guess he forgot." Damselfly took a handful of popcorn out of the bag she was holding and shoved it into her mouth. The oversized t-shirt she wore displayed a cartoon crow with a knife in its beak, an odd pairing with her hot pink sweatpants.

"He's not like you, Damselfly," Saturn said. "He doesn't forget things."

Julian turned around to face the elevator. No point sticking around, especially if all the other two had to offer was bickering. He had a job to do.

"Where are you going?" Damselfly protested through her mouthful of popcorn. She swallowed. "I was going to make all of us pasta for lunch."

"I'll be back soon," Julian said as he started toward the elevator. Not that he wanted to eat Damselfly's cooking. "I'm going to go find Storm Warning's body."

"City's taken it," Saturn said. "They've already announced a funeral."

Julian paused. *Damn it.* "When?"

"Tonight, at seven."

"Then I'm going to my apartment for a few hours." Julian sighed. "Guess I have a funeral to get ready for."

"Wait!" Damselfly took to the air and flew into Julian's path, wings fluttering. She dropped to the ground in front of him. "We should tell you what we know about the stormoid." Her gaze darted expectantly to Saturn, and Julian got the feeling she didn't actually know much at all.

Before Saturn had the chance to help Damselfly out, Julian glanced back at her. "Saturn can just email me the information, right?"

"Sure." Saturn walked toward them, grabbing her suit jacket off the back of the couch as she passed. "You should also take this scanner." She pulled a small electronic device from one of the jacket's pockets and held it out to Julian. It was a bit smaller than the average phone, and a screen took up its entire surface. "Point it at Storm Warning's body and turn it on, and it will show you the stormoid."

Julian slid the scanner into his pocket. "Thanks."

"I'll send you my files on the stormoid when I get back to my apartment," Saturn added.

Damselfly huffed. "Fine. Screw you guys. More pasta for me, then." She flew into the kitchen.

Julian felt a twinge of guilt as he resumed his walk to the elevator. Damselfly was the only one who didn't have a home outside the Complex, or another identity to use. Her wings couldn't bend or fold, so it simply wasn't possible for her to hide them.

He let Saturn enter the elevator first. As he followed, he hit the button for the ground floor. The only button.

The door slid shut, leaving them in silence. After a long moment, Julian asked, "Did you see the fight?"

"I saw the highlights on the news," Saturn answered, sounding a little distracted. "Work ran late for me last night. But it looked like you did great."

"Thanks."

They were quiet the rest of the way down. When they stepped out of the alley, they went separate ways. Saturn headed toward the nearest subway station, and Julian started the walk to his apartment. It would take nearly half an hour, but he found the stroll enjoyable in the spring weather.

He took an even longer route today, one that would take him past the scene of last night's fight. The city had brought in equipment to dismantle the walls he'd left up. Julian had taken a few sections down before disappearing the night before, not seeing any point in keeping everyone hostage after accomplishing his goal. But he'd been too exhausted to deal with all of them.

Back at his apartment, with plenty of time to kill before the funeral, he found himself checking the news frequently. He was concerned when he heard heroes had come in from New York to help with funeral preparations, but it sounded like they were gone by the afternoon. Good. More heroes were the last thing they needed in New Atlas.

Well, the last thing Julian needed.

Finally, the time came for him to leave. For attire, he went with a simple suit. He'd briefly considered showing up as Citadel but decided the better option would be to assess the scene without drawing attention. He doubted Blazar wanted the public knowing about the stormoid, anyway.

So, Julian told himself, he was simply going to the funeral see where they buried Storm Warning. He would return once it was dark. The Fallen Heroes Cemetery had guards, of course, but they were to keep out civilians.

Not him. He could get in and out without anyone ever knowing he was there.

It was a long walk to the cemetery, but crowded sidewalks were more tolerable than a crowded subway. Julian followed the masses through a tall iron gate. He'd never been here before, and as he passed statues of heroes who'd died long before his time—before Blazar even—a discomfort he couldn't shake settled over him. He didn't belong here.

Was he the only villain to ever visit? Or had others come to watch heroes they'd killed be put in the earth?

Julian found a spot near the edge of the crowd where he could see the casket from. Ropes blocked off the area around the burial site, and the only people allowed in were cemetery guards, police, a few reporters, and the mayor.

Location was good. A feel for the area would be even better. Julian closed his eyes, letting the earth below steady him for a moment before he sent his senses rolling through the dirt. Good. It wouldn't be difficult to manipulate the ground here.

When he opened his eyes, Julian caught a glimpse of blue moving through the crowd. Blue hair, pulled back in a braid. Even though she was facing away from him, he recognized the girl from the cafe.

The girl who'd approached Storm Warning's body after his death.

She was different. Noticeably different. Taller, for starters. And she looked like she'd somehow packed a six-month gym routine into a day. Even the long sleeves of her black dress couldn't completely hide that. Someone walked next to her, a person in a suit with blonde hair up in a ponytail.

Julian followed the two through the crowd. He tried to keep his distance, but it was difficult to avoid losing them with so many people around. He was forced to move closer, to shrink the space between them.

When the two finally stopped in a thinner part of the crowd, the girl's friend turned his head and noticed Julian watching. Julian looked away, but when he dared to glance back, the man was elbowing the blue-haired girl. He jutted a thumb toward Julian, and the girl looked his way. Their eyes met.

And then she was walking toward him.

Julian only had seconds to think up an excuse for following her. "I owe you a dollar." He reached into his pocket, praying he had a bill on him somewhere.

She laughed. "I don't want you to pay me back."

Julian paused. "No?"

"It's a dollar! I don't need it."

Julian wondered if he should bring up the height thing. There might be another explanation, the timing only a coincidence, but...could she have the stormoid?

She had approached Storm Warning's body. But how would she have taken it? Or even known it existed? Intuition could only be trusted so far, but she didn't strike Julian as the type of person to pursue a source of power like that.

Before Julian could decide where to take the conversation, she held out a hand. "I'm Charlotte, by the way."

"Julian." Julian pulled his hand from his jacket pocket to shake hers. Electricity jumped between them, making him flinch.

"Sorry!" Charlotte yanked her hand back. "Static electricity, I guess."

A small smile touched Julian's lips. He decided not to mention that there was no way she could have built up a charge out here on the grass.

"Charlie!" Charlotte's friend walked up to join them. There was something in his expression that Julian suspected was amusement. Oddly, it put him on edge. He flexed the hand Charlotte had shocked and slid it into the pocket of his suit jacket.

"Oh, uh, this is Spencer," Charlotte told Julian. "He's my cousin. And roommate."

"Nice to meet you." Spencer gave Julian a quick nod before glancing at Charlotte. "They're about to start the service."

As the words left his mouth, a hush fell over the crowd. Charlotte nodded, waved goodbye to Julian, and followed Spencer back to the spot the two had picked out. Julian remained where he was, turning his attention to the casket carrying the fallen hero.

A microphone had been set up in front of the casket. Mayor Song stood in front of the mic, and once the cemetery quieted, he spoke. "For the past decade, New Atlas has been beyond fortunate to have a hero as great as Storm Warning as our protector and guardian."

Julian spent the next few minutes unable to take his eyes off the casket, barely processing the mayor's eulogy. Had he really caused all of this?

Time passed in a blur.

Finally, the mayor's speech drew to a close. "I cannot tell you what will come next," Mayor Song said. "I can only promise that I will do my best to keep New Atlas a city that Storm Warning—that any hero—would be proud to serve."

The casket was lowered into the earth. Dirt filled in the hole. As soon as they were allowed to approach, civilians crowded the plot, tossing flowers onto the freshly disturbed dirt.

Julian sat on a bench along one of the cemetery's paths and watched the crowd thin. People streamed past him, talking quietly as they headed for the gate. After half an hour, a few still lingered, but they'd moved on to looking at memorials for other heroes. They couldn't stick around much longer. The place closed at sundown, and the red sky was darkening quickly.

And then Julian could do what he had to do. Maybe the stormoid had been taken from Storm Warning's body already, but he had to be sure.

He supposed he should leave now and come back once it was dark. He rose to his feet. But instead of heading directly for the gate, he walked to the headstone over Storm Warning's grave.

Julian shoved his hands in his pockets and stared at the hero's name carved into the stone. He had to admit that some part of him would miss fighting Storm. Their battles hadn't always ended with broken ribs and bleeding wounds. Julian often got away before things got too messy, and sometimes he even escaped with whatever money or prize he'd been after.

And Storm Warning, to his credit, was a fun opponent. He was clever, kept Julian sharp, and occasionally managed a decent joke or two between his high-and-mighty speeches.

But that part of Julian's life was over now. And it was for the better. There was nothing standing between him and whatever he wanted to take from the city. He and the other villains could rob the wealthy without fear of Storm Warning swooping in. Lord Saturn could steal whatever tech she wanted from the city's manufacturers. Everything New Atlas produced was at their fingertips.

Footsteps approached at Julian's right. Someone moved to stand next to him. Charlotte.

Julian glanced up at her. "What are you still doing here?"

"I could ask you the same thing." Charlotte smiled.

Fair enough. Julian glanced around. Not many people left... No, even if Charlotte did have the stormoid, he needed to be disguised as Citadel when he took it. He couldn't have her knowing he was a villain, now that she'd seen his face. And knew his name.

He let his eyes briefly look over her arms as she folded them. If it really was her who'd taken the stormoid, he'd have to fight her for it. How long would it take her to master Storm Warning's powers, if she had them?

"Is it just me, or are you taller than you were when we met yesterday?" Julian asked.

Charlotte flushed. "Uh, you might be remembering wrong." She tucked a piece of loose hair behind her ear. "I'm guessing you saw the fight last night?"

"You could say that."

"I was there. In person. I saw him fall." Charlotte turned to stare at the headstone. Her expression darkened. "I wonder what he's going to do next. Citadel, I mean."

What was he going to do next? He wouldn't need money anytime soon. The only thing he'd cared about for a long time was defeating Storm Warning. Now that he'd accomplished that...

"I suppose he'll want to brag for a while," Julian replied with a shrug. "He must be pretty proud of himself."

The last rays of sun lit up Charlotte's brown eyes as she lifted her chin. "Well, I guess someone's going to have to take Storm Warning's place."

Now they were getting somewhere. Julian raised an eyebrow. "You think there's someone who can?"

"I bet there is."

He studied her for a long moment. She tried to hide it, but there was confidence there. Determination. She really thought she stood a chance against him.

Her head turned suddenly, and for a moment Julian thought she was looking at him. But no, she was looking past him, at the sky darkening over the city.

"The sunset's beautiful," she said. "Kind of a nice send-off."

Julian followed her gaze, even though the view was something he'd seen a million times before. But the clouds were nice, he supposed, with the light hitting them the way it did.

"I should get home." As Charlotte backed away from the grave, she added, "Maybe I'll pay for your coffee again one of these days."

Julian chuckled. "Sure." *Or maybe we'll run into each other somewhere a little more exciting.*

After one last wave, Charlotte turned around and walked toward the gate. Alone, Julian noted. He wondered where her cousin had gone.

Julian stood by the grave for another minute before leaving. He waited outside the cemetery until darkness blanketed the city, and then he waited a little longer. Finally, he shrugged off his suit jacket, slid his half mask onto his face—just in case—and approached the cemetery's metal fence.

A tunnel opened in the earth, clearing the way for him to walk under the fence. He stayed far below the surface to avoid graves, but he still carved his path carefully, reaching ahead through the dirt with his senses to make sure he didn't run into anything.

He emerged from the ground next to Storm Warning's headstone. According to Saturn's email, the scanner would be able to detect the stormoid through the casket, but six feet of dirt was too much.

"Sorry, Storm," Julian said as he pulled the device from his jacket. "But I have to be sure."

Dirt lifted itself out of the grave and hovered in the air overhead, exposing the casket. Julian powered on the scanner and held it out. The screen lit up. An outline of Storm Warning's body appeared.

No stormoid.

Julian had a new target now.

He returned the dirt to the grave, leaving it just as he'd found it. After exiting his tunnel outside the cemetery, he filled that in, too. No one would ever know a villain had visited the hero he'd killed.

CHAPTER FIVE

The city streets were even busier than Charlotte expected during her walk back to the apartment. As usual, she was admiring shop windows and plants growing on apartment balconies, but she was also on high alert. While none of the villains had made a move yet, that could change at any moment.

Instead of going straight back to the apartment, Charlotte took a different turn and headed to Dove Park. She wasn't ready to sit alone in her room all night. It would be nice to watch the people walking by for a while.

Dove Park—a small stretch of grass and trees nestled between two buildings—didn't attract many visitors, surprisingly. It offered a view of Beebalm Street at one end, while the other side was hidden away and strangely quiet. The park was also in the perfect place to be flooded with the afternoon sunlight that found its way in between buildings. It was too late for that now, but lights from surrounding windows kept Charlotte from feeling uneasy in the darkness.

As Charlotte sat on one of the benches, watching the last of the light fade from the sky, she couldn't help but think about Julian. It was crazy enough that she'd happen to run into him at both the cafe and the funeral. What were the chances of seeing him again?

She sighed and rested her chin in her hand, trying to convince herself she didn't care that much. She would have given that dollar to anyone who needed it. Admittedly, she'd already seen the guy reaching for his card, and he certainly didn't seem to need the money, but...

Damn it, she'd thought he was cute.

Unfortunately, Spencer figured that out pretty quickly when Charlotte told him the story after running into Julian at the funeral. Spencer insisted he looked like he'd walked right out of a shady organization in a spy movie. Charlotte couldn't really see it. At least Spencer eventually conceded that he was "sort of pretty."

What did Julian really think about Charlotte's change in appearance? He hadn't pressed the matter after she'd brushed off his question about her height, but there was no way he believed he'd simply misremembered her, right? Unless he really wasn't paying attention at the cafe.

Based on the fact that she'd broken the door off the microwave—leaving maintenance perplexed—and that carrying the stack of textbooks she'd accumulated felt like lifting a feather, Charlotte definitely had superhuman strength. But she hadn't been able to summon any of Storm Warning's other powers. What if she didn't have them, after all? Maybe whatever that orb was just gave people muscles.

Suddenly aware of how hungry she was, Charlotte stood up, stretched, and glanced up at the sky. The idea of picking up food somewhere was tempting, but she had leftovers to finish.

Ugh. Why had she wandered so far from the apartment? It would take fifteen minutes to get back the usual way.

Or she could cut through alleyways. She'd been too terrified to take them before, even during the day, but she could handle anyone she ran into now, right? The big villains weren't known for hanging out in back alleys.

Charlotte made it a couple of blocks without any trouble. Halfway through a particularly long alley, though, something moved above her. She halted and looked up.

A figure stood at the top of a fire escape. The cape, the mask— Charlotte's heart skipped a beat. "Citadel." Apparently, big villains *did* sometimes hang out in back alleys. Eyes narrowing, she lifted her fists, though he had to have heard the tremble in her voice. "What do you want?"

Citadel chuckled. He grabbed the railing and jumped over. A pillar of stone broke through the ground in front of Charlotte to catch him and bring him down to her level. "Bold of you to be walking around alone so soon after Storm Warning's death."

"I don't need him to protect me." Charlotte managed a relatively steady tone, but she couldn't stop the slight trembling in her hands. "And doesn't someone as big and powerful as yourself have better things to do than stalk random civilians?"

"I'm flattered."

"Don't be."

"Let's cut to the chase, then." Citadel began circling Charlotte. She turned to follow, not wanting her eyes off him for even a second. "Are you the one who approached Storm Warning's body after he died?" he asked.

"I think you have me mistaken for someone else," Charlotte told him.

"No, I don't think I do."

Stone spikes emerged from the ground, forming a circle around Charlotte. "What the hell?" she exclaimed as they trapped her in a makeshift cell. "Let me go!"

Citadel stopped in front of her and leaned forward. "I think you took something that belonged to Storm Warning," he said, his voice low.

"Oh, and let me guess, you want it?" Charlotte slammed a fist against one of the spikes. To her surprise, a hairline crack appeared. Her victory was short-lived as she realized how many more blows it would take to break even one. And her hand stung with pain where she'd hit the stone.

"I'll do whatever it takes to get my hands on the stormoid," Citadel said. "I'm sure that's not surprising."

Stormoid? Is that what the floaty liquid orb was called? "I don't have it," Charlotte insisted. Was there a chance he'd believe her?

"I don't believe you."

"What makes you say that?" The wind picked up, freeing stray pieces of hair from Charlotte's braid. When Citadel didn't respond, she added, "You don't know anything about me." She hit the closest spike again. A rush of energy flooded her arm as it swung through the air.

Sparks jumped from her hand when it made contact. More cracks ran up the stone. Bigger cracks.

Shit. Of all the times for powers to show up.

Citadel smirked. "Seems I was correct."

"I wouldn't sound so smug, if I were you," Charlotte snapped back. "Storm Warning beat you plenty of times."

"Oh, I'm terrified." His voice was, unsurprisingly, thick with sarcasm. He straightened up and gestured at her. "You clearly have no idea how to use your powers."

"You don't know that!"

Citadel laughed and took a few steps back. He held out his arms. "Strike me down, then."

Charlotte glared at him. What was the secret? Maybe she needed to calm down, but that was hard to do with a supervillain staring her down. She tried bringing back that feeling of energy coursing through her body. Nothing.

"See? You're in over your head," Citadel said, arms lowering. "Now, all we have to do is figure out how to get the stormoid out of you."

"I'll never give it to you." Not that Charlotte even knew how. Could she make the stormoid leave her body if she wanted? Or would Citadel have to cut her open, like he did Storm Warning? The thought sent a chill down her spine. And a buzz of energy.

Bright light flashed overhead, and then a clap of thunder shook the alleyway. Charlotte yelped in surprise. Citadel looked up. Dark clouds were converging above them, far too low for clouds to form naturally.

A second strike of lightning broke through the clouds and hit Citadel. He flew backwards and collided with a wall before sinking to the ground. Charlotte laughed. "How's that for striking you down?"

Citadel pushed himself off the concrete and staggered to his feet. "Not bad." He lifted a hand. The stone spikes surrounding Charlotte grew taller and leaned in, giving her little space to move.

Panic closed in with the spikes. Charlotte did her best to fend it off with a few steadying breaths, then pressed her hands against two of the spikes and pushed. The next thing she knew, electricity was dancing around her, turning the world a blinding white. The air cracked.

The stone spikes exploded, and the light faded a moment later. Charlotte lowered her arms and swept her gaze over the rubble. Citadel took a step back as stray fragments of stone bounced across the ground around him. It was hard to be sure, with half his face hidden, but he looked surprised. Maybe even a little scared, but that could have been wishful thinking on Charlotte's part.

Still, she grinned at him. "You were saying?"

After a moment, Citadel shook his head and laughed. "Well, this should be fun. I do love a challenge." He rose to his full height. "This isn't over." A stone pillar burst from the ground to lift him into the air.

"Sure!" Charlotte called after him. "It's gonna end with you in prison!"

She had no idea if he heard her. He disappeared onto the roof of the building without another word, leaving behind the pillar. Another mess for city workers to clean up. Fists clenched, Charlotte stormed past the pillar to the other end of the alley.

Maybe Citadel wasn't scared of her, yet. But she was going to figure out her powers and make him fear her.

CHAPTER SIX

Julian had been thrilled to find Charlotte still outside after the funeral, and even more so when he'd confirmed she had the stormoid. But now he had an entirely new challenge: getting it from her. He'd sliced up Storm Warning countless times in battle without the stormoid emerging. Would it only come out if the host died? Julian certainly didn't want to kill Charlotte, only take her power. What was he supposed to do if death was the only way?

He probably should have kept fighting her, maybe taken her prisoner, but he was still worn out from raising the walls. He needed a few more days of rest before he'd be ready for a real fight.

"I assume you have my stormoid?" Blazar asked when Julian entered the Complex the following morning.

"There's a...complication," Julian told him. "It left his body."

Blazar's nostrils flared, but he calmed his expression quickly. "Someone must have taken it, then. I don't suppose you know who has it?"

"Not yet," Julian lied. He had the situation under control. No need to explain every detail to Blazar, as long as he got the thing eventually.

"You need to find it quickly, before whoever took it figures out how to use its power." Blazar sighed as he moved into the kitchen.

"Don't worry. I'll find it." Julian walked to the couch and sat down. Resting an arm on its back, he turned to look at Blazar. "Besides, even if their powers do start developing, I already defeated Storm Warning. And he had years of experience."

Blazar selected a glass from one cupboard, and a bottle of whiskey from the one next to it. "Yes, you certainly got lucky, didn't you?"

Lucky? Julian frowned, barely giving any thought to the oddity of whiskey so early in the day. "Come on, you think it was a fluke? I spent months planning those walls—"

"I'm not denying you put a lot of work into that fight, Julian," Blazar said. He poured his drink and approached the couch. "Or that you deserved your victory. But don't let it get to your head. You have to keep your guard up, or some cocky hero's gonna come along and knock you off your feet."

He had a point, Julian supposed.

"Understood?" Blazar asked.

Julian nodded. "Of course."

"Is that Julian I hear?" Damselfly sang as she flew in from the hallway.

Before Julian had a chance to greet her, Blazar spoke. "Go fetch Saturn for me. We're having a meeting." He took a sip of his drink.

Groaning, Damselfly turned around and returned to the hall. When she reappeared a minute later, Saturn trailed behind her, reading something on her phone.

"The four of us are going to take everything from the Marigold Bank on Beacon Street this afternoon," Blazar informed them. His stern tone left no room for debate. "When we're done, we'll burn it to the ground. It's about time we make a statement."

Julian held back a sigh. So much for a break.

Damselfly lit up. "Really? It's been forever since we all did something together. I was starting to think you all were just doing your own thing now." She nudged Julian with her elbow. "Especially mister superhero-killer over here."

"I thought it would be good to do something big," Blazar continued. "Show the city what they're in for. Sophia, you've got your monitoring systems in place around the city in case company shows up from out of town?"

Saturn glanced up from her phone. "Of course."

"Good. Everyone be ready by three." Blazar gestured for Saturn to follow him as he strolled toward the hall, drink still in hand. "We just have some technical details to work out."

"What are you going to do with your share of the money?" Damselfly asked as the two left.

Julian shrugged. Maybe he could update his room here at the Complex, or get a new car, or—

"I'm going to get the new Joybox," Damselfly said before he could come up with an answer. "The 2020 model is supposed to be awesome."

"A video game console? That'd be pretty easy to just...steal," Julian said. "Didn't you hit up the mall a couple weeks ago?"

"All the stores are sold out," Damselfly explained. "I have to order it online."

"And you've already blown through most of the money in your account, I'm guessing?"

"That's none of your business." Damselfly circled the couch and sat down next to Julian. She picked up the remote. "Now, if you're not using this, I'm going to watch TV."

"Fine by me." Julian stood up. "I'll be in my room until the bank robbery."

"Boring," Damselfly muttered. She flipped to another station.

The show's narrator spoke with way too much enthusiasm. "Today on Haunted Weddings, one woman is turning her bachelorette party into a séance—"

Julian left the living room. In the hallway, he paused next to Blazar's door. He could just make out Blazar's voice, but the man was talking too quietly for Julian to catch whatever he was planning. Julian moved on to his own bedroom.

He booted up his computer, hopped onto the library's database, and began putting together a list of books that might help him with the stormoid. He'd hoped to do this in person today, but with the robbery interrupting his schedule, it would have to wait until his next shift.

It was difficult to figure out where to even begin looking for information, given how little Julian had to go off of. He had no choice but to cast his net wide. Books on Storm Warning, local legends and history, types of superpowers...

By the time Blazar knocked on his door and told him to be ready in ten, Julian didn't feel like he'd made much progress. Hopefully, it would be easier to work when he was actually in the library.

He put on his Citadel costume, grabbed his half mask, and headed out to the living room.

Lord Saturn was the first to emerge, after Julian. The base of her costume was a white bodysuit covered in pockets to hold her various pieces of tech. A gold belt held spherical bombs around her waist, which she called the "moons of Saturn." Bulky brown rocket boots allowed her to fly.

And, of course, there was her helmet. It was a large sphere resembling the planet Saturn, complete with a flat ring that floated around it, apparently held in place by some sort of magnetic field. Even though her head wasn't visible from the outside when she wore it, she could see the world around her, run scans, and take recordings, all thanks to the tiny cameras embedded in the outer layer.

Damselfly appeared next. "Blazar always lectures us about being ready on time, and he's always the last to show up," she complained. Her black helmet and body armor were also designed by Saturn. Two narrow slits in the armor were perfectly positioned to let her wings through, and any inner components visible through gaps in the armor glowed a matching bright blue. On the helmet were two massive, deep red compound eyes resembling a real damselfly's, along with antennae.

"Relax, Damselfly," Saturn said. "He'll be out any second."

Julian moved to the window and watched the traffic below. A couple of minutes passed before he heard footsteps behind him.

Blazar entered the living room, his head freshly shaved. His red supersuit had a white stripe running down each side and a simple, pointed collar lined with shiny gold material on the inside. The same material was used for the logo on his chest: swirling lines that formed a rough circle, a simplistic representation of the type of galaxy he'd named himself after.

Long white gloves nearly reached his elbows, while his simple white boots came halfway up to his knees.

"Follow my lead," Blazar ordered. He lifted a red mask with flame-shaped edges to his face. "When we're done, Lord Saturn and Damselfly will leave with the money while I burn the place down. Citadel will cover me."

After everyone voiced their agreement, Blazar led the team to the elevator. To the alley. Once outside, Julian lifted himself to the roof with a stone pillar while Lord Saturn and Damselfly flew, and Blazar raced up the side of the building with incredible speed. Together, they made their way to the north end of the city, where their target waited.

By the time they reached Marigold Bank, people had taken notice.

Blazar jumped from the building across the street from the bank and landed in the middle of traffic, sending cars swerving. In addition to being able to move fast enough to generate massive fires, he was nearly invulnerable. Dropping from heights barely hurt, and it took an incredible amount of force just to bruise him.

Julian followed him down from the roof. Saturn and Damselfly joined them, and the four stormed through the bank's front doors together.

Blazar swept his arm through the air in a blur, unleashing a wave of fire that scorched the walls. People dove for cover. More than a few screams echoed through the bank lobby.

"Bring us all of the money in this building," Blazar ordered. "Every bill, every last coin. And don't worry about not being able to open your vaults." He gestured to Saturn. "She'll get them open for you." She'd also be able to disable the dye packs that would otherwise make the money unusable.

The tellers scrambled to meet Blazar's demands. Saturn followed a pair of them out of the lobby in what was presumably the direction of the vault.

Julian had once asked Blazar why he bothered getting tellers to fetch the money when Saturn could just break into the vault and let the team in to grab everything themselves.

"If we can make them do the work for us, all the better," Blazar had replied. "Why should we have to carry all the money out of the vault when they can bring it to us?"

The bank customers congregated as far from the villains as physically possible, in a corner opposite the front doors. Some were still shrieking in fear, while others demanded Blazar let them go. Julian wanted to commend their bravery, but only an idiot would try to give Blazar orders.

"Citadel, Damselfly, get them to shut up," Blazar snapped.

Julian rolled his eyes under his mask. "We don't need them, do we? Let's just throw them out of here."

It took Blazar a moment to answer. "Fine. But as soon as Saturn gets back, I'm starting the fire. Be ready to cover me."

Julian focused his attention on the wall behind the crowd. There was a lot of material he couldn't manipulate, but just enough stone was present in the construction for him to work with. One of his fists clenched at his side. The wall exploded outwards, sending a spray of debris into the alley behind the building. The sound of approaching sirens drifted into the bank.

"Get out of here," Julian ordered. The civilians didn't have to be told twice. While they rushed to get out of the building, an explosion sounded nearby. The ground trembled.

A minute later, Saturn returned. The tellers followed with boxes of money. Damselfly took some of the boxes, yanking them from the tellers' hands with a little more aggression than necessary. Saturn stacked the rest in her arms. A girl working at the front desk added a large bag of coins to the pile.

The four villains exited the bank. The employees hurried out behind them and ran off in different directions. Blazar didn't give them a second glance.

While Damselfly and Lord Saturn took to the air with the money—aided by Saturn's gravity assists to handle the weight—Julian stepped into the street and crossed to the middle before turning around. He knew better than to stand anywhere close to Blazar when he started a fire.

Blazar rapidly faded into a blur as he circled the building. Flames rose in his path. After a few moments of running, he caught fire himself.

"Citadel!"

Julian whirled around at the sound of his name. Everyone else had abandoned the block or ran into other buildings to hide. Who the hell was brave enough to confront him?

A figure stepped onto the sidewalk. "Citadel!" they yelled again, and this time Julian recognized the voice. Charlotte. She'd pulled her hair up under the black hood of her jacket and hidden the lower half of her face with a white cloth mask, but it was definitely her. Judging by the bravado with which she spoke, she was trying to sound intimidating.

Okay, with the lightning jumping through the air around her, she admittedly was a little intimidating.

"Shit," Julian muttered. He couldn't let Blazar see her. He pulled up a wall of stone behind him, cutting them off from the bank. Once that was taken care of, he lifted his chin, put on an air of confidence, and strolled toward her. "Didn't think we'd be meeting again so soon. You got a hero name yet?"

"My name is the last thing you should be worried about." Charlotte lifted a hand. The wind picked up, but the lightning faded. Smoke from Blazar's fire moved in, helped by the wind, obscuring the world around them.

"That all?" Julian stopped and folded his arms. "Bit anti-climactic."

Charlotte's raised hand tightened into a fist. A blast of lightning cut through the air and missed Julian by a few feet.

She still had no idea what she was doing. This was going to be too easy. Julian laughed.

Eyes narrowing, Charlotte charged at him and swung her fist. He sidestepped the blow without much effort. "Nice try, but I think you need more practice—"

The next blow struck him square in the jaw. He staggered a couple of steps to the right.

Charlotte shook out her hand. "Ouch," she muttered.

Julian rubbed his jaw. "Not bad." She may not have thrown a proper punch, but there was definitely an abnormal amount of strength behind the blow. Not enough to damage his jaw, thankfully.

"I don't need compliments from you, asshole." Charlotte stretched out her fingers and pointed her palm toward Julian. Sparks jumped from her hand. No lightning followed.

Julian took another step toward her, and a gust of wind pushed him back. He stepped out of the air current and continued his approach. "You're not in control at all, are you?"

Charlotte swung again. He dodged the blow. While he was distracted, she stomped on his foot.

"Ow!" He jumped back. "Rude."

"I don't think I'm the rude one here."

"Well, I don't know if 'rude' is the best word to describe robbing a bank," Julian said.

"God, you villains are annoying." Charlotte lifted her fists into a defensive position.

Julian could end this whenever he wanted, but he was starting to have fun. All the thrill of dancing around with Storm Warning, with much less pain.

But he had Blazar to worry about.

Julian grabbed Charlotte's shoulder with one hand and summoned a blade of stone in the other. She yelped in surprise and tried to step out of his grasp, but spikes of stone burst from the ground around her feet to block her escape.

Julian hesitated at the alarm in her expression. Then, for a heartbeat, all he could hear was Blazar's voice. *You certainly got lucky, didn't you?*

Maybe Storm Warning had been having an off day. Not feeling well. He could have been tired. *Be honest. You* did *get lucky. Storm Warning kicked your ass every other time you fought him, assuming you didn't run away first.*

No one was watching. No one would know Julian had beaten another hero with Storm Warning's powers. And Charlotte couldn't be considered to be on Storm Warning's level, anyway. Not yet.

That's not the point, Julian reminded himself. The mission was to get the stormoid for Blazar.

But wouldn't it be good to remind the city not to mess with him and the other villains? To show them that there was no point trying to replace Storm Warning? And wouldn't it be nice to prove to Blazar that Storm Warning's death hadn't been a fluke? Despite his mentor's jabs, Julian really had earned that victory. He'd worked hard to make those walls work, even if there'd been a little luck on his side, too.

All of this flashed through Julian's mind in the span of a few heartbeats. Charlotte twisted in his grasp, still trying to break free. She'd managed to mask any traces of fear she may have felt. Instead, pure rage burned in her eyes.

Julian released his hold on her and stepped back. The spikes he'd built crumbled. "Why don't you try fighting me when you actually know what you're doing?" The foundations of a plan were forming in his mind.

"What?" Charlotte exclaimed as he turned around. "Get back here, I'm not done fighting you!"

Julian paused and glanced back. "I'm giving you a second chance. Don't wait around for me to change my mind." He thought for a moment. He needed to push her in the right direction, but he couldn't make it obvious. "Better figure out what exactly it is you've got inside of you."

CHAPTER SEVEN

The New Atlas Library—specifically the Warbler Hill branch—was the only place Julian could find any real peace in the city. His apartment was nice, but it overlooked a busy street, and his neighbors loved inviting loud friends over at all hours of the day. And even quiet days at the Complex were hard to enjoy knowing they could be interrupted at any moment by Blazar's arrival.

Julian was shelving books the morning after the bank robbery when Charlotte came in.

He hadn't really expected her to come. Not so soon, anyway, and maybe not at all. But he was undeniably grateful, given that his other plan had been to hang around the cafe and hope she showed up there at some point. Apparently, that little jab about her needing to get information had done the trick.

Charlotte's face lit up when she spotted him. "Oh, hey, it's you again!" A few people nearby glanced her way. "Sorry," she added, lowering her voice. She hurried over to Julian.

"What are you doing here?" Julian asked.

"Uh...researching something. You?"

"I work here."

"You're a librarian?" Charlotte rested a hand on her hip and looked him up and down. He wasn't sure what she was looking for, exactly. Maybe she didn't think he was dressed the way a librarian should. "Huh. Wasn't expecting that."

"What did you think I did?" Julian asked.

"I don't know." She chuckled. "My cousin said he was getting secret agent vibes, though. Or mob boss."

The corner of Julian's lip turned up in a slight smirk. "Sorry to be more boring than you expected."

"Nah, boring's good. Especially the way my life's going right now." Charlotte leaned in. Her voice dropped even quieter. "Speaking of which, can you help me? I'm looking for information."

"What kind of information?"

"Uh, okay, don't hate me," she said, rubbing the back of her neck. "I'm not completely sure. I'm trying to learn about a...I guess you could call it an artifact? I don't know if that would be history or physics. Oh, maybe books on the city's heroes would work better. For example, Storm Warning..."

Once Julian started this half-formed plan of his, there was no going back. Charlotte knew his name now, and where he worked. If this failed, the only way out was...

Well, he'd cross that bridge when he got to it. Or burn it.

"I know what you're looking for," Julian told Charlotte before she could stumble over her words any further. "I've been waiting for you."

"What—?"

Julian held up a hand. "Follow me. I can explain what's happening to you."

With only a few people working upstairs today, the office in the northwest corner of the building was sure to be empty. Julian used the walk to run through his idea one more time, hoping the story was believable.

Of course it was. Charlotte didn't know any better. She had no reason not to believe him, right?

Julian gestured for Charlotte to enter the office, then pulled the door shut behind him. "The artifact you took from Storm Warning is called the stormoid."

Charlotte, who'd started examining the books lining the shelf along the right wall, whirled around. "I didn't take it on purpose, I swear—"

"Relax, you're not in trouble," Julian told her. "When the host dies, the stormoid chooses a new one. My job is to show you how to use your powers."

Charlotte's brow furrowed. Julian masked his apprehension. *Come on, come on...*

"So, I was...chosen?" Charlotte asked.

Julian had to be careful answering this. His first idea was to train her for a public fight with Citadel, a fight he would then win. Hopefully. But he had another option to try, something that might work out better in the long run: turn her to his side. Make her a villain.

Then, not only would Julian have obtained the stormoid for Blazar, but he'd also have saved him the trouble of finding and preparing a new host. If Julian returned to the Complex with a fully trained villain, Blazar would have to admit that Julian was on his level.

"There's a lot we don't know about the stormoid," Julian answered. "But I believe it simply chooses a host based on vicinity."

"So, have you been following it around from host to host?" She squinted at him. "Did you train Storm Warning?"

He didn't look nearly old enough to say he'd trained Storm Warning. Julian supposed he could lie and say he was an ageless being, but he decided to go a different route. "No, I'm only twenty-four," he said, which might have been the first true thing he'd told her, besides his name and job. "My predecessor trained Storm Warning. And he taught me what he knew about the stormoid, so that I could train whoever found it next."

"And how did you know I have it?" Charlotte asked, brow furrowing. "Or that I would come here?"

Julian was grateful he'd thought of answers to most of her potential questions before her arrival. "I have a way to track it. And I was hoping you might come looking for information, but I would have found you soon enough, if you didn't."

"This is crazy!" Charlotte paced back and forth in front of the bookshelf. "I still can't believe it happened to me, of all people."

"Things happen without reason all the time," Julian replied. Blazar had told him that more times than he could count. "The world's a chaotic place." *People wind up in the wrong place at the wrong time, they die, and you get left behind.*

"Why did I even go up to his body in the first place? That was stupid. But I thought he was still holding on, you know?"

"If you need a few days to process—" Julian began.

Charlotte stopped. "No. Every day that passes is another day for those villains to hurt people. I have to start as soon as possible."

A smile touched Julian's lips. "Good."

"Great!" Charlotte put her hands on her hips. "Uh, I'm free tonight. Well, I have an assignment to finish, and then I'm free."

Tonight? The full weight of what Julian was trying to do hit him. "Sure," he forced himself to say. "I'm done here at five."

"I could meet you here then!"

"Perfect." Julian opened the office door. "Anything else I can help you with?"

"If you have any books on the stormoid I could read, that would be nice," Charlotte said as passed him.

"Nothing that convenient, unfortunately," Julian replied. He followed her out of the office. "But maybe I can find something in my files for you."

"Figures." Charlotte sighed. "In that case, I guess I'd better get back to homework."

They reached the main floor of the library, and Charlotte waved. "See you tonight!" she exclaimed. This time, she ignored the annoyed glance a nearby patron threw her way. Julian held back a sly smile as he waved back. Could he really train her?

Of course he could. How different could it possibly be from using his powers, even if they did have a different origin? And what better way to figure out her weaknesses? Besides, if at any point he decided this wasn't going to work, he could always fight her for the stormoid as Citadel.

Julian glanced around the library. Everything he'd told Charlotte about the stormoid was a lie, but there had to be real information on it somewhere, right?

52

CHAPTER EIGHT

Five o'clock dragged closer at a painfully slow pace. After finishing up a portfolio assignment for one of her graphic design classes, Charlotte wound up pacing around the kitchen and annoying the hell out of Spencer while he sat on the couch.

For the time being, Charlotte decided not to mention her encounters with Citadel to Spencer. The last thing she needed was a lecture on walking around the city alone. But she did share every last detail of what Julian had told her at the library.

"I wonder how long it'll take me to get as good as Storm Warning was," Charlotte said. "Probably more than a few weeks, right?"

"These aren't piano lessons, Charlotte." Spencer's hands twisted his hair into a braid as he spoke. "You're dealing with a huge amount of power."

"Pretty sure you don't learn piano in a few weeks, either," Charlotte pointed out.

"Can we back up a little? I thought you ran into this Julian guy at a cafe *before* you got Storm Warning's power orb...thing."

"Stormoid. And that was just a coincidence. I guess."

Spencer finished his braid and twisted an elastic into place at the end. "But how did he figure out it was you?"

"He said he could track it. Which makes sense, considering his whole job is to take care of it." Charlotte paused her pacing to offer a half-hearted shrug.

"Then why doesn't *he* take on its powers?" Spencer asked. "Why does there have to be a random guy following around whoever has the stormoid?"

"Because the stormoid went into my blood!"

"And there's no way you could give it to him?"

"Why would I do that?" Charlotte rested her hands on the counter behind her and leaned back. "Look, this happens all the time in the movies, right?"

"What does?"

"Someone gets cool new powers, and a mentor shows up to teach them how to use them!"

"Usually the mentor is, like, an old wizard dude," Spencer said. "Not a librarian who looks like he'd rather be out stabbing people." He raised an eyebrow.

Charlotte rolled her eyes. "He doesn't look scary!"

"I didn't say that! He just—" Spencer sighed. "I don't know. I'm worried about you. This is a lot to happen so quickly."

Charlotte wanted to insist she was fine for the millionth time, but she stopped herself. Instead, she said, "I know it's a lot. But I have to do this." She flashed a smile that she hoped was reassuring. "I promise I'll be careful, okay?"

Spencer still looked apprehensive. "And you won't push yourself too hard in training?"

"Of course."

"Okay," Spencer said. "It's just that the villains outnumber the heroes around here. I don't want you in over your head."

Charlotte nodded. "I'll take it slow." She glanced at the clock. Two more hours. "I'm going to take a nap," she told Spencer. "See you in a bit."

Spencer reached for the TV remote. "Sweet dreams, then."

If only. When Charlotte drifted off to sleep, she quickly found herself enveloped in shadows and lightning. The world trembled around her and—

Citadel was there. Attacking her. Disks of stone flew at Charlotte's face, and despite how vivid the dream was, she had no control over her body. More lightning flashed.

And then she was falling.

Charlotte jerked awake, stomach still doing somersaults. As she sat up, she swore she heard one last rumble of thunder. She glanced at the alarm clock on her desk. More time had passed than she'd expected. She'd need to leave soon to make it to the library on time.

She got ready quickly and headed out to the kitchen. Spencer had moved to the table, where he had one of his many physics textbooks open in front of him, though his gaze was on the phone in his hand.

"See you later." Charlotte waved goodbye as she reached the door.

"I might be meeting with some of my classmates to work on our group project," Spencer said. His eyes narrowed. "If they can get their shit together, that is. But I shouldn't be out too late, so I'm sure I'll see you at some point."

"Sounds good." Charlotte stepped outside and paused to take in the late afternoon sun. God, she loved spring. The end of the school year was near, the weather was pleasant, and there was something about golden hour that made her feel like she was on vacation.

When she arrived at the library, Julian was already standing out front. She waved. He returned the gesture and descended the steps to meet her.

"Do you have a cool training facility or something?" Charlotte asked.

"That would be nice, but unfortunately, no." Julian shrugged off his jacket as the two set off down the sidewalk. "I was hoping I'd have more time to sort that part out before I had to train someone. But there's a place just outside the city that should work until I find something more permanent."

"You have a car?" Charlotte asked.

"I do, but I don't use it much."

Spencer would probably lose his mind if Charlotte told him she was letting this guy take her outside of New Atlas. But she was pretty sure she could kick Julian's ass if things went south. She was the one with superpowers, after all.

"Have you tried using your powers at all?" Julian asked.

Charlotte hesitated. Should she tell him she'd fought Citadel? Twice, technically. She decided to leave that part out for now. She didn't need him thinking she was an idiot. "Yeah, a few times," she replied. "I've been able to summon electricity, but I can't make it go in the direction I want it to. I think I've also made it windy, but that might have been just...wind."

To her relief, Julian didn't ask her to elaborate on where exactly she'd been summoning electricity. "That sounds like a good start," he said.

They entered a parking garage. Julian pulled a key from his pocket. At the press of a button, the headlights of a sleek, black Porsche lit up.

"Whoa," Charlotte said as they reached the car. "You got this on a librarian's salary?"

"It was a gift from my...father." Julian opened the driver's side door and climbed in.

Hm. People who called their dads "father" tended not to be on the best terms with them, in Charlotte's experience. She slipped into the passenger seat. "How far are we going?" she asked.

Julian started the car. "Not far. Shouldn't be more than a twenty-minute drive, if traffic's still decent."

That made sense. They were already pretty close to the western edge of the city. As they pulled out of the garage, Charlotte tapped her fingers against her lap. She wanted to ask more questions about the stormoid, but Julian seemed a little lost in thought.

Before she could decide whether or not to try and start a conversation, Julian spoke first. "You said something about finishing a school assignment. Do you go to NAU?"

"Oh, yeah, I do!" Charlotte replied with more enthusiasm than she'd meant to. "I'm studying graphic design." She threw Julian a sideways glance. "You're not much older than me. Are you in school?

"No." After a moment, he added, "Not right now."

"The library thing does seem like a pretty sweet gig."

"I guess it is," Julian said, a slight smile on his lips. "But graphic design sounds fun."

"It is. Usually."

Julian lifted an eyebrow. "Usually?"

Charlotte found herself rambling about the annoying guy in her color theory class who'd interrupted three of her presentations. Then the professor who gave vague guidelines for assignments and later insisted no one had met the requirements. And, of course, last month's disastrous group project that had ended with someone throwing a guy's phone out the window.

Every few minutes, she'd trail off, fearing that Julian had tuned her out. But he'd proceed to ask a follow-up question or two that encouraged her to keep going, and he even chuckled at the dumb jokes she threw in.

They eventually took a freeway exit just outside the city limits, drove up a winding road through a heavily forested area, and ended their journey in an empty gravel parking lot. Julian put the car in reverse and rested a hand on the back of Charlotte's seat as he turned to peer through the back window. The vehicle rolled back. Charlotte's eyes lingered on Julian for a moment before she followed his gaze out the window.

"Yeah, this should work." Julian hit the brakes, threw the car in park, and turned off the engine.

"Ooh, this place is nice!" Charlotte said as she climbed out. She turned in a circle, taking in the nearby trees and the dancing patterns of shadows their leaves cast on the ground.

Julian closed his door. "No one really comes to this spot, since the main road goes right past it to all the marked sites."

"Well, maybe that's a good thing." Charlotte walked to a small patch of flowers at the edge of the lot and dropped to one knee to examine them. "It's beautiful out here."

She looked up to find Julian watching her. "Yeah, I suppose that's a nice...bonus." He lifted an eyebrow. "Are you going to be okay tearing it up a little?"

Charlotte stood up. A nearby clearing of dirt, presumably set aside for a campsite that had never materialized, looked like a large enough space to throw some wind and lightning around. And it would be a good challenge to try and stay in there, right?

"Yeah. Let's do this," Charlotte said, starting toward the clearing.

Julian joined her, and when they'd reached the center of the space, he moved to stand a few feet in front of her. "You said you can summon electricity on command, right?" he asked.

"Uh, sometimes."

"Sometimes?"

It had mostly happened when she was in danger, whether by accident or by running into it deliberately. "I've tried to recreate the feeling I get when it does work, and nothing happens," Charlotte said, instead of elaborating on what had made the powers surface in the first place. "I'm not sure how I actually made it happen the first time."

"Well, that's your first problem. You're trying to summon a feeling, and not the power itself," Julian said. "Close your eyes."

Charlotte did as he asked.

Julian was quiet for a moment. "Can you feel it inside you?" he asked. "The stormoid?"

Charlotte tried to sense it and found nothing. "I don't think so."

"Hm. Okay." There was the soft sound of footsteps, and Charlotte got the sense Julian was circling her.

"It seems like my powers only come out when I feel a strong emotion," Charlotte told him.

"That's not surprising, but you should be able to master it no matter what state you're in." Julian paused at her right. "Storm Warning could summon a full-on storm while perfectly calm."

"That's a lot."

"Don't worry about being at that level, yet. Don't stress about trying to use any of your powers. Just stand still for a moment."

Charlotte took a deep breath. "Okay."

"I think you're struggling to bring out your power because you expect it to feel a certain way," Julian said. "Try to forget about that. Reach for your power, but don't think about how it's supposed to feel or get frustrated if it doesn't work right away."

"Should I try for a bolt of lightning?" Charlotte asked.

"Maybe try starting with something smaller."

Charlotte could almost hear the smile in his voice. Still keeping her eyes closed, she held up one of her hands and willed a small amount of electricity to dance across her palm. For a painfully long moment, there was nothing.

Then, there was water hitting her skin.

Charlotte opened one eye. A tiny cloud had materialized a foot above her hand and was spilling rain onto her skin. As she watched, lightning dropped from the cloud to strike her palm. There was even a light breeze grazing her skin.

"I did it!" Charlotte exclaimed, both eyes opening wide. It hadn't been exactly what she'd intended, but the tiny cloud was too cute for her to be anything but delighted.

Julian grinned. "You did."

Charlotte's face flushed. She cleared her throat. "They feel different from each other," she said. "The water, the wind, the lightning—I can sense them each as a different component."

"Good," Julian said. "Focus on those differences. You need to be comfortable with each one separately."

Charlotte was able to maintain the mini storm for a minute before it died out. After that, she spent another ten minutes just making rain clouds. It started feeling like a pointless exercise pretty quickly, but Julian assured her it was a good place to start. And once she'd gotten the hang of making them appear, he directed her to push them around the clearing.

"It might feel like a waste of time right now," Julian said. "But once you understand how to manipulate the clouds, you'll be able to apply that to your more...dangerous powers."

By the time the setting sun blanketed the forest in oranges and reds, Charlotte had been able to muster a cloud the size of a large dog and keep it raining for nearly three minutes straight. It was a better record than she'd expected to set coming into this.

"We won't stay out much longer," Julian told her, stopping her from forming another cloud once the last one dissipated. "I just want to do one more assessment real quick." He pushed up the sleeves of his shirt.

Charlotte's heart skipped a beat. Sheesh. She was going to need to try harder to stay focused on the superpower thing.

Julian continued, oblivious to the slight heat in her face. "There's more to a fight than using your powers. I'm going to train you in combat as well." He walked forward until they faced each other only a few feet apart. "Let's see where you're at first, though. Throw a punch at me."

"What?" Charlotte exclaimed. She took an instinctive step back. "I can't punch you!"

Julian laughed. "Why not?"

"I don't want to hurt you!"

"Don't worry about that."

"Are you sure?" Charlotte raised her fists slowly. "I have super strength."

"Trust me, I can handle it." After a moment, he added, "The details aren't important, but I'm also stronger than an ordinary human."

That piqued Charlotte's interest, but she decided to hold off on pressing him for more information. She curled her hand into a fist.

"Hold on," Julian said. "Hold out your hand."

Charlotte did, and he gently took it. He made minor adjustments to her fingers as he spoke. "Put your thumb here and adjust the angle slightly. Like this." He brushed his thumb over her knuckles. "Try to make contact here, all right? These two are the strongest."

Charlotte pressed her lips together and nodded. Julian pulled away and took a step back. "Whenever you're ready," he said.

Not giving herself any time to hesitate, Charlotte swung. Her fist met Julian's jaw. He staggered to the side.

"Sorry!" she exclaimed.

Julian responded with a short laugh. He wiped his arm across his face as he straightened up. "That was great. You've got a lot of strength. You just need to learn how to channel it properly."

"Okay." Charlotte grimaced. "Are you going to make me punch you again?"

"Not right now. We'll dive more into combat next time. But today was a good start." Julian started toward the car. "I'll try to find us somewhere in the city where we can train. Maybe a basement somewhere."

Charlotte laughed as she caught up to him. "That would be great. But it also sounds a bit ominous."

"Sorry," Julian replied, a hint of a smile on his lips. "I'll come up with a better way to describe it."

On the drive back, Julian laid out a rough outline of what he hoped to accomplish next time: basics of combat, manipulating electricity, hitting a target she was actually aiming for... Charlotte eagerly nodded along to all of it.

"I can drop you off outside your building," Julian said as they reentered the city. "If that's all right."

"Oh, sure, I'll direct you to my street corner," Charlotte replied. "It's kind of a tight street. I won't make you drive all the way down. It's a short walk, anyway."

As her block neared, Charlotte asked the question she'd been dwelling on since they'd left the forest. "Did you ever get to meet Storm Warning?"

A second passed. Another. "Yes," Julian answered. "A few times, to get a feel for how he used his powers." Maybe the delay came from his concentration on the road, but Charlotte swore there was some hesitation in his expression.

Still, she asked another. "Do you know his real identity?" Before Julian could respond, she quickly added, "I don't expect you to tell me, of course. Just curious."

"No, I didn't know his real name. I might have found out at some point, but I guess that won't happen now."

"Right."

A couple of minutes later, Julian slowed. "Here?"

"Yeah, this is perfect." Charlotte pulled out her phone as he brought the car to a complete stop. "Here, let me give you my number so we can work out a schedule. My classes are all over the place, but most days I'll be free either in the morning or late afternoon."

After that was taken care of, Charlotte threw her door open and hopped out. She spun around and bent over to peer back into the car. "Have a good night!"

Something flashed across his face. Surprise? Whatever it was, it was gone so fast, Charlotte thought she might have imagined it. He smiled. "You too."

CHAPTER NINE

Training Charlotte was going to be easy. She was already in a better place than Julian had been when he started trying to control his abilities. And thankfully, the same principles Julian used to master his abilities seemed to work for her.

Now, his biggest issue was time. Blazar was going to be impatient when it came to the stormoid. Julian would have to come up with a way to keep him from worrying. Charlotte certainly wasn't going to reach Storm Warning's level before Julian fought her for the stormoid, but he just needed her to *appear* as strong as the previous hero had.

As Julian laid in bed that night, he recalled how Blazar had helped him learn to use his powers. Blazar had started with similar techniques—telling Julian to relax, to calm his mind—for a month or so. That had been much more difficult for Julian than it would be for Charlotte, considering Blazar took him in right after his parents' deaths.

Julian had already known about his abilities at thirteen. Once rocks started popping up around him and cracks appeared in the driveway when he was upset, his mom sat him down and explained that there were some strange genes in her family. Power came and went through the generations, varying in strength.

All Mom could really do was move dirt around and create a handful on occasion. Sometimes flowers appeared in their yard when no seeds had ever been planted. And when it came to injuries, she had a resilience that bordered on unnatural.

But before she could teach him much, there'd been the big battle between the hero Sunbeam and the villain Incinerator—both dead now, and Julian couldn't help but wish he'd been the one to kill them. Julian's childhood home had been one of many in the New Atlas suburbs that were caught in the crossfire.

Julian had only survived because of his powers. He didn't tell anyone, but it was clear that something miraculous had happened when first responders pulled him from the rubble. When he arrived at the New Atlas Child Services office to be dealt with, his case wound up in the hands of Blake Sullivan.

The infamous Blazar.

While Julian had been alarmed to end up in a supervillain's care at first, Blazar had given him everything he could ever want in his home at the Complex. For the first time in his life, Julian got whatever he asked for.

"It was a blast from the hero that destroyed your home," Blazar reminded him, soon after taking him in.

"They said in the news that the fight was the only way to stop Incinerator," was Julian's reply.

"Sure, sure, collateral damage is inevitable. But what's the point, then? You do everything right and people still get hurt." Blazar stood with his hands clasped behind his back, staring at the city through one of the living room's massive windows while Julian sat at the kitchen counter.

"Heroes and villains are titles thrust on us by the people," Blazar continued. "I embrace it, sure. I take what I want, and that makes me a villain in their eyes. But some people are born with wealth and influence. We're born with abilities. Life gives everyone different assets, it's up to us to make use of them." His head turned. The city lights illuminated his profile. "Am I any different than the man who inherits a company, the man who reaps the benefits of the work done by his employees?"

He said that like many of those people weren't villains, too. A different kind of villain, sure, but villains all the same.

Not long after that, Blazar offered to help Julian with his powers. "I won't tell you what to do with them," he'd said. "But I hate to see power go to waste."

It started with the relaxed sessions, with Julian being told to clear his head. To focus on feeling his power before he tried to wield it. Blazar did that until Julian could control when the stones appeared in his hand, when the cracks appeared in the ground.

Then the sessions consisted of Blazar racing in circles around him, throwing fireballs his way, forcing Julian to learn to make shields of stone or risk burns. And he did get burned quite a few times. Until he got better.

Julian couldn't use his powers against Charlotte in training. She'd figure out his true identity in a heartbeat. But he'd hated every moment of fighting Blazar, anyway. Had it helped? He wasn't sure. He'd trained alone a lot, too.

Well, he could always stage a few smaller fights between Citadel and Charlotte to build her up. And get a feel for her fighting style, while keeping it simple himself. Saving his best tricks for the real show.

Lying in bed at his apartment, Julian closed his eyes. Blazar's voice was always in his head these days. "No one owes you anything," he'd always say to teenage Julian. "If you want it, you have to take it for yourself."

Blazar was right. No one owed Julian a victory. And Blazar didn't owe him his respect. Julian was going to have to be ruthless to earn it. To earn the city's fear.

And after that, he could have...

Anything, really.

Julian hated thinking about the day his parents died, the day he lost his home, but every once in a while, the memory hit him hard. Tonight it was back, demanding he relive every detail.

He hadn't used his powers on purpose. All he remembered was the world crashing down around him, and then darkness. When he was pulled out hours later, he realized he'd shaped a space in the rubble around him to protect himself.

Julian's eyes shot open. Of course! There had to be somewhere in the city where he could carve out a space underground to train Charlotte in.

It was a bit harder to get to sleep after that, itching with the urge to start researching locations, his mind racing with places to start. But there was no reason to rush. Better to get some much-needed sleep.

He texted Charlotte the next morning to sort out their next session, which they planned for Thursday. Good. That would give him a couple of days to find and prepare a training room.

After he dressed and ate breakfast, he walked aimlessly around New Atlas, focused on the world beneath him. With his senses, he traced tunnels and sewers and pipes and sprawling sections of earth and stone. Eventually, he settled on an area not far from the library, underneath a small plaza. There was nothing interesting around to draw unwanted civilians in, and there was a spot behind a wall where he could hide an entrance.

Perfect. He'd come back tonight to shape the room, and—

Julian's phone buzzed. He opened it and sighed. A text from Blazar. *Come to the COVE as soon as you can.*

With nothing else to do at the moment, Julian supposed he'd better deal with this now. *On my way,* he texted back. It seemed like a waste for Blazar to call him all the way to the Complex just to ask about the stormoid. Hopefully Blazar wanted something else.

When Julian entered the Complex, Blazar and Saturn were in the living room, wearing their villain suits and talking—arguing, really—with each other in hushed tones.

"—I tried to find a place that would have everything," Saturn said. "It just doesn't exist. We'll have to make three stops."

Blazar closed his eyes and pinched the bridge of his nose. "It'd be easier to go farther and hit one place—"

"I'm telling you, there's nothing!" Saturn folded her arms. "Don't ask for my help if you're going to turn around and act like I don't know what I'm talking about."

Julian cleared his throat. "Is something wrong?"

"Damselfly's hurt," Blazar said, burning gaze still locked with Saturn's.

Julian's heart dropped to his stomach. "Badly?" he asked, his blood running cold. Was she—?

"She'll be fine," Saturn said, glancing at Julian before shooting Blazar a glare. "Don't give him a heart attack, for god's sake."

"He knows what happens in this business."

"Exactly!"

Blazar rolled his eyes and faced Julian. "Damselfly tried to kidnap the mayor last night."

"Alone?" Julian asked incredulously.

"Yeah. Ran into some wannabe hero who did a number on her. Look, she'll be fine, but Saturn wants someone here to keep an eye on her and make sure she doesn't drop dead."

"Just take her food when she gets hungry, and check on her wounds," Saturn said. "Her arms were bleeding pretty heavily, so some of those bandages might need to be changed. Don't forget to add disinfectant."

"Where are you two going?" Julian asked.

"I'm working on a new plan, but I need some parts to make it work," Blazar said.

"*I* need the parts," Saturn corrected. "I'm the one who actually knows how to build your ideas, Blake."

"Well, good luck," Julian said as he passed them. Neither responded. When Julian reached the hall, he paused and glanced back.

Blazar had a hand resting on the side of Saturn's face. "You know I wouldn't be here without you. I need you."

Saturn's eyes narrowed. "You need my tech."

"You're ridiculous." Blazar's voice lowered, but Julian could still hear him. "Come on, Sophia. You know we can pull this off. New Atlas will bow to us. And after that, we'll move on to other cities. No one will be able to stop us."

Saturn didn't respond.

"You say people don't listen to you?" Blazar pressed. "Make them listen to you."

Julian continued into the hallway and walked to Damselfly's door. He knocked. "Hey, it's Julian. Can I come in?"

"Do you have food?" Damselfly called.

Julian sighed. "What do you want?"

"Ice cream."

Julian returned to the living room. Blazar and Saturn were gone. He grabbed a container of chocolate ice cream and a spoon from the kitchen before returning to Damselfly's room.

She sat in bed, eyes fixed on her TV. Bandages covered her left arm, her right forearm, and more were visible at the neckline of her baggy t-shirt. Julian didn't have a chance to speak before she stuck out a hand. He handed her the ice cream and spoon.

While Damselfly popped open the container and dove in, Julian grabbed the chair sitting next to her desk and dragged it to her bedside. "How'd they get through your armor?"

Damselfly swallowed. "Blazar didn't tell you who I fought?"

"Nope."

"It was Collider."

Julian frowned. "I've heard the name, but none of us have fought them before, right?" He wasn't even sure of the hero's gender. Maybe their costume hid it even from people who did encounter them—it wasn't a bad idea play it extra safe when it came to hiding your identity. It just took some extra work.

"Nope. No one knows much about them, and they don't talk much," Damselfly said. "But their power is density manipulation. They can make themselves really strong, or light enough to float, or phase through objects entirely. Like my armor."

Even if that were true, it would take a lot of skill to injure Damselfly like this. They'd need to phase the part of their body passing through her armor while keeping whatever weapon they used solid in order to cut through skin.

"Blazar could have killed them." Damselfly looked up. "You could have."

"Maybe," Julian said. "They sound like they're pretty good. I'm surprised we haven't dealt with them before." Maybe it was the loss of Storm Warning that had encouraged Collider to try their luck against a COVE villain.

"Well, it was only a matter of time, right?" Damselfly set the ice cream container on her nightstand. She pulled her legs to her chest and rested her chin on her knees. "I'm not good enough to be a villain, and I can't be a normal person either."

Julian had no idea what he could say that would make her feel better. And she'd know if he lied. "Damselfly, you've accomplished plenty," he tried.

"So what? I'll never be like you or Blazar."

"Who says you have to be like us? It doesn't matter."

Damselfly rolled her eyes. "If it doesn't matter, then why are you all so obsessed with beating the biggest heroes? You made such a big deal out of killing Storm Warning."

Julian leaned back in the chair. "Well, it means we don't have to worry about him interfering with our plans anymore. I've cleared the way for...whatever it is Blazar is working on."

"At least admit you like bragging about it." Damselfly sighed. "It's all about reputation."

Julian couldn't argue with that. If it were only about convenience, he'd have taken the stormoid from Charlotte already.

His phone buzzed in his pocket. Expecting something from Blazar, he pulled it out. It was a text. But not from the villain.

Damselfly leaned over. "Who's Charlotte?"

"What? No one."

Wrong answer. Damselfly lifted an eyebrow. Julian groaned internally. He had told so many lies already. Why couldn't he have said she was a coworker?

"She's clearly someone," Damselfly said, a sly grin crossing her face. Well, at least she wasn't sad anymore. But this might be worse.

"And who do you think she could possibly be?"

"A girl," Damselfly sang.

"Well, yeah, obviously." Julian leaned away from Damselfly and unlocked his phone. "And so what if she is?"

"Do you like her?"

"No! Who even said I'm into women, anyway?"

Damselfly rolled her eyes. "Nice try, but you told me you're bi at the Christmas party last year."

"What? I don't remember that."

"Eh, I'm not surprised. You were pretty drunk," Damselfly said. She let out a short laugh. "You accidentally broke one of Blazar's fancy glasses, and he was pissed." Leaning back against her pillows, she added, "But I'm probably the only person who remembers all that, since you were very insistent I didn't drink anything."

Oh. That did sound familiar. And not surprising. Despite his size, Julian had always been a lightweight to an *embarrassing* degree. He was glad he'd at least had the sense to keep alcohol out of Damselfly's hands. Saturn hadn't let him drink at the Complex parties when he was a teenager, either. He was grateful for that, now.

There had been more villains at the parties, back then. Some had established themselves in New Atlas before Blazar invited them to join the COVE, while others had been legally adopted by him. Like Julian.

So many had been killed in the years after Blazar brought Julian in. For a moment, Julian found his mind wandering to all those days Blazar had come to the Complex to announce that someone else was gone. All of the funerals.

Damselfly returned to pestering Julian about Charlotte, bringing him back to the present. "Come on, the least you could do is tell me about her!" she said. "I don't get to go out and talk to people like you do."

"Why do you even care?" Julian asked.

"You know I love drama. And this is a million times better than the stuff on TV."

"And a million times more boring," Julian told her. "Seriously. It's nothing."

"Uh huh." In the blink of an eye, Damselfly snatched his phone from his hand. "I'm sure that's why your last text to her says... 'Looking forward to seeing you Thursday.'" She shot him an amused look. "First of all, do you seriously text like that?"

"What's wrong with the way I text?" Julian asked.

"You sound like an old person."

Julian grabbed his phone back. "Excuse me?"

"Hey! What did she say after that?" Damselfly demanded.

Julian glanced at the text he'd just gotten from Charlotte. *Can't wait!* "I don't think I need to reply to it."

Damselfly leaned forward to peer at the screen. "Sure, I guess not. That exclamation point seems pretty excited, though."

"I'm serious, this is...work-related. It's a professional exclamation point."

The truth about his plans might get Damselfly to leave the matter alone, but Julian wasn't completely sure he could trust her with that. Not yet.

Damselfly finally relented and turned her attention back to the TV. "If you say so." Her smug smile made it clear this wouldn't be the last Julian heard of it, though.

He stared at the phone screen for a long moment before returning it to his pocket. *Yeah, right.* Charlotte was certainly likeable, but he knew better than to let himself get too close. Train her, fight her, take back the stormoid. It was a simple plan, and it would be a waste of a perfect opportunity if he screwed this up.

Damselfly fell asleep at some point. Julian took that opportunity to switch from her reality show to the news. After discussing a car crash on the freeway outside New Atlas for a minute, they cut to an aerial shot of a factory.

"There was an attack here earlier tonight," the reporter said. "New Atlas supervillains Blazar and Lord Saturn broke in and caused extensive damage before robbing the warehouse. The company has not yet disclosed what was stolen. This comes shortly after a similar break-in at another facility twenty miles away..."

A third attack was covered not long after. And only half an hour after that, the sound of the elevator door opening echoed through the Complex. Julian went out to meet Blazar and Saturn.

"Got what you needed?" he asked.

"Sure did." Blazar tossed a black duffel bag onto the kitchen counter. Its contents clanged against each other.

"Careful," Saturn murmured.

"Damselfly's asleep," Julian told the two. "Her bandages look fine. I'm going to head home."

"You could spend the night here," Blazar suggested.

"I work early tomorrow," Julian lied. "And I need a few things at my apartment."

"Suit yourself." Blazar moved to the cupboards, likely in search of a drink. "Any progress finding the stormoid?"

"I'll let you know as soon as I have something concrete," Julian replied. "But I've been following a few leads on people who were near Storm Warning's body after he fell."

Blazar nodded. "Good."

Julian left the Complex with mixed emotions. On the one hand, he was relieved to have Blazar's attention off him, if only for a little while.

On the other, leaving Damselfly under Blazar's care had him feeling strangely guilty.

CHAPTER TEN

The walk from campus back to Charlotte's apartment was going great, until she dropped her tablet.

Trying to answer emails while walking was probably a bad idea.

"No, no, no," she muttered as she bent down to pick it up. The screen was shattered, barely clinging on. Charlotte pressed the power button. It lit up, to her relief, but using it was going to be a nightmare now. She doubted she'd be able to draw at all.

She cradled it in one arm as she threw open the door to the apartment. "Spencer? You here?"

"Kitchen!" Spencer called.

Charlotte walked into the kitchen, where Spencer was making a sandwich. "How were your classes?" Charlotte asked.

"Surprisingly good. My magnetism exam went well," Spencer answered. "And my calculus professor approved my extra credit assignment."

"Oh, congrats!"

"How was your morning?"

Charlotte held up the tablet. "I think this about sums it up."

Spencer winced. "Does it still work?"

"Barely." Charlotte set the device on the counter and sighed. "I have jus enough money to get groceries for the rest of the year. I can't buy a new tablet until I start working this summer."

Spencer closed up his sandwich. "Can your parents help you?"

"I can't ask them for a new tablet, they're still paying off the car they had to buy last year." Charlotte sighed. "It's fine. I'll figure something out. I'm pretty sure the art department has tablets they rent out." They'd be old as hell, but that was better than nothing.

Spencer cleared his throat. "You're meeting with Julian later today, right?"

"Oh, right!" Charlotte perked up. "Yeah, I'll leave in a couple hours. Which reminds me, I wanted to practice a little more before then."

"In here?" Spencer asked.

"Yeah! All I've been doing is making small clouds." Charlotte held out a hand, and sparks jumped from her palm. "Oh, uh, and that. Sometimes."

"Just don't set the place on fire. Or flood it."

"Roger that."

As Charlotte headed for her room, Spencer called after her, "Hey, aren't you supposed to be able to fly?"

Charlotte stopped in the hallway. "Uh, maybe?" she called back.

"You haven't tried it yet?"

"No."

Charlotte entered her room and pulled the door closed behind her. She blinked, and she was somewhere else entirely.

She stood on the roof of a building. A storm brewed in the sky above her. As her head tipped back, a bolt of lightning broke through the clouds and struck the ground in front of her. She tried to look around, but the body she was in refused to cooperate. She had a feeling it wasn't her own, although there was something familiar about being in it.

Whatever was happening to her, she snapped out of it within seconds and found herself back in her room. She looked around frantically, wondering if something had triggered the vision, but nothing looked out of the ordinary.

Had she fallen asleep...standing up? Was that something that could happen?

No, it had to be related to the stormoid. But if so, what was it she was seeing? Charlotte would have to ask Julian about it when she saw him. In the meantime, she did have a portfolio statement to work on.

While Charlotte typed away on her laptop, she kept part of her focus on maintaining a dark cloud over her bed. She would have kept it closer to her, but her clouds tended to let out bursts of electricity or rain when she got annoyed, so it seemed best to keep it away from the computer.

Finally, she let the cloud fade away, stretched out her arms, and rose to her feet. She still had plenty of time before she needed to meet Julian at the library, but if she left now, she could take the longer route around a block filled with stores and restaurants. After throwing on shoes and saying goodbye to Spencer, she set out.

A lot of stores tempted Charlotte on her walk. After passing up a plant shop and a stationary store and some cute clothes in window displays, it was an electronics store that ended up drawing her in. She told herself she was just going to take a look as she entered, knowing deep down she wouldn't be making a purchase here anytime soon.

Charlotte looked over the tablets, comparing models and checking out reviews. She was distracted from her shopping when a man in a nice suit entered. He walked to a cabinet of laptops—the most expensive models in the store—and waved over an employee to unlock the door for him. Charlotte watched him check the gold watch on his wrist as the employee approached. Must be nice, she thought, to just buy a new laptop without thinking twice.

Well, she'd been here long enough. Time to go meet Julian.

Her heart quickened as she turned onto the street with the library. God, she only hoped she could make it through training without embarrassing herself. It was bad enough that she felt like she sucked at using her powers, despite Julian's insistence she was doing well. The fact that she was so easily distracted by him made matters a hundred times worse.

Charlotte shook off the thought. *Figure out your powers now, figure out your feelings later.* Saving New Atlas from villains was more important than worrying about whether or not she had a chance with Julian.

CHAPTER ELEVEN

When he had time to spare between his usual library tasks, Julian dug around the city archives for information on Storm Warning. Maybe the stormoid wasn't public knowledge, but it was possible there was a detail somewhere that could provide a hint about its origin. Books written on Storm Warning would be even better, but most of them had been checked out after his death, with hold lists a mile long.

If news articles and websites didn't yield anything useful, Julian supposed he could track the borrowers down and steal the books. That might be overkill. But he wanted every last piece of information he could get. Even if he figured out how to take the stormoid from Charlotte without issue, more intel would be helpful for whoever Blazar gave it to.

Plus, Julian had no idea how to go about containing the stormoid once he took it from Charlotte. She said it had entered her blood and there hadn't seemed to be a way to stop it. What would have happened if there was no one nearby for the stormoid to enter?

Blazar had assumed the stormoid would remain in the host's body until someone deliberately removed it. What else could he be wrong about?

Julian set aside a few articles about a battle between Storm Warning and a villain called Pitfall that looked promising, along with an interview Storm Warning had done nearly a decade earlier. He'd have to read them later. After his training session with Charlotte.

Today, she was already waiting on the steps by the time he stepped outside. "Sorry I'm a few minutes late," he told her. "Busy day."

"Oh, no worries! I was a little late, too," Charlotte said, dismissing the apology with a wave of her hand. "So, where we headed?"

"I found a place nearby that I think will be perfect."

Julian led her to the plaza above the new training room. His hastily installed door still remained in place in one of the connected alleys, and his key unlocked it without issue.

After carefully shaping the room, he'd brought in some extra lamps from his apartment. The place still looked rather unwelcoming after that, so he threw in an old rug, but that hadn't helped much. "I did my best to make it...nice," he said as they entered, surprised to find he was a little embarrassed by how dingy it looked. "But I guess there's no point bothering with interior design if you're going to be tearing the place up."

Charlotte laughed. "I don't care, as long as we'll be safe down here."

"Of course." Granted, if the place collapsed, Julian would be forced to reveal his powers. Hopefully, it wouldn't come to that.

"How did you find this place?" Charlotte began circling the room, her eyes sliding over every inch.

"I went through some old city maps," Julian told her. "It used to be a storage room."

She ran a hand along one of the walls. "Huh. Doesn't look that old."

Maybe Julian should have put a few cracks in the concrete to make the place seem older. Oh, well. Charlotte would probably forget that detail once they began training. And it wasn't as if he could add dust and grime. "Let's get started," he said, hoping to distract her from her investigation.

Practice went well for about twenty minutes. But the longer Julian tried to have Charlotte keep a small shower of rain going, or maintain a steady flow of electricity, the more frustrated she became.

"Damn it," she cursed after her electricity flickered out for the twentieth time.

Maybe it was Julian's imagination, but she seemed more irritated with herself than usual. "I understand why you're stressed," he said. "But there's no rush to figure this out." Well, there was, and they both had different reasons for wanting her to improve quickly. Reminding her of that wouldn't make her better, though.

"It's not the powers that are stressing me out. I've had a long week." Charlotte reached up to adjust her ponytail. "And I dropped my tablet earlier today, and it's broken, and I need it for school, but I have no idea what I'm going to do because I don't have the money to buy a new one right now." The words tumbled out, taking on a frantic pace the longer she talked.

"Not enough money?" Julian frowned.

"Yeah, I mean, I'm not exactly swimming in cash." Charlotte lowered her arms and sighed. "I have a few ideas. I'm just going to be stressed until I get it sorted out."

Now this was something Julian could work with. Could he push her in another direction? Remind her that she had the power to take any tablet she wanted? He couldn't do it as Julian. But Citadel could use this.

Charlotte pressed her hand to her forehead. "Ugh, I have a project I need to finish by Monday. Maybe I can borrow someone else's."

Monday was too soon for a fight with Citadel, but the money issue was still something Julian could work with later. "I think I could find you a tablet to use," he said.

Charlotte perked up. "Really?"

"Sure, I bet someone in my family has one lying around that they don't need." He probably could take one of Damselfly's or Saturn's and they wouldn't even notice.

"That would be great!" Charlotte exclaimed. She quickly added, "If you're sure."

"Of course," Julian said with a wave of his hand. "Now, let's get back to lightning."

After a few attempts that ended with Julian getting shocked, he was able to talk Charlotte through guiding the lightning in a steady arc between her hands.

"Good," he said, watching the electricity jump from one palm to the other. The next step would be figuring out how well she could aim.

Charlotte looked up at him, her warm eyes reflecting the lightning as it faded from her hands. "It's not as easy as clouds, but it's getting there." A smile crossed her face as she added, "Thanks."

It took Julian a moment to find his train of thought. "Let's finish up with some more combat practice," he said, wondering if the electricity had hit him harder than he'd realized. "Once you've improved a little more at both, we can start combining them."

"That sounds dangerous," Charlotte said. "For you, I mean." She grinned.

"Well, I have a few ideas." Julian had no ideas. Maybe he could find some kickboxing dummies for her to attack? That sounded like a problem for him to deal with tomorrow. He lifted his fists. "For now, show me how you would attack me. Try not to electrocute me."

"No promises," Charlotte said with a smirk. She threw a punch. At least she'd shed her reservations about hitting him.

Julian dodged, barely. Charlotte swung again, and he held up a hand to catch her fist. "Can you block?" he asked.

"Block?"

He swung at her, deliberately slowing himself so he could test her reaction time and pull back if needed. She caught on quick and ducked. As she moved, she pulled her hand free from his and darted to the right. By the time he was turning around to face her, she was throwing another punch.

This one caught Julian in the chest and sent him stumbling back. Charlotte paused, hesitation creeping into her face. He nodded as he straightened up. "Keep going," he said. "You're doing well."

She pressed forward. Julian focused on dodging as he moved backward, letting her gain ground until he hit the wall. When she swung again, he reached up to grab her arm. "Not bad, but you're easy to dodge," Julian told her. "You need to focus on not giving your next move away."

"How am I giving myself away?" Charlotte asked.

"You'd do fine against most people, but a trained fighter can figure it out from the way you shift your weight. And you need to get faster."

In the silence that followed, Julian realized how close Charlotte's face was to his. He let go of her arm, and she took a step back, still breathing hard. "How do I get faster?" she asked.

Julian straightened up and cleared his throat. "Practice. You're still adjusting to your new strength. If you have a gym you can go to, maybe with kickboxing bags, that would be a good thing to do when you have time."

"Got it." Charlotte nodded. "Anything else?"

"Now's a good time for a break," Julian said. "But you should try building up the amount of time you can keep electricity going on your own. Next time, we'll start target practice."

While Julian turned off the lamps, Charlotte climbed the stairs and opened the door at the entrance to let light spill in. Julian caught up with her, and they stepped out of the tunnel.

"Hey, Julian," Charlotte said as they left the plaza.

Julian didn't like the way his heart quickened at the way she said his name. Residual adrenaline from their practice fight, he tried to tell himself. "Yeah?"

"I haven't tried flying yet. Should I...start working on that?"

As much as he wanted her to get started on that, he had a feeling she wasn't quite ready. "Might be too ambitious to try that so soon. Let's get you more control over the other elements of your power before you go jumping off buildings." Julian glanced sideways at her. "It could be worth seeing if you can levitate a few feet off the ground, though. Somewhere indoors," he emphasized. Hopefully she wouldn't go crashing through any ceilings.

"I have tried that!" Charlotte exclaimed with a ferocity that took him by surprise. "I haven't felt anything at all."

"Keep trying. I'm sure you'll figure it out soon." He needed her to.

They walked to the next block together. Julian started toward the crosswalk, but Charlotte stopped and gestured to the right with her thumb. "Well, my apartment's that way, so I guess I'll see you later," she said.

Julian nodded.

"Good night!" Charlotte added as she turned around.

"Good night," Julian called back.

As he walked, Julian contemplated the best way to get Charlotte a tablet. Borrowing one still seemed plausible, but he was beginning to lean toward simply buying her a new one. It would be easiest, really, and money wasn't an issue for him. So why not?

Julian stopped in front of an electronics store. Closed already? He'd been ready to buy a tablet for convenience's sake, but maybe he could come back in a couple of hours and break in.

No, bad idea. If Charlotte heard about a break-in happening right before he gave her a new tablet, she might think it was more than a coincidence. With a sigh, Julian turned around. It was a much farther walk, but he knew of another store that was open until one a.m.

The place was crowded as hell, and the song blaring over the store radio was one Julian had already heard too many times this week. Another reason the library was the best place in the city.

Still, he made his way to tablet display and looked them over until he found a model that looked like the best one out right now. As he reached for a box, he noticed that the shelf to his left had the same model in different colors. Including a shade of blue similar to Charlotte's hair. Julian grabbed that one instead.

A man stepped up to the shelf next to him. After sweeping his gaze over the options, he glanced at Julian. "Excuse me, is that the last one in that color?" the man asked.

Julian shot him an apprehensive look. "I think so."

"Would you consider trading me?" The man picked up a box of the same model in black. "My toddler loves blue."

"Do toddlers even know colors?" Julian asked, raising an eyebrow. "And what does a toddler need a tablet for, anyway?"

"What do you care what color it is?" the man asked. "You're a grown man."

As if Julian wasn't allowed to coordinate colors. "It's not for me, it's for...a friend," he said. If only he were in costume. He wouldn't even need to make verbal threats. People would simply stay the hell away from him.

He was ready to just walk away, but deep down, he knew Charlotte wouldn't care what color the thing was. With a sigh, he held the box out to the man. "Fine. Take it."

The man's face lit up. "Really?"

"Yes. Quickly, before I change my mind."

Despite Julian's abrasiveness, the man smiled at him as he took the box. "Thank you. Really, it means a lot."

"Sure. Just don't let the damn thing raise your kid." Julian grabbed a black tablet and headed for the checkout counter.

As he approached, an employee waved to him. "Excuse me, sir, but I think I have something you might be interested in." She held out a box to him. "It's a case for the tablet, same color as the other one you were looking at."

A case was a good idea, seeing as how Charlotte had dropped the last one. Julian accepted the box. "Thank you."

"And I can ring you up over here, if you're ready," she added.

Julian followed her to the cash register. As she scanned the items, she said, "This is a nice one. Whatcha using it for?"

"It's a gift, actually," Julian said without thinking.

She lifted an eyebrow. "Expensive gift. Is it for a family member? Partner?"

"Coworker," Julian lied.

The employee laughed. "I wish my coworkers liked me this much. You can go ahead and swipe your card."

After the payment processed, the employee set his items in a bag, tossed in the receipt, and held it out to him. "Well, if you ever need help with anything else, I'm here most days," she said with a sly smile.

Julian took the bag. "Sure. Thanks." Maybe he sounded a little curt, but he was too tired to care.

His mind raced the entire walk home, jumping around between the stormoid, training, Blazar, and Charlotte. Inside his apartment, he set the bag from the electronics store on his dining table and sank into one of the chairs.

Julian stared at the bag. The money was nothing, compared to what he had. Still, he hadn't had to do this at all. In fact, *not* helping Charlotte might have helped push her toward joining him as a villain. It was the kind of lesson Blazar would teach him.

But he'd done it anyway. And he couldn't deny that ever since they'd left the training room, his mind kept wandering back. Not to work out what techniques might help her improve, or come up with ways to assess her aim or teach her combat, but to relive the way she smiled triumphantly when she succeeded, or laughed when he said something she apparently found funny, or the intensity she fought with when they practiced combat—

Okay, fine. Maybe he liked her. It was hard not to. Sure, she had that "it's my responsibility to save the world" mentality that he usually found annoying, but she somehow managed to pull it off without the insufferable self-righteousness most heroes had.

Damn. The more he thought about it, the more unlikely it seemed he'd be able to convince her to give villainy a try. That could be fun, but if it didn't happen, he had to go through with his original plan.

He could set his feelings aside for the plan. If he could kill Storm Warning, he could do anything. Though, he hadn't cared about Storm Warning like he did Charlotte. Even if Storm had been a fun fight, and the least annoying of New Atlas's heroes, and maybe even easier to deal with than Blazar in a bad mood.

Julian frowned. Did he...miss Storm Warning?

He shook his head. Overthinking wouldn't get him anywhere. He couldn't control his feelings, but he could control his actions. And that would be enough to see this through.

It had to be enough.

CHAPTER TWELVE

The morning after their first training session in the underground room, Charlotte got a text from Julian asking what her schedule was for the day.

Classes all day. I won't have time for training, she told him. *Sorry!*

Do you have five minutes? he asked in reply.

When she told him she was between classes at the moment, he asked her to meet him at the south edge of campus. She found him standing in front of his car, scrolling through his phone with one hand. He had something tucked under his other arm.

When Julian noticed Charlotte approaching, he stepped away from the car and lifted his sunglasses. "I have something for you," he told her. He held out a tablet.

"Oh!" Charlotte exclaimed. She took it from him and looked over. Wow, this was a nice model. "You found me one to use."

"It's yours to keep."

She looked up at him, eyes wide. "What? You didn't buy this, did you?"

"Really, it's nothing." That seemed to be as close to an answer as she was going to get.

"This one's really expensive." Charlotte glanced at the tablet again. "And you got a case for it and everything." The case was her favorite shade of blue, though she'd suspected he'd picked it based on her hair. Which was...sweet.

"I figured the less you had to worry about, the more you could focus on training. Really, don't worry about it," Julian insisted.

Charlotte threw her arms around him before she could second-guess herself. "Seriously, thank you. You're a lifesaver."

"Well, I wouldn't say that," he muttered. After a moment, he used one of his arms to somewhat awkwardly return the hug. "But you're welcome."

Charlotte stepped back. "Okay, I have to get to my next class. Thanks again!"

Julian was already climbing back into the car. "Of course. I'll see you soon." The last thing Charlotte noticed before the door closed was the small smile on his lips.

They managed to fit in three sessions the following week. By Friday, Charlotte had moved on to firing small bursts of lightning at the punching bags Julian brought in. And she was doing much better fighting him hand-to-hand. She only put a fraction of her strength into her blows, but she still knocked him off his feet every now and then.

He took the hits surprisingly well. And as she improved, he picked up speed.

Friday evening, while Julian turned off the lamps, Charlotte asked the question that had been on her mind for a few days. "So, when do I put on a costume and go out to fight villains?"

She was expecting a "you're not ready yet" from Julian, but surprisingly, he didn't shut the idea down. "Did you have a costume in mind?" he asked.

"Oh, no, not really." Charlotte rubbed the back of her neck. "I should probably hide my hair, though."

"Agreed." Julian crossed the room to meet her by the stairs. "I have some costume pieces and suits that haven't been used. We can take a look at them one of these days."

One of these days. Charlotte nodded and moved to take the first step up the stairs. She'd barely lifted her foot when the world around her disappeared, and she found herself hovering far above the city of New Atlas.

With a cry of surprise, she dropped to her knees in the real world. But in her mind, she was in a dark room, then sitting at a desk, then standing on the roof of a building. At the other end of the roof, facing her, was Citadel.

And then the basement returned.

"Charlotte? Are you okay?" Julian dropped to one knee next to her. As Charlotte came to her senses, she noticed his hand hovering above her arm. He pulled it away as she looked at him.

"I don't know. I saw something," she told him. "Flashes."

"Visions?" Julian asked.

"Maybe? It felt like déjà vu. Like I've experienced it before. But there's no way." She looked up at him. "I saw Citadel. I was standing on a roof with him."

Julian's gaze darkened. "Strange."

"You don't know what it is I'm seeing?" Charlotte asked. "It's related to the stormoid, right?"

Hesitation took over Julian's expression. "I don't know exactly what it is, but I'll do some research. Maybe there's information I missed somewhere." He rose to his full height and, after a moment, held out a hand to help her. Charlotte's heart missed a beat or two as she took his hand and let him pull her up, knowing damn well she didn't need his assistance.

Their hands stayed together a moment longer than they needed to. As Julian pulled his away, he said, "Let me know if you see anything else."

Charlotte nodded. She could almost still feel the sensation of Julian's skin against hers. "I think—I think I might have experienced that before. The first time it happened while I was asleep, so I thought it was just a weird dream," she said. "But I've been seeing storms, and I had a vision where Citadel was attacking me."

Alarm flashed across Julian's face. "I'll get to the bottom of this," he promised.

As Charlotte followed him up the stairs, she wondered if she could figure out how to trigger the visions on purpose. Maybe if she saw more of them, she could figure out what they meant.

CHAPTER THIRTEEN

Julian entered the library shortly after midnight. As he turned his key and pushed the back door open, he wondered if there was any source of information on Storm Warning he hadn't checked yet. Now, on top of trying to understand how the stormoid-host bond worked, he needed to figure out what the hell Charlotte was seeing in these visions.

There had to be a lead somewhere. Something. Anything. Maybe he should go back to Storm Warning's early days.

Or maybe he should try figuring out Storm Warning's real identity.

On the bright side, Julian wasn't as pressed for time as he'd initially feared. Over the past week, Blazar had been too wrapped up in the plan he was concocting to pester Julian much about the stormoid. Or about "keeping the city in check," as he put it. Whatever he was working on had to be big.

Julian circled the library. He nabbed a book on Storm Warning that was waiting to be picked up by the next person on the hold list, a few magazines that promised interesting pieces on the hero's abilities, and a few articles he'd sent to the printer on his way over. He picked a couch on the first floor to sit on, turned on a lamp, and picked up the book.

This book, after detailing the stories of Storm Warning's first public appearances and his rise to fame, had a chapter speculating about his powers. A few interviewers had asked Storm about them on the rare occasions he stopped to answer their questions, but he always said he didn't have much information to share—likely to prevent any villains from learning something they could use against him.

But based on what little Storm Warning *had* said, and what people saw when he fought villains over New Atlas, various scholars had put forward theories about the origins of his abilities. Maybe one of the historians or physicists had something worth investigating.

Julian could eliminate all of the ideas that assumed Storm Warning was born with his abilities. Besides those, there were still plenty of suggestions thrown around about hypothetical storm phenomena that might give a person powers, and comparisons to heroes in other parts of the world with similar powers. But most of the chapter's page space was devoted to an interview with one particular historian. The historian described the legend of an unnaturally massive pearl called the Eye of the Storm.

The Eye had allegedly spent thousands of years being carried around the world by its hosts, to whom it granted storm summoning abilities. The most recent stories suggested it made its way to North America in the 1300s, but the trail ran cold a couple of centuries before the present day.

The idea that Storm Warning's power came from the Eye hadn't gained much traction because most of the academic community doubted it existed at all. Sure, there were much stranger things known to be real, but in a world full of fantastic artifacts and objects, it could be difficult to differentiate the real stories from the made-up ones.

Julian set aside the book, opened his laptop, and searched for papers by the historian. He found one detailing all of the information they'd compiled on the Eye of the Storm and printed it.

While he waited for the pages to print, he hopped onto the city's website and scanned the most recent obituaries. He'd been studying them since Storm Warning's death, hoping he'd stumble across someone who could plausibly be Storm Warning's alter ego. But if Storm had anyone in his life who knew his true identity—even just those other superheroes— they'd wait to announce his death as long as they could after Storm Warning's public fall.

They might try to avoid it altogether, but it was hard to keep that kind of thing off the internet entirely. If Storm worked somewhere public, especially, his untimely death was bound to wind up in an article.

After a few minutes passed and Julian didn't find anything interesting, he rubbed his forehead and leaned back. That was enough for tonight, he decided. He'd read more about the Eye tomorrow and hope he found something useful.

Julian returned the Storm Warning book to the hold shelf, grabbed the paper he'd printed, threw on his jacket, and left the library.

One last stop before he could go home and rest.

He entered the Complex quietly, not wanting to explain himself to anyone who might be here tonight. He wasn't sure he could come up with a great reason for taking extra costume pieces and unused suits. Thankfully, he didn't run into anyone. Less than five minutes after he'd arrived, he was leaving with a box.

Whatever costume Charlotte went with, they'd have to make modifications, both to fit her powers and to ensure the pieces wouldn't be recognized by the other villains. Julian opened his messages with Charlotte as he walked into his apartment. His thumb hovered over the keyboard. No, it was almost two a.m. Setting up their next session could wait until the morning. He left the box of costume pieces on the table and went to bed.

After hours of restless sleep, Julian woke to sunlight streaming through his bedroom window. He couldn't remember much from his dreams, only that he'd been fighting something. It left him mildly unnerved, but he dismissed the feeling, grabbed his phone as he climbed out of bed, and walked out to his kitchen.

He typed out a message to Charlotte as he walked. *You free anytime today? I have something new I want to try.* There was a decent chance she was busy, and it would be a while before he got a response. He opened a cupboard below the counter and bent down to grab a pan.

As he straightened up, his phone buzzed. He grabbed it and read the response from Charlotte. *I have some assignments to work on, but I'll be free around 2:30! I can meet you at the library, if that works for you?*

Sounds good, he texted back.

See you then!

He mentally planned the training session as he cooked himself an omelet. Charlotte's aim still wasn't perfect, but she was comfortable manipulating lightning and wind, and she'd mastered summoning clouds. It was time to put the pieces together and try something bigger.

CHAPTER FOURTEEN

While Julian waited for two-thirty to roll around, he studied the paper he'd brought back from the library. The more he read, the more he was sure this legendary Eye of the Storm was the stormoid. Unfortunately, there was no information on how to remove it from a person who was carrying it.

He did run across one interesting detail, though. According to a journal allegedly belonging to someone who'd hosted the Eye in the 1700s, the Eye carried the memories of all its former hosts, and the present host could access them.

If this really was the stormoid, then Charlotte had all the information Julian needed. She could see if the stormoid ever left a living host in the past, and how it had happened. But he couldn't rush this. He needed to get her to answer his questions without questioning why he was asking them. As soon as she got suspicious, it was all over.

That was fine. They needed more time before she'd be ready for the big fight. Until then, all he had to do was encourage her to unlock more memories.

At two o'clock, Julian left his apartment and walked to the garage to pick up his car. He pulled up along the curb in front of the library and got out to wait for Charlotte.

"You brought your car," Charlotte noted when she arrived.

"We're going back to the clearing in the forest," Julian told her. "It's time you tried something bigger."

Charlotte grinned. "Hell yes."

As they neared the city limits, Charlotte's phone buzzed. She checked the screen, and a smile crossed her face. "Finally!"

"What's that?" Julian asked.

"Oh, it's my mom." Charlotte glanced up from the phone. "I haven't seen my parents since I turned twenty-two a couple months ago."

"Happy late birthday," Julian told her.

"Thank you." Charlotte laughed. "Anyway, my mom's been saying she and my dad would come visit soon for, like, a month now, but stuff kept coming up. She caught the flu, and then their basement flooded, and my dad has this work trip next week he can't miss—anyway, they'll finally be able to come down in a couple of weeks." She tapped the screen and chuckled. "She sent me a photo of them in front of this weird deer statue at the park by their house."

Julian didn't want to take his eyes from the road for more than a second, but he did allow his gaze to flicker briefly to Charlotte's screen, just long enough to glimpse the photo of her parents: a woman with long waves of brown hair and tanned skin, and a tall man with dark brown skin and a shaved head.

"Do your parents live in New Atlas?" Julian asked.

Charlotte shook her head. "They're about an hour north."

"Ah."

"You...mentioned your family when I told you my tablet broke," Charlotte said. There was a hint of caution in her tone that suggested she wasn't sure if she should be asking about this. "Do they live in New Atlas?"

"Yeah, they do," Julian said. After a moment, he added, "Well, they're my adopted family. My real parents died when I was a kid."

"Oh, I'm sorry," Charlotte said. "Are there a lot of people in your adopted family?"

"Besides my parents, I have...I guess she's like my younger sister." Julian briefly wondered how Damselfly would react if she heard him call her his sister. "There used to be more of us, but everyone else moved away years ago."

"Well, that's nice that you have them."

"Do you have any siblings?" Julian feared if he let the conversation stay on his "family" too long, he'd accidentally let something slip that would reveal he was lying to her.

"Nope. Only child," Charlotte replied. "Quite a few cousins my age, though. I spent a lot of time with my dad's side of the family growing up."

They entered the freeway. Buildings turned to trees. Charlotte told a few stories about her cousins, including one where a girl had gotten in trouble at a birthday party for starting a marker war.

Julian laughed. "One of my friends in elementary school did that," he told Charlotte. "He said you got bonus points for drawing on people's faces. The teachers were furious when we all went back inside."

God, that felt like another life.

"So, what exactly do you want me to do today?" Charlotte asked as they rolled into the gravel parking lot.

Julian parked the car and threw open his door. "It's about time you summoned a real storm," he said as he started toward the edge of the lot.

Charlotte followed him. As they left the gravel behind, she asked, "What if I can't do it yet?" Her excitement from earlier was starting to sound more like anxiety.

Julian stopped in the center of the clearing. Turning to face her, he said, "Charlotte, you've done amazing so far. Even if you don't get it right away, I know it won't take long for you to figure it out."

Charlotte flushed. "Okay. Okay, you're right. I can do this."

As Julian stepped back, he found himself wondering if her heart jumped the same way his did when their eyes met. He wanted to believe that the look in her eyes was what he thought it was, but—

The wind picked up around them, snapping Julian from his thoughts. He took another step backward as dark clouds formed above the clearing, not much higher than the tops of the nearby trees. He tipped his head back. The first drop of rain to fall hit his forehead.

More rain followed, falling inside a perfect circle around Charlotte. She held out a hand and laughed. Lightning cracked and jumped through the clouds but didn't come down to touch the earth.

Julian grinned at her. "Like I said. Amazing."

Charlotte smiled back. Despite the fact that the rain fell even harder where she stood, Julian crossed the gap between them. Another burst of lightning lit up the clearing.

She laughed. "Oh my god, we're drenched."

"I may not have thought this through," Julian admitted. Truthfully, he didn't care in the slightest that his shirt was rapidly becoming soaked. Charlotte had come so far with her powers in just a couple of weeks. This plan of his actually had a chance of working.

The smile fell from his face as he thought about what that meant. Charlotte without the stormoid.

It's not as if things had to end. As long as she was alive—no, could he really bring himself to still see her after he took her powers? Would she want to see him, even if she didn't know he was Citadel?

Charlotte didn't notice his change in expression. Didn't notice that he felt sick. She had tipped her head back to study the clouds above her. "I feel like I really know how to control the parts of the storm," she said. "I'm not very precise, but with some practice—"

"Right. Practice," Julian cut her off without meaning to. "Let's have you try moving the entire storm around as a unit."

"Oh, sure. Okay." Charlotte's gaze flickered to him. She looked concerned for a moment, but it passed.

The clouds drifted north, moving about an inch a second. The rain moved with them, and lightning still cracked occasionally. Charlotte and Julian moved to the edge of the storm and followed behind it.

"Good," Julian said as they walked. "Now see if you can control how much rain is falling."

They worked for another hour, with Julian pushing Charlotte to manipulate every last aspect of the storm. The strength of the wind, the diameter of the circle that the rain fell in, the height of the clouds—ideally, she'd soon be able to summon a storm way up in the sky where they normally formed. She struggled with most of it, but it was clear she'd be able to get the hang of it with a few more practice sessions.

Finally, Julian had Charlotte dismiss the storm, and they headed back to the Porsche.

"I have one last thing for you," Julian told her as they reached the car. He opened the trunk and grabbed the box of costume pieces.

Charlotte took the box from him. "You got me a costume?" she asked, eyes widening as she opened it.

"Not exactly," Julian said. "There's a lot of stuff you could use to put together a costume in there, though. I figured you'd want to pick it out yourself."

"Wow." Charlotte dug through the box. "Yeah, I could definitely use some of this."

"I grabbed a few things you could use to hide your hair," Julian continued. "Some suits and jackets with hoods, and a couple of helmets. There's also shoes, gloves, oh, and there should be a few capes, too."

Charlotte chuckled. "I don't think I'll use a cape, but thanks."

"Why not?" Julian lifted an eyebrow.

"No offense to anyone who has one," Charlotte said. "Storm Warning's was cool. I'm just not a fan, personally." She paused. Smirked. "Although, I would like to strangle Citadel with his own cape one of these days."

Julian laughed and hoped Charlotte couldn't hear the nerves behind it. "I'd love to see that."

A buzzing sound came from nearby. Julian turned and realized he'd left his phone sitting on the floor of the trunk. He grabbed it and found he had a text from the woman who scheduled shifts at the library.

"The library needs me to swing by and cover for a couple of hours," he told Charlotte. He typed out a reply to let the other librarian know he'd be there soon.

"Well, now I feel worse about drenching you in water," Charlotte said.

Julian assessed his clothes. "My pants aren't too bad. I think they'll be dry by the time I walk in." He tugged at the bottom of his shirt. That was a completely different story. "It's fine, I have some clean shirts in this bag." He reached for the duffel bag that the costume box had sat next to.

While Charlotte carried the box around to the front of the car and climbed into the passenger seat, Julian peeled off his wet shirt and shrugged on a long-sleeved black button-up from his bag. As his hands reached the top buttons, he glanced up briefly. Just long enough to see Charlotte looking back at him. His gaze darted back down.

Julian tossed the bag back into the trunk, closed it, and walked to the driver's door. Once he'd pulled out of the parking lot, Charlotte spoke.

"You think I'm ready to fight Citadel?" she asked, looking up from the box in her lap.

Julian's grip on the steering wheel tightened. "I think you'd hold up just fine, but..."

"You don't think I can beat him?"

"He did kill Storm Warning," Julian reminded her. He threw a quick glance at her and couldn't help but grimace at her anxious expression. "But I don't think you need all of Storm Warning's experience to do well against Citadel," he said. "Storm Warning beat him a lot." *A lot.* "I'm just saying you need to remember what you're up against."

After a long moment, Julian added, "And even if you do beat Citadel, there are other villains. There's always going to be something else to fight."

Charlotte let out a weak laugh. "Is that supposed to be encouraging?"

No. "Just...remember you're not responsible for defeating them all." *You're not responsible for anything.* "It will always be up to you to decide what you do with your life."

They left the woods and entered the freeway.

"Can you tell me about Storm Warning?" Charlotte asked. "What was he really like?"

Julian searched his memories, wondering if it mattered whether or not he lied. He settled for sharing his real impression of the man. "He was funny."

"Really?"

"Oh, yeah. And relentlessly optimistic," Julian said. "He was also one of those types to question why the villains did what they did. I think he believed he might be able to turn some of them to the good side."

"Did it ever work?"

A heartbeat passed. Another. "I don't know."

Charlotte looked back down at the box. "I'm afraid I won't be able to take his place."

"Don't think about it like you're replacing him," Julian told her. "You have his powers, but that's it. It's okay if you do things differently."

"I just hope I get it right."

CHAPTER FIFTEEN

Charlotte carried the costume box into her apartment, eager to take a closer look at her options. Despite what Julian had said about not rushing things, she was getting impatient. Sure, she probably couldn't beat Citadel yet. But she had the power to start helping people now. Maybe that meant only stopping smaller criminals for the time being, but that would be good practice. And she'd rather test her powers on people who were hurting others than Julian, even if he insisted he could handle it.

After carefully examining everything in the box, Charlotte began assembling a costume. Julian had also suggested on the drive home that she find a way to customize the pieces, if she could. She already had some ideas. She laid out her selections and dug around in her desk drawers until she found her paints and brushes.

About an hour later, while Charlotte was trying it all on together, the front door opened. Good, Spencer was here.

Charlotte slid on the dark blue-green helmet and walked out to the kitchen. "What do you think?" she asked, pointing at the silver lightning bolt she'd painted on the front of the helmet. A transparent visor protected her eyes, leaving only the lower half of her face exposed.

In addition to the helmet, she wore gray plants and a matching zip-up vest, both accented with white stripes. She also wore a long-sleeved shirt the same color as the helmet underneath. The dark blue shoes she'd picked looked like high-top sneakers, but they were made of some of the sturdiest material Charlotte had ever touched. All of the costume's material felt remarkably strong, in fact.

Spencer lifted an eyebrow when he saw Charlotte. "Not bad. Where'd you get all that?"

"Julian gave me a box of costume stuff to try."

"So, he thinks you're ready to be a hero?"

Not exactly. "Pretty much. Training's going really well." Charlotte adjusted the helmet. "I'm going to start small, of course, but I think I'll pick it up quickly."

"I don't think being a superhero is something you pick up quickly."

Charlotte laughed. "What are you, an expert on superheroes?" she teased.

Spencer set his bag on the table and sat down. "No, I just—it feels like you're moving pretty fast, is all."

"I have to get out there eventually." Charlotte slid the helmet off. "You know, like how birds have to push their babies out of the nest?"

"Terrible metaphor, but sure," Spencer said. "Wait, you're not planning on going out tonight, are you?"

Charlotte shrugged. "I thought I might just...see what's going on. Hang out on some rooftops."

Spencer squinted at her. "Have you figured out how to fly yet?"

"Uh, okay, maybe not rooftops. But I could walk around some dark alleys," Charlotte replied. "I just want to get a feel for the superhero thing." She tensed as she watched Spencer look her costume over one more time. If Spencer was really that worried, maybe she shouldn't go out.

"Okay," Spencer finally said. "Fair enough. But please tell me you're at least going to eat dinner first."

Charlotte let out a small sigh of relief. "Yeah, of course."

"Great. I have stuff to make mac and cheese, if you want."

"Sounds great. Thanks."

While Spencer started cooking, Charlotte grabbed her phone, took a seat at the table, and checked her messages. Nothing. Julian hadn't told her to go looking for trouble, but he hadn't exactly discouraged it, either. It sounded like Citadel was his only concern.

Twenty minutes later, Spencer set a bowl of mac and cheese in front of Charlotte. As he sat down with his own bowl, he said, "You mentioned training was going well?"

"Yeah, I summoned a small storm today." Charlotte took a bite of the pasta.

"Julian must be a good teacher, then."

Charlotte tried to stop the heat from rushing to her face as she swallowed. "Yeah, he's pretty great. He said he's impressed with how quickly I'm learning."

Spencer smirked. "You ever gonna bring him here?"

"Oh, I don't know." Charlotte stared down at her dinner. "I'm not sure he's interested in hanging out outside of training."

"But he said he's impressed with you?" Spencer pressed.

"It's basically his job to say that."

"He also bought you a tablet."

"I'm pretty sure he's rich," Charlotte said. "I don't think it was that big of a deal for him."

"Okay, sure."

Charlotte rolled her eyes. "Believe me, you'll be the first to know if he asks me on a date."

"I better be," Spencer replied with a laugh.

The two finished dinner, and Charlotte offered to clean up so Spencer could start studying for a physics exam. After she was done sticking dishes in the dishwasher, Charlotte worked on some logo designs for an assignment until the sky turned black.

Finally, she stood up, stretched, and waved to Spencer. "I'm going to head out for a bit."

Spencer glanced up. "Stay safe. Call me if you need anything."

"Of course." Charlotte grabbed her helmet and put it on, ensuring all of her hair was tucked underneath it. "I mean, let's be real, I probably won't run into anything crazy." New Atlas wasn't exactly a high crime city. She'd have to be in the right place at the right time to find a lowlife criminal attacking someone, and the bigger villains stuck to grander crimes.

"Hopefully," Spencer muttered.

Charlotte took the door outside and hurried down into the alley next to their building. Instead of taking the usual ten-foot walk to the sidewalk, she moved deeper into the alley, to where it connected with another block of apartments.

She kept to the shadows as she wandered, listening hard for any signs of distress. It didn't take long for her to suspect that for every glamorous fight that wound up on the news, heroes spent a dozen boring hours waiting around for something to happen.

She was in the middle of an alley a few blocks from her apartment when a thud sounded overhead. She stopped and looked up.

Citadel stood above her, balanced on the railing of the fire escape. Lights from the building behind him illuminated his figure and glinted off his golden mask.

"Are you stalking me?" she spat at him. "What the hell are you waiting for? Just fight me already!"

"I wanted to see what you'd do with your powers," Citadel said.

"Besides kick your ass?"

"Cute." Citadel laughed. "I was hoping you might realize I wasn't worth the trouble."

Charlotte glared. "What's that supposed to mean?" The more Citadel talked, the more certain she was that something about his mask was altering his voice, even though it didn't cover his mouth.

Citadel jumped from the railing and landed a few feet in front of Charlotte. "Come on," he said as he rose to his full height. "Do you really want to get hurt again and again trying to stop me? What have I ever done to you?"

"Kill Storm Warning."

"I meant to you, specifically."

Charlotte held her ground, even as he took a step toward her. "You rob banks and hurt people for money!" she exclaimed.

"I don't get your type." Citadel shook his head. "You could do the same. Stop worrying about paying bills. Take whatever you want."

That would be nice, wouldn't it? To just take groceries instead of scraping the bottom of her bank account to pay for them? Charlotte shook her head. "Not if it means hurting someone else."

Citadel folded his arms. "Depends on who you steal from."

"Maybe." Charlotte's eyes narrowed. She admittedly might not feel too bad about stealing from a rich CEO, but she wasn't ready to resort to that yet. "But you're not playing Robin Hood, stealing from the rich and giving to the poor. You're taking whatever is in front of you for yourself." Too angry to be scared of Citadel, she stepped forward and jabbed a finger into his chest. "And you don't care what gets destroyed in the process."

"And why should I?" Citadel demanded. "No one cared about destroying my home, hero or villain."

Charlotte paused. "What?"

"No one cares, Storm," Citadel said. "You can play hero all you want, but no one's going to come along and reward you for it." His head tipped to the left. "How can you not just take what you need? What you want? I don't understand what's stopping you!"

"Back up," Charlotte said. "Your home was destroyed?"

"This isn't about that."

It wasn't an excuse for terrorizing the city, but maybe if Charlotte could get to the bottom of what this guy's deal was, she could get him to leave innocent people alone. Was that what Julian had meant when he said Storm Warning tried to understand the villains? "I'm sure people cared," she said. "If heroes were involved, they must have felt awful—"

"I don't care if they felt bad about it," Citadel said. "What, is some public apology supposed to make me feel better?"

"You can't take that out on other people! That's not anyone else's fault." Charlotte flung out an arm. "If your problem is with heroes, then fine. Fight heroes. Maybe take some money while you're at it. But if you threaten people's lives, I'm going to..."

Citadel leaned in. "You're going to what?"

"I'll kill you, if I have to."

"Kill me?" To Charlotte's annoyance, the corner of Citadel's mouth turned up in a smug smile. "You really think you can do it?"

"I'll sure as hell try."

The smug expression dropped. Citadel took a step back. "You should reconsider your place in the world. And I'm not just saying this to get you off my back. You could use your powers to live a better life."

"Oh, because you're just living the dream, aren't you?"

Citadel didn't respond. He turned around and walked in the other direction.

Oh, hell no. She wasn't going to let him just walk away from her again. Charlotte stormed forward and grabbed his stupid cape as it billowed behind him. With one swift motion, she yanked him backwards. Citadel landed on his back with a grunt of pain.

"I don't need people's thanks. Or a reward." Charlotte moved to stand over him. "God, what happened to you that made you think it was your right to hurt people?"

Citadel groaned as he sat up. Rubbing his shoulder, he said, "Okay, that's a little much. I'm not trying to hurt people, I just...take things."

"And you hang out with Blazar. He's got the highest casualty rate of any of the city's villains." Charlotte folded her arms. "What's your relationship with him, anyway? Do you work for him?"

That struck a nerve. "I don't work for him, I work with him," Citadel said indignantly. "Sometimes. We mostly do our own thing."

"Sure."

"Look, I wouldn't do things the way Blazar does, personally, but his methods aren't my business."

"Well, I'm going to make them *my* business," Charlotte hissed. She lifted her chin. "Once I'm at full power, no villain in this city is going to get away with hurting civilians."

Citadel's demeanor shifted entirely. He was on his feet in a heartbeat. "You can't fight Blazar. You'd never win."

"What do you care?" Charlotte asked, a grin creeping onto her face. "Scared I might hurt your friend?"

"I'm serious," Citadel said, no trace of his usual bravado. "Stay clear of him or you're going to end up dead."

"So, you're giving me advice now?" Charlotte rested a hand on her hip.

"Enough of this," Citadel said. "I have more important things to do. Stay away from the big villains, if you know what's good for you."

Before he could turn away, Charlotte lifted her hands. Her powers surfaced. Electricity jumped from her palms to Citadel.

A wall of stone rose between them, shielding Citadel just in time. Charlotte darted to the right. As she came around the wall, Citadel swung a hand at the side of her head. She ducked and swiped her leg at his ankles. He stepped back, and she missed.

"You'll have to be faster—" Citadel started.

Charlotte took him by surprise with a knee to the stomach. It wasn't something Julian had taught her, but one of the moves a campus gym instructor had shown her last week while she trained with the punching bags.

Citadel staggered backward. Before he could retaliate, Charlotte swung her leg again. This time, she knocked him to the ground. She dropped to one knee next to him. Brought her face close to his. "You know why I really don't want to be like you? Because there are some things you can't just take from people," she said. "Steal the entire world, if you want. It's not going to make anyone like you."

Cracks appeared in the ground, separating a square of concrete beneath Charlotte. One side of the square lifted, sending her tumbling onto her back.

Citadel pushed himself up and leaned over her. It was his turn to move in too close. "You think there's no one out there who'd want someone capable of giving them the world?" he asked, voice low.

"If it's stolen? Maybe." Charlotte shoved her shoes into his chest, knocking him backward. "But then it's not you they want, is it? It's your power."

Citadel rolled and sat up. "Who says I need someone to care about me, anyway?"

"It's a better reward than money."

Citadel snorted. "You're saying you'd rather have someone care about you than be able to afford rent?"

"Okay, no," Charlotte admitted as she stood up. "Obviously, I want both. But being selfish is only going to get you one of those things."

Citadel was back on his feet, too. He strolled forward and grabbed her arm. She stumbled back into the wall behind her.

"You're just assuming that no one likes me," Citadel said.

"Well, you do seem insufferable." Charlotte let an electric shock roll though her arm. Citadel yanked his hand back. She stepped to the right and circled him.

"I have friends," he insisted as he turned around to face her.

"Other assholes? Like you?"

"Oh, shut up." Even as he said the words, shaking his head, Charlotte realized there was a hint of a smile on his lips. "And personally, I find heroes lecturing me about my life choices more insufferable."

"Oh, am I getting on your nerves with all of my self-righteousness?" Charlotte asked sarcastically. "I can take you straight to prison, if you prefer."

"This has been insightful, actually." Citadel laughed. "Really, this was fun."

"Let's see if you're still having fun in five minutes." Charlotte swung her fist, aiming for Citadel's jaw. He jumped out of the way, but lightning jumped from her other hand as she lifted it. The blast of electricity struck him in the side. He stumbled right into Charlotte's next blow.

Citadel pressed a hand to his jaw where her fist had struck him. "Aren't you supposed to be able to fly?"

"What makes you think I can't?" Charlotte asked.

Citadel chuckled. The ground trembled. A pillar of stone broke through the concrete and launched him into the air. "Come and get me, then!" he called.

Charlotte glared up at him, silently hoping this would be the moment when her flight powers kicked in. Her feet remained firmly planted on the ground. "Okay, plan B," she muttered to herself. She lifted a hand and fired a bolt of lightning at the pillar.

Massive cracks raced up the stone to Citadel's feet. Before he could react, Charlotte smacked the side of her fist against the stone. The entire pillar crumbled.

Citadel grunted in pain as he hit the concrete. Still, he rolled and was back on his feet in a heartbeat. Charlotte raced forward to meet him. He swung at her. She ducked, grabbed the front of his suit, and shoved him into the nearest wall.

The air above the alley cracked. A bolt of lightning dropped from above to strike Citadel. He gasped and sank to his knees.

"Either you're holding back, or I'm better than I thought," Charlotte said.

Citadel laughed weakly. "Bold." A blade of sharp stone appeared in his hand. He jumped up and swung. Missed again. Maybe the pain from the fall was slowing him down.

As Citadel swung his weapon again, Charlotte reached out to grab his arm. And missed. The sharp stone sliced through the sleeve covering her upper arm. Sliced through skin. Charlotte cried out in pain.

To her surprise, Citadel dropped the weapon and stepped away from her. Her arm still stung, but she pushed through the pain to lunge at him. Lightning raced across her skin. He grunted as they crashed to the ground together, Charlotte landing on top of him.

"Come on, is that all you've got?" Charlotte growled at him.

Citadel didn't answer. After a moment, he pushed her off and climbed to his feet. "If you were smart, you'd stay away from me." He turned around. "And Blazar."

Charlotte rose to her feet. "I'm not done with you!" She summoned a current of wind to push him back toward her. "Get back here!"

Citadel whirled around. "I said stay away, Charlotte!"

Her heart stopped. "You—you know my name?" she stammered.

There was a beat of silence. The lower half of Citadel's expression gave nothing away. Charlotte wished she could see his eyes.

"Don't worry," he finally said. "I have no interest in revealing your secret."

To be honest, part of her had already feared he would figure out her identity sooner or later. He knew what she looked like under the helmet, after all, and the blue hair wasn't helping.

Charlotte ran forward to attack him again. Another pillar erupted from the ground carried him up to the roof above.

"Come back!" Charlotte yelled.

But he was already gone.

Charlotte fumed the entire walk back to her apartment. The only reason she hadn't beaten him yet was because he kept running away. *Coward.* If she could fly, she'd be able to stop him.

Every step worsened the pain in her arm. She clutched it as she climbed the stairs, afraid of what she would see when she finally looked. At the apartment door, she took a deep breath before slowly pushing it open. "Spencer? You here?"

Silence.

Had Spencer said he was meeting up with his class group tonight? Charlotte couldn't remember. She made her way to the bathroom, poked around the drawers until she found the first aid kit, and stumbled into her room.

She'd felt the blood trickling down her skin since the fight, but she didn't realize how bad it was until she shrugged off her vest and pulled up her sleeve. Her heart skipped a beat. *Oh, god.*

Charlotte fumbled with the roll of gauze for five minutes, trying in vain to wrap the wound on her own. Finally, with a shaky hand, she grabbed her phone. She scrolled to Spencer's contact and started typing out a message.

Halfway through, she stopped and deleted what she'd written. If Spencer saw how injured she was, he'd never let her hear the end of it. Though to be fair, Charlotte had been planning to fight easier opponents than Citadel.

She scrolled up, and her last message to Julian caught her eye. No, she couldn't call him with this. Besides, he'd be as concerned as Spencer.

But Citadel knew her name. She had no idea what to do about that, even if he insisted he wouldn't tell anyone. He was a villain. It was inevitable he'd use her identity against her.

Charlotte fell back onto her back and buried her face in her other arm. The pain was worse, now. Throbbing. She wiped away the tears stinging her eyes, sat up, and grabbed the gauze. When the next attempt at wrapping her arm failed, she angrily chucked the roll at the wall.

She grabbed her phone again and tapped the call button next to Julian's name. Maybe she'd leave out a few details, but she couldn't hide this from him. They would train again in the next few days, anyway, and he'd certainly see her injury then.

The phone rang. Once. Twice. Maybe calling was stupid. What if he didn't pick up?

There was a click. Julian answered. "Charlotte?"

CHAPTER SIXTEEN

Julian limped into the Complex elevator. He wasn't sure exactly which blow from Charlotte had caused the injury, but it wasn't even the worst. Of all the places on his body that were sure to be bruised tomorrow, the worst spots of stabbing pain were behind his right shoulder, his stomach, and his upper back. God, she was strong. She'd definitely been holding back during training.

When Charlotte started rambling about doing the right thing even if there was no reward, Julian really thought it would give him the push he needed to go through with the plan. It was a reminder of just how far apart their worlds really were.

But...

He couldn't stop thinking about how easily she charged in to fight him. Was it brave? Or stupid? Or both? She was new to this, and he'd been a villain for years. He'd killed Storm Warning. She should have been terrified.

Julian entered the Complex and went straight to his room to change out of his costume, as well as grab a few books that needed to go back to the library. He found himself frozen in the bathroom, staring at himself in the mirror, the realization finally dawning on him that this wasn't going to work. Not because it was a bad plan. He was sure that if he fought Charlotte in front of the whole city, he'd get exactly what he wanted: fear from New Atlas, respect from Blazar, and the stormoid.

His hands tightened around the edge of the counter. *Idiot.* He'd barely scratched Charlotte and he felt awful. He didn't even feel bad when he hurt the other villains during the occasional sparring session.

How could he admire someone so reckless? She cared so much about the people of New Atlas, most of them people she would never know personally. What lengths would she go to for someone she did know? Someone close to her?

Not him. Not Citadel. Not unless he...

Not unless he became someone very different.

Julian lifted a hand and ran it through his hair. There had to still be a way to get the stormoid from her. Without hurting her, because that was apparently off the table now. He had a starting point. Somewhere in all of the information about the stormoid there had to be something useful. And he still had to ask Charlotte about her memories.

It's not that big of a deal, he tried to tell himself. Once the stormoid was out of her, this whole mess would be over. No more training. No more talk of fighting Blazar.

Damselfly was in the kitchen when Julian went back out, sitting on the counter with a bag of chips in her hand.

"You haven't been around here much the past week," she said. "And Blazar and Saturn are so busy with their plan, they haven't been in much, either. I'm bored."

"If you're bored, go rob a bank," Julian told her.

"I'm bored of robbing banks!"

The sound of voices came from just outside the front door. Blazar and Saturn. *Speak of the devil,* Julian thought. He and Damselfly turned to watch the two enter.

"What are you two up to?" Blazar asked. Saturn strolled past him, holding a duffel bag that Julian could only assume was more stolen equipment.

"Is that for the plan you're working on?" Julian asked.

Blazar's only answer was a nod.

"Is there anything I can help you with?" *Something to distract me?*

"Just focus on getting the stormoid," Blazar said. "You know, I heard on the radio that there was some rogue lightning not far from here. Maybe you should go investigate." His gaze moved to Damselfly and her bag of chips. "Damselfly, I thought I told you I didn't want you eating junk food all the time."

"Pretty sure my stupid DNA can handle it," Damselfly muttered.

"I'm just saying. Maybe you'd win more fights if you cared about what you put in your body."

Damselfly glared at him. Her eyes began to glisten.

"Blake," Saturn said, her tone stern. She paused in the middle of the living room and glanced back.

Blazar sighed. "I'm sorry, Damselfly, I've had a stressful day today. Eat whatever you want. It's your life."

Before anyone could make any further attempts to defuse the situation, Julian's phone rang. All eyes moved to him as he pulled it from his pocket.

Charlotte.

He swallowed. "I have to take this," he said, starting towards the balcony. He was dimly aware of the other villains still staring as he stepped out, pulled the door shut, and answered the call.

"Charlotte," he said. "Are you okay?"

"I'm fine. Sort of. Sorry to call so late, but—" She sounded more upset than Julian expected. "Citadel knows I have the stormoid. I think he's been following me, and I—he attacked me tonight."

Was she only calling to tell him this? "Are you hurt?"

"Not that bad, but...I have this cut on my arm I don't know how to deal with. I'd ask Spencer for help, but he's not here."

The cut from his blade. Julian grimaced. He'd hoped the wound wasn't deep, but he hadn't been able to tell during the fight. "Okay, I—" He glanced through the door into the kitchen. Blazar and Saturn were talking to each other now, but Damselfly was still watching him. "I can leave to come meet you in a few minutes." He hesitated. "Did you want to meet somewhere?"

"I probably shouldn't leave. I'll text you the address to my apartment."

"Okay." Julian took a deep breath, hoping to steady his racing heart. "I'll be there as soon as I can."

"Thank you," Charlotte said. After a second, she added, "I'm sorry."

"It's okay," Julian told her, fresh guilt welling in his chest. "I'll see you soon."

After hanging up, he stared at his phone for a long moment before shoving it back in his pocket and heading inside. He headed straight for the elevator, hoping to get out of the Complex without any trouble.

"Where are you going?" Blazar asked as Julian passed him.

Julian paused by the door. "To investigate that lightning you mentioned."

"Who was on the phone?"

"Library."

"You were on the phone with a building?"

Damselfly laughed. Saturn shot her another stern look. Blazar didn't take his eyes off Julian.

"It wasn't anything important, just someone asking if I could take their shift tomorrow," Julian told him.

"Okay. One last question." Blazar's arms folded. "Are you okay?"

Julian frowned. "I'm fine."

"Really? Because you have a slight limp."

Julian was saved by a beep from Saturn's phone. "Blazar," she said, holding it up. "Come on, I think I've found somewhere we can get batteries."

Damselfly rolled her eyes as the two walked toward the hallway. "Pretty sure they sell those everywhere."

"Not that kind of battery," Julian muttered, watching them disappear around the corner.

"It's called a joke, moron." Damselfly reached into her bag to grab another chip. "Who really called you? Was it that girl?"

"What girl?"

"You know exactly who I'm talking about." Damselfly glared at him. "Look, Julian, why are you so freaked out about it? Congratulations on having a life! I'm happy for you."

"Freaked out about it? I'm a supervillain, remember?" Julian walked the rest of the way to the elevator and hit the call button with a little more force than necessary. "And happy for me? Why do you care?" He glanced back.

"I don't know, because we've known each other for years? It's obvious you've been happier the past couple of weeks. When you're here, you're nicer." Damselfly glanced down. "And I can't leave this place unless I'm going to commit a crime."

Had Julian been nicer to her these past couple of weeks? "I'm sorry," he said. "But that's not my fault."

"I never said it was." Damselfly slid off the counter and stormed toward the hallway. "Good night, Julian."

Julian couldn't deal with Damselfly's latest emotional crisis right now. He could apologize to her later. He wasn't entirely sure what he was supposed to be sorry for, but he felt guilty for some reason, so he'd have to figure that out.

Fifteen minutes later, Julian stood in front of Charlotte's door. After triple checking he had the right number, he took a deep breath and knocked. Why the hell was he nervous? Maybe this was the moment where he got the stormoid. This could be a good thing. Right?

The door opened. Charlotte had a blood-soaked towel pressed to her arm. "Hey, Julian," she said weakly.

His eyes widened. He stepped inside and closed the door behind him. "Come on, you should be sitting down."

"My room's this way." Charlotte turned around and led him to a hallway. "I've got the first aid stuff out already."

Julian followed, doing his best to hide his limp. He could already feel some pretty good bruises forming on his own body.

They entered Charlotte's room. Julian's gaze quickly swept over the desk and her new tablet, the box he'd given her, the extra costume pieces strewn across the floor, a container of paint, and finally rested on the nightstand where the first aid kid sat. Charlotte sat down on the edge of her bed as he walked over and picked up a bottle of disinfectant.

"Did you clean it yet?" Julian asked.

"Huh?" Charlotte eyed the bottle. "Oh. No, not yet."

Julian hesitated a moment before he sat down next to her, uncapping the bottle. "All right. Let's take a look."

Charlotte lowered the towel, and he winced.

"That bad?" she asked.

"You're going to be fine." Julian gently grabbed her arm with one hand. With the other, he poured the disinfectant onto her wound.

Charlotte flinched.

"Sorry," Julian said. "But the last thing you want is an infection." He paused. "How exactly did this happen?"

"Citadel summoned a stone blade and sliced me with it," Charlotte muttered. She looked up and managed a sly smile. "But I got some pretty good hits in, too."

She sure did. Julian's back ached as he leaned in to examine the wound. "I bet you did great."

"Thank you." Charlotte sighed. "I wish you could see me in a fight. Then I could really impress you."

"I'm already impressed." Julian looked up to ask a question, but momentarily forgot it when he saw the way Charlotte was looking at him.

"You're impressed by me?" she asked softly.

He swallowed. "Of course. You're doing far better than I ever could have hoped." He stared at her for another moment before remembering what he was doing. "Do you have any washcloths? Small towels?"

"Yeah, bathroom's just across the hall. Check the top drawer."

Julian crossed the hall to the bathroom, dampened a cloth in the sink, and returned to Charlotte. He wiped away the blood and grime as carefully as he could, but she still winced in pain at the worst of it. The slight trembling in his hands didn't help.

Maybe, he admitted to himself, he didn't need to be this close.

There was still a steady trickle of blood coming from the wound. "What did you say happened when the stormoid left Storm Warning's body?" Julian asked, trying to keep his voice light.

"It came out of the wound in his chest as a silver liquid." Her expression darkened. "You don't think it's going to leave me, do you?"

"No, I don't think so. Storm Warning got cut up plenty of times. I was just...curious." Julian dabbed at the last of the blood before setting the washcloth down and grabbing the disinfectant bottle again. He poured a little more on the gash.

"You have bandages?" he asked.

"There's a roll of gauze over there on the floor," Charlotte replied.

Julian stood up and crossed the room to grab it. He decided not to ask how it wound up there. "You're going to need something better for a wound this deep." He returned to the bed, grabbed the kit, and dug around until he found a thicker bandage roll.

Charlotte held out her arm. Julian sank back on to bed next to her as he unrolled the bandage. "Could you lift your arm up a little higher?" His voice was starting to weaken. Maybe it was his imagination. Charlotte obliged, and he began wrapping the bandage around the wound. After a minute, he tore it off from the roll and secured the end.

"Thank you," Charlotte breathed. "For everything. Really, you didn't have to come here."

"It's nothing. Really." Julian willed his gaze to move up, to meet Charlotte's eyes. "You..." He trailed off.

She leaned forward an inch. Two. Three. "Julian, I was wondering—"

A door opened in the distance. "Charlotte!" a voice called from the front of the apartment. "You here?"

Charlotte jumped to her feet. Her gaze darted around the room frantically. "Uh, yeah hang on—" She grabbed a jacket off the back of her desk chair and shrugged it on, hiding her bandages. "Julian's here too!"

Julian rose to his feet. "I—"

Charlotte was already out the door. He followed her to the kitchen, where Spencer was digging through a backpack he'd set on the table.

"I'm going to kill my group members," Spencer muttered, pulling a laptop from the bag. His gaze moved from Charlotte to Julian. "Julian! Good to see you." His tone was chipper enough, but he looked exhausted. And annoyed. Julian wondered what his classmates had done to piss his off.

Julian gave him a polite smile. "Good to see you, too, Spencer." He glanced at Charlotte. "I should head out. I have to open the library tomorrow morning."

"Oh, sure," Charlotte said. "I'll walk you to the door."

They paused in the entryway. Julian lowered his voice. "Are you sure you're going to be okay?"

Charlotte nodded. "I'll let you know if anything changes." She smiled, which was reassuring.

"Okay. Sorry, I don't mean to worry you. You should be fine now." Julian hesitated. "Were you going to say something before Spencer came in?"

Charlotte flushed. "Oh, I don't remember. I was feeling pretty lightheaded for a minute there."

"You should probably get some rest, then." Julian found the door handle and opened it.

"I'm going to bed as soon as you leave," Charlotte assured him. "Have a good night."

He stepped outside and looked back. "You too, Charlotte."

The door clicked shut. Julian cursed under his breath as he started his walk home.

CHAPTER SEVENTEEN

Charlotte didn't wake up dead, so her day was off to a good start.

The bandage had turned dark red, but the bleeding had long stopped. Per the instructions Julian texted her that morning, she swapped it for a clean dressing and added more disinfectant. Wrapping up the new bandage was a challenge, but she was able to get it on without asking Spencer for help.

Throughout her classes that day, she kept checking her phone. She wanted to ask Julian the question she'd been too afraid to follow through with the night before, but she wasn't sure how to go about it. Wasn't sure if she *could* do it.

Around noon, Charlotte stopped by one of the campus cafes to grab a coffee. As she eyed the front counter, debating whether or not to grab a bagel too, someone tapped her shoulder. She jumped and turned around.

"Sorry, didn't mean to scare you," the man said. He held her wallet out to her. "But I think you dropped this." He wore a suit, and he looked to be in his early forties. His short hair was a reddish blonde. He definitely wasn't a student, but he didn't look like a professor either.

"Oh!" Charlotte frowned as she took it, wondering how it'd fallen out of her bag. She must have stuck it in the wrong pocket. "Thanks."

"I'm sure student life is hard enough without having to worry about losing your wallet."

Charlotte laughed. "Yeah." She stepped forward as the line moved, and the man followed. "I'm guessing you're not a student?"

The man chuckled. "No, I was here getting approval to put up posters. My company is redoing our website, and we wanted to hire a graphic design intern."

Charlotte's face lit up. "Really? I'm majoring in graphic design."

"Well, what a coincidence." The man pulled a business card from his pocket and held it out to her. "Why don't you shoot me an email later, and we can see about getting you an interview."

Charlotte took the card. "Wow, that would be great. Thank you."

"What did you say your name was?" The man extended his hand.

"Oh, um—" Charlotte shook it. "Charlotte Hathaway."

"Pleasure to meet you, Charlotte." The man smiled. "I'm Blake Sullivan."

"Thank you, again. I'll email you as soon as I get a chance." The line moved again, bringing Charlotte to the front. The cashier waved Charlotte over.

Today was going surprisingly well.

As she sat down to drink her coffee, she pulled out her phone and opened her messages with Julian. A new one had come through while she was ordering. *How are you feeling?*

Pretty good, she typed. After a moment, she added, *Just getting coffee before my last class.*

Seconds dragged by. And then, *Can I call you real quick?*

Sure. Charlotte stepped outside and walked to an empty bench nearby.

The phone lit up with Julian's call a moment later. "Hi!" she answered, her voice coming out more excited than she'd intended. Lowering it, she asked, "What's up?"

"I wanted to check if you were still up for a training session today," Julian said. "We can go easy, but maybe it would be better if you took a break for a couple of days."

May as well go for it now. "Say, what do you do besides work?"

"Hm?"

"When you're not at the library or training me. I don't think you've mentioned doing much else."

"Well, I guess not much, recently," Julian said. "I've been doing a lot of research on the stormoid—"

"I think maybe you're the one who needs a break."

"What?"

The incredulousness in his tone made Charlotte laugh. "Come on. Just a few hours where we don't worry about saving the city."

There was a pause. "We?"

Charlotte struggled to keep her tone confident. "Yeah, I mean, we both cleared our afternoon for training, anyway. I just thought maybe we could walk around for a while. Could be a nice change."

"Yeah," Julian said after a moment. "Yeah, that sounds...nice. Does four o'clock still work for you?"

"Sounds great," Charlotte replied, her heart hammering in her chest. "See you then."

It was hard to focus during her art history class. The moment the lecture ended, Charlotte was out of her seat and headed for the door. Walking home faster wasn't going to put her any closer to four, but she still found herself rushing up the stairs into the apartment.

"How were classes?" Spencer asked as she walked in. He sat at the counter with his laptop open.

"Not bad. You?"

"All right."

Charlotte set her bag on the counter. "Good. You got any group projects or anything tonight?"

"Nope. What about you? Do you have training today?"

"I'm meeting Julian at four," Charlotte said. She shrugged off her jacket. "Oh, and I ran into this guy at the cafe—"

"Whoa," Spencer said. "What happened to your arm?"

Oops. Charlotte glanced at the bandage. "Oh, uh, it's not a big deal. This was just the only thing that would cover it."

Spencer's eyes narrowed. "How did it happen?"

Charlotte's shoulders sagged. "While I was out last night…" She sighed. "I ran into Citadel. He knows I have the stormoid."

"He attacked you?"

"Not exactly." Charlotte set her jacket next to her bag. "He's been taunting me, mostly. I'm the one who started the fight." She folded her arms. "Honestly, I did pretty good. He ran away."

Spencer lifted an eyebrow. "You get in a few good hits?"

Charlotte grinned. "Quite a few, actually."

"Good," Spencer said. "Well, I'm glad you're not dead. Try to stay that way."

"Will do." Still excited about the internship opportunity, she quickly explained her encounter with Blake Sullivan to Spencer, who wished her good luck. Then, Charlotte grabbed her bag and jacket and started toward her room.

"You know you don't have to defeat Citadel to prove yourself, right Charlie?" Spencer called after her.

Charlotte paused at the entrance to the hallway. She turned around slowly. "Yeah, I know."

"Most people forget that smaller heroes are important, too," Spencer said, his gaze still on his laptop screen. "The big shots don't have time to patrol the streets at night where nothing happens most of the time."

After yesterday, Charlotte wasn't surprised.

"Stopping criminals on the streets gets left to the heroes who can't deal with the supervillains," Spencer continued. "Or don't want to. But it matters just as much to the people they save."

"I get it," Charlotte said. "It's okay to start small."

"And it's okay to stay small, if you want," Spencer added. "But whatever choice you make, make sure it's your own."

Charlotte nodded.

CHAPTER EIGHTEEN

It was stupid to say yes to Charlotte, but Julian didn't care. Screw training. *One day off,* he told himself. One day off, and then he would go back to searching for a way to take the stormoid from her without hurting her.

He was a villain. He did what he wanted. And right now, he didn't want to take the stormoid or scare the city or steal money. Right now, he wanted a goddamn break.

Standing in front of his mirror, he rolled up the sleeves of his shirt and examined his skin. The bruising wasn't bad on his forearms. Like the scratches he'd picked up getting thrown against bricks and concrete, the worst of it was on his sides and back.

Nothing Charlotte would see. Probably.

Before his thoughts could wander too far in that direction, the alarm on his phone went off, informing him that it was almost four.

He'd sent Charlotte the address to his apartment building earlier, and she was waiting out front when he stepped outside. Her hair was down today, and he realized he'd never seen it not in a ponytail. His pace slowed.

"Hey!" She waved.

"Hi." Julian shook himself, finished descending the steps, and stopped in front of her. "Did you have anywhere in particular in mind?"

"Not really. I kinda just wanted to walk around." Charlotte shrugged as they started down the sidewalk. "Although there is a park near my apartment that gets really good sun."

Julian chuckled. "Isn't there sun everywhere?"

"I guess," Charlotte replied. "But the buildings block so much of it. This park's in the perfect position to get light."

"You sure care a lot about the sun, for someone with storm powers."

Charlotte flashed him a grin. "Sun's good for you. And plants. It's science."

When Julian laughed, she elbowed him. Right in one of his bruises. He barely managed to keep his reaction from showing on his face. He forced his pained grunt into a short laugh.

"I'm serious, they've done studies on it," Charlotte added.

Julian's apartment was only a few blocks from the northern edge of the city proper, and they wound up walking in that direction.

"Are you telling me keeping plants in my office would be good for me?" Julian asked.

"Honestly? Yes."

After another chuckle, Julian turned the conversation to her day. Charlotte ended up explaining one of the assignments she was working on this week. When she mentioned how much better her new tablet was than her old one, he smiled.

They turned a corner. Something up ahead caught Charlotte's eye, and her face fell. Julian followed her gaze. His heart sank.

Right. They were on Beacon Street. This was where Marigold Bank used to be.

They wordlessly continued walking to the site. The rubble had been cleared away, leaving an empty lot of dirt.

"I hate looking at this," Charlotte said with a sigh. "I know they have to wait for the money to build a new building, but it looks so...sad."

"Was this...your bank?" Julian asked tentatively.

"No. But I feel bad for everyone who did go here."

Julian felt a twinge of guilt in his chest. He wasn't incapable of that sympathy for strangers. He knew he'd felt bad for people on the news when he was younger, but it seemed to have...faded over the years.

Maybe he'd simply gotten good at ignoring it.

He tried to imagine how those bank customers might feel right now, imagined their frustration at having to travel farther to another branch, the employees who would need to find new work. The money was insured, of course, and losses would be repaid by the government. But it would still be an immense burden for everyone involved.

Charlotte, meanwhile, moved her attention to the next street sign. "Oh, there's Beebalm Street! I'm taking that as a sign we should go to Dove Park."

"Dove Park?" Julian asked, taking a moment to process what she'd said.

"It's the one near my building I mentioned," she explained. "Oh, it is about ten blocks south. Are you okay with walking that far?"

Julian gestured down the street. "Lead the way." His limp was all but gone now, and he'd exerted himself with far worse aches.

Charlotte grabbed his hand and pulled him forward.

She started telling him about how she'd found the park a couple years earlier, and how most people didn't notice it was there and there was a bigger one nearby anyway with a playground that all the parents took their kids to and damn it, it was hard to think with her fingers entwined in his.

It wasn't as if he hadn't attempted relationships before. He'd held other people's hands in his. But he hadn't felt anything quite like this in…a long time. It probably should have scared him.

Thankfully, Julian found his senses again before they arrived at the park. It was definitely the kind of place he would have walked right past on his own. A pizzeria was positioned almost directly in front of the entrance, and the open gate leading in was easy to miss.

He and Charlotte walked across the grass to a sunlit patch in front of one of the many trees. Charlotte sank into the grass, pulling Julian with her. Julian gently rested his free hand on a small stretch of dirt next to him, letting the feeling of the earth below steady him. His other was still entwined with Charlotte's.

She closed her eyes. "I usually come here when I'm stressed about school to sit in the sun for a while."

"If you're stressed, aren't you worried about having enough time to get everything done?" Julian asked.

Charlotte shrugged. "Sure. But what's an hour? It helps me focus better after, anyway."

Her eyes stayed closed. Julian stared at her. He'd seen her a million times, and he already thought she was pretty, but this felt new. The afternoon sun on her skin, her curls of hair hanging around her face—

Her eyes opened. Julian's first instinct was to look away, but her gaze locked with his, and he couldn't bring himself to break away.

And then her eyes were glowing white.

"I'm seeing something," Charlotte said, panic rising in her voice. Her hand broke away from his. "Someone's attacking me—"

The sight sent a jolt down Julian's spine. "It's okay." He moved in front of her and placed his hands on her shoulders. "Whatever you're seeing, it can't hurt you."

"Wait." Charlotte took a deep breath. "I'm—in a garden, I think. But the man next to me, his clothes look...old."

"Old?" Julian frowned.

"Yeah, like he's from the nineteen-hundreds." Charlotte squeezed her eyes shut again, hiding their bright glow. "And—" She gasped.

"Charlotte?" Julian fought not to tighten his grip on her.

Her eyes opened. The glow faded. "It changed. The man I was with attacked me, but he was wearing a costume. It was all black and gray, and he had a cloak with a hood and a mask with a white face painted on it." She frowned. "But somehow, I knew it was the same guy."

"I figured it out," Julian told her. "It's memories. You're seeing memories of the previous stormoid hosts."

"Memories?" Charlotte's brow furrowed. "Oh. That explains why I saw Citadel."

Julian shifted uncomfortably. "This man in the costume, was he a villain? A hero?"

"I'm not sure."

The description sounded familiar, but Julian wasn't sure why. Had he come across it during his research and forgotten? There had been a lot of late nights. And plenty of random details to miss.

Julian lowered his hands. "When I get home tonight, I'll do some research and figure out who you saw."

"There was something else," Charlotte said. "I remember that I was wearing red gloves."

Red gloves. Julian nodded. "Got it."

"Sorry to freak you out."

"Don't worry about me," Julian said. "Are you sure you're okay? You said he was attacking you."

Charlotte looked down. "I know it wasn't real, but—" She held up a hand, and Julian realized she was shaking. "I really felt like I was going to die for a second there."

"It was sort of real," Julian told her. "It happened to someone."

"Good point." Charlotte managed a weak smile. She laid back on the grass. "I just need a minute, and I'll be fine."

Julian adjusted his position. His hand brushed over the spot on the ground where it had rested a few minutes earlier. He frowned. The earth felt different. He'd always been able to sense variation across soil, but he'd never paid it much attention, since dirt wasn't useful to him. But the ground felt richer than it had when they sat down.

He shrugged it off as he laid on his back next to Charlotte. Even though they were in the middle of the city, the most prominent sounds were chirping birds and the trees rustling with the occasional breeze.

"I'm starving," Charlotte finally announced.

The corner of Julian's mouth turned up in a smile. "Want to get food somewhere?"

"I'd love to, but—" Charlotte sighed. "I have leftovers to finish. And an art assignment. Sorry."

Julian sat up. "Don't worry about it." Disappointed as he was to say goodbye, he had a new lead to investigate.

They left the park, and Julian considered reaching for Charlotte's hand again. He decided against it. They only had a short walk before she'd split off to go to her apartment, anyway.

"Oh, look!" Charlotte exclaimed. She paused in front of a flower shop to admire the plants growing in pots out front. "I love going into this place. Even though I never buy anything."

"Why not?" Julian asked as he stopped next to her.

Charlotte shrugged as she straightened up. "It's not really a great use of my money." She laughed. "It's fine. I just like looking at them."

They walked together for another minute before parting ways. Julian watched Charlotte set off toward her apartment, and it wasn't until he lost her in the crowd that he continued up Beebalm Street. His various aches worsened at the mere thought of the walk ahead, but he pushed forward.

When he arrived at his apartment, he went straight to his desk and gathered up the research he'd collected on the Eye of the Storm. The historian had compiled a list of supers with storm powers who'd been operating in times and places that lined up with legends about the Eye. It was hard to confirm which ones received their powers from the Eye and which ones had acquired them some other way, but the details from Charlotte's vision could narrow Julian's search.

Finally, after more than an hour of reading, he found a match. The man in black and gray was likely Shadowmaster, a superhero who could create darkness and transform it into blasts of energy. He'd lived in the Midwest in the mid-1900s, and not long into his career, he'd developed a very public rivalry with a villain named Red Tempest. A villain with storm powers who wore red gloves.

It had all ended with a huge battle over Chicago. Details were hard to confirm, given the lack of cameras, but the story had an interesting conclusion. Eyewitnesses claimed that Shadowmaster had pulled a silver orb from Red Tempest's chest.

It would take more digging to figure out how the stormoid had gotten from there to Storm Warning, but Julian didn't care to follow that trail right now. What really mattered was that the stormoid could be removed. Red Tempest hadn't died after losing it; he'd been locked up in prison.

Red Tempest. Julian leaned back in his chair. He wondered what Charlotte was going to think of this. The stormoid host wasn't the hero in this story. He was the villain.

CHAPTER NINETEEN

The next day at the library, when he wasn't doing actual work, Julian searched for more accounts of the final battle between Red Tempest and Shadowmaster. When nothing turned up, he switched to looking for information on other battles between them.

That yielded results. Their rivalry, from their first public fight to that last battle, spanned over a decade. And shortly before Red Tempest's first appearance, another hero had vanished. Another hero with storm powers.

Julian became so invested in trying to untangle their story that he almost forgot about the stormoid itself.

His phone buzzed around noon. A text from Charlotte. He frowned as he picked it up. A photo?

It was the park they'd been at yesterday. It took him a moment to realize what she was showing him: a small patch of blue flowers at the center of the photo. Her message read, *New flowers popped up! :)*

That fast? Julian stared at the photo. The flowers were only where they'd been sitting. Where his hand had been, specifically.

Had he...done that?

Well, if that was some ability he didn't realize he had, it wasn't exactly useful. Still, he was smiling as he typed his response. *That's good. Are you stressed about school?*

Stressed about an internship interview I have tomorrow, actually, Charlotte replied. *But it would be really great if I get it.*

Good luck! Julian's hand, to his dismay, trembled slightly as he set the phone back down. And yet he was still smiling like an idiot.

After work, once the sky had gone dark, Julian donned his Citadel costume and full mask and took to the rooftops. He kept out of sight of the people walking below as he made his way to the lot where Marigold Bank used to stand.

This block was made up of businesses that had closed hours earlier, so besides passing cars, the street was empty. Julian dropped to the ground at the back of the lot, out of reach of the streetlights. He focused his senses on the ground below. The dirt. It was dead, full of old stone and rubble. How had he done it in the garden?

All he'd been thinking about was Charlotte.

He knelt down, peeled off a glove, and rested a hand on the earth. In theory, he'd be able to do this—whatever he was doing—without making physical contact, but he could figure that part out later.

After a long moment of nothing, the dirt responded to him. Something shifted. The same energy Julian used to create stone was transforming the earth. Sensation overwhelmed him as his power spread across the entire lot.

Once he was done, he rose to his feet. The lot didn't look any different than it had when he arrived, but he could feel a difference. Whatever that meant for the dirt, he'd just have to wait and see.

"Citadel."

The voice speaking behind him was a new one. Deep. Warped. Julian turned around slowly.

The figure approaching him was covered in sleek pieces of metal armor so shiny Julian could see his own reflection on every surface, right down to the metal gauntlets hiding the figure's hands. Their face was hidden under a smooth helmet that was just as reflective all the way around, save for the narrow slit they watched him through. Something about the helmet's shape seemed to be the cause of their warped voice.

"Who are you?" Julian called to the figure.

"Name's Collider." They lunged forward with speed that was surprising, but not superhuman. Before Julian could move out of the way, though, they had a hand around his ankle.

Then, he was flying through the air. For a brief moment, he felt impossibly light.

He smacked into the sidewalk on the other side of the lot, next to the street. By the time the world stopped spinning around him and he was able to look up, Collider was standing a few feet away.

Shit. Where had they been all these years? Fighting muggers in dark alleys? They were good.

Julian pushed himself up. "Do you have a specific problem with me, or are you just in a bad mood?"

"Little bit of both." Collider hit him with a roundhouse kick to the jaw, sending him crashing back against the ground.

Julian rolled, jumped to his feet, and backed up, gaze fixed on Collider. It was impossible to make any real assessments about them with all of that armor. The only way he'd learn anything was by fighting.

Collider took a step forward. Then another. Julian moved forward to meet them and threw a punch. His hand went right through them. *Shit.* How was he supposed to hit someone who could phase through matter? Or, rather, phase matter through them?

To make matters worse, whatever transformation he'd done to the lot had drained his energy. He wouldn't be able to generate large amounts of stone for a few hours, at least.

Collider returned his attempted blow with a kick to the chest. Julian soared backward and hit the ground in front of an empty office building. The landing knocked the air out of his lungs.

Collider was halfway to him when he finally managed to suck in a breath. He climbed to his feet and watched them stroll forward slowly, blatantly unafraid. Besides Storm Warning, no one had ever fought him with this much confidence.

Well, running was an option. Julian had run from Storm Warning on occasion, though that was typically when he was seriously injured and without backup. Embarrassing, but it was better to live and fight another day than die at the hands of some minor hero most people didn't give a second thought.

Julian turned and darted between two buildings. He followed the alley to the next street, one that had restaurants mixed in with offices and businesses, though they all appeared to be closed, too. Footsteps behind him warned that Collider was giving chase.

He crossed the street and entered another alley, where he slowed and glanced back. Collider was just stepping onto the sidewalk. Julian summoned a stone pillar and made it halfway up the building to his left before he ran out of steam. He nearly stumbled off.

Collider reached the base of the pillar. They pulled back their arm and punched it with enough force to split it in half vertically. Julian jumped and reached for the railing of a fire escape. His ribs slammed against metal bars. He gasped.

Below him, Collider's head tipped back to watch as he struggled to pull himself up. After a moment, their feet left the ground and they drifted into the air, toward Julian. He heaved himself over the railing and landed hard on the metal stairs.

"Come on, just tell me what you want!" he demanded as he pushed himself upright.

Collider dropped onto the railing. "Well, I don't suppose I could get you to agree to give up being Citadel forever."

"Oh, sure, let me think about that for a second." Julian was low on energy for generating material. He could still move things around, though. He focused on the ground far below. Concrete was so hard to work with, but it was his only option. He raised a platform of pavement.

"Should I take that as a no?" Collider folded their arms.

Julian waited until the last possible second to jump to his feet and vault over the railing. As he hit the platform, he pushed it even harder, forcing it to carry him high and fast.

Collider jumped into the air to follow. If they had to lower their density to float, at least they wouldn't be able to hit him up here.

Julian's platform carried him over rooftops, faster than Collider could move. Thank god. He eyed the maze of streets and alleys and buildings below, searching for a good place to drop. He picked a small parking lot behind a diner. The platform brought him down to the pavement a little faster than intended. The rough landing sent him stumbling.

He found his balance, raced to the back door of the diner, and tried the handle. It was unlocked, saving him the trouble of breaking it. As he stepped inside, he formed a small disk of stone and flung it into a dumpster on the other side of the parking lot. A loud clang reverberated through the air. Julian pulled the door to within an inch of the frame and watched Collider drop into the lot next to the dumpster.

"Come on, Citadel, you're really gonna run?" Collider turned in a slow circle. "You can't hide forever. If you want this city so damn bad, you're gonna have to get through me and the other heroes."

What other heroes? Julian's heart hammered against his aching rib cage. He forced his breathing to steady as he watched Collider, silently hoping they wouldn't come this way.

A minute passed. Another. Finally, Collider took to the air and vanished into the night.

Julian waited another minute or so before daring to pull the door shut the rest of the way. He turned around and found himself face-to-face with a diner employee staring at him with wide eyes, a garbage bag clutched tightly in her hands.

"Not a word," Julian muttered as he passed her.

CHAPTER TWENTY

Julian staggered into the Complex. He removed his mask and tossed it on the kitchen counter as he entered.

Damselfly, Blazar, and Saturn were sitting on the couch. Equipment and printed diagrams were strewn across the coffee table, and Saturn was working on her laptop.

Julian frowned. "What are you all doing?"

"Explaining a mission to Damselfly," Blazar said. He looked Julian over. "What the hell happened to you?"

Julian grabbed the edge of the counter and leaned back against it. "Collider." Every breath exaggerated his pain. He tipped his head back and held in a groan.

Damselfly shot Blazar a glare. "See? I told you they were strong!"

"And what were you doing fighting Collider?" Blazar asked, ignoring Damselfly's comment.

Julian forced his head to lower so he could meet Blazar's eyes. "They attacked me." He had an idea and added, "While I was following the guy who I think might have the stormoid."

Blazar lifted an eyebrow.

"I'm not completely sure yet, but I was able to confirm he was around some of the reports of lightning and rain," Julian continued, his pulse quickening. Lying to Charlotte was one thing. Lying to Blazar just might get him killed.

But he didn't feel as guilty, lying to Blazar.

"And Collider attacked you while you were following him?" Blazar asked.

Julian nodded.

"Did they say why?"

"Nope." A fresh twinge of pain shot through Julian's abdomen. He pressed a hand to the spot. "But they seemed pretty full of themselves."

"Maybe they want to replace Storm Warning," Damselfly suggested.

"Maybe," Blazar muttered. He rose to his feet and glanced at Damselfly. "Get this taken care of soon."

Damselfly nodded.

Julian went to his room to change and grab his first aid kit. Blazar and Saturn were gone by the time he made it back out to the living room. He walked to the couch where Damselfly still sat, his eyes on the papers scattered across the table in front of her.

Julian sat down next to her. "What does Blazar want you to do?" he asked as he turned his attention to the scrapes running up his arms. Where to even begin?

Damselfly picked a game controller out of the mess of equipment and papers Saturn had left on the table and pressed a button. The pause menu up on the monitor disappeared, launching her back into the shooter game she was playing. "I'm supposed to destroy a restaurant on Quail Street and Eighty-Third."

That was close to the edge of the city. Like Marigold Bank. Julian picked up his bottle of disinfectant. "Destroy it? You're not stealing anything?"

Damselfly shook her head. "Blazar said it's in the way."

"In the way of what?"

She shrugged. "I guess he needs to do something in that spot for his big plan."

Why hadn't Blazar explained this plan to Julian yet? He tipped the bottle and winced as cold liquid ran over his open wounds. He worked in silence for a few minutes, leaving only the sounds of gunfire and explosions from Damselfly's game to fill the room.

"Hey, I'm sorry if I upset you when I left the other night," Julian finally said. "I was in a hurry. I know you hate being stuck here."

Surprise flashed across Damselfly's face. "Uh, thanks." She glanced at him. "We don't really apologize to each other around here, though."

Julian lifted an eyebrow.

"I mean, we're villains," Damselfly added as she turned her gaze back to the monitor.

"Yeah, but we're supposed to be on the same team." If they didn't have each other, what did they have?

Besides all of their stolen money, that was.

Damselfly fell quiet and didn't speak again until Julian had finished bandaging himself up. "You know, this game's got a two-player mode, and I have another remote," she told him. "If you want to play a match with me."

Julian watched her fire at a character on screen and send them falling off the edge of a building. "Sure," he said. "Are you playing online?"

"Not right now. Controller's right there." Damselfly pointed to the shelf next to the monitor where she kept all of her games and remotes.

As Julian sat back down with the controller, he asked, "Do we fight each other, or are we on the same team?"

"We could do either, but since you've never played, I should probably help you." She shot him a sly grin. "It wouldn't be any fun beating someone who doesn't know what they're doing."

"I think I can figure out a video game," Julian said. "It's just shooting the enemy, right?"

Damselfly laughed. "Yeah, sure. And taking into account blind spots, weapon and armor stats, grenades, map layout—"

"Okay, okay," Julian cut her off. "Just tell me what to do."

Julian died fifteen times before he finally lasted long enough to kill an enemy. Then, while he was relishing in his first victory, a fiery explosion killed him again.

"Told ya," Damselfly said. "You have to watch out for those grenades."

After that, Julian slowly got the hang of the game. He was nowhere near as good as Damselfly, but his kill count gradually went up while the rate at which he died decreased.

"If you could have your wings removed, would you?" Julian asked, after one of the matches ended in a victory for their team.

Damselfly shrugged. "Does it matter? Saturn doesn't think it's possible."

"Why wouldn't it be? Doctors can amputate limbs just fine."

"I guess it's all tangled up with my nervous system," Damselfly replied as she started the next match.

"But Saturn's an engineer, not a doctor." Julian frowned. "We should have a real surgeon should take a look."

"Well, if you happen to find one, let me know."

Julian had no idea where to find a surgeon who'd be willing to help villains without reporting them to authorities, but he knew they existed. Blazar had to know at least one. In fact, when one of Julian's first fights had ended badly, Blazar had taken him to a secret hospital to get patched up.

But since then, going to a regular hospital under his civilian identity had been sufficient for anything he couldn't deal with on his own. Julian had no idea how to go about finding the secret hospital, if it still existed.

Damselfly's wings twitched. Despite how fragile they looked, they were remarkably strong. Strong enough to carry her, of course.

"I wasn't the only one at the lab that made me, you know," Damselfly said quietly. "I had a brother. But he...didn't make it."

Julian jumped out of the way of enemy gunfire. His pulse quickened. "I'm sorry."

"When they picked us up from our foster home and told us they were taking us to this lab for experiments, I was so excited," Damselfly continued. "I wouldn't have to go to school anymore, and I was going to have these cool superpowers, and it was supposed to be the best thing that ever happened to me." She shook her head. "I'd do anything to go back now. I'd rather still be failing math tests and getting hit in the face with dodge balls."

After a long moment, Julian dared to ask a question he'd been holding on to for two years. "How old were you? When you were taken to the lab, I mean?"

"I was ten."

Julian's hands tightened around his controller. She'd spent four years there.

He'd been seventeen when he went out into the world as Citadel for the first time. Damselfly had been only fourteen. She'd joined the team on her first mission only a couple of months after Blazar brought her back from the lab.

Blazar had caught wind of the experiments the lab was doing and decided to take a look for himself. Damselfly was the only surviving test subject, and he'd broken her out while Saturn stole tech. Afterwards, the two had burned the place to the ground. The arson bit had purely been for fun, according to Blazar.

One of the enemies nailed Julian with a headshot. He sighed and leaned back against the couch. "There has to be someone who can do something," he said. "If that's what you really want, I mean."

Damselfly nodded. Hesitation crossed her face. "Could you...not tell Blazar about any of this? I think he'd be mad if I said I wanted to get rid of my wings."

Blazar would absolutely be furious, considering all the trouble he'd gone through to get Damselfly in the first place. "I won't mention it," Julian said. "I think I owe you, anyway."

Damselfly grinned. "You mean for not snitching about your girlfriend?"

Julian rolled his eyes. "She's not my girlfriend."

"Whatever you say."

CHAPTER TWENTY-ONE

The ten minutes Julian spent standing on his balcony were him stalling, and he knew it. He had to go to the empty lot and see if his transformation had done anything, but he was afraid of what he would find. Though, he wasn't completely sure if he was more afraid of finding nothing, or of finding...

Something.

Julian finally forced himself to stop people watching and leave the building. As he turned the corner onto Beacon Street, he braced himself. There wasn't going to be anything out of the ordinary. And if there were, so what?

It would make Charlotte happy.

He stopped in front of the empty lot and stared, unable to hide his stunned expression. Patches of grass had popped up around the lot. Along with a variety of flowers.

"Incredible, right?" an older woman said as she passed. "I wonder who did this."

Julian slid his hands into his jacket pockets. He wanted Charlotte to see this. He wanted to *see* her see it. He could already imagine her excitement. Even though the small amount of walking he'd done today made last night's injuries feel like hell, he pulled his phone from his pocket to text her as he walked away from the lot.

Do you have time for a training session today? he asked.

Her reply came a minute later. *I'm on my way to my internship interview right now, but we could meet after! If you come by Dawn's at 1:30, I should be done.*

Julian put the name into his phone's map. It was a bookstore with a cafe, and it was only about a five-minute walk from his apartment. Perfect. He replied to Charlotte. *Sure, I'll meet you then!*

Half an hour later, Julian opened the door to Dawn's and walked into the cafe portion of the store. The first thing he saw was Charlotte standing up at a table in the far corner, shaking the hand of the man across from her. Her face lit up when she looked past him and saw Julian. She smiled.

Julian waved, a grin crossing his own face. His excitement only lasted a moment. Then, the man turned around, and Julian's blood turned to ice in his veins.

Blazar gave him a cold smile.

"Julian!" Charlotte rushed to him and, to his surprise, hugged him.

He could barely look at her, unable to tear his gaze from the man walking toward them. "I—hi, I wasn't—"

Charlotte stepped back before he could fully get his thoughts back on track.

Julian met her gaze and tried to avoid looking at Blazar. "Is your interview done?" he asked. "I know I'm a little early, I didn't want to interrupt—"

"Your timing's perfect, actually, we just finished."

Blazar stopped next to Charlotte. "I have some other interviews lined up this week, but I'll let you know as soon as we've made our decision," he told her. His gaze flickered to Julian, his expression unreadable.

"Thank you again, Mr. Sullivan," Charlotte said. "I look forward to hearing from you!"

Blazar left without saying a word to Julian, leaving him terrified. What was this? A threat? A power move? Coincidence? No, a threat was far more likely. But why? There was no way he knew Charlotte had the stormoid.

Charlotte waved a hand in front of Julian's face. "Hey, are you okay?"

He supposed he would have to wait and find out. His next trip to the Complex might wind up being very unpleasant.

"Sorry, I'm fine. Just a little distracted." Julian gave Charlotte his full attention. "What was the interview for, exactly?"

"An internship with his company. I'd be helping them redesign their website."

"That's great!" Julian hoped he sounded enthusiastic enough. He and Charlotte walked to the door.

Charlotte held up her phone. "He seemed to like my portfolio, so I think I have a chance."

Julian leaned over to peer at her screen as she scrolled through logo designs and cartoon drawings and thumbnails for posters. "Oh, wow," he said. "Those are really good."

Charlotte flushed and lowered her gaze, a smile crossing her face. "Thanks." She returned her phone to her pocket.

Julian glanced around anxiously as they approached the closest intersection. Would Blazar linger in the area to watch them?

"Are you okay?" Charlotte asked. "You seem stressed."

"It's nothing. I'm just a little out of it today, I guess." Julian ran a hand through his hair. "Before we head to the training room, I had something I wanted to show you. We'll have to turn left up here."

"Sure," Charlotte said, confusion on her face even as she smiled at him.

Julian could barely hide his excitement as they approached the lot. When they stopped in front of it, Charlotte grabbed Julian's arm, her eyes widening with surprise. "Oh my god." She laughed. "This is amazing."

Julian grinned. Like a damn idiot. "Saw it when I came by this morning. No one seems to know what happened."

A few other people paused on the sidewalk around them, admiring the new flowers. Charlotte stepped into the lot and knelt next to a cluster with petals a similar shade of blue to her hair. "Well, whoever did it, they have great taste."

Julian chuckled. "I agree."

They made their way to the training room after that. A couple days prior, Julian had dragged in some kickboxing dummies and lined them up in a row at one end of the room. As he turned on the lamp, he told Charlotte, "I brought those in for target practice. See if you can hit them with the lightning."

Charlotte crossed the room and eyed her targets. "So, I just blast them with electricity?"

Julian leaned back against the wall. "Just do whatever feels right," he answered with a shrug as he folded his arms.

Sparks jumped from Charlotte's hands as she shook them out. Once she'd warmed them up, she lifted them and aimed her palms at the dummies.

Some of her blasts missed, but her aim improved with every attack. One by one, the dummies fell to the ground and sent a cracking sound through the air. Some landed in one piece. Others were split down the middle by the force of Charlotte's lightning.

"Good," Julian said once she'd knocked them all down. He helped her pick up the dummies that were still whole. "Back up a few feet and try hitting these ones again."

Charlotte kept going until she was knocking down dummies from the other side of the room. Her aim wasn't perfect, but she hit far more than she missed. Finally, she completed a round where she knocked down every dummy on the first try.

As she moved to put them upright again, Julian held up a hand to stop her. "I think that's good for today," he said. Fighting her was a bad idea right now, given the state he was in, but he lifted his fists anyway. "How about a quick match before we go?"

Charlotte smirked. "Sure."

This was a really bad idea.

She charged and threw a punch. For the next minute, Julian focused solely on dodging her blows. It took all of his effort to match her speed. Finally, he had an opening. He swung a fist, aiming for her shoulder.

Charlotte dodged, swept her leg across the floor, and caught his ankle. Julian stumbled. While he was focused on keeping himself from falling, she grabbed him and pushed him into the wall. Julian grunted in pain.

She stopped and relaxed her grip. "Are you okay? I'm sorry, I didn't think I threw you that hard—"

"You didn't, it's fine." Julian straightened up. "I'm already injured."

"What?"

"It's nothing." Julian tugged at the bottom of his shirt sleeve, which was a mistake. Charlotte's gaze landed on a bruise just visible at the edge of the fabric. She gently took his wrist and pushed the sleeve back, exposing more bruised skin. And the bandage covering a particularly bad scrape. Julian sucked in a sharp breath.

"What happened?" she asked.

"I was attacked," he told her, which was technically the truth. "Honestly, I'll be good as new in a few days. I'm mostly just sore."

Charlotte's eyes widened as she looked up at him. "Why would someone attack you?"

Now he had to lie. "I think they were looking for information on the stormoid." Julian tried to sound nonchalant. "But there's nothing for you to worry about. I didn't tell them anything."

"I'm not worried about me. I'm worried about you."

Julian's stomach turned. Fresh guilt washed over him. "Really. I'm fine."

Charlotte leaned forward, bringing her face closer to Julian's. "Well, if I were there, I would have destroyed them."

"I'm sure you would have." Julian tipped his head down ever-so-slightly. He wanted to move closer. Close the gap between them. His next thought was to berate himself for having such a terrible idea.

Before he could make up his mind, Charlotte stumbled backwards and pressed a hand to the side of her head. Her eyes closed.

"Charlotte?" Julian rushed to her side as she sank to her knees. "Charlotte, what's wrong?"

"He's attacking me again. The guy in black." Charlotte grimaced. She took a slow breath and opened her eyes. No glow. The vision was already over.

Right. Julian had nearly forgotten about what he'd found in his research. "I think I know who he is," he told Charlotte. "He was a hero called Shadowmaster. And the memory belongs to Red Tempest."

Charlotte frowned. "Red Tempest?"

"I don't know much about him. Only that he and Shadowmaster were rivals for a decade. But the stormoid host...he was the villain," Julian explained. "He terrorized Chicago until Shadowmaster finally beat him. And at the end of their last battle, Shadowmaster took the stormoid from him, somehow." He hesitated. "Did you see it happening? Shadowmaster taking it from you?"

"He was about to, I think," Charlotte murmured. "I could actually feel the stormoid in my blood. Just below the surface." Her gaze lowered to the floor. "Do I have to see these memories? I don't want a villain in my head!"

Julian moved to rest his hand on her shoulder but stopped himself short. "You're not him. You're just seeing what he saw," he told her gently. "I know it's hard. But remembering those things might help you."

They stood up together. Charlotte rubbed her arm. "I guess you're right."

"Let me know if you see anything else," Julian said. "I'm not entirely sure how Shadowmaster was able to take the stormoid without killing Red Tempest, but it's something we should figure out. So we can prevent it from happening to you," he quickly added.

"I guess I'll try to relive it, then," Charlotte said. "I'll let you know if I learn anything."

Julian couldn't blame her for sounding hesitant. If she felt everything the host felt when she relieved their memories, then she would feel Red Tempest's pain, too.

The flashes coming to her seemed random. Did the stormoid have a mind of its own? Was it showing her these memories deliberately? And if so, why these ones, specifically?

CHAPTER TWENTY-TWO

Julian and Charlotte left the training room and walked west. Charlotte had an evening class she had to get to, and Julian offered to walk with her to the edge of campus, despite his exhaustion.

They were a block away when Charlotte stopped and groaned. "I left my phone sitting by the stairs," she said.

"Do you want to go back for it?" Julian asked.

"I don't have enough time. Class starts in ten minutes." Charlotte sighed. "Sorry, you need to go home and rest, but I'll need it by tonight—"

"I'll go get it for you now," Julian said. "I'll be back here before class is over."

"No, Julian, you should—" Charlotte stopped herself. "All right, but I need you to do something else for me."

"Anything." The word left Julian's mouth without thinking.

Charlotte grinned. "Go get dinner first, okay? There's no rush. Sit down for a while."

"I promise, I'm fine," Julian told her. But sitting down did sound nice. "How long is your class?"

"Just bring my phone by my apartment later. I'll be home by seven."

"Sure thing." Julian paused. "Will you be hungry after class? I could bring you food, too."

"Don't worry about me. I've got food at home." Charlotte waved as she took a step back toward campus. "I'll see you later, Julian."

Julian waved goodbye and turned around. Even though he'd promised he'd get food first, his first stop was the training room. He grabbed Charlotte's phone off the floor, slid it into his jacket pocket, and stepped back outside.

After that, he found a small diner down the street to eat at. He was surprised he'd never heard of it before. The sandwich he ordered was one of the best he'd ever bought in New Atlas, and the soup was pretty damn good, too. Maybe he'd bring Charlotte sometime.

Even after he was done eating, he had time to kill before Charlotte would be home, and there was no point walking all the way to his apartment just to turn around and come back. May as well pick somewhere close to her apartment to wait.

Dove Park sounded like the perfect choice.

Instead of the grass, Julian picked one of the benches to sit on. He didn't realize he was dozing off until someone said his name.

"Julian."

Julian jerked awake and sat up as Saturn strolled toward him, dressed in civilian clothes. "Sat—Sophia?" Julian glanced around the park. He couldn't see anyone nearby, but better safe than sorry. "What are you doing here?"

"Following you."

"What? Why? How long?" Had she seen him and Charlotte enter the training room?

"I found you near the university campus," Saturn answered. After they'd left the training room, then. "And Blazar asked me to. He probably would have followed you himself, but he had something more important to deal with today." She sat down on the bench next to Julian. "He knows you're seeing that girl."

"It's not...like that." The lie felt wrong on Julian's tongue.

"Who is she?"

"What does it matter to you?" A glare replaced Julian's anxious expression. "You're not entitled to every detail of my life."

"Maybe not, but Blazar's planning something big. If you're distracted, you could ruin this for all of us." Saturn's eyes narrowed. "He wants to make sure you're still focused on the stormoid."

"Of course I am! And I barely know her." Julian rose to his feet. "Tell Blazar if he has a problem with my personal life, he can talk to me himself."

He started to walk away, but he only made it ten feet before Saturn called after him, her voice softer this time. "Julian, wait."

Julian stopped. Sighed. Turned around.

Saturn stood up. "Julian, you're free to do whatever you want. I'm not going to stop you from seeing her. But I am going to warn you that this isn't going to end well."

"What makes you so sure?"

"It never does for us. I learned that the hard way. I don't—" She cut herself off and shook her head.

"You think I don't know that?" Julian's fists clenched. "I've been here before, too. But I want it to be different this time."

"You say that now," Saturn muttered. "You really think it could last for someone like you? Someone like Blazar?"

Julian was quiet for a long moment. "I'm not like Blazar," he finally said.

"But you want to be."

Julian was starting to think that it didn't matter what he wanted. He simply...wasn't Blazar. He forced himself to hold Saturn's gaze. "You chose to work with Blazar, you know," he said. "I didn't."

Saturn's eyes narrowed. "Now is not the time to start having regrets."

"Regret? Me?" Julian took a step back. "You're the one who keeps helping him. You do all the work for his plans, and for what? What has he ever done for you?"

"His plans are going to change things for all of us," Saturn said.

"And what is he planning?" Julian demanded. "If I knew what was going on, I'd be happy to help."

"I can't tell you, yet."

"Why not?"

Saturn didn't answer. Julian's mind raced. "You don't know what he's planning either," he realized.

"I know enough," Saturn replied.

"Yeah, enough to build what he needs you to build," Julian said. "The rest of us watched you two fight and make up for years. He pushes you away and then pulls you back when he needs you. Don't tell me you don't see it!"

"Don't start with that, Julian. He gave so many people a home. People who had nowhere else to go."

Exactly, Julian thought. *Nowhere else to go.*

No choice in the matter.

"And what about you?" he asked. Saturn was a grown woman with a successful career. Surely she wasn't dependent on Blazar for a life.

"He gave me a home, too." Saturn folded her arms. "What do you think my life is like outside of the Complex? My mother passed away before I was old enough to walk. And my father left me to start a tech company on the west coast, only to drop dead too!"

"I'm sorry," Julian said, surprised by Saturn's outburst, but his voice was still laced with frustration. "You have a job, though. You have another identity. You could do whatever you wanted."

For a moment, both of them were quiet. The wind picked up, rustling the leaves in the trees. A bird sang. Julian's heart pounded in his chest.

"Why do you care so much about the details of Blazar's plan?" Saturn asked. "That should be the least of your concerns right now."

"Because I don't know what comes after this!" Julian flung out his arms. "I keep waiting for everything to fall into place. I thought it would happen after I killed Storm Warning! I thought I'd finally made it!"

Saturn stared at him.

"I have to go." Julian turned around.

"We need you, Julian!" Saturn called. "Don't let us down."

Julian's hands tightened at his sides. He didn't say another word as he stormed to the park entrance. A few people on the sidewalk cast him apprehensive looks as he exited.

It took a few minutes to calm himself down. Charlotte was home now, waiting for him, he reminded himself. He could worry about Saturn and Blazar later.

Julian halted in the middle of the sidewalk, and it took him a moment to fully process what had caught his eye. He was standing outside the plant shop Charlotte had pointed out the other day. There were new bouquets sitting in vases on the table outside.

A mix of pastel flowers—pinks and blues and purples—drew his attention. Julian picked up the vase and carried it inside to pay.

Ten minutes later, he stood outside Charlotte's apartment. He took a deep breath. Knocked on the door.

When it swung open, Spencer was on the other side. Julian tensed. He wasn't entirely sure why.

"Charlotte! Julian's here!" Spencer stepped back. "Hey, Julian. Come in."

Julian followed him inside. Charlotte looked up from where she sat at the dining table, working on her laptop. "Thank you!" she said as she jumped to her feet. As she walked to meet him, her gaze darted to the bouquet, and her smile widened. "Flowers?"

Oh. Right. He'd forgotten he was holding them. "Oh, yeah, I just— it was on the way, and you mentioned—"

Charlotte hugged him. Julian winced.

"Sorry, I forgot you were hurt!" As Charlotte stepped back, Julian found his gaze flickering to Spencer. Spencer looked away, back to his textbook, but something in his expression put Julian on edge.

"It's okay," Julian said. He reached into his pocket to grab Charlotte's phone. As he held it out to her, he added, "I should get home, though."

"Yeah, please get some rest." Charlotte took the phone. "Hey, if it's all right with you, I could use a quick study break. Is it okay if I walk with you to the end of the street?"

"Of course."

Charlotte moved to open the door for Julian, and when he stepped back out into the evening air, she followed.

As they walked away from the apartment complex, Charlotte spoke in a low voice. "I remembered something else," she said quietly. "Not much, but I saw the stormoid leaving me—leaving Red Tempest."

"Oh." Julian watched her out of the corner of his eye, trying to gauge how she felt about the memory. She wasn't giving away much. "What was it like?"

"It hurt," she said. "I could feel the pain, too, and—" She frowned. "There was something else. A feeling. Emotional pain, I guess, at losing his power. But I snapped out of it before it ended, so I'm not totally sure."

Julian couldn't bring himself to press for the details of the stormoid itself, though he should have. He needed to know how it happened, if he was going to take it, but the mention of it hurting—

"Oh, heads up, there's a shortcut through this plaza here." Charlotte stopped and jutted a thumb to her right.

Julian paused. "Oh. What street's on the other side?"

"Maple. Here, I'll show you."

They entered the plaza. Offices wrapped around it, but trees were planted around the edge, hiding most of the buildings from view and casting long shadows across the ground.

"Have you figured out what's triggering the memories?" Julian asked as they walked. "Any sort of pattern?"

"I'm not sure yet," Charlotte said. "But I'm hoping I can remember how to fly one of these days."

"I'm sure you will."

In the center of the plaza was a fountain. Julian paused next to it. Charlotte stopped at his side and reached out a hand to touch the water. A sly grin crossed her face.

Julian lifted an eyebrow. "What are you—?"

Charlotte lifted her hand. Water formed a small sphere beneath her palm. With a flick of her wrist, she sent it flying at Julian's face.

It splashed against his forehead. He laughed in surprise as drops of water slid down his nose and cheeks. He wiped them away with the sleeve of his jacket. Since he'd mostly focused her training on electricity, he tended to forget she could manipulate other storm elements, too.

"Sorry," Charlotte said. Her smirk made it clear she had no regrets.

Julian swept his hand across the surface of the water, sending a spray at Charlotte. She laughed and jumped back. He took a step forward, pulling his arm back to try again. Charlotte's hand shot out and caught his wrist. With her other hand, she hit the water and splashed him again.

"Maybe I taught you a little too well," he teased.

"Aw, you scared?" She pulled his arm and turned him toward the fountain. He stumbled forward a couple of steps. His hands landed on the edge of the fountain, and he caught a glimpse of his reflection staring back up at him from the water. Grinning like an idiot, the echo of a laugh on his face—he never looked like this in the mirror.

"Sorry," Charlotte said, letting go of his arm. "That didn't hurt too much, did it?"

"No, you're fine." Julian straightened up and turned around. "I'll just get you back with this." He splashed the water he held in his cupped hand into her face.

Charlotte laughed as she wiped her arm across her face. "Okay, okay, truce?"

"Truce," Julian agreed.

Her eyes found his, shining like bronze in the evening light. A light breeze swept through the trees around them, making golden rays of sun dance across her skin. Stray pieces of her hair shifted with the wind.

Charlotte reached up to rest a hand on the side of his face, sending his pulse skyrocketing. "You have a pretty bad bruise right here," she murmured. She gently brushed a thumb over the spot.

Julian reached up and held his own hand over hers. "That's far from the worst one," he admitted.

"Next time you get in a fight, maybe let me know," she said, lifting an eyebrow. "I still owe you for patching up my arm."

Julian dared to lean in. He smirked. "You're hoping I get in another fight?"

"Maybe I'm just hoping..." Charlotte trailed off. Her gaze lowered. To his mouth.

"Hoping what?" Some part of Julian was fighting to hold himself back, but why? Wasn't that the point of all this? That he could do whatever he wanted?

But he wanted this in another world. A world where he wasn't Citadel.

The hand pressed to the side of Julian's face pulled him closer, and his own hand moved with Charlotte's. The gap between them was down to a few inches.

"You're not going to stop me, are you?" Charlotte asked, her voice low.

"Why would I?" Julian breathed.

The gap between their lips closed.

As his eyes drifted shut, Julian lifted his other hand to Charlotte's back. He couldn't think, could barely breathe, knew nothing beyond where Charlotte's skin touched his. Her other hand found his shoulder and they pulled each other even closer as they kissed again. And again.

"Charlotte," Julian stammered as he finally pulled away. "I should—" *I should go home.* He did have things to do. Work tomorrow. He kissed her again. "I should get going." And again.

Charlotte pulled back, grinning. "Sorry. You must be exhausted." The hand she'd had pressed to his face fell to her side.

Julian lowered his own hands. "Good night," he said, still breathless.

Charlotte took a step back. "Good night."

Julian stepped forward, took her face in his hands, and kissed her one last time, savoring the feeling of her lips against his. "Sorry. Good night for real," he said as he stepped away.

Charlotte laughed. "Okay. Good night for real."

Julian watched her walk away. Even after she was gone, it took him a minute to find the energy to start the long journey back to his apartment. But despite the aches that worsened with every step, and the exhaustion weighing down on him, he was smiling the whole way home.

CHAPTER TWENTY-THREE

A mix of exhilaration and relief lingered with Charlotte all the way back to the apartment. She'd been terrified Julian would pull away. That he would tell her she was wrong, that he didn't feel what she felt.

But she returned to the apartment feeling lighter than she'd felt in months. And she was still smiling when she walked in.

Spencer glanced up from his book. "Hey."

"Hey." Charlotte grabbed the vase of flowers Julian had brought and set them on the table as she sat down in front of her computer.

"Was Julian okay?" Spencer asked. "He looked a little...stiff."

"Oh, yeah, just a minor injury," Charlotte said, not really wanting to get into the issue of Julian being attacked, too. "He says it's not that bad."

Spencer lifted an eyebrow. "Well, you seem like you're in a much better mood than when you left."

Charlotte flushed. "Yeah, he kissed me," she said. "So, I guess he likes me after all."

"Oh, good. I was afraid you were going to need me to point out the flowers he brought you."

Charlotte laughed. "Okay, okay." She leaned forward to look at them again. Tracing a finger over the edge of one of the petals, she asked, "Hey, have you been past the lot where Marigold Bank used to be?"

"Uh, no, not recently. Why?"

"Oh, you should if you get a chance!" Charlotte told him. "Someone planted flowers."

"Cool," Spencer said. "But they're going to have to put a new building there eventually, aren't they?"

"Yeah, but at least it's nice in the meantime."

Spencer smiled. "All right, fair enough." His gaze swept over the flowers Julian had brought before returning to the textbook. He'd never been one for strong emotional reactions, and Charlotte genuinely appreciated that he wasn't the kind of person to make a big deal out of romantic endeavors. But she swore she saw apprehension in his gaze.

And truth be told…

Charlotte couldn't shake the growing feeling that there was more to Julian than met the eye. Something he wasn't telling her. The fight he'd been in seemed more important than he let on, too. Who else out there was after the stormoid? Who else knew that he was the one training her?

And then there were the flowers that had appeared in the park where they'd been sitting, and more flowers in the bank lot the day after…was it really just a coincidence?

Charlotte had no idea what to make of it all. But if there was something more going on, she really hoped there was a good explanation for it.

She spent the next hour or so finishing up various school assignments. After that, she dragged herself to her room, quickly got ready for bed, and collapsed on top of her blankets. She expected to drift off gradually as her eyes fell closed. Instead, she was plunged into another memory.

Charlotte stood in a grassy field, staring down a city skyline, wind whipping around her. Only, she wasn't Charlotte. She was Red Tempest. Shadowmaster stood in front of her, lifting a hand.

Black energy exploded from his palm and cut through Red Tempest's chest. Not deep enough to be fatal, but deep enough to knock him off his feet. Charlotte felt the stabbing pain, felt the thud of the ground as he dropped to his knees.

"Battle's over, Tempest," Shadowmaster said. "Do you have any idea how much damage your storm did to the city?" He moved forward to stand over Red Tempest. He lifted a hand and removed his painted white mask, revealing the face of a man in his late thirties underneath. It was a face that Red Tempest already knew.

"Serves them right," Charlotte felt her mouth scream. The pain twisting Red Tempest's heart in his chest wasn't just from his injuries. She'd never felt anguish like this before.

"Your problem is with me, not them." Shadowmaster's tone remained cool, but there was pain in his eyes, too. He shook his head. "Give me the Eye."

Somehow, Charlotte knew he was referring to the stormoid. She felt tears stream down Red Tempest's face.

"Please." Shadowmaster's voice softened. "You know it's over for you. Don't make me kill you."

"You wouldn't," Red Tempest spat. "You can't do it."

"I will. For them."

"You care about that damn city more than me?"

Shadowmaster didn't answer. Instead, after a long moment, he said, "You've done too much damage already." He extended hand and aimed his palm at Red Tempest. "Last warning. I will kill you."

Red Tempest lifted his chin. "Fine. Take it."

A new sensation abruptly took over. Charlotte could *feel* the stormoid moving in Red Tempest's blood. He was in complete control of it. The liquid travelled to the wound in his chest and spilled out. It formed a solid sphere of metal in the air between him and the hero.

There was no way for Shadowmaster to take it otherwise, Charlotte realized. If Red Tempest didn't give it up, Shadowmaster would have had to kill him to remove it.

Shadowmaster encased the stormoid in a cube of pure darkness. He grabbed it from the air with both hands. "I didn't want it to end like this, Thomas."

Red Tempest's real name.

"Me neither," Red Tempest said through ragged breaths. "But I made my choice."

"Was it worth it?" Shadowmaster asked.

Red Tempest responded with cold laughter. Shook his head. "Almost."

"Almost?"

"We could have had it all. Together."

"No. We couldn't." Shadowmaster gave him a sad smile. "You chose your greed over me."

Red Tempest's head lowered. "I should have made you kill me."

Charlotte's eyes flew open. She sat up in her bed, back in the present. Her hand moved to her chest and felt the pounding of her heart from beneath her ribs.

The physical pain was gone, but the emotional pain of what she'd just relived lingered for a few more minutes. Charlotte pulled her legs to her chest and rested her chin on her knees as she waited for it to fade.

She did have one less thing to worry about. No one could take the stormoid from her without her permission. And she sure as hell wasn't giving it up willingly.

If anyone wanted to take it from her, they'd have to kill her.

CHAPTER TWENTY-FOUR

Julian, in costume and wearing the mask that fully covered his face, observed from a rooftop as Damselfly attacked the restaurant. She had no idea he was watching. He'd almost offered his help to her directly but had decided against it. She rarely did things on her own, and he wanted to see how she'd handle it.

And if anyone showed up to fight her, he'd be there, ready to join in as Citadel. He wasn't in the best shape, but he had the energy needed to generate a few stone pillars.

Of course, it was hard to focus when his heart kept skipping beats. It had been a full day since they'd kissed in the plaza and he still couldn't keep his mind off Charlotte. Couldn't stop it from replaying their time together. Even the memory of her throwing him to the ground as Citadel was enough to make his face burn. He was torn on many things these days, but every inch of him was dying to see her again.

If only his second job weren't so demanding.

Damselfly dropped from the sky and flew straight through one of the restaurant's front windows. Julian winced, though he knew her body armor probably saved her from feeling much pain at all. And she was resilient even without it.

People were pouring out of the restaurant within seconds, some frantically making calls on their phones while others simply screamed. As the last of them trailed out, Damselfly broke out of the building through a different window. She soared into the air and hovered over the street, watching the restaurant. Waiting for it to blow.

The first blast took down the southwest corner of the building. The plan, as far as Julian knew, had been to plant Saturn's moon bombs around the restaurant and detonate them one after the other. After about ten seconds, the next bomb went off, bringing down another corner. A third and fourth followed. Only the center of the restaurant was left standing now.

Smoke spilled out of the restaurant's remains. Fires broke out across the rubble. While flames inched higher into the sky, someone emerged from an alley below Julian and started across the street.

Collider.

Headed straight for Damselfly.

Julian broke off a section of the roof he stood on and descended to the street. The small crowd of onlookers scattered at the sight of him. "Damselfly!" he shouted.

Damselfly looked down at him, and Collider turned around in the same moment.

"What are you doing here?" Damselfly yelled back, her voice slightly muffled by her helmet.

"Damselfly, get out of here!" Julian's gaze flickered to Collider. They were bound to target him if Damselfly left. Another fight between the two of them would likely end with hospital-worthy injuries, if he couldn't escape fast enough, but better him than Damselfly. He could take it.

"But the building—" Damselfly glanced back. "I didn't set off the last detonator!"

"I'll finish bringing it down and you can tell Blazar it was you." Julian's hands curled into fists. "Just get away from here!"

Damselfly hovered in the air for another moment before nodding and shooting up into the sky.

Julian lowered his gaze to Collider as they strolled toward him. "Ready for round two?" He raised his fists.

"Did we have a round one?" Collider paused. Their head tipped to the side. "Because all I remember is throwing you around until you ran away like a coward."

Julian's eyes narrowed under his mask. "If you're so brave, why haven't you taken on Blazar yet?"

"Oh, I will," Collider said. "Once I'm done with you."

They lunged. This time, Julian was ready. He dodged their first attack and summoned a staff of stone in his hand. Swung. The weapon moved right through them. They threw another punch, and he reached up to catch their fist.

The force of the blow was stronger than he expected. He stumbled but kept himself upright. One hand still on Collider's metal gauntlet, Julian swung his staff at their arm. The stone passed through them again.

It was going to be impossible to hit them if Julian didn't get the timing perfect. He took a step back and raised the staff, waiting for them to make the next move.

Collider lifted their leg to kick him in the chest. Bracing himself for the blow, Julian brought his staff down on their leg. Stone met metal with a clang.

His delight at finally landing a hit was short-lived. Pain reverberated through his arm and Collider's metal boot continued on to strike him right in the sternum. He staggered backwards, cursing.

Glass shattered behind Collider. They whirled around, and Julian followed their gaze as another figure jumped out of the building, carrying someone.

Charlotte. Wearing her costume.

"There's still people in there?" Julian asked in surprise. Who hadn't evacuated at the first sign of Damselfly?

"What, like you care?" Collider spun around and whacked him on the side of his head with a fist, sending him crashing to the ground. While he grunted at the sensation of air leaving his lungs, they stormed toward the building. "How many more?"

Charlotte set the man down on the sidewalk. "Just a few in the kitchen, I can—"

"I've got it." Collider marched past Charlotte and went right through a crumbling section of wall.

Julian sat up and rubbed the side of his head. It took a moment for the spots to clear from his vision.

Charlotte faced him as he climbed to his feet. "So, we meet again, Citadel."

Good thing he'd grabbed his full mask. At this point, Charlotte would probably be able to recognize him just from the bottom of his face. "I'm starting to think you're following me," he told her.

Charlotte rolled her eyes. "Pretty sure it's the other way around, asshole."

Julian held up his hands. "Not today. I'm serious."

"Right. You were just busy destroying this restaurant."

"Actually, that was Damselfly."

Collider reemerged from the building, carrying three people at once. They lowered the three gently onto the sidewalk and returned to where Julian and Charlotte stood. "Good to see I didn't miss anything exciting."

"You're Collider," Charlotte said blankly.

"And you are?" Collider rested a hand on their hip.

"The new Storm Warning."

"Well, you should probably come up with your own name."

"Yeah, I guess." Charlotte frowned. "Where have you been all this time, anyway?"

Julian backed away slowly, mentally planning his escape. The buildings on the other side of the street would be the best way to flee, but it would take a tall pillar to get himself up.

He froze and cursed under his breath. He'd promised Damselfly he'd finish bringing down the building, and he couldn't let her get in trouble with Blazar. Even if Julian told Blazar what happened, he'd blame Damselfly for not finishing the job.

Before Julian could think up a way to get the rest of the building down without Charlotte and Collider stopping him, a woman behind him caught his attention.

"Wait!" she tried to yell in the direction of Charlotte and Collider, but her voice was hoarse. Barely audible, even to someone as close as Julian. The distant sirens weren't helping.

The woman's gaze flickered desperately to Julian. She sat on the pavement, cradling an arm that bore a nasty scrape. "My friend's still in there. She was in the bathroom."

Julian glanced at the two heroes, who hadn't heard the woman. Convincing them to listen to him would take precious time. And the fire was spreading rapidly.

Walk away. He always walked away. The aftermath wasn't his problem. But...he'd never been this *close* to the aftermath. He wasn't supposed to stick around this long. And as flames danced in front of him, something inside of him felt sick.

He took a split second to look at Charlotte again. She'd go back inside in a heartbeat.

Damn it. Julian drew in a deep breath and charged toward the burning, crumbling remains of the building. The smoke embraced him, and he found another reason to be grateful he was wearing the full mask. It wouldn't save him from smoke inhalation, but it would help long enough to get him out of this unharmed. Hopefully.

The bathroom sign had survived the explosions. Julian ducked under it and stepped through a doorway.

A woman sat on the floor in the corner of the bathroom. Her eyes went wide when Julian entered. "Citadel," she stammered. She lifted an arm to hide her face. "Please don't kill me."

"I'm not here to kill you." Julian scanned the bathroom. "Anyone else in here?"

The woman shook her head. As Julian walked toward her, a second set of footsteps sounded behind him. He looked back.

Charlotte.

"Help me!" the woman exclaimed, fresh panic in her voice.

"I already told you, I'm not here to kill you!" Julian turned to face Charlotte. "What are you doing in here?"

"I'm here to save her." Charlotte's eyes narrowed. "From you, apparently."

"Did you both miss the part where I said I'm not here to kill her?"

"Sorry that I'm having a hard time believing you," Charlotte replied. "But can you blame me, given your track record?"

Before Julian could respond, the wall behind Charlotte collapsed. She yelped and jumped forward, narrowly dodging the rubble spilling across the floor. Nearly colliding with Julian. His heart quickened. *Damn. It.*

"Well, there goes our way out," she said as she moved to stand between Julian and the woman.

Julian forced his mind back on track. The smoke was getting worse, fast. "Use your powers to get the smoke out of here," he told Charlotte.

Charlotte pressed her lips together and nodded. A wind swept through the room, finding its way in through gaps in the wall and carrying the smoke out through openings on the other side.

"You're welcome," Charlotte said pointedly, shooting him a sideways glance.

Julian sighed. "Thank you. Now that I'm not on the verge of suffocating, I think I can get us out of here."

"That's a little dramatic."

"Honestly, I don't know what you expected from a man wearing a cape," the woman sitting on the floor said.

Charlotte laughed. "Good point."

Julian's face went red under his mask. "Do you want me to get you out of here or not?"

"Whenever you're ready," Charlotte replied with a dramatic sweep of her arm.

"I need you both to stand closer to me."

"Of course you do," Charlotte muttered. She walked to the woman and held out a hand. "Don't worry. I promise we're going to make it out of here." The woman let Charlotte help her up, and they both moved to stand next to Julian.

Julian, thankfully, had enough energy to form a dome of stone above them. Once it was in place, he closed his eyes and located the parts of the buildings he could feel. The parts he could manipulate. The stone, the brick, the concrete.

He shattered it all.

Rubble rained down around them. Smoke poured back into the bathroom and heat radiated off the burning fires. Jaw clenched with the effort, Julian kept his focus on the stone protecting them.

Once the building was done falling, he tossed aside the dome. Flames crawled toward them. "Let's go."

The woman tried to stand and immediately dropped back to the ground. "I can't," she said, her voice weak. She trembled violently.

Julian grabbed the woman, lifted her off the ground, and made his way toward the sidewalk.

"Wait—" Charlotte started.

"I've got her," Julian said. "Put out the fire." He glanced back. "You're the only one who can do it."

The rain started and Julian continued forward with the woman. Collider stood on the sidewalk, watching him approach with folded arms.

When he reached the pavement, Collider's arms dropped to their sides. "Put her down!" they demanded, storming toward him.

"Planning on it." Julian grunted as he bent over to carefully set the woman down.

Collider halted in front of him. "Why did you do that?"

Julian shrugged as he took a step back. "Couldn't have her in the way."

Collider moved forward, matching his step. "And where do you think you're going?"

Julian gestured to Charlotte as she joined them. "She needs to stick around a little longer to finish putting out the fires. I suggest you help anyone who might be injured." His gaze flickered to the woman he'd left sitting on the sidewalk. "Or you can chase me. Your choice."

He took another step back. Collider stared for a long moment before turning and kneeling next to the woman. "Are you okay?" they asked.

Julian ran to a nearby building and turned the corner, putting himself out of sight of Charlotte and Collider. He needed a minute to catch his breath before heading back to the Complex, but he couldn't have those two teaming up to fight him. He definitely would not win.

From here, he could just make out the heroes' voices as they spoke to each other, though he couldn't quite understand what they were saying. After a few moments, he dared to peer around the corner.

The two heroes had moved into the middle of the street. The sirens of first responders were much louder now, not more than a block away. Time to go. But...

Collider shrugged. "Take it or leave it, but I think Stormbringer would fit."

"Huh." Charlotte rested a hand on her hip. "I like it."

Julian chuckled. Then immediately winced in pain. But even as he pressed a hand to his side, he was only thinking that he did like the name for Charlotte.

CHAPTER TWENTY-FIVE

Julian walked slowly to the hidden elevator, moved slowly as he pressed the button for the Complex. In the weeks since he'd killed Storm Warning, he seemed to dread every trip here more than the last.

He forced himself to step inside when the door opened. No Blazar. No Saturn. Just a very angry Damselfly.

"Why'd you send me away?" Damselfly demanded as he entered. She flew out of the kitchen, a can of soda in her hand. "We could have taken Collider on together!" She gestured wildly with the can and sent soda splashing into the air.

Julian moved to the couch. "No, we couldn't. Another hero showed up." He removed his mask and set it on the coffee table as he sat down.

"Who?"

"They don't have a name yet." He leaned back. Grimaced in pain. "But...they have Storm Warning's powers."

"Oh!" Damselfly exclaimed. She dropped to the ground with a soft thud. "You found the person with the stormoid. That's good!"

"No. It's not."

"What? Why? Now you just have to take it from them, right?"

Julian sucked in a deep breath and turned his head to look at her. "Damselfly, what would you do if you had to fight someone you didn't want to hurt?"

"Well, I don't think I have anyone like that." Damselfly rubbed her arm. "I mean, I can't imagine I'd ever have a reason to fight any of you."

Julian moved his gaze to the blank TV monitor. His faint reflection stared back at him. "I made a mistake," he said. A series of them, really. One after the other. And deep down, he'd known all along he was making them.

Frowning, Damselfly set her soda can on the counter and approached the couch slowly. "Julian, you're kind of...freaking me out. What's wrong?"

"It's better if you don't know yet. I don't want you getting in trouble with Blazar." Julian forced himself to stand. "Speaking of, do you know when he's coming by next?"

"He said he'd come by tomorrow morning to talk to me about how the restaurant thing went," Damselfly replied.

"I'm going to stay here tonight, then." Julian sighed. "I have to talk to him." He had to deal with the man eventually. Better sooner than later.

Damselfly lit up. She clapped her hands together. "Cool! I can make pancakes for breakfast."

Julian felt nauseous at the thought but forced a smile. "Sounds great."

He headed to his room to change. When he returned to the living room, Damselfly had that shooting video game of hers going again. She pointed to the second controller sitting on the coffee table, among bags of candy and empty soda cans. "You in?"

"Just a few rounds," Julian told her as he sat down. "I'm exhausted. And tomorrow's going to be...busy."

"What, did you clear your entire schedule to talk to Blazar?" Damselfly asked. She popped a piece of chocolate in her mouth. As she chewed, she added, "That's probably a good idea, actually. It usually takes a couple of business days to recover from a conversation with him."

Julian chuckled. "I hope not. I have something tomorrow evening." *Hopefully.*

"What do you want to talk to him about, anyway?" Damselfly asked.

"This...thing he has planned," Julian said. "I'm not going to help him with anything else until he tells me what it is."

Damselfly let out a low whistle. "Well, it was nice knowing you."

"Oh, please. Blazar's tough, but he's not unreasonable." Even as the words left his mouth, though, Julian wasn't sure he believed them.

Damselfly hesitated. "And...the stormoid?"

"I need to hold him off a little longer on that," Julian told. "I need to figure out a new plan."

"What was your old plan, exactly?"

"It doesn't matter."

They played in silence for a while after that, besides the occasional string of curses from Damselfly. Finally, after one of the matches ended in a victory, Julian set the controller down and rose from the couch.

"I'm off to bed," he said. "Good night."

Damselfly nodded as she started a new single player match. "Good night."

The next morning, Julian was awoken by the smell of something burning. He quickly dressed and hurried out to the kitchen, bracing himself for the worst. Whatever that was.

"Relax, I put the fire out as soon as it started," Damselfly said as he entered. "We're on attempt two."

"Great." Julian sat down at the counter. "But just so you know, I like my pancakes medium rare."

"Ha, ha." Damselfly rolled her eyes as she added flour to the bowl in front of her. She mixed it for a minute before moving to pour it out onto the pan behind her.

"Wait," Julian said. "That looks too runny."

"Don't backseat cook, Julian." Still, Damselfly paused. "How do I fix it?"

"Start with another half cup of flour."

After she'd mixed in the new flour, Damselfly held the bowl out to him. "Better?" she asked. He nodded.

While Damselfly poured the batter into the pan, Julian pulled out his phone, opened his messages with Charlotte, and stared at the keyboard. Every minute or so, he'd started to type out a message, only to shake his head and back up.

"What's up?" Damselfly asked after his fourth failed attempt.

"Huh?" Julian glanced up to find her standing directly on the other side of the counter, staring at him.

Damselfly gestured to his phone with her spatula. "You look—" The end of the utensil spun in small circles. "—anxious."

"I'm not anxious."

Damselfly leaned forward and peered at his screen. "Ha, I knew it! You're texting Charlotte."

Julian groaned. "It's not—I'm—"

"Come on, what's the deal? You've talked to her a bunch already, right?"

Julian set the phone down and buried his face in his hands. "Yes," he muttered.

"Hm. Let me get this straight." Damselfly set her elbow on the counter and rested her chin on her hand, swinging around the spatula with her other hand. "The man, the *supervillain* who killed Storm Warning, who's robbed a dozen banks and won and lost a hundred battles, is nervous about texting a girl?"

"That's very dramatic. And I'm not nervous." Julian lifted his head and leaned over to eye the smoke coming off the griddle. "And please keep your eyes on the pancakes."

"Sure." Damselfly turned around and flipped one of them over. The other side was nearly black. "Look, I know I don't get out much, but I watch a lot of TV."

"I've noticed."

"Clearly, you don't know what you're doing."

Julian snorted. "I know what I'm doing, okay? I've been in relationships before."

"Really?"

"Okay, well, not *long* ones." The supervillain thing made it hard. Randomly disappearing to help Blazar with his plans didn't help. And according to some people, he was apparently a "selfish asshole" who "never thought about anyone besides himself."

If only that were true. It used to be, he could admit now, but these days he was always thinking about Charlotte. And worrying about Damselfly, and wondering what Blazar was planning and why Saturn still bothered helping him.

Julian sighed. "I just keep thinking—this is a bad idea. I'm Citadel."

Damselfly scooped one of the pancakes onto a plate and added more batter to the pan. "Would you rather be Citadel? Or would you rather...?"

Be with her.

Damselfly was the only person he'd dare have this conversation with. She was the only villain to ever even hint that she'd rather have a normal life.

"I can't just leave all of this behind," Julian muttered.

"Why not?" Damselfly asked. "Oh, right, you'd be poor if you didn't steal stuff, wouldn't you?"

"No, no, I could..." Julian trailed off. He could make an honest living, right? It'd be a lot more work, but he liked the library. He could work more hours, or pick up another job somewhere else, or go to school.

Really, he may as well quit while he was ahead. No villain lasted forever.

His gaze dropped to the phone in front of him. He had to stop being an idiot. They'd spent plenty of time together already. They'd kissed, for god's sake. He grabbed the phone. *Are you busy tonight?*

But even if he did quit being Citadel, there was always a chance Charlotte would find out eventually. His other identity was too deeply entangled with the past few years of his life. His chest tightened. He'd have to tell her himself, wouldn't he? How could he possibly expect her to look past that? Even if he convinced her he didn't want to be Citadel anymore—

Damselfly set a plate with two charred pancakes in front of him. "Julian, whatever happens, whatever you choose...just don't leave me here alone, okay?" She smiled, but it didn't reach her eyes. "I mean, without you around, Blazar would be a hundred times more annoying."

"Of course I wouldn't just—leave," Julian said. Would Blazar even let him? Blazar knew where he lived. He'd insisted on coming by to see the place after Julian moved in. Julian couldn't run from him. Not in New Atlas.

No, no, of course Blazar would let him go. He'd never forced Julian to be a villain in the first place, technically. He'd strongly encouraged it, was all. Very strongly.

The phone buzzed with Charlotte's response. *I'm free after 5 :)*

Julian thought back to what Damselfly had said a minute earlier. How could someone who'd killed a superhero, someone who had an entire city living in fear of him, someone who'd always taken what he'd wanted...how the hell could he be nervous?

Because he had something to lose.

Damselfly noticed the message. "So, what do you have planned?" she asked, shaking Julian from his thoughts.

He glanced up. "Well, unlike you, I actually know how to cook."

"Rude." Damselfly stuck her tongue out at him.

Despite the fact that the outsides were black, Julian tore off a piece of one of the pancakes and tried it. He lifted an eyebrow. "You know, if it weren't burned to hell and back, I think this would be pretty good."

"You're just saying that."

"I'm serious. Try actually paying attention to them this time." Julian nodded to the stove behind her. "And turn the heat down a bit."

Before Damselfly could make another attempt, the elevator door opened. Blazar barged in, Saturn trailing behind him.

"I need everyone on a mission tonight," Blazar announced. "We're burning down an office building. It'll take a while, and I'll need help keeping firefighters at bay."

Julian returned his phone to his pocket and slid out of his seat. "What? Why?"

"To make room for our new home!" Blazar spread a map across the coffee table, bumping Julian's mask and sending wrappers drifting to the ground. "Enough hiding. We're going to build a giant tower."

"And make ourselves an obvious target for heroes?" Damselfly asked skeptically.

"There won't be any heroes around to fight us!"

Blazar had truly lost it if he thought heroes wouldn't come in from across the country. Julian followed Saturn to the table and took a closer look at the map. It was of New Atlas. Several places at the edge of the city had been marked with red X's, including the former site of Marigold Bank and the restaurant he and Damselfly had destroyed.

And near the center of the map was—

Blazar pointed to the giant red circle. "These three buildings here have to go."

Julian stared at the spot. That was...

That was right where Dove Park was.

Julian's hands tightened into fists. "I can't tonight," he told Blazar.

Blazar looked up and stared at him incredulously. "Can't? What other obligation could you possibly have?"

"Library...work."

"You have got to be kidding me."

"You want my help?" Julian asked. "Tell me what your big plan is."

"You don't need to worry about the details," Blazar said. He brushed a hand over a folded corner of the map to straighten it out. "I have everything under control."

Julian's jaw clenched. "Stop acting like you're doing me a favor by keeping things from me. Tell me what you have planned or I'm not helping you anymore."

"Julian." Blazar kept his tone light, but his frustration was clear. "Come on. We need you on this."

"Well, I don't need you," Julian snapped.

That did it. Blazar's entire demeanor shifted. He rose to his full height and looked down at Julian. Damselfly glanced away. Saturn lowered her gaze to the map.

"Don't forget everything I've done for you, Julian," Blazar said.

"Believe me, I haven't." Julian backed away from Blazar, toward the door. "But you don't get to control my entire life just because you saved me." Though Julian wasn't sure he'd call it saving anymore. As his hand found the elevator button on the wall, he added, "And stop stalking me. My personal life isn't your business."

"I just want you to remember where your priorities lie," Blazar said.

Julian glared at him. "I know exactly what my priorities are."

He stepped back into the elevator. The door slid shut, cutting him off from Blazar.

If Julian did leave the Complex for good, he wanted to leave on good terms. But he was beginning to fear that would be impossible.

CHAPTER TWENTY-SIX

Charlotte paced back and forth in the living room, occasionally stopping to look at herself in the mirror or check the time or glance at her phone again.

Spencer had left an hour earlier to work on a lab report on campus, leaving Charlotte to anxiously wait for her date with Julian alone. She picked up her phone and stared—for the millionth time—at the text message Julian had sent after she'd told him she was free that evening.

Want to join me for dinner tonight? I'm making chicken risotto.

When Charlotte responded with an enthusiastic yes, he'd sent her his address and told her to plan for seven, since he had to take care of a few things at the library. It was only 6:30, but Charlotte didn't see the point in trying to get anything else done right now. Her ability to focus on anything else was completely shot.

A few minutes later, while she was staring at the message again, a new text from Julian popped up on the screen. *Dinner will be ready soon!*

Thank god he'd learned to start using exclamation points in his texts. Charlotte had feared she sounded crazy the first few times they'd arranged training sessions. She replied to let him know she was on her way, grabbed the gift bag sitting by the door, and stepped out of the apartment.

She was halfway to Julian's apartment when something made her pause in the middle of the sidewalk. She wasn't sure what had her feeling so unsettled, but she found herself anxiously scanning the faces of everyone passing by. After she turned in a few circles and couldn't find anything out of the ordinary, she brushed the feeling off and kept going.

Ten minutes later, she stood in front of Julian's door, triple checking that she had the right number. Like at her apartment, his door opened directly outside, but he was on the fifth floor. The walkway outside was nice, with potted plants lined up against the side of the building.

Charlotte slid her phone into her jeans, took a breath to clear her thoughts, and knocked.

The door opened quickly. "Come in," Julian said. "It's almost ready."

"It smells amazing," Charlotte told him as she entered. She held up the bag. "Here, I have something for you."

Julian looked surprised as he took the bag from her. "Thank you. What—?" He reached in and took out the potted succulent.

"I thought you could use something to keep you company at work." Charlotte grinned. "Here or at the library or wherever. And those are supposed to be easy to take care of."

Julian chuckled. "You don't think I can handle a plant?"

"Better safe than sorry." Charlotte glanced around the entryway she'd stepped into. "And I don't see any in here, so I can't say I'm blown away by your experience."

"I guess I can't say I've kept plants before. But I'll keep this one alive for you." Julian held the pot out to her. "Mind carrying this into the dining room for me?"

"Sure."

Julian led Charlotte through the living room into the kitchen. He picked up a spoon off the counter and gestured through an archway into the next room. "I'll be right over, if you want to take a seat."

Charlotte entered the dining area, set the succulent in the middle of the table, and slid into a chair. She watched Julian push up his sleeves as he moved to stand over the stove. Watched him lift the pot, scoop the risotto into two bowls, carry them over to the table.

"Can I get you anything to drink?" Julian asked as he set the bowl in front of Charlotte. "Water? There's also a bit of white wine left over."

Charlotte glanced at the bottle of wine sitting among the other ingredients next to the stove. "Ooh, fancy," she said. "Yeah, I'll have a little of that."

Julian stepped away from the table and returned a moment later with forks and two glasses of wine. As he leaned over to set the glass in front of her, Charlotte's gaze briefly darted to a bruise at the edge of his collarbone, only visible thanks to the fact that the top button of his shirt was undone. Was that new? He would have told her if he'd been in another fight, right?

Charlotte picked up her fork and, suddenly aware of how hungry she was, took her first bite of the risotto. "Wow," she blurted. "This is incredible."

"Thank you." Julian's smile sent a rush through her. After a moment, he added, "I don't actually cook for other people that much."

"Really? I can't believe people aren't begging you to cook for them all the time." Charlotte took another bite, and Julian started on his own food. While they ate, she bragged about the grade she'd gotten on her last presentation. He followed with a story about an author they'd managed to get for a book signing at the library.

"You know, we still need posters to advertise it," he told her. "Maybe we could hire you to do them."

Charlotte blushed and looked down. "Really? You think they'd want me?"

"Sure. Your stuff's great." Julian lifted his glass. "And I'm sure I only saw a fraction of it."

"Poster design is a lot of fun," Charlotte said as Julian sipped his wine. "I'd definitely be interested."

"I'll figure out who's in charge of the event and talk to them," Julian promised.

Finally, Charlotte finished off her last bite. "Okay, consider this." She took a sip from her glass. "You make food again, but we take it to Dove Park and have a picnic."

Something flashed across Julian's expression. But before Charlotte could get a read on it, he smiled again. "Yeah. That sounds great." He ate his last bite of risotto and stood up. Reaching out to grab the succulent, he said, "Here, I want to put this on my desk in the living room."

Charlotte followed him back into the living room. They passed a couch and a coffee table and stopped next to a desk that looked out a window. On the other side of the glass, city lights glittered in the night. Charlotte admired the view outside while Julian set the plant down.

They looked at each other at the same time.

Julian took her hand in his and gently pulled her toward the couch. "I have something for you, too. Wait here. I'll be right back."

Charlotte nodded as she sat down. "I don't know how you're going to top a plant, though."

Julian laughed. "You're right, my gift's not nearly as good."

He left the room and returned a moment later holding a book. "I don't actually know if you'll be interested, but this was the only book on Storm Warning that didn't have a hold list," he said. "It's about his early days as a smaller hero."

Charlotte took the book and flipped through the pages. Photos of Storm Warning were scattered throughout, collected from news reports and security footage and social media.

"I don't know, maybe it could be...motivational," Julian continued. "Or something."

"Yeah!" Charlotte exclaimed. "This is cool!" She barely knew anything about Storm Warning before his time as New Atlas's biggest hero. She set the book on the coffee table and threw her arms around Julian. "Thanks."

"It's due in three weeks," he said.

Charlotte laughed as she pulled away. "Got it."

She lifted her eyes to meet his and felt her breath catch in her throat. Julian's hand moved to the side of her face. The sensation of his palm against her skin was enough to send her head spinning. When his lips crashed against hers, her mind was gone.

Charlotte closed her eyes and let him pull her closer. Not close enough. Her hand moved to his chest. She took a moment to trace her fingers across his exposed skin before finding the next button of his shirt to expose some more.

The doorbell rang.

She reluctantly pulled her lips from Julian's. They hovered an inch apart. "Are you expecting someone?" she asked quietly.

"No." Julian kept his eyes on her, a dazed expression on his face. "It's—it's probably not important." As he moved in to kiss her again, he gently pushed her back against the couch. They separated again, briefly, while he carefully positioned himself on top of her, and then Charlotte was overwhelmed by how much of his body was pressed against hers. Pleasantly overwhelmed.

His mouth moved to her neck. She reached back up to his shirt. Before she could start on the next button, a slight groan slipped from his lips. The fabric bundled in her clenched hand.

The doorbell rang again. And then again, only seconds later. Julian's kisses continued against her neck, relentless, inching toward her collarbone.

"They seem pretty persistent," Charlotte murmured.

Julian stopped and sighed, his breath hot on her skin. "Guess I'll see what they want."

It took him a moment to get up and walk into the entryway. Charlotte leaned over to watch. She could just see the front door from here, and she was dying to know who could possibly need something from Julian this late in the evening.

He opened the door. Charlotte's heart dropped to her stomach. She recognized the man on the other side of the door. The costume he was wearing.

Julian said the man's name, confirming her fear.

"Blazar."

CHAPTER TWENTY-SEVEN

*B*lazar.

Julian was going to be sick. His hand tightened around the door handle as he racked his brain for some course of action that wouldn't end with Blazar killing him. Or Charlotte.

"Julian!" Blazar exclaimed, his tone far too friendly. Why was he in costume? Had he walked up to Julian's door like this? Had anyone seen him?

"What are you doing here?" Julian hissed.

Blazar frowned. "You seem upset."

"I'm in the middle of something."

"Yes, I can see that." A smirk touched Blazar's lips. "Don't worry, I'm just dropping something off."

He shoved something into Julian's chest. Citadel's mask. *His* mask.

Blazar set the rest of the costume, neatly folded, on the small stand next to the door.

"I keep this at the Complex," Julian said, quietly enough that he hoped Charlotte couldn't hear him.

"Sure," Blazar said. "But I didn't want you to have to go all the way there before you come to help us tomorrow afternoon."

Blazar had rescheduled the destruction of the office buildings? Did he need Julian's help that badly? "I already told you I'm not helping you."

"Suit yourself." Blazar shrugged. "Just thought I'd give it one last try."

No, Blazar wasn't really here to get Julian's help. He wasn't here to return the costume. He must have been watching Julian's apartment. Maybe he'd followed Charlotte. Regardless, he knew she was here.

Blazar wanted her to know the truth.

Blazar wanted to tear them apart.

"Go," Julian said, with as much coldness as he could muster. "And don't come to my apartment without warning." That part came out a bit louder than he meant it to.

"Sure thing. Good night, Julian."

Julian's hand tightened around the edge of the mask. The moment Blazar turned around, he threw the door shut.

The silence that followed was suffocating. Julian's heart pounded against the walls of his chest, threatening to break him open. Slowly, he forced himself to turn around. To face Charlotte.

She was already on her feet, eyeing him with—an expression he couldn't read. "You—you know Blazar," she stammered. "Why do you know Blazar?"

"Please," Julian said. "Let me explain everything from the beginning. I promise I—"

"What's that in your hand?"

Julian swallowed. He held up the mask. Light glinted off the metal.

"I'm Citadel," he confessed.

The blast of lightning knocked Julian into the door behind him. As he sank to the floor, he caught a glimpse of Charlotte disappearing into the next room through the lights dancing in his vision.

Julian jumped to his feet, threw the mask aside, and ran after her. "Charlotte, wait!"

When he entered the dining room, Charlotte was throwing open the window. "Charlotte—" he started.

She flung a hand toward him. More electricity hit him and threw him into the table. One of the empty bowls clattered to the floor. A glass tipped over. Charlotte climbed through the window and dropped onto the fire escape.

Julian rushed to the window and followed her through. By the time his feet hit the fire escape, Charlotte was already on the landing a floor below.

"Charlotte, stop!" he shouted. "Please!"

Charlotte peered up at him through the gaps in the metal stairs. "Why? So you can kill me?"

"I'm not going to kill you!"

"Then what was the point of all this, huh?" Charlotte flung out her arms.

The alley, which was already dark, fell further into shadow as black clouds gathered above it. Julian's gaze flickered up to them before moving back down to her. "I can explain, if you would just let me—"

She was already racing down the stairs again. Julian cursed and followed.

He lost sight of her when she jumped off the fire escape at the bottom. When he reached the last step, he turned and found her standing in the middle of the alley, hands raised. Another blast of lightning struck him. Julian fell from the fire escape and landed on his back on the pavement with a loud groan of pain.

The first drops of rain fell on his face.

Struggling to get air back in his lungs, Julian pushed himself up. "Charlotte. Please." More electricity threw him into the wall.

"Why aren't you fighting back?" Charlotte demanded. A gust of wind whipped her hair around her face. The rain came down harder.

Julian sat up. Leaned his head back against the wall of the apartment building. "I can't."

Charlotte's eyes narrowed. "I don't get it. Don't you want to kill me?"

"I don't want to kill you." The words came out between ragged breaths. "I never did. I was trying to get the stormoid."

"Of course," Charlotte said, her voice cracking. "I'm such an idiot."

"No, Charlotte, you're not—it's more than that—"

Lightning flashed overhead, briefly illuminating the alley, briefly illuminating Charlotte. "What did you even want it for?" she asked. "Were you going to take Storm Warning's power for yourself?"

"Blazar's the one who wanted it," Julian told her. "He was going to train a new villain."

"Well, then why did you train me?" Charlotte's hands lifted and tightened into fists in front of her. "All you did was make me stronger."

Julian's clothes were soaked through with rain now, and the drops streaming down his face blurred his vision. "I trained you because I—" His voice was breaking. He was choking on his own words. He dropped his gaze to the ground. "I wanted to—I had to prove I didn't get lucky when I killed Storm Warning." He sucked in another ragged breath and winced as the motion sent pain shooting through his back, his ribs, his chest. "I thought it would be enough for Blazar. But it wasn't."

Charlotte was quiet for a moment. There was another flash of lightning in the clouds above. "Julian, you can't take the stormoid from me," she said. "It's impossible."

"But Shadowmaster—"

"Shadowmaster didn't take it from Red Tempest!" Thunder boomed with Charlotte's exclamation. "Red Tempest gave it up to him willingly!"

Julian looked up, eyes going wide. "He did?"

"He did," Charlotte said. "But I am never giving it to you. So if you want to take it from me, you'll have to kill me."

All of this, this quest to get the stormoid, his determination to take it from her without hurting her—

All for nothing.

"Come on!" Electricity danced across Charlotte's skin, jumping between her fingers. "Aren't you going to fight me?"

All Julian could do was stare at her blankly. "I can't."

"What the hell are you talking about? You could fight just fine when you brought down that restaurant yesterday!" Charlotte took a step toward him. Another. "Get up. Let's end this here."

Julian shook his head. "You don't understand. I can't." He swallowed. "I can't hurt you."

"You—wait," Charlotte said. Her hands lowered. The arcing electricity vanished. "No, no, this was all a trick. You tricked me to get the stormoid. You don't actually *like* me."

"I'm sorry."

Slowly, realization dawned on Charlotte's face. "No. No." She was taking slow steps back now. "That's impossible. You're—you're supposed to hate people like me." She squeezed her eyes shut.

"I know. But I don't," Julian said weakly. "I like you, Charlotte. I was ready to give up being Citadel for you."

For a long moment, the only sound was the falling rain.

Charlotte's eyes snapped open. A white glow illuminated her face.

"Charlotte?" It took him a few seconds longer than it should have, but Julian mustered the strength to get back on his feet. "Charlotte, what are you seeing—?"

A powerful blast of wind rolled through the alley. Julian staggered back into the wall under its force. The rain came to a sudden stop. The clouds above Charlotte parted.

Charlotte took to the air and disappeared into the night sky.

CHAPTER TWENTY-EIGHT

In the stormoid's memories, Charlotte saw herself taking flight. Again and again and again and again.

And when she opened her eyes, she was hovering in the air, far above the glittering city of New Atlas. She yelped in surprise. Her heart dropped to her stomach, and she dropped ten feet. Twenty.

Charlotte frantically waved her arms. Then, for a brief moment, she was soaring over the clouds in the daylight.

A heartbeat later, she was back in the present. Falling. Somehow, a coherent thought broke through her panic. *You can fly. You can do this. Focus.*

She spread her arms out to either side and forced them to stop shaking. Her descent slowed. Slowed until she was hovering perfectly still in the air. After floating frozen for a long moment, she cautiously adjusted herself so that she was upright.

Okay. Great. Now to get back on the ground without falling to her death. Charlotte eased into a gradual descent. Her pace was unbearably slow, but she was too terrified to push herself any faster.

As finer details appeared on buildings and individual people became visible on the street below, Charlotte realized that her slow drop to the ground would draw way too much attention. She halted again and assessed her options. Finally, she accepted that she'd have to land on a roof and find a way down from there.

She selected a nearby skyscraper and made her first attempt at moving horizontally. It was surprisingly easy to move in the direction she wanted. Controlling her speed was a bigger challenge. When Charlotte dared to push herself a little faster toward the roof, she found herself shooting forward. In a panic, she threw her arms out in front of her and came to a jarring halt.

She was floating about thirty feet above the roof she'd been aiming for. Eager to be done with this mess, she eased herself down until she was close enough to drop to the concrete unharmed. The moment her feet thudded against it, she stumbled to the center of the roof and sank to the ground.

She should go home. Tell Spencer what happened. Oh, god, she had to tell Spencer that Julian was Citadel. Spencer was going to think she was an idiot for not figuring it out after spending so much time with him.

Charlotte rolled onto her back and buried her face in her hands, trying to hold back her sobs with little success.

She had to tell someone else too, right? The authorities? She knew Citadel's secret identity. And...he knew hers. Was it safe to go out as Stormbringer knowing that a villain could expose her to the world and put everyone close to her in danger?

She had to. She had to find a way to be a hero and stop Citadel.

What Charlotte hated more than anything else was that, deep down, she still wanted him. He'd actually cared about her. Everything he did for her, everything he'd said...he'd really meant all that, hadn't he?

Unless this was all another elaborate trick. But why not just take the stormoid from her in the alley?

The look on his face, the pain...her stomach turned at the memory. It was real. It was absolutely real.

Charlotte let her arms drop to the ground at her sides. She couldn't bring herself to get up.

Slowly, pieces came together. Julian approaching her at the funeral, after her transformation. Him not fully understanding the stormoid. Telling her she should try to relive memories of it being taken from Red Tempest.

And Citadel, backing off after he'd cut her during their fight. Citadel knowing her real name.

Fresh tears stung Charlotte's eyes. Had she been stupid not to see it before? Or had she been ignoring the little things on purpose, not wanting to look too closely and realize Julian was hiding something.

She rolled onto her side. Her hand moved to the spot on her arm where the cut had been, where Julian had bandaged her up with trembling hands, his face so close to hers she thought she might lose her mind. The mark he'd left was almost gone now.

Her eyes closed again. She needed to go home. Spencer would be worried. Was he in danger? Would Julian go after him? Charlotte didn't want to believe he would, but Citadel had done a lot of awful things in his life.

Exhaustion weighed down on her, stopping her from getting up, from even reaching for her phone. For a long moment, all she knew was the cool concrete pressed against her skin. Then darkness.

Then, blinding sunlight hitting her face.

Charlotte sat up, heart pounding in her chest. Frantically, she pulled her phone from her pocket and checked her messages. Nothing. Nothing from Spencer. Nothing from Julian.

She jumped to her feet and ran to the edge of the roof. As she reached it, she realized she couldn't fly down to the sidewalk in broad daylight.

Before she could find an alternative, someone on the street below shouted, "Hey, watch where you're going!"

Curious, Charlotte scanned the sidewalk until she spotted a man pushing his way through the crowd with surprising aggression. She frowned as she realized she recognized him. Blake Sullivan. The man who'd interviewed her for the internship.

He was walking away from Charlotte, toward an intersection. When he reached it, he turned left and disappeared behind the next building over.

Charlotte took a deep breath and a step back. Then, she raced forward and jumped, willing her abilities to carry her over to the next roof.

To her relief, when she stepped off the ground, she lifted up into the air much faster than she had the night before. A little too fast. She overshot the spot on the next building where she'd hoped to land. Instead, her feet hit concrete only a few feet from the roof's opposite edge. The edge above the street Blake had entered.

Charlotte slowly leaned forward to peer down at the sidewalk below. Blake was still walking fast, but he had a phone in his hand now. As he held it up to his ear, he took a sharp turn into an alley.

Charlotte followed the edge of the roof to the corner of the building where the alley started. Below her, Blake walked up to a door and stopped in front of it. One hand moved into his jacket pocket.

"What the hell do you mean Julian's there?" Blake growled into the phone.

Charlotte's heart jumped. No way. He couldn't possibly mean the same Julian.

"I'm on my way up right now," Blake said. "Don't let him leave."

But Julian had met Blake, briefly. And he'd looked like he'd seen a ghost.

Blake hung up the phone, pulled a key from his pocket, and stuck it in the door. When the door swung open, it revealed a metal elevator door on the other side. After a moment, that opened, too.

Charlotte backed away from the edge of the roof, her head spinning. She lifted her gaze up to the top of the building opposite the alley. The building Blake had just entered. It was taller than the one she currently stood on, and it looked like an unassuming office building, with dark windows and the occasional balcony. Was this where he worked?

If it was, why the hell was he accessing it with a secret elevator?

Charlotte fired off a quick text to Spencer to alleviate any concern he might have, if he was waiting around for her. *I'll be back soon.* She didn't have the energy to add anything else right now.

As she returned the phone to her pocket, she looked back up at the building. At the top floor. Through one of the windows facing her, she could just make out figures moving around. There were three of them, and one was gesturing wildly while the other two watched.

And then, a fourth figure entered.

CHAPTER TWENTY-NINE

Julian expected he'd wake up to police arresting him, with heroes for backup. Or Blazar would be there to kill him. Or maybe Charlotte would come back to drag him off to prison herself.

Or kill him.

No, she wouldn't kill him.

Would she?

Regardless, Julian woke up to bright sunlight on his face and a dull headache. He lazily lifted an arm to shield his face from the light. He'd fallen asleep on the floor, a few feet from the couch. After the confrontation last night, it had taken what little energy he had left just to drag himself back up the stairs and inside.

He sat up. His gaze flickered to the coffee table where Charlotte had left the book on Storm Warning.

When Julian had seen it come in at the library, he'd initially taken it to look at himself. Flipping through it, though, he'd realized Charlotte might enjoy it. And encouraging her to become a hero was supposed to be part of the plan, anyway. Not that he cared much about the plan anymore. Even before things went south last night.

Next to the book was the empty wine bottle that he vaguely remembered bringing with him from the dining room. He reached out and grabbed it. Nope, not empty. Not yet.

Julian was lucky no one had come for him yet, but he couldn't sit around forever waiting to see what happened. The Complex might be the only safe place for him. But if he saw Blazar right now...

He wasn't sure what he'd do.

No, no, he had to deal with Blazar sooner or later. *Let's get this over with.*

Julian climbed to his feet, still holding the bottle. He'd let Blazar push him around for years, believing that Blazar knew what was best for him. But that bastard just wanted another kid with superpowers working for him.

Still dressed in what he'd been wearing the night before, his shirt still damp from the rain, Julian pulled on his shoes. He'd been terrified of Blazar when the man adopted him. When had that terror turned to admiration? Was it when Blazar taught him to use his powers by throwing fire at his face? When he sent him out to rob a jewelry store to pay for his high school courses—courses Blazar made him take online?

Or was it when Blazar told Julian that if he kept it up, he'd make a fine supervillain someday? One that Blazar would be proud of?

Julian downed the last of the wine, slammed the bottle down on the stand where Blazar had left his costume, and stepped outside.

His mind wasn't present for most of the walk. It seemed as if only a few moments had passed before he found himself standing in front of the elevator to the Complex. It carried him up at a pace that was somehow too slow and too fast all at once.

When the door opened, Julian stormed through it. "Where is he?"

Damselfly sat at the counter, eating cereal. Saturn was on the couch examining the blueprints laid out in front of her. Both of their heads snapped toward Julian at the same time.

"Julian?" Damselfly asked. Concern crept into her expression as she looked him over. "What are you doing here?"

"I'm looking for Blazar," Julian answered. He shot Saturn a pointed look. "Where. Is. He?"

"He should be here any minute." Saturn rose to her feet. "I thought you weren't going to help us, though."

"I'm not."

Damselfly slid out of her chair. "Julian, what's wrong? What happened?"

Julian couldn't bring himself to give her an answer, or even look at her. His vision was starting to blur.

"I'm calling Blazar," Saturn said, pulling out her phone.

"Good." Julian's hands tightened into fists.

Damselfly approached him slowly. "Julian?" she asked, her voice painfully quiet. "Did Blazar do something?"

"Damselfly, you should leave the room." He didn't want her around if Blazar was going to get angry. And he didn't want her to see Blazar beat the shit out of him, if that's what this came to.

Saturn spoke into her phone. "Are you on your way? We have a problem. Julian's here."

"I'm not leaving," Damselfly said. "Not if you're going to say something stupid to Blazar."

"I'm not letting him get away with this," Julian replied. He finally glanced her way. His stomach turned at the fear on her face. Voice faltering, he whispered, "Please go."

Damselfly stood her ground.

"Yeah, he's pretty upset," Saturn said. "Blake, what did you do?" A moment later, her gaze darkened. "Fine," she muttered. She hung up and set her phone down.

"Where is he?" Julian repeated, attention back on Saturn.

"Almost here. We don't have much time." Saturn moved toward him. "Julian, tell me what's going on. Let's figure this out before he gets here." Somewhere under her cold exterior, he thought he might have heard a trace of softness. Wishful thinking, maybe.

"You can't help me, Sophia." Julian gestured angrily as he spoke. "You've never been able to help any of us. Not even yourself."

"Julian, think this through. Whatever you have to say to Blazar, it can't be worth—"

The elevator door opened. "Julian!" Blazar said, his voice dripping with fake enthusiasm. "What are you doing here?"

Julian whirled around to face him. "What the hell were you thinking?"

A cold grin spread across Blazar's face. "Whoa, Julian, you look like you were struck by lightning or something."

Rage blinded Julian. Wiped away his thoughts, all of the words waiting on his tongue.

He screamed and lunged at Blazar.

In the blink of an eye, Blazar was behind him. He struck Julian in the back. Hard. Julian couldn't stop his fall, couldn't stop himself from hitting the ground face-first.

Blazar rolled Julian onto his back with his foot. "What the hell was your plan, Julian? I thought you were smart. Smart enough to know you could never beat me."

"Why?" Julian gasped, struggling to catch his breath. "Why can't you just let me live my own damn life?"

"And let your power go to waste?" Blazar shook his head. "I couldn't give up on you that easily. You're not the strongest, but you're still useful." He paused. "Or, at least, you were."

He reached down, grabbed Julian by the front of the shirt, and lifted him into the air. In the blink of an eye, they were standing by the door to the balcony. Nausea washed over Julian. He grabbed at Blazar's arm in a desperate attempted to free himself.

Blazar kicked open the door to the balcony. Damselfly screamed something unintelligible.

"Blake!" Saturn shrieked. "What are you doing?"

Blazar ignored them. He stepped outside and lifted Julian higher into the air. "You could have had everything, Julian," he said. "Money, New Atlas, the entire world."

Julian's grip on Blazar's arm tightened. "What the hell would I do with the entire world?"

Blazar's arm burst into flames. Julian yelped and let go. Blazar moved him over the edge of the railing.

"Was it worth it?" Blazar demanded. "Losing it all? Losing your family?"

Did Blazar want Julian to beg for his life in his last moments? Apologize? Say he regretted it all?

"I'd do it all again," Julian hissed. "Fuck you."

Blazar let go.

Julian watched Blazar grow smaller as he fell. By the time he summoned a pillar to catch himself, he'd be falling too fast, and he didn't have the mind to find stone nearby that he could use, and his stomach was in his throat and Damselfly was still screaming and he was going to die—

Something slammed into him. Arms wrapped around him. Before Julian could process what was happening, he was hitting concrete. Rolling across a roof.

When the world stopped spinning, he opened his eyes to find Charlotte standing over him.

"Charlotte," he gasped as he sat up.

Her head was turned toward the building that housed the Complex. She'd carried Julian to a roof out of sight of the balcony, but he had no doubt that Blazar had seen his rescue.

"Blake Sullivan is Blazar, isn't he?" Charlotte asked.

Julian nodded.

"Great. That makes two people lying to me about their identity." Charlotte turned to look at Julian. "I'm going to take him down."

"Charlotte, please," Julian begged. He moved onto his knees. "You can't go after him. He'll kill you."

"I have to do something."

"You can't!"

"Don't tell me what I can and can't do." As Charlotte took a step toward Julian, the air around her cracked. A pool of water materialized above him and fell into a short torrent of rain.

"Lovely," Julian muttered once the rain cleared. He ran a hand through his sopping hair. "Just as my shirt was finally dry from getting thrown off a building."

"I have to stop Blazar," Charlotte repeated.

Julian rose to his feet. He nearly collapsed again but, after stumbling a few steps to the left, managed to find his balance. "I don't think he knows you have the stormoid. He was following you because he knew I was…seeing you." He swallowed. "If we get out of here now, you can hide from him. He'll never have to know, and you'll be safe, and—"

"I'm not giving up," Charlotte cut him off. She looked down, and Julian realized that she was still wearing clothes from the night before, too. "But we'll retreat for now. I have to find Spencer, anyway." She turned around and headed for a door that led into the building beneath them.

Julian jogged to catch up to her. The sudden movement made his head spin. "Why'd you save me?"

"I need you—"

His heart skipped a beat.

"—to tell me what Blazar is planning." Charlotte glanced at him. "He is planning something, isn't he?"

"Something big," Julian affirmed with a nod. "But I have no idea what. He refused to tell the rest of us. All I know is that he had to tear down the bank and the restaurant to make it work. And…" He hesitated. "He's going to destroy more buildings this afternoon. The ones around Dove Park. He wants to build a new base there."

They reached the door. Charlotte grabbed the handle. "We'll find a way to stop him," she muttered. "We have to."

The door was, surprisingly, unlocked. This clearly wasn't a high security building. Or a busy one. Julian and Charlotte found their way down a maze of floors without running into anybody.

Julian was grateful they didn't have to come up with an explanation for why they were wandering around the place. Or why he was sopping wet. He was also grateful there was no one around besides Charlotte to see him stumble a few too many times as they descended the stairs.

The exit they found on the first floor spit them out in an alleyway. Collider stood on the other side of the alley, leaning back against the wall, their arms folded. Though they wore their reflective metal helmet, the rest of their armor was nowhere to be seen. Instead, they were dressed entirely in black, from their leather jacket down to their combat boots. A plain gray backpack was slung over their shoulder.

Julian's heart dropped to his stomach, though there was no way they could possibly know he was Citadel—

"Collider?" Charlotte's eyes widened.

Collider moved their hands to the sides of their helmet. "Well, look who it is," they said. The helmet lifted as they spoke, and their warped voice transitioned to something far more ordinary. Something *familiar.* "Stormbringer and Citadel."

Julian's eyebrows shot up in surprise. Charlotte's expression was equally stunned.

"Spencer?" Charlotte exclaimed. "You're Collider?"

CHAPTER THIRTY

The first thing Spencer did was punch Julian in the face. Charlotte barely processed Julian staggering back into the door behind they'd come out through, rubbing the side of his face.

"May as well have a permanent bruise right there," he muttered.

Charlotte blinked. Spencer Higgs, her cousin—and roommate for the past three years—was Collider. And she hadn't suspected a thing.

"We can't stay here," Spencer said. "We need to get somewhere safe." He eyed Julian for a moment before facing Charlotte. "Is he coming with us?"

Charlotte forced herself to focus. "He has information on Blazar," she said slowly, trying to pick apart her whirling emotions from the facts. "And since Blazar just tried to kill him, I'm assuming he'll be willing help us defeat him."

"I don't think that's possible," Julian said under his breath. "But sure. He's just going to kill me anyway." He took a step forward and swayed. "So, where are we going?"

"Do you think we'd be okay to go back to the apartment?" Charlotte asked Spencer.

Spencer shook his head. "I don't know what the chances are Blazar's figured out who you are, but it's not worth the risk." He slid his helmet into his backpack and zipped it up. "Besides, I have somewhere better we can go."

Charlotte and Julian followed Spencer to the end of the alley. They spent a grand total of thirty seconds traversing the sidewalk before Spencer took a sharp turn and led them down a set of stairs into a subway station.

At the bottom of the steps, Julian tripped and barely stopped himself from falling.

"Are you injured?" Charlotte asked quietly. The hand she'd nearly reached out to help him clenched at her side.

"No," Julian muttered. "Not any more than I already was."

Spencer glanced back and lifted an eyebrow. "I can't believe we were scared of him."

Julian shot him a glare. "You're lucky I was low on energy the night you attacked me. If I'd been able to generate stone, I would have won."

"Sure."

"Wait, you two fought?" Charlotte asked, brow furrowing.

"Apparently," Julian said. To Spencer, he asked, "If you really think you're strong enough to beat me, why didn't you try before?"

"Why bother when Storm Warning had you under control?" Spencer shrugged. "It left me free to deal with the smaller villains popping up."

Spencer walked the group to a narrow hallway that led away from the station's main corridor. The three left the crowd of subway travelers behind and entered a cooler, quieter part of the station.

"How did you figure out who he was, anyway?" Charlotte asked. "I didn't get the chance to tell you."

"I'll explain everything when we get to the base." Spencer came to a sudden stop and rested a hand on the wall to his right. "Hm. Not quite," he muttered. He slid his hand a few inches to the right. "Here we go."

He pushed his hand forward. A small section of the wall sank in half an inch before clicking into place. Spencer pressed a finger to a spot in the center of the rectangle. A short beep echoed in the narrow space.

A section of wall behind the group sank into the floor, revealing a dark passageway. Spencer gestured for Charlotte and Julian to enter first. As he followed the two in, he pressed a button on a panel just inside the new opening. The wall slid back into place behind them. Fluorescent lights flickered on, illuminating the hallway.

Spencer moved to the front of the group and continued down the hall. A minute of walking brought the three to a long flight of stairs. At the top was a surprisingly ordinary-looking door.

"The base is above ground," Spencer said as he reached for the handle. "It's part of a bigger building. But this is the only way to access it."

On the other side of the door was...an apartment. Directly ahead, more stairs led up to another floor. To the left was a living room with a TV and couch and chairs. There was a dining area to the right, and a kitchen just visible on the other side of a counter. It was hard to believe they were in a secret superhero base.

Spencer set his backpack on the floor. As he straightened up, he pulled back the sleeve of his leather jacket, revealing a watch on his wrist. "The others should be here soon."

"The others?" Charlotte asked.

Spencer gestured to the couch in the living room. "Sit down. I'll explain everything."

Charlotte settled onto the couch first, and Julian took a seat at the other end. Spencer didn't look happy that he was dripping water onto the furniture but didn't say a word as he moved to stand in front him and Charlotte.

"First, Charlotte, I was planning to tell you that I'm Collider," Spencer said. "You getting superpowers complicated things, and I decided to wait and see how you did before telling you anything."

Charlotte nodded. "I guess that makes sense." She hadn't felt any sense of betrayal or anger at the revelation, just—awe? Despite rarely making the news, Collider had always seemed like a pretty impressive hero.

Julian leaned back against the couch. "So, how did you figure out I was Citadel, if Charlotte didn't tell you?"

"I suspected something was up from the beginning," Spencer told him. "The story about the stormoid and a random guy being in charge of training the host felt off. But Charlotte kept telling me about how the training sessions were going well and she was getting more powerful, so I started thinking I might have been wrong about you." He folded his arms.

"And then I kicked Citadel's ass at the bank lot, and you were injured when you dropped off Charlotte's phone the next day."

Charlotte frowned. "The bank lot?"

Julian rubbed his forehead. "Yeah, I was there—" His eyes closed. "I figured out I could manipulate dirt and make—make flowers grow."

"You did that," Charlotte realized. "You did it when we were at the park, too."

"On accident. But yes."

Spencer cleared his throat and focused on Charlotte. "I still wasn't completely sure he was Citadel, and I didn't want to say anything to you until I could prove it. I was also trying to figure out what his plan was." He glanced at Julian. "Why were you training her, anyway? All you did was make her stronger."

"Yes. Well aware." Julian's eyes stayed closed. "It was a very complicated plan. I wouldn't expect you to understand—"

"He was going to fight me in public to prove himself to Blazar," Charlotte explained. "And then take the stormoid from me."

"He was going to kill you?" Spencer asked, his voice rising sharply.

"No," Charlotte said, maybe a little too quickly. "He...never wanted to kill me. He's not a threat to us."

"Yes, I have no interest in hurting either of you," Julian added with a wave of his hand.

Charlotte sighed. "You could sound a little more opposed to the idea."

"My apologies. I was just thrown off a building, so I might be lacking in emotional energy right now." His eyes opened and moved to her. Briefly. Then they were on the ceiling.

The door opened behind Spencer, and the sound of voices spilled into the apartment as three people entered. They all wore costumes.

"Hey. You three." Spencer waved a hand to catch their attention. The group fell silent. "Come meet Stormbringer."

To Charlotte's surprise, their faces lit up.

"You finally brought her?" a woman asked.

It took Charlotte a moment to realize she recognized the hero. "You're Airborne, aren't you?" she asked as she rose to her feet.

The woman nodded as she reached up to pull her bright green hair down from its ponytail. A moment later, she pulled the hair from her head entirely, revealing it was a wig and that she had short curls of black hair underneath. The suit she wore was a darker shade of green, though it was still lighter than her dark brown skin. Her gloves, boots, belt, and the simple mask around her eyes were white.

"You know Airborne's powers already, right?" Spencer asked.

Charlotte nodded. Airborne could make anyone near her fall violently ill, turning most villains into an easy target. Stronger ones could resist her power, but ordinary people were no match.

"You can call me Wendy," the hero added as she removed her mask. She cracked a small smile, and there was a gleam in her brown eyes. "Or Dr. Fleming."

Spencer nodded to the hero standing to Wendy's left. "And that's Jackrabbit. You've probably heard of them, too."

Jackrabbit waved. They were dressed in brown leather and fur-lined boots. The tan helmet protecting their head had two large rabbit ears extending from the top and a set of small antlers between them. The helmet was open at the front to expose a pale, freckled face and hazel eyes.

If Charlotte remembered correctly, Jackrabbit had fairly average super strength and speed, but they were well known for their powerful legs that allowed them to jump higher than most buildings in New Atlas.

"Name's Jack Richards," they said. "Jackie's fine too. Whatever. And yes, that was a 'them' Spencer introduced me with." Their voice had a masculine timbre to it, but it wasn't very deep.

Julian piped up from the couch. "Antlers? Shouldn't your name be Jackalope, then?"

"Jackalopes aren't real."

"So?" Julian lifted an eyebrow.

Jack shrugged. "My power doesn't come from the DNA of a made-up animal. It comes from rabbit DNA."

Despite everything, Charlotte couldn't help but exchange a confused look with Julian.

Spencer was already introducing the third hero. "And Cactus here is new—"

"*The* Cactus," the girl corrected. As she spoke, the spines protruding from her green skin retracted, and her skin changed to a light brown. She removed a white cowboy hat from her head, letting short waves of brown hair fall to her chin. The rest of her costume—all brown leather and white denim—was reminiscent of the old west, right down to the white cowboy boots.

"Right, sorry. This is The Cactus," Spencer said.

"What's wrong with just Cactus?" Charlotte asked.

"Someone in Arizona's using that name," The Cactus replied. "And since everyone else is dropping names, I'm Cassidy Castillo."

Charlotte nodded. "I'm Charlotte—"

"Hathaway," Wendy finished, resting a hand on her hip. While the other two heroes looked to be college age, she was definitely older. Forties, maybe? "Yep, Spencer told us all about you." She looked past Charlotte, to the couch. "And who's this guy?"

"Oh, that's just Citadel," Spencer said dismissively. "Don't worry about him."

"Citadel?" Cassidy yelped, jumping back. "What's he doing here?"

"He's going to help us defeat Blazar."

Charlotte glanced at Julian. He was still assessing the heroes through narrowed eyes.

"Okay," Jack said. "But what is he doing *here*? On our couch?"

"And why does he kind of look like a lost puppy?" Wendy added.

"Lost puppy?" Julian said indignantly.

"Yeah, with your hair a mess and your clothes sopping wet," Wendy gestured to him. "How did that happen, anyway?"

"I got rained on."

Jack frowned. "There hasn't been any rain today."

Wendy folded her arms. "Did the rain unbutton his shirt, too?" she muttered under her breath. Charlotte felt her face flush.

"You know I killed Storm Warning, right?" Julian snapped.

"Uh, yeah," Cassidy said. "Could we maybe try not to piss off the supervillain sitting on our couch?"

"Relax, he's not going to hurt any of us," Spencer said. "And if he lays a finger on anyone, I'll kick his ass. Again."

Julian rolled his eyes.

Spencer continued. "But if he doesn't want us to throw him out on the street to fend for himself against the most dangerous man in New Atlas, he's going to start making himself useful. Now." He turned to face Julian. "Julian, what can you tell us about Blazar?"

CHAPTER THIRTY-ONE

Julian didn't get the chance to even begin talking about Blazar before he was interrupted.

"We can't fight Blazar," Wendy said, shaking her head. "He'll kill us all."

"Yeah," Cassidy added. "We don't do supervillains trying to take over the world, or stopping apocalypses, or alien invasions, or—"

"None of those things are going to happen," Spencer cut her off. "And there has to be a way to hurt him. Everyone has a weakness."

Charlotte cleared her throat. "Julian?"

Julian sighed. "Well, his speed is terrifying, but he can burn himself out quickly if he's not careful," he said. "And he's not entirely invincible." He glanced up at Charlotte. "He did come back from a battle badly injured, once. It was a fight with Storm Warning. But he never told me the details."

"So, Charlotte's capable of hurting him," Spencer said. "And killing him, hopefully."

Julian nodded. "If Charlotte can find that fight in the stormoid memories, maybe she can remember how Storm Warning hurt Blazar and do it again."

"But it could take me years until I'm strong enough to hurt him!" Charlotte protested. "Storm Warning had way more experience."

"And you have that experience inside of you," Julian reminded her. "In the stormoid."

"Charlotte, I don't want to put this all on you," Spencer said. "And I definitely wouldn't blame you if you wanted to walk away. But whatever you choose, I'm not giving up. If Blazar wants New Atlas, he'll have to go through me."

Charlotte looked to Spencer and lifted her chin. "Then I'm not giving up, either," she said, her gaze burning with determination.

Julian lowered his own gaze, trying to steady his racing heart. The last thing he wanted to see was her in a fight with Blazar. "I don't know what Blazar has planned for the city, but I do know what he has planned for today." He quickly explained what he knew about the office buildings Blazar wanted torn down.

"That's our mission, then," Spencer said. "We'll go to Dove Park, wait for Blazar to show up, and defend the office buildings."

"Lord Saturn and Damselfly will be there, too," Julian added. His stomach turned at the thought of Damselfly, the memory of her screaming as Blazar dragged him out onto the balcony. "Saturn's overwhelmingly loyal to Blazar, but Damselfly..." He trailed off.

"What about Damselfly?" Spencer pressed.

Quietly, he said, "Please don't hurt Damselfly."

Spencer folded his arms. "Why not?"

"She doesn't deserve any of this. She's only sixteen." He swallowed. "I promised—I promised I wouldn't leave her with Blazar."

Spencer was silent for a long moment. Finally, he said, "All right. We'll do what we can."

"Are you sure we can handle those villains?" Cassidy asked. "Storm Warning's the only one who was able to handle them in a fight."

"Well, we've never gotten everyone together to fight them at the same time," Wendy pointed out. "We do outnumber them, and apparently, one of their own will be on our side."

"And it sounds like we might be able to win over Damselfly, too," Jack added. They slid off their helmet as they spoke, revealing curly blonde hair underneath.

Julian rose to his feet and ignored the subsequent pain that coursed through his body. "I'm not letting Damselfly fight Blazar."

"How about we ask her what she wants to do, when the time comes?" Spencer suggested.

Julian took a deep breath. His ribs ached. "Fine." The matter could be dealt with later.

"It's settled, then," Wendy said. "Everyone get an early lunch, and then we'll head out to monitor the park."

"My costume's at my apartment." Julian's gaze flickered briefly to Charlotte. "It's dangerous to go there now, but as long as I'm quick, I think I'll be okay." Blazar had better things to do than wait around Julian's place all day.

Now that he thought about it, he would need to call out of work at the library until this was all over, too. He could probably get away with telling them he was sick until they'd dealt with Blazar. Or until Blazar killed them all.

"Fine. Charlotte and I will go with you," Spencer said.

Julian's eyes narrowed. "It would be safer if I went alone."

"I'm not letting you out of my sight." Spencer turned to Charlotte. "We should stop by our place, too. Grab anything you might need in the next few days."

Charlotte nodded.

"You three get food out," Spencer told the other heroes. "We'll eat when we get back. We shouldn't be gone for more than an hour, tops." He paused. "But before we go, Julian, come with me."

"What? Why?"

"We have a ton of costume stuff upstairs," Spencer said. "Along with other clothes we've collected over the years. You're going to change into something that isn't drenched, so that we don't attract the attention of everyone we pass. Charlotte, you come too. We need hats and sunglasses."

"I don't wear hats," Julian told him.

"You do today. Come on."

Julian and Charlotte followed Spencer up a flight of stairs. While they stepped off into a hallway on the second floor, the stairs continued upward, indicating the apartment was even bigger than Julian expected.

The third door on the right led into a room filled with racks and dressers of clothes. "How big is this place?" Charlotte asked as she opened a random drawer.

"Pretty big," Spencer replied. "We've got four floors, and the top three are mostly empty bedrooms and bathrooms. It was designed with more heroes in mind." He paused. "We're hoping to grow our ranks, eventually."

"Have you tried recruiting Wrecking Ball?" Charlotte asked.

"Yeah. He wasn't interested in being a team player." Spencer shrugged.

Julian searched the racks until he found a pair of black pants and a blue shirt that looked like they would fit him. They would at least work until he got his own clothes from his apartment. As he turned around, Spencer tossed something to him. He barely caught the baseball cap. With a sigh, he put it on.

"I'm going to find us some sunglasses," Spencer said. "Charlotte, could you run downstairs and grab my phone? I left it in the dining room when I came by this morning." With a glance at Julian, he added, "We'll come down and meet you by the front door."

Charlotte's gaze darted to Julian. Back to Spencer. She shrugged. "Sure thing."

The moment Charlotte was gone, Spencer crossed the room and stopped directly in front of Julian. His eyes narrowed. "If you hurt her—more than you already have—I'll kill you."

"You have nothing to worry about," Julian said, his tone bitter. "I'd let her kill me before I hurt her again."

After letting the silence that followed linger for a moment that was painfully long, Spencer said, "You really care about her, don't you?"

Julian's hands tightened around the clothes he'd grabbed. "Was that not obvious?"

"Forgive me for thinking you were just a damn good liar." Spencer turned around and walked to the door. "Go ahead and change. Come downstairs when you're done." He paused. "And Julian?"

"Yes?"

"Her last boyfriend got into Harvard law. And the girl she dated before that was a model."

What was he trying to say? That Charlotte could do better? "They both sound wonderful," Julian said, laying the sarcasm on thick. The relationships had ended for a reason, after all.

Spencer lifted an eyebrow. "At least neither of them killed a superhero."

"And neither of them are going to help you defeat Blazar." Julian dismissed Spencer with a wave of his hand. "I'm going to change now, so—"

"I'm going." Spencer stepped out, and the door clicked shut.

When Julian made his way back downstairs, Spencer and Charlotte were waiting by the door, talking quietly. The other heroes ignored Julian as he walked through the kitchen, except Cassidy, who gave him a nervous look as he passed.

Once they'd left the base and reentered the subway station, Charlotte spoke. "The other heroes seem...nice," she said.

"They're great heroes," Spencer said. "It's just hard to get them organized, sometimes. I don't blame them for being busy, but they're not great at communicating when they need help. Or can't make it to the base for a meeting." He sighed.

"What are you going to do about your classes?" Charlotte asked. "I assume going to campus is too dangerous right now."

"I've had all my professors for previous classes, and they know I'm a good student. Shouldn't be too hard to work something out," Spencer said. "Do you think you'll be okay?"

"Yeah, mine are all reasonable enough. I'll tell them I had a family emergency."

Julian trailed behind the two, half-listening to their conversation. Spencer threw frequent glances back to make sure he was still there.

They stopped by Charlotte and Spencer's place first. While the two packed their bags, Julian hovered by the front door, thinking back to the last time he'd been here. To what had happened after.

After a few minutes, Charlotte and Spencer emerged from their rooms, and the three set off for Julian's apartment. He moved to the front of the group when they reached the building and led the way up to his door. He braced himself as he opened it, fearing he'd see Blazar standing inside.

To his relief, the place was empty. Everything was right where he'd left it. He reached for his costume off the stand by the door and ignored the empty wine bottle sitting next to it. As he picked up the stack, he realized Blazar had shoved his half mask in with the other costume pieces, too.

Julian's gaze darted around as he walked farther into the apartment, and he spotted his full mask lying on the floor where he'd thrown it the night before. He picked it up.

"I'll go pack a bag," he said. He glanced back at Charlotte and Spencer. Sarcasm creeping into his voice, he added, "Make yourselves at home."

He found a duffel bag in his closet and threw in as many clothes as would fit on top of his costume, along with some toiletries. After one last look around his bedroom, he left and returned to the living room. He found Charlotte and Spencer sitting on the couch.

Julian nodded at the Storm Warning book on the coffee table. "It's still yours for three weeks, if you want it."

Charlotte silently took the book and tucked it into her bag.

Spencer jumped to his feet. "All right, let's get out of here."

They stepped out of the apartment, and Julian immediately froze. "Shit."

"What? What's wrong?" Charlotte asked.

"Surveillance drone." Julian pointed to the drone hovering above the building next to his. "It's one of Saturn's."

"Then let's go, before more company shows up," Spencer said. He moved past Julian, and Charlotte followed.

Julian went down a few steps before stopping again. "Wait. I forgot something."

Spencer turned around. "Come on, Julian," he groaned. "Whatever it is, it can't possibly be—"

Julian shoved his duffel bag into Spencer's arms. "I'll be right back."

"Julian, wait," Charlotte said.

"I'll be right back," Julian repeated. "Promise." He jogged back up the stairs and hurried into his apartment.

He returned to them a minute later, carrying the succulent Charlotte had given him the night before. "Didn't want this dying," he said. Despite his bravado, he couldn't bring himself to look at Charlotte to see her reaction. He grabbed his bag back from Spencer and continued down the stairs. "Now come on. We don't have all day."

CHAPTER THIRTY-TWO

When they returned to the superhero base, Spencer took Julian and Charlotte up to the third floor and gave them empty bedrooms to use. Julian set his succulent on the windowsill, changed into his Citadel costume, and grabbed his half mask.

He stepped out of the room at the same time Charlotte stepped out of hers down the hall, dressed in her Stormbringer costume. Her gaze met his for a brief moment before dropping to the floor.

"I have a few questions for you," she said.

Julian walked until he was standing next to the wall opposite her. He nodded. "Go ahead."

"Everything about being a protector of the stormoid and learning from some predecessor and having the job of training me...you made all that up," she said plainly. Not really a question.

"Yes."

"And everything you said about your adopted family?" Charlotte asked.

"I guess I was referring to the other villains when I said that."

"And the thing about your father buying you your Porsche?"

"That was a lie. I bought it myself." Julian shrugged and folded his arms. "You seemed suspicious that I could have gotten it working at the library." Maybe taking this more seriously would improve his chances of making Charlotte hate him less, but acting casual was the only thing keeping him together right now.

Charlotte's eyes darted up to meet his. "Did you steal the tablet you gave me?"

"I thought about it," Julian admitted. "But no. I paid for it."

"Was the money you used stolen?"

"Could have been library salary."

Charlotte took a deep breath. Closed her eyes. "And you pretended to be interested in my life?"

Julian's casual facade slipped. "That...wasn't pretend." He swallowed. "I liked hearing you talk."

Her eyes opened. Grief burned in them, like fire trapped in smoky quartz. "At the restaurant. When we were both in there and everything was collapsing—why'd you go back in to save that woman?"

"I'm not entirely heartless," Julian said. "I'm—I was just selfish."

"But would you have done the same thing two weeks ago?"

Probably not. But Julian didn't have to say it out loud. Charlotte's face made it clear she knew what he was thinking.

After a moment, he did say, "I'm a thief, not a killer."

Charlotte let out a cold laugh. "Not a killer? Did you forget how this whole mess started?"

Julian shook his head. "Storm Warning's different from a civilian. He chose this life, and he knew the risks."

"So, you don't feel bad about killing him?" Charlotte took a step forward, her expression darkening. "You don't feel even a hint of guilt?"

Julian fell silent. Finally, quietly, he said, "I don't know anymore."

Charlotte took a shaky breath. "Let's go. Blazar could attack at any time."

Julian nodded.

They walked downstairs to the dining room. Spencer sat at the table, dressed in his metal Collider armor. The other heroes were gathered around the table, too. They all looked up when Julian and Charlotte entered.

"Is it a good idea, taking him out like that?" Wendy asked. "We don't want to scare people."

"We shouldn't be dealing with many civilians," Spencer said. "Dove Park's usually empty. And all that really matters is that we keep those villains from tearing down the office buildings."

"Don't forget to eat!" Jack exclaimed. They gestured to the plates of food laid out on the table. "And make sure you're hydrated. I'll have water bottles in my bag, but I can only carry a few."

Julian walked to the table, frowned, and picked up half a sandwich. "What is this? Turkey?"

"Turkey, mayonnaise, and American cheese," Jack said.

"Excuse me?"

"What, you have a problem with our food?" Spencer asked.

"Yes, I have a problem with your food." Julian set the sandwich down and ventured into the kitchen, where he began opening cupboards. "Do you have any cooking ingredients?"

"No one actually lives here, we just hang out here a lot," Spencer said. "Well, I guess you, me, and Charlotte live here now, since you've endangered our lives."

Julian barely heard that last comment. "You could do so much better stocking this place up." He moved onto the fridge. It was empty except for a few slices of cheese, a half-empty container of turkey, and a gallon of milk that he suspected had gone bad. "I'm not surprised you're a bunch of college students."

"Wendy's a surgeon, actually," Cassidy said. "She took my appendix out last year."

Spencer rose to his feet. "How about we worry about groceries *after* we stop Blazar from destroying a bunch of buildings?"

"Fine." Julian threw the fridge door shut. "But if I'm going to be stuck living here, I'm going to be cooking food that's actually edible."

"Do you know how to cook?" Wendy asked skeptically.

Julian glanced at Charlotte.

Charlotte sighed. "Yeah, he's pretty good," she said. "I guess if he's going to be hanging around, we may as well put him to work."

Spencer smirked. "I agree."

"You ate food Citadel made?" Cassidy asked incredulously as she and the other heroes stood and made their way toward the door. "Weren't you afraid it might be, I dunno, poisoned?"

"I didn't know he was Citadel at the time," Charlotte replied, shooting Julian a look.

Julian ignored the look and drifted to the back of the group. Twenty feet down the hall from the apartment's entrance, Spencer paused and opened another hidden panel in the wall. "This exit will take us out in an alley near the park," he explained.

"How many hidden doors do you have?" Julian asked.

"Plenty that we're not going to tell you about," Spencer replied. He pressed his finger to the wall, and a gap opened up behind him.

As Julian continued to trail behind the group, he watched Charlotte and Spencer talk to each other quietly, inaudible with the other heroes chatting much louder. He wasn't sure he had a prayer of getting Charlotte to...not hate him. But if he did want to get on her good side, he would have to get on Spencer's good side, too. That might be even more difficult.

What would be the point, though? What waited for him at the end of this? Assuming they were able to kill Blazar before he killed them, Julian would have to face a group of heroes who knew his secret identity. They wouldn't just let him walk away.

Julian swept his gaze over the group. He'd heard stories about them all on the news at least once—except for The Cactus—but it was hard to be sure how much of a threat they were. Collider turned out to be much more powerful than he'd expected. The three new heroes were all wild cards.

Maybe they did have a chance against Blazar.

Or maybe this would end in more dead heroes.

At the end of the tunnel, they all climbed up a ladder and emerged in a dark alley. Jack slid on their helmet, Wendy tied her wig back up into a ponytail, and Cassidy's skin went all green and spiky. From the alley, it was a short walk between buildings to Dove Park.

As soon as they entered the park, Spencer spoke, his voice warped by his helmet. "Everyone spread out. Find a place to watch from where you won't be seen," he said. "When the villains show up, we'll all move out at once. Stick together in pairs. Stormbringer and Airborne, Jackrabbit and The Cactus, and Citadel's with me."

Julian didn't see the point in arguing. He nodded. While the other four headed off to different sides of the park, he fell into step next to Spencer.

"So, are you in charge of everyone?" Julian asked as they walked toward one of the buildings.

Spencer shook his head. "No one's technically in charge. Wendy and I make most of the group decisions, though."

Julian lifted an eyebrow before realizing Spencer couldn't see his face through his mask.

"Let me guess," Spencer said. "You all did whatever Blazar told you to do?"

"He's the oldest and most experienced," Julian said. "And he owns our—the villains' base."

They stopped at the foot of the building. "I'm going to lower both of our densities and lift us up to that balcony," Spencer said. "We can use that tree growing in front of it to hide."

"Fine."

Spencer grabbed Julian's arm, and a moment later he felt lighter than air. In a way that made him sick to his stomach. The two drifted upward until they reached the balcony. Spencer grabbed it and pulled them both over the railing.

Gravity returned suddenly and with full force. Julian slammed into the balcony while Spencer landed gracefully on his feet.

"Little warning next time?" Julian pushed himself up.

"Oops," Spencer deadpanned.

They moved to a corner of the balcony obscured by the massive tree next to it. Julian peered through the leaves above to watch the sky.

"Any idea which direction he's going to come from?" Spencer asked.

"West, most likely. Our base's entrance is up that way."

After that, they waited in silence. Julian was used to waiting, but today, being alone with his thoughts was the last thing he wanted.

Then again, facing Blazar would probably be *slightly* more unpleasant.

After nearly forty-five minutes, the silence over Dove Park was finally broken. Lord Saturn dropped from the sky and slammed into the ground in the middle of the park. Damselfly descended a moment later, coming to a stop about ten feet above the grass.

A flash of red cut across the park, headed for a building opposite the one Julian and Spencer waited at.

Julian jumped up onto the balcony railing as the other heroes emerged from hiding below. He took a deep breath and jumped. A platform of stone materialized beneath his feet to carry him down.

"Blazar's going to circle the buildings at full speed and start a fire!" Julian shouted. "Saturn's got bombs, too. Don't let her activate moons around her belt. And find a way to distract Blazar." He glanced at Charlotte, who stood twenty feet away from him. "We're going to need rain."

Charlotte nodded. "On it." She shot straight up into the air and held out her arms. Clouds gathered overhead.

Saturn reached for one of her moons. Wendy was already racing forward to meet her. As she drew close, Saturn dropped to one knee and pressed a hand to her stomach.

"Who are you?" Saturn demanded as rain started to fall. One of her shaking hands inched closer to the bombs on her belt.

Wendy stopped ten feet in front of her. "Name's Airborne."

"And I'm The Cactus!" Cassidy shouted as she joined Wendy. She flung her arm in a wide motion, firing off a volley of cactus spines that embedded themselves in Saturn's suit. Saturn yanked back the hand hovering at her side.

While the others dealt with Saturn, Julian ran toward Damselfly, not yet sure what he'd say when he reached her. It didn't matter. Before he could even open his mouth, Blazar slammed into him and sent him flying.

Julian hit the ground and rolled across the grass. When he came to a stop, he pushed himself up off his stomach quickly, but had to pause to wait for his head to stop spinning. It took a moment for his vision to clear.

When it did, the first thing he noticed were the blue flowers growing in the ground a few feet in front of him. His flowers.

He glanced back. Blazar was strolling toward him, a wide smile on his face. "Really, Julian?" he asked. "Have you sunk so low as to team up with a band of pathetic heroes?"

Blazar would have to be careful with how he used his speed if he still planned to burn down multiple buildings. Bringing down just one had always been draining for him.

"Bring it, old man." Julian jumped to his feet and lifted his hands. He raised a wall of stone in the same moment that Blazar shot forward. Blazar dodged the wall at the last second, circling around it and crashing into Julian as he came around the corner.

As they went down, Julian summoned a blade and drove it upward into Blazar's chest. He put all of his strength into it and barely broke skin. Blazar laughed. Pushing Julian aside, he said, "Nice try, but you'll be lucky if that got a drop of blood out of me."

Gritting his teeth, Julian swung again. While Blazar's attention was on his weapon, he summoned a second blade in his other hand and swiped at Blazar's side. The blow that would have sliced open any ordinary person's arm barely left a scrape on Blazar.

"Come on, Julian," Blazar said. "You know how annoying it is to replace the suit. Could you try not to tear it up so much?"

"Why the hell did I ever look up to you?" Julian hissed.

Blazar shrugged. "I've got money, power, respect..." He pulled back his fist. "And I don't give up everything I have for the first girl who looks my way."

Julian dodged the blow. Barely. Blazar's fist was a hair away from grazing the side of his face. He was lucky Blazar threw punches at ordinary speed—to save energy, Julian assumed. Or maybe he just didn't want to completely obliterate everything he hit.

The ground beneath Blazar turned to stone. Julian lifted the front end of the stone, launching Blazar backwards. He landed in one of the several puddles that had formed across the park and sent a spray of water into the air.

Julian chuckled. "Looks like the weather's not in your favor, Blazar. I don't see how you're going to burn these buildings down now."

Blazar disappeared in a blur and reappeared behind Julian a moment later. "Don't be an idiot, Julian," he said, anger finally audible in his voice. "What do you think these heroes are going to do with you when they're done with you? Let you go?"

"I don't care what happens to me, as long as you go down."

"Really? All because I ruined your chances with some girl?"

"No." Julian whirled around to face him. "This is because you ruined *me*."

"I helped you!" Blazar grabbed Julian and threw him into the ground. "You ungrateful son of a—"

Jack dropped from the sky. Their boots collided with Blazar's left shoulder, and both of the supers hit the ground. By the time Blazar was sitting up, Jack had already launched themself back into the air.

Blazar followed Jack from the ground at a normal pace. He only made it ten feet before Spencer crashed into him with enough force to send him staggering sideways. When Blazar regained his balance and turned to swing at Spencer, his fist passed right through him.

While Blazar was distracted, Julian searched the park and found Damselfly still hovering in the air, watching the fight. He sprinted toward her. "Damselfly!" he shouted.

Damselfly swooped toward him with startling speed. He slowed. Started to back up. "Damselfly, what are you—?" he started.

Her feet hit his chest. His back hit the ground. Gasping in pain, all he could do was watch as Damselfly moved to stand over him. She ripped off her helmet so that Julian could see the tears brimming her eyes. "You said you wouldn't leave me!"

"I didn't want to!" Julian found the strength to sit up. "You saw what Blazar did!"

"And now I'm stuck with him and Saturn and you're gone!"

"Come with me, then," Julian said. "Please."

"I can't! He'll kill me! He already wants to kill you!" Damselfly lifted her arm, apparently to wipe her tears, before realizing the metal body armor wouldn't do any good. She sniffed. "I'm—I'm scared."

"Please. Come with us," Julian tried again. "I promise I won't let him hurt you—"

He glimpsed a red blur in the corner of his vision. Blazar appeared next to Damselfly and grabbed her arm.

"Come on," Blazar said. "We're going home."

They vanished.

"Blazar!" Saturn shouted. Her rocket boots turned on and launched her into the sky.

Julian climbed to his feet and watched Blazar and Damselfly disappear from sight, watched Saturn disappear over the next building. His fists clenched at his sides. A stone platform formed beneath him and lifted him into the air.

"Come back!" he screamed.

CHAPTER THIRTY-THREE

As the villains vanished from the park, Charlotte returned to the ground. She let go of the clouds and the rain and the lightning and allowed her storm to fade.

Julian was the only one in the air now, hovering on his platform of stone, his gaze fixed in the direction Blazar and the others had gone in.

"Good news," Jack said as they and the other heroes gathered around Charlotte. "We stole all of Lord Saturn's moon-bomb-thingies." They lifted their armful of bombs.

Cassidy lifted her hands and took a step back. "Uh, maybe be careful with those?"

Wendy and Spencer didn't pay the bombs much attention, so the two must have decided they were stable enough to carry around. They both quickly shifted their focus to Julian, but Wendy was the one to address him. She cupped her hands around her mouth and shouted, "Citadel, let's go! They're retreating. We won."

"No," Julian said, still staring into the distance. "I have to save Damselfly."

"What?"

"Come on, Julian," Spencer said. "We don't have time for this."

Julian looked down at the heroes, fury burning his gaze. "I'm going to get her."

His platform shot into the air, carrying him away.

"Well, now what?" Wendy rested a hand on her hip. "We can't just wait around for him to come back. People are going to start showing up to see what happened."

Charlotte's jaw clenched. "I'll go get him."

Spencer glanced at her. "Are you sure? Because I'd be happy to go knock some sense into him—"

"No. I'll do it." And truth be told, Charlotte wasn't entirely sure Julian needed sense knocked into him right now. She took a deep breath and let herself lift off the ground. It was one thing to hover in the air and summon a storm. Flying across the city to chase Julian would be something else entirely. She really hoped she didn't end up smacking into a building. "I'll meet you in the alley we came out of!"

"Okay," Spencer said. "Be careful."

Charlotte nodded before flying straight up. Once she was high enough, she scanned the sky for Julian and spotted him in the distance, moving west. She aimed herself toward him and surged forward. It only took a few seconds to catch up.

"Julian!" she shouted. She tried to slow herself gradually but found herself jerking to a sudden stop. Her stomach lurched. Thankfully, her sense of balance returned quickly.

Below her, Julian came to an equally abrupt halt and stumbled forward across his platform. He looked up. "Charlotte?"

She eased forward and down until she was hovering next to him.

"Please don't try to stop me," Julian said.

"Then let me come with you," Charlotte replied. "It will be faster. And—I can't let you get killed before you help us beat Blazar."

Julian was quiet for a moment. His eyes seemed to be searching her face for...something. "Okay. Okay. Sure," he finally said. "Can you keep up with me flying?"

Charlotte hesitated. "Maybe if I had more practice, but—"

"Stand on here with me." Julian took a step to the left, leaving a spot open on the platform for her. She dropped to the stone.

"You should probably hold on." Julian held out his arm.

Charlotte was in agreement. She grabbed his forearm. "Ready when you are."

They shot forward, and Charlotte yelped involuntarily. She definitely would have flown off if she weren't holding on to Julian. They soared over skyscrapers, occasionally moving up to avoid the taller ones. Finally, they slowed. Julian brought them down toward a familiar building.

Right. This was where Blazar had thrown Julian off a balcony.

Charlotte's heart was still racing as the platform eased to a stop. "I don't see any of them."

"They're either back inside already, or on their way up in the elevator," Julian muttered.

"So, what's the plan?"

"We fly in, grab Damselfly, and fly out." Julian's voice carried a surprising amount of confidence.

"That's a terrible plan!" Charlotte exclaimed.

"How is it terrible?"

"For starters, Blazar's faster than both of us." Charlotte gave the top floor of the building a nervous glance. "By the time we figure out where Damselfly is, he'll be attacking us."

Julian sighed. "Well, do you have a better idea?"

"We could…" Charlotte's eyes narrowed as she continued to study the building. "Wait, I do have an idea." She hadn't paid Damselfly much attention at the park, but she had noticed something when she'd darkened the area with her storm clouds. "Damselfly's armor glows, right?"

"Yeah, a little," Julian said. "Why?"

"I'm going to blind them." Charlotte lifted her hands. "I'll put clouds around the windows. I think I can make them thick enough to keep any sun from getting in."

"What about the lights inside?" Julian asked.

"I bet if I blast them with enough lightning, they'll go out."

"Okay," Julian said slowly. "Okay, this could work. But Saturn's got a backup generator in place, so we'll still need to move fast."

"Got it." Charlotte focused on the air around the top of the building. Black clouds manifested in front of the windows, heavy with rain she forced them to hold in. "I'm going to fry them. Ready to take us in?"

"Ready when you are."

Charlotte grabbed his arm. She summoned as much electricity as she could muster and unleashed it on the Complex.

Through the windows running down the building, she and Julian watched lights flicker out, one floor at a time.

"Oops," Charlotte said.

"The rest is just offices. They'll be fine. Let's go."

Julian moved them forward again. The stone platform flew through the black clouds and hit glass. The window ahead shattered. They followed the torrent of glass shards inside. Once in, Charlotte closed the gap they'd passed through in the clouds behind them, plunging the Complex into darkness.

"What the hell?" Blazar's voice cut through the black.

Ignoring the chill his voice sent down her spine, Charlotte turned her head, searching. A faint blue glow caught her eye.

The platform moved toward the glow. Charlotte reached her arms out. When they reached Damselfly, she threw her arms around the girl and pulled her onto the platform. Though Charlotte was mostly used to her super strength, she was still surprised by how easy it was to lift her, body armor and all.

Damselfly let out a small yelp of surprise before falling quiet. One of Charlotte's hands returned to Julian's arm, while she kept the other wrapped around Damselfly. "Go!" she hissed.

They were almost back to the window when the lights flickered on.

"Sophia!" Blazar shouted. "Stop them!"

Charlotte didn't dare look back. She kept her eyes on the empty window frame as it moved closer. Closer. Something whizzed through the air behind them. They exited the building, knocking a few more shards of glass out of the frame as they passed through.

A moon of Saturn landed on the platform. The bomb rolled to Charlotte's foot and bumped against her shoe.

It didn't detonate. She stared at it, frozen, heart racing, barely able to breathe. Any second now, she was sure, everything would blow up and—

Damselfly reached down to pick the bomb up. Her bug-eyed helmet hid whatever emotions might have shown on her face. "Saturn didn't activate it."

Charlotte glanced at Julian. "Did she do that on purpose?"

"I don't know," Julian said. "Let's just get the hell out of here."

He carried them back to Dove Park and lowered them to the grass. They stumbled off the stone platform, all breathing hard.

Julian straightened up and removed his mask. He laughed. "Charlotte, you're a genius," he said. "That was incredible."

Charlotte turned away, face heating. "I'm just glad it worked."

His expression fell. He nodded. "Thank you," he said, his voice quieter. "It means a lot."

Damselfly removed her helmet, revealing a grin spread wide across her face. "So, this is Charlotte?"

"No." Julian whirled around to face her. "I mean, it is, but she's not—"

Charlotte cleared her throat to cut him off. "I told Spencer we'd meet him in the alley."

"We should get going then." Julian slid his mask back into place. Damselfly followed his lead and put her helmet back on. As Charlotte led the way to the alley, Julian fell into step at her right, and Damselfly moved to the other side of him.

Spencer waited in the alley, still dressed in full armor, leaning against one of the buildings with his arms folded. Damselfly froze when she spotted him. "Collider," she whispered, her voice shaky. She took a step back.

Julian held out a hand toward her. "Damselfly, he won't hurt you. I promise."

Damselfly still didn't move.

"Oh, right," Spencer said. He stepped away from the wall. "I forgot about my fight with her."

Seriously? Spencer had fought Damselfly, too? Charlotte wondered if any of his meetings with classmates had been real.

"Spencer, could you take your helmet off, please?" Julian asked.

Spencer obliged. As he removed his helmet, he said, "Not surprised your best friend is the kind of person who would attempt to kidnap the mayor."

Julian rested a hand on Damselfly's shoulder. "Does it matter anymore? She failed, and I saw how bad the aftermath was." He lowered his voice and said something to Damselfly that Charlotte couldn't hear. Damselfly took off her own helmet.

Spencer's expression softened. "All right, Damselfly," he said as he tucked his helmet under his arm. "I'm sorry I roughed you up so much. I didn't realize you were so...young."

"I'm not a baby," Damselfly muttered. "But whatever. Sorry I tried to kidnap the mayor, I guess."

Julian frowned. "Why did you try to do that, anyway?"

"I dunno. Ransom?" Damselfly shrugged and walked forward. "Now let's go already. I'm tired of standing." Although she'd switched to a confident act with startling speed, she kept as far from Spencer as she could while the group entered the secret passage.

Charlotte moved to walk at Spencer's side. "Where are the other heroes?" she asked.

"Already back at the base."

Sure enough, Wendy, Jack, and Cassidy were all sitting on the couch when Charlotte and the others arrived. While the four poured in, the heroes rose to their feet.

Wendy folded her arms. "Wow. You actually got her back."

"She's younger than I expected," Jack noted. Damselfly shot them a glare.

Cassidy, whose skin had returned to its natural color, shifted nervously. "So, we're bringing in another villain?"

"What's her name again?" Jack asked. "Dragonfly?"

"This is Damselfly—" Julian started.

Damselfly cut him off. "Harper."

Julian frowned and glanced at her. "What?"

She lifted her chin. "My name is Harper Reed."

CHAPTER THIRTY-FOUR

Charlotte found the door to Julian's room open and the room itself empty. She moved her gaze farther down and across the hall, to the room Spencer had assigned Harper to. As she approached the ajar door, Julian and Harper's conversation became audible.

"—because we can't get any of your stuff from the Complex," Julian was saying. "But if there's anything else you need, the heroes can get it from the store." Before Harper could respond, he added, "Not video games."

"Then what am I supposed to do?" Harper asked. "Sit around all day waiting for Blazar to find us and kill us?"

"That's not going to happen."

Charlotte nearly moved forward to get their attention when Harper spoke again. "So, what happened with Charlotte?"

"What do you think?" Julian replied. "She found out I was Citadel."

"But you're helping the heroes, now!"

"I'm the only one who can help them beat Blazar. Doesn't change the fact that I killed Storm Warning."

"Oh."

After a few moments of silence passed, Charlotte knocked on the door frame. "Julian? Wendy's back with the groceries you wanted."

The door opened the rest of the way. "Come on, Dams—Harper," Julian said.

Harper followed him out of the room, dressed in jeans and an oversized t-shirt she'd found among the extra clothes, with slits cut in the back to let her wings through. Her chin-length black hair was still damp from when she'd taken off her helmet during the rainy fight at Dove Park.

The three walked downstairs to the kitchen, where Wendy was unloading the grocery bags she'd brought in. Julian assessed the food. "Good. Looks like you got everything."

Charlotte elbowed him in the side.

"Ow," he muttered, moving his hand to the spot. After a moment, he sighed and looked up at Wendy. "Thank you."

"The vodka's coming home with me," Wendy said.

"Fine by me." Julian said picked up the bottle and inspected it. "I only need a little for the pasta sauce."

"You're putting that in the pasta?" Harper asked incredulously.

"The alcohol cooks out. Did you not know—never mind." Julian set the bottle back down and started rolling up the sleeves of his shirt. "Harper, find a knife and a cutting board. You're going to chop onions."

"I don't think you want my help," Harper said. "Unless you're looking for more reasons to make fun of my cooking."

"No, I'm going to show you how to cook."

"Do you need us to do anything?" Spencer asked.

"Just give me space," Julian said with a wave of his hand. "I'll let you all know when it's ready."

After one last glance at Julian, Charlotte followed Spencer and the other heroes into the living room, where they found places to sit on the couch and chairs.

"Hey, Spencer," Charlotte said as she settled onto the couch next to him. "If you don't mind me asking, how did you get your powers?"

"It was an accident in one of the physics labs my freshman year," Spencer replied with a small smile. "I could explain what happened in more detail, but—"

"I don't think I'd understand a word of it." Charlotte laughed. "That's cool, though." Spencer's freshman year was the year before she'd moved in with him, and the year before she started at NAU after her gap year. She was only a few months younger than him, and if she'd started university right after high school, she'd be a senior alongside him.

"It took a few months to get the hang of it," Spencer said. "Before that, I accidentally walked through some walls. And slammed into others." He chuckled. "But I was able to make my costume by decreasing the density of metal so that I could manipulate it, and then making it dense again to protect me."

"Charlotte, you have the same powers as Storm Warning, right?" Wendy asked.

Charlotte nodded. "His power comes from this ancient artifact. I was by his body after he died, and it moved from him to me," she explained. "What about the rest of you?"

"When I was a kid, I got really sick. Doctors had no idea what it was," Wendy replied. "When I recovered, I had my powers."

"I volunteered for a medical research study to help pay my tuition," Jack said. "Wound up getting an infusion of genetically modified rabbit DNA—among other things—that gave me my abilities."

Cassidy shrugged. "Mine's a family thing."

Charlotte's brow furrowed. "Everyone in your family can turn into cacti?"

"Pretty much."

They chatted for half an hour about their first fights and the struggle to control their powers. Finally, Harper peered into the room from around the corner.

"Julian says it's ready," she said.

The heroes moved into the dining room and crowded around the table. A few stools had to be pulled over from the counter, but they managed to fit everyone. Barely.

"Guess we'll have to get a bigger table," Jack said.

Julian opened his mouth but changed his mind about whatever his planned response was. He set the pot of pasta down in the center of the table. Harper came over with a stack of bowls and distributed them.

Charlotte scooped some of the pasta into her bowl and took her first bite. Damn it, it was just as good as the risotto. Maybe even better.

"So, Harper," Spencer said. "I don't suppose you know anything about Blazar or his plan that Julian didn't already tell us."

"I might." Harper shoved a bite of pasta into her mouth.

Spencer lifted an eyebrow.

Harper swallowed. "He was yelling about it on our way back up to the Complex, after we left Dove Park," she continued. "He was mad at Lord Saturn, because she said she wouldn't be able to get the generators online until Friday morning."

Julian frowned. "What generators?" he asked.

"These giant contraptions she started building in her room. I have no idea what they're for," Harper said. "But once they're done, she's going to put them at the sites of the buildings we destroyed. Marigold Bank and the restaurant. There's also one going up in a parking lot at the south end of the city, and one at the baseball fields on the east side.

"So, we have five days to figure out what these generators are for and how to stop them?" Wendy asked.

"Sounds like it," Spencer muttered.

Julian drummed his fingers against the table. "I have an idea," he said after a moment.

Spencer sighed. "Let's hear it."

"Let's kidnap Lord Saturn."

"Kidnap?" Jack exclaimed.

Cassidy's eyes widened. "*Lord Saturn?*"

"Sure," Julian said with a shrug. "She doesn't have any superpowers, just her tech, so it'll be easy. We can grab her from the car manufacturer she works at."

Charlotte glanced at Spencer. "What do you think?"

Spencer twirled his fork around. "I think it might be our best shot at figuring out Blazar's plan." His gaze moved to Julian. "But do you really think she'll give us information?"

Julian glanced at Harper. "I think it's worth a try," he said.

Harper didn't respond. She lowered her gaze to her food and took another bite.

"Okay," Spencer said. "I guess we're planning a kidnapping tomorrow."

"Oh, by the way, you nerds don't have to worry about Dove Park anymore," Harper said. "Blazar said it was time to 'focus on his plan' and 'the new headquarters could be built once the city belonged to him.'" She made quotes in the air with her fingers as she spoke.

Spencer chuckled. "Great."

A few moments of silence passed after that. Julian cleared his throat. "Wendy, you're a surgeon, right?"

Harper looked up, surprise flashing across her face.

"Cassidy mentioned it this morning," Julian added.

"Yes, I am," Wendy said. "But I'm surprised you remembered."

"I remembered because I wanted to ask—" Julian glanced at Harper. "I think Harper might have a question for you."

Harper's wings twitched. "Do you think it would be possible to...remove them?"

Wendy's brow furrowed. "Your wings?"

Harper nodded. "Saturn said it wasn't possible because of my nervous system, or something. But she's an engineer, not a doctor." She rubbed her arm and looked down again. "Julian said I should try asking a real surgeon."

"I'll see what I can do," Wendy said. "But I won't be able to tell if they can be removed just by looking." She thought for a moment. "I have to meet with some patients at the hospital tomorrow morning. You could come with me, and once my consultations are done, we could do some scans." Her gaze darted to Harper's wings. "We can take my car and use a back entrance. I should be able to keep anyone we can't trust from seeing your wings."

Harper's face lit up. "That would be great." After a moment, she added, "Thanks—thank you."

Julian looked to Spencer. "Is that okay with you?"

"Sure," Spencer said. "Once they're done at the hospital, we'll meet back here to discuss grabbing Lord Saturn."

Everyone finished eating not long after that. The other heroes gathered up their things and prepared to leave for the night. Jack hovered by the table for a moment before pointing at what little pasta remained in the pot. "Hey, can I take these leftovers home to my boyfriend?"

"Sure, help yourself," Julian said with a wave of his hand as he walked back into the kitchen. He began rounding up the dishes scattered across the counter. Jack grabbed a container from one of the cupboards and dished up the rest of the leftovers.

While Charlotte remained at the table to check her emails—the last of her professors had accepted her request to miss a few classes, to her relief—Harper gathered up the bowls and forks left behind and set them on the counter in front of Julian. "Can I go watch TV now?" she asked.

Julian hesitated a moment, eyeing the assortment of dirty dishes. "Yeah, go ahead," he said.

"I'll be here at seven tomorrow morning to grab Harper," Wendy called as she followed Jack and Cassidy out of the base. The door clicked shut behind her.

Spencer paused by the table, next to Charlotte. "I'm going to go shower," he said to her quietly. "Make sure those two don't burn the place down, will you?"

Charlotte managed a weak laugh. "Sure thing."

Spencer headed upstairs. Charlotte rose to her feet. She threw a quick glance into the living room, where a commercial for a racing video game blasted on the TV while Harper watched, Then, she pushed in her chair and walked into the kitchen. To Julian.

"Did you need something?" Julian asked as he set the last of the dishes next to the sink.

"I was going to offer to help with dishes," Charlotte told him.

Julian froze. "Sure," he said after a second. "Could you dry them after I hand them to you?"

Charlotte tried drawers until she found a dish towel and moved to stand next to him at the sink. Julian started washing one of the measuring cups.

"How old were you when Blazar took you in?" Charlotte asked as he handed it to her.

"Thirteen." Julian glanced back toward the living room. "Harper was fourteen." He picked up a bowl and submerged it in the water. Began scrubbing. "But she was in a lab for four years before that."

Charlotte tried to remember being thirteen. Ugh. Middle school.

Julian rinsed the bowl and held the bowl out to her. "I have a question for you, now."

Charlotte took it. "Okay."

"Why did you give me a dollar that day at the cafe?" he asked. "The first time we met."

"I would have given it to anyone," Charlotte said with a shrug, hoping he couldn't hear the half-truth of it. "It was nothing, really."

"I was already pulling out my card. I didn't need it."

Charlotte's heart pounded in her chest. She finished drying the bowl and set it on the counter to start a stack. "I know," she said quietly.

"Then why—?"

"I wanted—" Charlotte swallowed. "I wanted an excuse to talk to you, you know." She kept her eyes fixed on the sink. "And then I saw you again at the funeral, and you happened to work at the library too, and as ridiculous as it sounds, deep down I thought—I thought there might be a reason for it." Her eyes began to sting. She blinked, willing herself to hold in her tears.

Julian held out another bowl. She lifted a shaky hand to take it.

"I was—I kept wondering what would happen if I told you that I was Citadel," Julian whispered. "Or that I didn't want to be him anymore."

What would she have said to that? If he'd told her before Blazar forced him to confess? Charlotte would have still been furious, but maybe—

If he really wanted to be a different person—

Maybe she could forgive him. Maybe. Charlotte's hand tightened around the towel. The thought made her feel...guilty? What did she have to forgive him for, besides lying about his identity? She wasn't the one he'd stolen from. She wasn't the one he'd killed. Would it be wrong of her to let that all go?

"Let's just focus on Blazar right now, okay?" she finally said. "I don't think I can deal with anything else until this is over."

Julian nodded.

They finished cleaning and drying the dishes in silence. As Charlotte set the last bowl on top of the stack, Julian opened one of the drawers and reached for the pile of forks she'd made.

"I'll put everything away," Julian said. "You can go."

Charlotte headed up to her room. It had been a long day, and tomorrow promised to be busy, too. Still, the full weight of her exhaustion didn't hit her until she sat down on her bed.

Her body was tired, but her mind was still racing. She grabbed the bag of stuff she'd brought back from her apartment and reached in to find a change of clothes. Her hand brushed the library book on Storm Warning. She hesitated a moment before pulling it out and setting it on the bed by her pillow. After that, she quickly changed and moved into the bathroom to get ready for bed.

When she returned, she picked up the Storm Warning book and opened it. Though she didn't plan on reading for longer than a few minutes, she quickly found herself drawn into the stories of his first battles. The early speculation around his abilities.

It didn't take long for her to stumble across the account of his first encounter with Blazar. He was the first hero in years to dare take the man on, and though he'd come away from the fight injured, he'd scared Blazar off.

Charlotte was pulled into a memory. To her relief, it wasn't a battle. In fact, it was a very odd change of pace from the other memories. She walked through a hallway lined with lockers and filled with students who looked high school age.

"Mr. Park." A boy waved his hand as he approached. "What's with the arm brace?"

The man whose memory Charlotte was seeing spoke. "Fell out of a tree trying to get my cat down," he said with a chuckle. Charlotte got the sense it was a lie. "Are you ready for the exam today?"

The boy nodded.

As the memory started to fade and the sensation of the bed returned to Charlotte, she caught a glimpse of a banner draped across the wall of the hallway. Big blue letters spelled out the name of the building she stood in.

Skyline High School.

CHAPTER THIRTY-FIVE

The moment Julian reached the bottom of the stairs the following morning, Charlotte was talking to him, waving her hands animatedly. "I think I figured out Storm Warning's identity!" she exclaimed.

Julian rubbed his eyes. "You know his real name?"

"Well, no, not exactly," Charlotte said. "I know his last name. But I know where we can go to find out who he was!"

Julian glanced at the clock on the oven, still trying to process what Charlotte was saying. It was almost nine a.m. "Did Harper leave with Wendy?"

Charlotte nodded. "They won't be back until one, at least. It took some convincing, but Spencer thinks it would be okay if we went to Skyline High School to take a look."

"Skyline High School?"

"I had a memory of being there, as Storm Warning. I think I was— he was a teacher," Charlotte said. "One of the kids called him Mr. Park."

"And you're sure this was Storm Warning and not one of the other hosts?" Julian asked.

"Pretty sure," she said. "I was reading the book you gave me."

She was?

"It seems like memories are triggered by me reading about them. Or by experiencing a similar event myself," Charlotte continued. "Anyway, it might be a slim chance we'll find anything useful, but we do have time to kill before the other heroes get here. At the very least, I might be able to trigger some more memories and find something we can use against Blazar."

"And you want me to come?" Julian asked skeptically.

Charlotte rubbed her arm. "Spencer had to run some errands and didn't want you left here alone."

"He still doesn't trust me?"

"Can you blame him?"

"No," Julian admitted. "Okay, Skyline High School it is." His stomach was already starting to turn. Before everything fell apart, he'd hoped he'd be able to figure out Storm Warning's identity because he thought it might help him with his plan. Now he was surprised to find he dreaded the idea.

It was easier to kill a man without a face or a name.

They left the base and took the passage to the exit in the subway station. "Will we be able to get back in?" Julian asked as they stepped out of the gap in the wall.

"Yeah, Spencer added my fingerprints to the database." Charlotte turned around and pressed her thumb to a spot on the brick wall. The gap closed. "And showed me a couple more entrances."

"Sounds like you were up early."

"I had a hard time sleeping."

Julian had, too, but decided not to mention it. "Which way are we going?"

"The school's on Blue Street, near Fifth. We should probably take the subway up a few stops."

As they made their way to the platform, Julian asked, "Did Spencer mention who built all those passages for them?"

"Some engineering friends of his helped build them a few years ago," Charlotte replied. "I guess they've all graduated now."

The subway ride was uneventful. When they reached their station, Julian and Charlotte walked up to the street level and headed north. From there, another five minutes of walking brought them to the front steps of the high school.

They entered behind a group of students and stepped into a large foyer. On the other side of the space, beyond the students milling about, was a long table with a white tablecloth. Bouquets of flowers covered the table. In the center was a framed portrait of a smiling man with light skin and blonde hair. A blue banner hung over it.

In memoriam.

Julian forced himself to keep up with Charlotte as she approached the memorial. When they reached it, she studied the portrait. "Is that...him?" she finally asked.

Even without the mask, Julian was sure it was. He nodded and lowered his gaze to read the name at the bottom of the photo. Oliver Park.

"He was a chemistry teacher," Charlotte said quietly. She ran a finger along the small plaque propped up next to Oliver's picture.

"Can I help you two with something?" a polite voice asked. Julian and Charlotte turned around. The man standing in front of them was tall and broad-shouldered and dressed in a suit with a simple blue tie. His graying hair was slicked back, and the wrinkles in his bronzed skin suggested he was in his late fifties.

"We were just here to see the memorial," Charlotte said.

The man gave them a sad smile. "Did you know Oliver?"

"Uh—" Charlotte glanced at Julian.

Julian cleared his throat. "Sort of."

"I'm Ray Mayweather, one of the school administrators." The man held out his hand. Charlotte shook it first, then Julian.

"I'm Charlotte," Charlotte said.

"Julian," Julian added.

"Pleasure to meet you," Ray said. "I was very close with Oliver."

Julian exchanged a look with Charlotte, and they seemed to be thinking the same thing. *Close enough to know his secret?*

"We know a lot about him," Charlotte said slowly. "Things most people don't know."

Ray nodded. "Why don't we talk in my office?"

Julian and Charlotte followed him into a hallway and to a door. A card next to the door had Ray's name on it. The school bell rang as he grabbed the door handle.

"You caught us between classes," he said, pushing it open. "The next period starts in a minute."

Inside the office was a desk with a computer monitor, a few filing cabinets, and another door. Ray sat down behind the desk and gestured to the two chairs across from it, against the wall by the door. "Have a seat."

For a brief moment, Julian was flashing back to that time in middle school he'd been called into the principal's office after getting caught skipping class with his friends to see a movie. He couldn't even remember what movie it had been, now.

"It sounds like you know about Oliver's other job," Ray said as Julian and Charlotte sat down.

Charlotte nodded. "We know he was...Storm Warning."

"And...how do you know about him?" Ray asked. "As far as I'm aware, he only told me and a few other superheroes."

Julian frowned. *Other* superheroes?

"I have the source of Storm Warning's power," Charlotte explained. "We've been calling it the stormoid, but I guess it's actually—"

"—The Eye of the Storm," Ray finished with her, nodding. "I helped the heroes from New York make funeral arrangements, and when we realized it was gone from his body, we were afraid Citadel had gotten his hands on it. I'm glad that wasn't the case."

"Me too," Charlotte said, shooting Julian a sideways glance. Julian lifted his eyes to the ceiling.

"You must be that new hero people have been seeing around, then," Ray said. "The woman you saved at that restaurant said you're calling yourself Stormbringer, right?"

"Yeah," Charlotte said. "I'm Stormbringer."

Ray turned his gaze on Julian. "And you are?"

"I'm..." Julian glanced at Charlotte as he trailed off. His instinct was to lie, but what if she didn't want him to? He couldn't help but think it would be a bad idea to tell this guy the truth, though.

Thankfully, Charlotte came to the same conclusion. And she managed to technically avoid lying. "He's not a superhero, but he has powers, too," she said. "He helped me learn to control mine."

"Well, I'm just glad the Eye wound up in good hands," Ray said. "Have you had to deal with Citadel at all?"

"A few times. I think I've got him under control," Charlotte said. A hint of a smirk touched her lips. Julian was slightly embarrassed to feel his face heat. Yeah, "under control" was one way of putting it.

Charlotte continued. "Actually, we came here today because I was hoping to unlock one of Storm—one of Oliver's memories. A battle with Blazar."

"I would stay far away from Blazar, if I were you," Ray replied, frowning. "At least until you have a better handle on your abilities."

"I don't really have a choice," Charlotte said. "We found out he's planning something. We don't know exactly what it is, yet, but it's happening Friday morning."

Ray's expression darkened. He let out a heavy sigh. "I guess it was inevitable. He's been getting bolder, and now with Storm Warning gone, he must think no one can stop him."

"I'm going to stop him," Charlotte said. "Me and some other heroes."

Ray rose to his feet. "Sounds like all I can do is help you access those memories, then. I have a box of Oliver's stuff you can take. Mostly photos and teaching awards, but there are some notebooks from his house that I think are journals." He walked to the other door in the room and opened it, revealing a small closet.

As Ray grabbed a box off one of the shelves, Julian brought himself to ask the question that had been a weight on his tongue since they'd entered Ray's office. "Did Oliver have a family?"

"Two cats," Ray said. "Which my daughter adopted after his death. Other than that, he devoted most of his time to teaching and giving extra help to students who needed it." He returned to where the two sat and held the box out to Charlotte.

"Thank you," Charlotte said. She stood up and accepted the box. Julian rose, too.

"I'll make some calls to my friends later today," Ray said. "There are other heroes here in the state who might be able to help. But New York's a busy place, and they could be tied up with other problems."

"We'll take any help we can get," Charlotte said.

"I'd offer you my assistance, but it hasn't meant much since I lost my powers."

Charlotte's eyebrows went up. "You had powers?"

Ray nodded. "I was born with them, but I was in a real nasty battle about—" He thought for a moment. "—six years ago. Put me out of commission for nearly a year, and I never fully recovered my abilities. I'm simply not strong enough to save anyone anymore." He sighed. "The way the battle ended, everyone thought I'd been killed. I decided it was easier to let them think that."

Julian's stomach turned. No, no, no, this sounded too familiar—

"Do you mind me asking who you were?" Charlotte asked.

"Sure." Ray smiled. "I was Sunbeam."

Sunbeam.

Shock jolted through Julian's entire body.

An invisible pressure followed, tightening his chest, crushing his lungs until he couldn't breathe.

Ray frowned. "Julian, are you all right?"

Sunbeam.

Julian's blood was ice in his veins. The world spun around him. He saw Charlotte turn toward him out of the corner of his eye, but he couldn't bring himself to look at her. All he could do was fumble for the door handle and stagger out into the hallway.

CHAPTER THIRTY-SIX

Charlotte's heart hammered in her chest as she watched Julian disappear into the hallway. What the hell just happened?

"Is he okay?" Ray asked.

"I—I'm not sure." Charlotte shifted the box to one arm and grabbed the door before it could swing shut. She followed Julian into the hall. "Julian?"

Julian hadn't gone far. He'd sunk to the floor halfway down the hall, his back to the wall and his eyes fixed on the empty space in front of him. Charlotte approached slowly and set the box down before moving to sit next to him.

"Julian," she said softly. "What's going on?"

Julian was still staring at nothing. "He's been alive the whole time," he said, his voice quiet. Empty.

"Sunbeam?"

Julian closed his eyes. "He was supposed to be dead. When I heard about the battle that killed him, I thought—I thought I could finally move on." Cracks formed in his voice, letting something darker spill out. Pain. Grief.

"What did Sunbeam do?" Charlotte asked. She suspected she already knew the answer. Something Citadel had told her. Something Julian had told her.

"There was this big battle with Incinerator. And when Sunbeam fired the blast that finally knocked him out—" Julian hid his face in his hand. "It was my house. He hit my house. He killed my..." His voice faltered.

"I'm sorry," Charlotte whispered. "I'm so sorry, Julian."

Julian lowered his hand. His gaze flickered to her, briefly. Then to the floor. "Sometimes I think it's worse, that he didn't mean to do it," he said. "That it was an accident. I'm not supposed to hate him, because he was trying to do the right thing, right? He saved people. Except..."

"I know."

Julian abruptly climbed to his feet. He rested a hand against the wall next to him and took a ragged breath. "I need to get out of here. I can't—I can't breathe."

A door opened behind Charlotte. She stood and glanced back as Ray stepped out of his office.

"Is everything okay?" Ray asked.

Charlotte's gaze returned to Julian. His eyes were closed again. She reached down and grabbed Julian's wrist as she looked at Ray again. "We're fine," she said. "We should be going. Thank you for all your help."

"Of course," Ray said, though his expression still held concern. "If you need anything else, feel free to drop by." He went back into his office and pulled the door shut.

"Come on. Let's go outside," Charlotte said gently. She bent down to pick up the box before leading Julian to the nearest exit.

She found some outdoor seating in a nearby plaza shaded by trees. She took Julian to the most secluded table she could find, and they sat down. He rested his arms on the table in front of him and stared at nothing.

He was quiet for nearly ten minutes. Charlotte tried not to stare, instead watching squirrels scavenge the ground nearby or glancing at the occasional passing car. But her gaze kept darting back to him. To his blank expression. His empty eyes.

"I was sixteen when they said on the news that Sunbeam was killed," Julian finally said. "And then Incinerator broke out of prison and died in another fight a few months later." His gaze moved up to the trees. "And that was that. I was supposed to be over it."

"You don't just get over that kind of thing," Charlotte said.

"Blazar disagrees."

"I'm guessing he didn't get you a therapist."

There it was. The barest hint of a smile, cold as it was. "Does he seem the type to want to talk about feelings?"

"Other than anger? No, he doesn't."

Julian shook his head. "I shouldn't have lost it in there. Seeing him shouldn't have set me off out like that."

"It's okay." One of Charlotte's hands inched toward Julian's. "Julian, it's a totally reasonable reaction. You weren't expecting—"

Julian's demeanor shifted. "Don't," he said softly, pulling his hand back. "Don't try to make me feel better because you think you have to. Let's just be done with this."

"What?" Charlotte frowned. "Julian, if you want to talk about it, I'll listen."

"Why?" Julian asked, his gaze meeting hers. "You hate me."

Charlotte's heart dropped.

"I don't..." She trailed off, feeling her throat starting to close. Did she hate him?

"Can you honestly say you don't?"

Charlotte took a deep breath. "I don't hate you, Julian." And it was true. She rested a hand on his shoulder. "I'm still angry about what happened. But if you want to help us defeat Blazar, then I'm going to work with you and—"

Julian moved his arm away. "I know you're trying to help, but..."

"But what?"

"Charlotte, it hurts when you look at me."

The words sank in. Clawed at Charlotte from the inside.

Julian squeezed his eyes shut. "And I know it's my fault. I deserve it. But I'd rather you avoid me than—than try to help me when I know how you really feel about me now."

"I can't just pretend you don't exist, Julian," Charlotte said, her voice barely more than a whisper. "We have to work together on this."

Slowly, Julian rose to his feet. "Let's just get back to the base," he said. "I need some time alone before we kidnap Saturn."

Charlotte stood up with him.

"At least I can still make Blazar pay for what he did to me," Julian muttered.

They headed for the sidewalk. Charlotte thought carefully for a few minutes before speaking.

"I'm sorry for what Blazar did to you," she finally said. "But you were thirteen, not three. It's not like you didn't know stealing was wrong." After a pause, she added, "And you chose to kill Storm Warning."

Julian was quiet for a long moment. "I know it doesn't change anything, but you know that feeling you get when you screw up? Like you just stepped off a cliff?" he asked. "I felt that right after Storm Warning fell."

He let the confession hang in the air a moment before continuing. "But it was supposed to be a victory. I was supposed to be happy. So I convinced myself I was."

Charlotte tried not to stare at him on the subway ride back, tried not to study his every expression like she had earlier. She hadn't realized how much she'd been doing it until she was stopping herself every few minutes.

Her mind raced as they stepped off the train, as they entered the secret hallway and walked to the fingerprint scanner. She opened the passage with her finger and let Julian step in first before following him.

When they entered the base, Charlotte finally voiced what she'd been thinking.

"Julian," she said, stopping him before he could reach the stairs. He turned around. "You said last night that you thought about telling me you didn't want to be Citadel anymore."

Julian's only response was a solemn nod.

"Maybe that's not the right thing to do. I don't know if you should walk away from all of this. Maybe you should—" Charlotte swallowed.

"Maybe instead of hiding for the rest of your life, you should become a hero."

"A hero," Julian repeated blankly.

"You took New Atlas's protector away," Charlotte told him. "If you really, really want to make things right, then you need to be the one to protect them, now."

"I don't know if I can do that," he said quietly. "I'm not—I don't know if I'm strong enough."

"You won't be doing it alone," Charlotte said. "You have the rest of us heroes on your side."

"Do I?"

"As long as you're trying to make up for what you've done, I promise you'll at least have me."

Julian stared at her. "Okay."

He turned around and went upstairs.

Charlotte moved into the living room and sank onto the couch with the box of Oliver's belongings. The first thing she took out was a photo of him with a group of students in lab coats. She carefully set it on the table and reached back in.

Within minutes, she had it all spread out across the table. Five photos, three plaques bearing the title Teacher of the Year, a very old chemistry textbook, some pens with the high school's name on them, and a stack of notebooks.

They were indeed journals, after all. Accounts of fights with villains, starting with the first time he stopped a guy holding up a gas station. And before that, Oliver detailed how he'd found the Eye of the Storm in a jar while helping clean out a neighbor's attic after their death.

Charlotte dove into the first journal, eagerly taking in every word. Maybe she should have skimmed until she found the fights with Blazar, but she couldn't resist seeing Storm Warning progress from an ordinary guy who found the Eye in an attic to the powerful hero New Atlas remembered him as now.

She didn't stop reading until a little after one, when the door to the base opened and Wendy and Harper walked in.

Charlotte set down the notebook and rose to her feet. "How'd it go?" she asked.

"Great," Wendy said. "It should be a simple procedure to remove the wings, if she really wants it done."

"Really?" Charlotte looked at Harper. Harper was staring off into space, her expression unreadable.

Julian emerged from the staircase. "Did I hear that right, Harper? Wendy can remove your wings?"

Harper nodded, still quiet.

Julian walked up to her. "That's good news, right?"

The dam broke. Harper burst into tears.

"She lied to me!" she sobbed.

"Hey, hey, hey." Julian dropped to one knee and placed his hands on Harper's shoulders. Eyes on hers, he asked, "Who lied to you?"

Tears ran down Harper's face. She wiped them away with the long sleeve of her shirt. More took their place. "Saturn told me I was going to be like this forever! Why would she say that?"

Julian kept his expression steady as he pulled her in and wrapped his arms around her, carefully avoiding her wings. "I'm sorry, Harper. I don't know." Once her face was in his shoulder, he let his own emotions show. The same anguish Harper was feeling. And a hint of something else.

Rage.

"I hate her!" Harper cried into his shirt.

"It's okay," Julian murmured, keeping his voice steady. "It's okay."

Charlotte moved closer to Wendy. "Did Harper say anything when you told her?" she asked quietly.

"She was excited for a minute, and then she got quiet," Wendy replied. "She didn't talk much on the way back."

Julian masked his dark expression and pulled away from Harper. "Come sit down at the table," he said as he stood up. "I'll get you something to eat." Glancing at Wendy, he asked, "Do you know where the others are?"

"Spencer just texted. He said he'd be here with Jack and Cassidy in about twenty minutes," Wendy answered.

Julian nodded. With one hand on Harper's shoulder, he guided her into the dining room and pulled out a chair for her. She sniffed as she sat down.

"What do you want?" Julian asked.

"Can you make pancakes?" Harper's voice was hoarse.

"Sure. I can do that." Julian glanced at Charlotte and Wendy. "Either of you want any?"

"I'll have some," Charlotte said.

"May as well make enough for everyone," Wendy added.

Charlotte sat down at the table, leaving a chair between herself and Harper. "Are you going to have Wendy remove them, then?"

"Yes." Harper sniffed and wiped her face again. "But I want to beat Blazar first."

Julian set a mixing bowl on the counter in front of him. "Harper, you don't have to do that. We can deal with Blazar."

"No." Harper lifted her chin. "I want to help you. I have to."

"Okay, then." Julian moved to the cupboard he'd stowed the cooking ingredients in.

By the time Spencer and the others arrived, Julian had a large plate of pancakes sitting on the table for them. Spencer raised an eyebrow. "Bit of a jump from pasta."

"You weren't here, so Harper got to pick," Julian said.

"All good. I love pancakes," Spencer said as he sat down. "Hey, Harper."

Harper sniffed. "Hi."

Spencer looked to Charlotte, his question clear in his expression.

"Wendy said she can remove the wings," Charlotte explained. "Harper's going to have it done after we beat Blazar."

"Oh, congrats!" Jack said as they took a seat.

Harper flushed. "Thanks."

Cassidy joined the table. "So, what are you going to do after you have them removed?"

"I—" Harper folded her arms and rested them on the table. "I want to go to high school, actually," she said quietly. "But I guess I'm a few years behind."

"I bet you could get caught up." Julian entered the dining room with a stack of plates and set them on the table. He slid into the empty chair between Harper and Charlotte. "Maybe you could start this fall, if you're willing to work over the summer."

Harper nodded.

"That means you can't pay video games twenty-four-seven—"

Harper punched Julian's arm. "I know, old man." She looked away, but Charlotte caught her smile before she did.

And then, for a heartbeat, she was looking at the Julian she'd known before. Before he turned out to be Citadel.

"Okay," Spencer said, drawing the table's attention. "It's about time we discuss this plan to kidnap Lord Saturn."

CHAPTER THIRTY-SEVEN

Two years earlier—and one week after the Complex had lost two of its stronger villains in a fight with some New York City heroes—Blazar had brought Harper home. Julian had been in the kitchen trying to figure out what the hell he was doing wrong with his cheesecake recipe when they returned.

"We're back from the lab," Blazar announced as he entered. He turned and spotted Julian. "Ah, there you are."

"How'd it go?" Julian asked, looking up from the pan he'd pulled from the oven.

"Saturn's on her way up with the girl," Blazar said. "She had some equipment to deal with."

"Girl?"

"The lab only had one surviving test subject by the time we got there." Blazar moved to the counter and briefly glanced at the cheesecake. "She's only fourteen, but if we train her right, she could be useful. She can fly."

The door opened again a moment later and Saturn entered, with Harper trailing behind. Harper wore simple white pants and a matching shirt with the number twenty-eight on the front in black print. Her blue wings fluttered behind her as she looked around the Complex.

"We're calling her Damselfly," Blazar said.

Julian held up a hand. "Nice to meet you."

Harper's head turned toward him. She approached the counter. "'Nice to meet you?' What are you, forty?"

Julian glanced at Blazar, who let out a cold laugh. "Yeah," Blazar said. "She's got quite the personality."

Julian folded his arms. "What about that made me sound forty?"

"I dunno. Only old people ever say that to me." Harper rested her arms on the counter and leaned forward. "Who are you, anyway?"

"I'm Citadel."

Blazar circled the counter and clapped a hand on Julian's shoulder. "Julian here's been with us for, what, nine years now?"

Julian nodded.

Saturn paused behind Harper. She adjusted the duffel bag slung over her shoulder. "Blake, did you want to look through the equipment we took from the lab?"

"Absolutely." Blazar stepped away from Julian. "Damselfly, make yourself at home. Julian can show you around, and there's an empty room next to his waiting for you." He paused at the entrance to the hallway. As Saturn passed him, he added, "And we'll discuss your training tonight after dinner."

As soon as they were gone, Harper's eyes moved to the pan in front of Julian. "Is that cheesecake?"

"Yes," Julian answered. "But it's not good, I screwed something up—"

Harper grabbed a stray fork he'd left on the counter and took a bite anyway. "Seems fine to me," she said through a mouthful.

Julian chuckled. "What were they feeding you at that lab?"

"I dunno. Rabbit food?" Harper took another bite of the cheesecake. "Can I finish this?"

"Knock yourself out." Julian told her, smiling for the first time in a week.

Two years later, Julian and Harper were in costume, hovering in the air above the car manufacturing plant Saturn worked at.

"Are you sure you want to do this?" Julian asked. "I could grab her myself."

Harper shook her head. "I'm here to back you up. I'm not leaving."

"Okay." Julian glanced behind him, at the woods next to the plant. It was technically in New Atlas, but it sat at the very outskirts of the city, beyond the grid of skyscrapers. Somewhere below them, the other heroes were waiting out of costume with an SUV Jack had borrowed from their parents. Since the kidnapping of Sophia Novak would appear to be a civilian abduction to the rest of the world, they figured it would be best if no heroes were spotted at the scene.

If this worked out how Julian was hoping, though, no one would know who had taken her at all. He lifted his phone to his ear.

"Any sign of her?" Charlotte asked.

"Not yet," Julian replied. "But if she's working her usual shift, we have another few minutes."

Sure enough, not long after five o'clock rolled around, the plant's front doors opened, and Saturn stepped out. But she wasn't alone. She walked with a group of four people. Isolating her would be tricky.

"Now, Charlotte," Julian said into the phone.

Thick, dark clouds rolled across the parking lot. As soon as the employees were hidden from view, Julian lowered his stone platform into the storm. Harper followed, wings buzzing.

Julian jumped off of the platform near where the employees shouted in blind panic. He could only hear one set of footsteps running through the clouds. He followed the sound. Seconds later, a figure appeared in front of him. As Saturn looked back, he could just make out her face through the mist.

"Sophia, stop!" Julian called to her. "There's nowhere to run."

She slowed. "What are you trying to accomplish, Julian? Even if you take me, Blazar already has what he needs."

"You're going to tell us exactly what it is he's planning."

"No. I'm not." Saturn backed away from Julian. And bumped into Harper. Before Saturn could react, Harper's arms wrapped around her, and the two lifted into the air.

Julian summoned his platform, hopped onto it, and followed. He caught up with Harper and a wide-eyed Saturn high in the air.

"Julian," Harper gasped. "I can't keep carrying her—"

Julian lifted the platform to meet Harper's feet. She set Saturn down. Saturn yanked herself free from Harper's grasp.

"Where are you taking me?" Saturn demanded.

Julian ignored the question. "If you don't want to fall to your death, hold on to one of us."

After a moment's hesitation, Saturn reluctantly grabbed Julian's arm. He carried them away from the manufacturing plant before the clouds finished fading, safely out of sight of the other employees. Moments later, they were dropping into the trees, where the other heroes waited next to the SUV.

"Wendy?" Julian called.

"On it," Wendy said, taking a step forward as the platform hit the ground. Saturn immediately blanched and pressed a hand to her mouth.

Cassidy walked up to Saturn, clutching a bandana in her hands. While most of her skin was its usual brown, her hands had turned green and grown small spines. Careful to avoid touching Saturn with them, she lifted the bandana and tied it around Saturn's head, blindfolding her.

Julian unfastened his cape and removed his mask. As he tucked them under his arm, he turned to Jack. "You're sure this place will work?"

"My family owns the cabin," Jack said. "And there isn't anything else nearby. No one will interrupt."

Charlotte dropped to the ground next to the SUV. "Did the clouds work?" she asked as Julian approached.

Julian nodded. "They were perfect." He grabbed a rear door and held it open. Wendy and Spencer guided Saturn into the third row of the vehicle.

Once they were settled, Jack pushed up the second row of seats. Julian, Harper, and Charlotte climbed into the vehicle, with Harper in the middle. Jack circled around to the driver's side, and Cassidy took the passenger seat next to him.

During the half hour drive to Jack's family's cabin, Jack chatted quietly with Cassidy, while Wendy and Spencer had their own conversation in the back. The middle row stayed quiet.

Saturn, thankfully, realized there was no point in fighting. When they reached the cabin, she allowed herself to be led inside. Spencer tied her to a chair in the living room before removing her blindfold. The heroes gathered in a circle around her.

"I'm not telling you anything," Saturn said. "This is a waste of time."

Julian grabbed a second chair and dragged it over so that he could sit across from her. "You said Blazar has what he needs, but Harper said he can't do anything until Friday morning."

Saturn frowned. "Harper?" Her gaze moved to someone behind Julian. "Oh. Damselfly."

"That's not my name," Harper hissed with surprising aggression.

Saturn's expression darkened. "It's not too late," she said to Harper. "Come back with me. These heroes are using you."

"And you weren't?"

Julian looked back at Harper for a moment before returning his attention to Saturn. He leaned forward in his chair. "This isn't about her. Or me. What are the generators for, Saturn?"

"Like I said, I'm not telling you anything," Saturn said.

"You're really that loyal to Blazar?"

"You've clearly misread our relationship, Julian."

"No. Because it's the same as the rest of us," Julian replied, shaking his head. "He convinced you that you could rule the world. But he was never going to let any of us have something he wanted for himself."

"Blake and I are equals," Saturn said defensively. "I've known him since we were in elementary school. We founded the Complex together."

Julian frowned. He'd known the two had known each other for a long time, but that was even longer than he'd thought. "You would always have chosen him over us," he realized.

Saturn's expression was as cold as ever. "You're not my children, Julian."

"Blazar acted like he was our father."

"And I told him that was a bad idea."

Julian let out a bitter laugh. "You thought he would listen to you?"

Anger flashed across Saturn's face.

"I still don't get it," Julian continued. "Why do you do what he asks? Harper and I and the other villains—he took us in because we had nowhere else to go. Our only option was to help him. But you had your own life, and you're a genius. You could do anything."

"I'm a genius because of him." Saturn's voice softened. "I learned to build and create things for him. Because he had powers, and I wanted to join him."

"Was he always like this?" Julian asked.

Silence.

"He always found villains who'd lost something," Saturn finally said, looking away from Julian. "Our families, our homes—we were willing to take from the world because it had taken from us."

Julian's hands, resting on his legs, tightened into fists. She knew what she was. No delusions. No trying to convince herself it was her right to fight back against the world.

"He always knew those were the kind of people he could get to work for him," Saturn continued. "But he's not like that. He doesn't have a tragic backstory or a dead family or a home destroyed by a superhero. His life was perfect. He had everything handed to him." Her gaze dropped to the floor. "And I guess that made him think he deserved more. When people stopped giving him what he wanted, he started taking it."

"You know he's awful," Julian said.

"Not to me," Saturn replied quickly. Her eyes were back on Julian in a heartbeat. "Who would say no to someone who promised them the world, whatever they did to get it?"

Before Julian could stop himself, his gaze flickered to Charlotte.

"You could have had it too, Julian," Saturn said, drawing his attention back to her. "So what if Blazar was the one in charge? We all could have been happy. Together."

"I wasn't happy," Harper blurted. She walked forward until she was standing at Julian's right. "And we weren't together! You all left me alone all the time!"

"We saved you!" Saturn replied, her voice rising to match Harper's. "We saved you from that lab!"

"You're villains! You don't save people!" Harper's eyes shone with tears. "I just wanted to go back to my old life."

"You would have been even more miserable. You would have gone back to bouncing around foster homes." Saturn's eyes narrowed. "This time without your brother."

Harper looked like she'd been shot.

Julian was on his feet in a heartbeat, blood boiling, fists tightening at his sides. "What the hell is wrong with you?" he shouted. Louder than he'd meant to.

"It's the truth," Saturn said plainly. Her lack of reaction made Julian angrier. "And even if those wings could have been removed, so what? Blake wasn't just going to let her go. She knew too much."

"Don't. I know that's a lie." Harper choked the words out. "They can be removed. And I'm going to get rid of them as soon as we stop Blazar."

"You'd give up your power?" Saturn's eyes widened as they moved to Harper. There wasn't just surprise there, but anger, too. Indignation. "After everything? I made that suit for you!"

"I'm going to burn it when this is over."

"It's fireproof."

"Then I'll blow it up! With one of your bombs!"

"Harper. Go," Julian said, trying to force some gentleness into the words. It didn't work as well as he'd hoped.

Harper glanced at him. "But—"

"Go." Julian looked around the heroes, finally taking in their concerned expressions. "Someone, please—"

"I've got her." Wendy stepped forward and rested a hand on Harper's shoulder. "Come on. Let's go sit down."

While they left the room, Julian dropped to one knee in front of Saturn. "You have no idea what you've done to her," he hissed.

"I was trying to help her," Saturn said. Did she really believe that? "Like I said, Blake wouldn't have let her go. Telling her the wings could be removed would have only made things worse."

"And why would you care about helping her?" Julian asked. "You never cared about us."

Saturn took a moment to answer. "That's not entirely true," she whispered.

"Then it wasn't enough. Not if you're choosing Blazar over us. Over the city and everyone in it."

"It never would have been a problem if you hadn't screwed up! If you'd just brought Blazar the stormoid—"

"That's not what it's called," Julian cut her off. Speaking quietly enough that none of the heroes could hear, he added, "And I found something better than that. Better than Blazar's approval."

Saturn lifted her gaze to something beyond Julian. Charlotte. "And then you lost it," she said. "Didn't you?"

"Maybe," Julian replied. "But I'm still not coming back. I don't want Blazar's world anymore." He rose to his feet and raised his voice. "Please, just tell us what the generators are for."

No response.

"Please," Julian repeated. "Sophia."

She looked up. "It doesn't matter. Blake has everything he needs, and you can't stop him," she said. "The generators are complete. They won't be charged until Friday morning, but even if I don't make it back, he'll be able to move forward with his plan." Quieter, she added, "God knows he's powerful enough."

"What do the generators do?" Julian asked.

Saturn sighed. "They're going to generate a forcefield. All of New Atlas will be trapped inside. And Blake's not going to let the city go until he gets what he wants."

Julian had held a few blocks ransom the night he'd killed Storm Warning. Blazar was going to hold the entire city ransom.

That bastard had stolen his plan.

"He's going to kill every hero that tries to save New Atlas," Saturn continued. "Or die trying."

Julian stared at her, stunned. "You do realize it's going to be the latter, right? Blazar's powerful. Maybe the most powerful person on the east coast. But if other heroes from around the country get involved, he doesn't stand a chance."

Saturn didn't respond. She was looking at the floor again. Of course she knew that. She wasn't stupid. Was she simply not brave enough to stand up to Blazar? To tell him he was going to get himself killed?

She didn't love him enough to stop him—if she really did love him at all. Maybe she hoped Julian and the others would get to him first, but surely she knew better than to assume they would let him live. Blazar wasn't the kind of villain you tried to lock up. He was far too dangerous.

As Julian started to turn away from her, Saturn looked up again. "Don't bother going to the Complex to destroy them," she blurted. "We moved them to a secure location while they charge up. You'll never find them. Not until it's too late."

Julian and the other heroes gathered in a tight circle.

"So," Julian said quietly. "Even if we fail, Blazar's definitely going to get murdered by all the other superheroes who show up."

Spencer shook his head. "Who knows how many will die before one succeeds, though? And how many civilians will get killed in the meantime?"

"We still have to stop him before he goes through with his plan," Charlotte added in agreement. "At the very least, generating the forcefield is going to cause a lot of destruction. And who knows what else Blazar will do while he waits for heroes to show up?"

"Probably kill people," Julian muttered. "He's going to want to get heroes to show up as fast as possible."

"Exactly," Spencer said. "So, if we can't get to the generators before then, we have to stop him Friday morning."

Julian turned his head to meet Charlotte's gaze. "I don't know what the rest of you were thinking, but—Blazar can't be kept alive at the end of this. He's too dangerous. Even if he's injured, he'll find a way to escape." He swallowed. "We have to kill him."

Charlotte responded with a solemn nod. "I know."

CHAPTER THIRTY-EIGHT

Charlotte and the other heroes moved into the next room of the cabin, where Wendy and Harper sat on wooden chairs by the window. Julian briefly explained what Lord Saturn had told him about the forcefield.

"It's Tuesday, and we have until Friday," Spencer added at the end of the explanation, folding his arms.

"Well, it's Tuesday night," Jack said.

"Yeah," Cassidy added. "And the forcefield thing is Friday morning, so really, we only have Wednesday and Thursday." Her eyes widened. "Oh my god, we have two days."

"We'll make the most of it." Wendy said, rising to her feet. She rested her hands on her hips. "Extra training, but not so much that we wear ourselves out. And Charlotte will try to find information on Blazar's weakness in Storm Warning's memories."

A thud came from the next room. A flash of light and the sound of a small explosion followed. Then, a window shattering.

Julian was the first to race toward the room they'd left Saturn in. Charlotte followed, and the other heroes were close behind. Smoke spilled out of the room as they entered.

"Saturn!" Julian exclaimed. He coughed and waved a hand in front of his face. "Sophia!"

Harper caught up to Julian and grabbed his arm. "It's no use. She's gone."

"Damn it." Julian whirled around as the smoke began to clear. The window facing the front of the cabin had been blown out.

"Should we go after her?" Charlotte asked.

"We'll never find her," Julian said, shaking his head. "I should have known she'd keep an explosive device on her." He walked to the chair, which had been split in half. The ropes they'd tied Saturn up with laid in a frayed pile on the floor. He picked up a charred piece.

"At least we got some information out of her," Spencer said.

Julian stared at the rope. "Yeah. I guess we did."

Charlotte took a cautious step toward him. "How much do you think she'll tell Blazar? About what we know now?"

He looked up at her. "Doesn't matter. If she says the generators can't be turned on until Friday, then they can't be turned on until Friday."

"Great." Spencer slid his hands in his pockets. "Let's find something to cover that window and get out of here. Jackie, let your parents know we'll pay for a new one."

Jack brought out a tablecloth and duct tape, and Wendy helped them secure it across the gap. After that, the heroes piled into the SUV and headed back to New Atlas.

"So," Spencer said from the backseat once they were on city streets. "Who's going on patrol tonight, again?"

"I have to go back to the hospital," Wendy said.

Jack turned into a parking garage. "I told my parents I'd drive them to the airport," they said. "And I definitely remembered to put that on the calendar, this time."

Spencer folded his arms. "Well, I can't go. I have to run to campus and take an exam."

"Wait, I'm going out alone?" Cassidy asked, her voice almost a squeak.

Charlotte perked up in her seat. "I can go with you!"

"That's a great idea," Spencer said. "Take Julian with you."

On the other side of Harper, Julian scoffed. "Thanks, but I think I'm going to go directly to bed."

Harper elbowed him in the ribs.

"Ow!" Julian rubbed his side. "What was that for?"

Harper leaned toward him to whisper something. She wasn't very good at it. Charlotte heard every word. "Go with her, dumbass."

Julian pushed Harper back a few inches. "Fine, I'll go," he muttered.

Charlotte turned to look out the window as Jack pulled into a parking spot, wishing she couldn't feel her face turning red.

While the others went their separate ways, Charlotte, Julian, Harper, and Cassidy returned to the base. Before Charlotte could go upstairs to change into her costume, Julian stepped into her path.

"If you don't want me to come, I'm happy to stay here with Harper," he said.

"Well, what do you want to do?" Charlotte asked.

Julian blanked. "I…"

Charlotte sidestepped in. "I doubt anything exciting is going to happen," she said. "But I think it would be good if you came." She headed for the stairs. "It's up to you, though! I won't snitch to Spencer."

When Charlotte came back downstairs, Cassidy was waiting by the door in her costume, adjusting her hat. No sign of Julian. Charlotte was surprised to find she was a little disappointed.

"Sorry." Julian walked into the entryway from the dining room. "Harper couldn't figure out how to use the microwave." He'd refastened his cape and had his half mask in hand. "I'm ready."

"Oh!" Charlotte cleared her throat. "Great. Yeah, let's go." She turned away and slid her helmet onto her head, over the hair she'd pulled up.

The three left the base and took the exit to the alleyway. "So, what exactly are we doing?" Julian asked. "Walking around dark alleys until we run into trouble?"

"Pretty much," Cassidy replied. "It'd be nice if we had a hero with super hearing or sight or something. Jack's got above-average hearing, but even they can only pick up stuff happening within a few blocks."

"I could fly up and keep an eye on things from above," Charlotte said. "I need more practice, anyway."

"That would be great!" Cassidy paused her stroll and glanced at Julian. "We'll split up down here, then. Everyone stay close, and call if you find trouble."

Charlotte nodded. With one last glance at Julian, she jumped into the air and flew up to a nearby roof.

She moved from building to building, surveying the world below, but her thoughts were elsewhere. Why had she told Julian she thought it would be good for him to come? Did she really think she could persuade him to become a hero after all of this?

And if he did want to, then what? Would the other heroes allow it? They seemed to be warming up to him, but Charlotte hadn't been able to bring herself to ask anyone what they wanted to do with him after they dealt with Blazar.

And what about Harper? She'd need someone to take care of her once her wings were gone. Julian would be the best person to do that.

After half an hour of circling city blocks, Charlotte sank to the edge of a roof and let her legs hang over the ledge. Seeing Julian and Harper together—she couldn't imagine tearing them apart. Especially after what Lord Saturn had said about Harper's brother.

A scream cut through the night, sending a jolt through her. Were they going to fight someone after all? She jumped off the building and flew in the direction the scream had come from. In an alley below, movement caught her eye.

A figure dressed in a black cloak was approaching a woman, who stumbled backwards in her attempt to get away from them.

Charlotte dropped to the ground between the woman and the cloaked figure. "Am I interrupting something?"

The figure reached up to pull back the hood of their cloak, revealing a girl whose face was hidden under a glittery silver masquerade mask. Piercing blue eyes met Charlotte's.

"Back off," the cloaked girl said.

"Not a chance." Charlotte raised her arm above her head and fired a bolt of lightning straight up into the air. Hopefully, that would draw Julian and Cassidy to her. She had a feeling she could handle this girl herself, though.

The girl's eyes widened. "Shit. You're Stormbringer."

Charlotte smirked. Good to know her name was getting around. "And you are?"

The girl reached into her cloak. "Call me Night Sword."

"Is that Knight with a K, or—?"

Night Sword frowned. "No, no K. Just Night." She drew out a massive longsword from under her cloak and pointed it at Charlotte.

A sword? Charlotte lifted her fists. Nothing she couldn't handle, right? "Great. Well, I can't just let you rob this woman, so—"

"I'm not robbing her." Night Sword rolled her eyes. "She works for a lab, and I'd like the serum she's carrying in her bag."

"Sounds like robbing to me," Charlotte said.

"'Robbing' makes it sound like I'm mugging her for whatever she's got in her wallet," Night Sword said indignantly. "This was a planned theft."

Why were villains always so weird about their plans?

"Char—Stormbringer!" Julian yelled as he ran into the alley. He came to a halt and looked Night Sword over. "Who's this?"

"Nothing I can't handle. Get this woman behind me somewhere safe," Charlotte ordered.

Surprisingly, Julian nodded. He ran past Night Sword, past Charlotte, to the woman standing next to the wall.

Night Sword lowered her blade a couple of feet. "Hey, isn't that Citadel?"

Julian glanced back. "Uh, yes, technically I am," he said.

"Dude," Night Sword said. She held out a hand. "I'm a huge fan."

"You have fans?" Charlotte asked, raising an eyebrow at Julian.

Julian shrugged. "Apparently. I don't think it's surprising, given the whole Storm Warning thing."

"But you're not even a villain anymore!"

Night Sword frowned. "He's not?"

"No." Julian sighed. "I suppose I'm not."

"Cool. Then I don't feel bad about this." Night Sword lifted her weapon and charged at Julian.

Charlotte hit her with a blast of lightning, sending her flying into the nearest building. Julian pulled up a stone wall in front of the woman, shielding her from the fight. "Stay here," he said before running to Charlotte's side.

A thud came from nearby. Charlotte turned as Cassidy jumped from a fire escape to the roof of a dumpster, and from there to the pavement. "Did I miss anything?"

"Just an attempted mugging," Charlotte said as Night Sword rose to her feet.

"It's not a mugging!" Night Sword sprinted toward them.

Cassidy took a step forward and launched a row of cactus spines from her arm at Night Sword. Night Sword lifted her weapon and swung, easily deflecting the spines. Charlotte raised a hand to fire off more lightning, but Julian stepped forward first. He extended a hand, and a sword of stone formed in his grasp. His hand tightened around the hilt.

He swung just in time to meet Night Sword's blade.

Night Sword flashed him a cold grin. "So, what made the great superhero killer Citadel switch sides?"

Julian swung again. She jumped back to avoid the blow. "Why don't you tell me what it is you're trying to steal, first?"

"Oh, that chemist's serum?" Night Sword asked. "It's supposed to give you super strength."

The woman, who peered out from behind the stone wall to watch the fight, piped up. "It's still in the trial phase! If you took it, you could die!"

"Or I could get cool powers!" Night Sword swung again. Julian ducked and slammed the side of his stone blade against her ribs, knocking her to the ground.

Julian moved to stand over Night Sword. Stone spikes rose from the ground around her and curved in, trapping her in place. "It was a nice effort, but I'm afraid your villain career ends here."

Charlotte rested a hand on her hip. "Great. Let's, uh, tie her up and drop her at the police station?" She glanced at Cassidy.

"That should be fine, since she doesn't have any superpowers. Saves us the trouble of going all the way to the super prison for a check-in." Cassidy walked toward the woman they'd saved. "Can you come with us to give a statement?"

The woman nodded. "Thank you." She took in Cassidy's costume. "You're The Cactus, right?"

"Finally, someone who knows my name!" Cassidy spun around. "You guys hear that?"

The woman leaned over to peer around her. "And I recognize Stormbringer, too, but—is that really Citadel?"

"He's helping us out. It's a long story," Charlotte told her. She glanced at Julian. "Maybe we should look into getting you a new costume."

"Hm? Oh, sure, maybe." Julian said, his mind clearly somewhere else.

Night Sword sat up and grabbed one of the spikes. "You didn't answer my question, Citadel. Why'd you give up being a villain?"

He lowered his gaze to meet hers. "Believe it or not, it's not always as fun as it looks."

"Yeah, he got tired of getting his ass kicked by heroes," Charlotte added, folding her arms.

"Hilarious." Julian took a step toward Night Sword. "Now, how are we getting her to the station?"

"You're not," Night Sword replied. She lifted her weapon and slammed the hilt against one of the spikes. Whatever the hilt was made of, it was much stronger than the blade. The spike exploded in a shower of fragments.

"I suppose I could have mentioned that I already have super strength, and was just looking for more," Night Sword said as she rose off the ground. "But you've wasted enough of my time already." She slammed the sword's hilt against another spike, clearing a path for her to escape.

CHAPTER THIRTY-NINE

Charlotte, Julian, and Cassidy rushed forward to stop Night Sword. Cassidy was the first to attack, unleashing an even greater volley of spines than before. Night Sword knocked most of them out of the air, but a few embedded themselves in her legs.

Night Sword's face twisted with pain. "Let's give you something to keep you busy," she hissed. She turned her weapon over in her hand and lunged at Cassidy, the tip of the sword pointed at Cassidy's chest.

Julian jumped into her path and summoned a shield of stone. The blade clattered against it. His jaw clenched.

Charlotte lifted her hands and drew her lightning to the surface.

Night Sword hit the stone shield with her hilt, and it exploded. Julian lifted a hand to shield his face from the spray of rubble. As his arm lowered, Night Sword's mouth moved. Whatever she said, it made Julian freeze. She lifted her weapon.

Lightning jumped from Charlotte's hands. The blade of the sword met Julian's arm.

Julian cried out in pain as the metal sliced through his skin. Night Sword pulled back her bloodstained weapon and swung again, this time at Julian's stomach. Charlotte's lightning hit her a moment later, throwing her backwards onto the concrete.

Charlotte rushed to Julian's side as he sank to his knees. "Julian," she whispered. "Julian, are you—?"

"I'm fine," he managed through gritted teeth.

Night Sword was back on her feet again, this time to run away. Cassidy sprinted after her. Charlotte watched them disappear around the corner before turning her attention back to Julian.

Julian pressed a hand to his bleeding stomach. "The wound's not that deep."

His hand was already soaked in blood. Charlotte grimaced. "You're bleeding a lot, Julian."

"I've had worse." He sucked in a deep breath. "Let's just get back to the base."

"Are you sure you can walk that far?"

"I have to." Slowly, Julian rose to his feet.

Cassidy reappeared at the end of the alley. "Sorry," she said. "I ran after her, but she got away."

Charlotte forced herself to think. "At least she didn't get the serum," she said. She looked at the woman still standing nearby, watching them with wide eyes. "Cassidy, take her and make sure she gets home safely. I'll get Julian back to the base."

"Sure." As Cassidy passed by them, she paused. "Thank you, Julian. If you hadn't jumped in the way, she would have—"

"Stabbed you in the chest?" Despite the amount of pain he seemed to be in, Julian smirked. "We'll find her again eventually. And now we know what to expect."

While Cassidy left with the chemist, Charlotte and Julian made their way to the alley with the passage entrance. She tried not to stare at him, but she kept eyeing his bleeding arm and the hand pressed to his abdomen.

They were almost to the front door when Julian stumbled. Charlotte reached out to grab him before he could fall.

"Thanks," he muttered. He shook his head. "I still can't believe she got me."

"Just because she's new, doesn't mean she's not good." Charlotte grabbed the door and threw it open. "And she did run away, so I'd call that a victory."

Julian chuckled, then immediately winced in pain. "Guess so."

They stepped inside. Charlotte still had one hand on his arm, and the other on his opposite shoulder.

"You guys back already?" Harper called from the living room.

"Yeah, Julian's injured. We need the first aid kit."

"Wait—" Julian started.

Harper was already sprinting into the entryway. "What happened?" Her eyes widened when she saw Julian. "Oh my god."

"I'm fine!" Julian insisted. "Get me some bandages and I'll be good as new."

"Is Spencer back yet?" Charlotte asked.

"No, not yet," Harper said. "Where's the first aid kit?"

Charlotte nodded toward a closet door off the dining room. "I think Spencer said there's one in there. Could you bring it up to Julian's room when you find it?"

While Harper ran into the dining room, Charlotte and Julian headed up the stairs to his room. Charlotte finally let go of him as he sat down on his bed. He pulled off his mask and tossed it aside. "I'd hate to bleed out all over my sheets."

"Here, wanna sit on the floor?" Charlotte held out a hand to help him.

"I've got it." Julian slid off the bed and sank to the carpet.

Charlotte swept her gaze over her room. Her attention settled on the windowsill, where the succulent she'd gifted him sat. It was much bigger than it had been when she'd bought it, despite how little time had passed, and a tiny red blossom had sprouted from its side. She suspected there was more than just a little extra sunlight at play.

The door that Charlotte had left ajar swung the rest of the way open. "Found it," Harper said as she walked in. She held out a small bag to Charlotte.

Charlotte took the bag and sat down on the floor next to Julian. "Do you wanna deal with this by yourself?" she asked as she opened it.

Julian pulled his bloody hand away from his stomach and winced. "I'm not going to be able to wrap my arm myself."

A door opened downstairs.

"I'll go see who it is," Harper said. She hurried out of the room.

Charlotte pulled a bottle of disinfectant out of the bag and a roll of bandages. "Okay," she muttered to herself.

Julian reached up to unfasten his cape. "You can handle blood, right?" he asked as he tossed it aside.

"Of course I can," Charlotte said, though her voice had picked up a faint tremble. "I was fine when you cut my arm open."

"You didn't seem fine." Julian's hands moved to the bottom of his suit's shirt.

Charlotte swallowed. "Okay, yeah, but it wasn't because of the blood." She lowered her gaze. "It did look like she cut you pretty deep, though."

Julian pulled his shirt up over his head, bringing his wounds into the light. Charlotte winced. There was even more blood than she'd realized.

"Here, I'll do it myself, it's fine—" Julian reached for the disinfectant.

"No," Charlotte said, determination setting in. She yanked the bottle away before he could grab it. "I've got it." She uncapped it, carefully took his arm in her hand, and tipped the bottle. Disinfectant poured onto the gash across his upper arm, mixing with the blood.

Julian flinched. Charlotte instinctively pulled back, lifting the bottle away from him.

"Charlotte," Julian said, his voice strained. "I need you to ignore how much pain I'm in and keep going. Okay?"

Charlotte nodded and went back to pouring the disinfectant on the wound. Tried not to focus on the muscle under her hand. Or on Julian's skin pressed against hers. The blood washed away.

She had to reposition herself to get to the gash on his stomach. Julian adjusted one of his legs to let her move closer. He leaned his head back against the bed and squeezed his eyes shut. The shallow rise and fall of his chest distracted Charlotte for a moment.

With a shaky hand, she resumed pouring.

"I should have been able to beat her," Julian said quietly. "Easily. But..." He grimaced as he trailed off.

Charlotte frowned. "But what?"

He shook his head. "Never mind."

Charlotte pulled back and put the cap back on the disinfectant. "It looked like she said something to you," she said. "Right before she got your arm."

Julian sighed. "She said—I don't know, something about how she wanted to kill the new Storm Warning and take my place." He lifted his head. His eyes found hers. "And—it was like looking in a mirror, for a second there."

"Oh," was all Charlotte managed to say.

Footsteps came up the stairs. Harper appeared in the doorway. "Spencer's back. Cassidy, too."

Already? The woman must not have lived far from where they'd fought Night Sword.

Spencer appeared behind Harper and squeezed past her, a small bag in hand. He tossed it to Charlotte. "There's a special medication in there. Put it on the wounds. It'll help them close up fast," he said. "It's expensive and hard to get, but we need him healed before the fight with Blazar."

"Thanks," Charlotte said. She reached into the bag and pulled out a white tube. "How'd your exam go?"

"Decent." Spencer looked at Julian. "Cassidy told me what happened," he said. "Sounds like you did good."

Surprise flashed across Julian's face. "Thanks."

"Sorry you got stabbed on your first shift." Spencer turned around and walked back to the door. "I told the other heroes to be here by nine for training. Try to be up by then."

"Sure thing," Charlotte told him. "Good night."

"Good night!" Spencer disappeared into the hallway. After one last glance at Charlotte and Julian, and a flash of what looked suspiciously like a smirk, Harper followed Spencer out and pulled the door shut behind her.

Charlotte twisted the lid off the medication and held the tube over Julian's arm. A fluorescent blue gel oozed out.

"This is safe, right?" Julian asked, lifting an eyebrow.

"I'd say there's a fifty-fifty chance it would give you superpowers, but you already have those," Charlotte said. "So, maybe it'll turn your skin blue?"

Julian laughed. He appeared to immediately regret it. "Ow," he said, wincing.

Charlotte couldn't help but chuckle. "Sorry," she said. "I'll try to be less funny."

Julian smiled, and it didn't fade even as she spread the medication across his arm, though he did flinch a couple of times.

"This...this isn't so bad," he said. "Right?"

Charlotte's eyes darted up to meet his. It wasn't. It wasn't bad at all. She managed a quick smile before glancing back at his arm to make sure she'd covered the wound.

Julian held out a hand. "Here, I'll put it on my stomach, if you want to start bandaging my arm."

"Sure." As Charlotte handed the tube to him, she let her hand linger against his a moment longer than she needed to.

They worked in silence for a minute, Charlotte wrapping his upper arm while he covered his other wound in medication.

"Thanks for letting me help you," Charlotte said as she tied off the bandage.

"Well, I'm not a complete idiot," Julian replied. He capped the tube and set it down.

Charlotte's gaze lowered to his stomach. She lifted the roll of bandages. "I think this part will be easier if you stand up."

Julian rose to his feet. She followed. Now that the panic from the fight was wearing off—and the blood washed away—her mind was starting to focus on other things. Like how extremely shirtless he was. She forced herself to move quickly as she bandaged up his abdomen.

Once she was done, she gathered up the first aid supplies and put them back in the bag. "Do you need anything else?" she asked.

When Julian didn't answer, Charlotte looked up to find him staring at her. "No," he finally said. "Sorry, no, I'm okay. Good night."

Part of her didn't want to leave him.

But he still had to be in a lot of pain, and they both needed rest, and she wasn't sure she was quite ready to move on from everything. Not yet.

She nodded. "Good night, Julian."

She stepped out into the hallway and returned to her room.

CHAPTER FORTY

Charlotte was the first one in the kitchen the next morning. She was starving, so she dug around in the cupboards until she found a loaf of bread. She stuck two pieces in the toaster.

By the time Julian entered a few minutes later, she had her toast on a plate. "Plain toast?" he asked as she picked one up, lifting an eyebrow.

"It has butter on it!" Charlotte protested. "We don't have any other toast ingredients."

"It looks a little burned." Julian rested his hands on the edge of the counter.

"Yeah, I think that toaster's got issues." Charlotte set the toast back down on the plate. "How are you? Your cuts, I mean?"

Julian straightened up and pulled back the bandage on his upper arm, revealing a scar. "That medication worked even faster than I expected."

"Told you that stuff's good," Spencer said as he walked in. He frowned. "Did something burn?"

"Your toaster sucks," Charlotte told him.

"Oh, yeah, that thing's basically decoration."

Charlotte glanced at Julian. "I hate to ask, but..."

He laughed and moved toward the fridge. "I'll make eggs. Go sit down."

Charlotte and Spencer sat down at the dining table. Charlotte pulled out her phone to check emails but kept throwing glances toward the kitchen. Toward Julian.

Spencer cleared his throat. When Charlotte looked at him, he had a sly smile on his lips. "Honestly, he makes a decent hero."

Charlotte's face burned. She looked down, starting to smile herself. "You think?"

"You still like him, don't you?" Spencer asked quietly.

"Now that I'm not totally pissed off at him anymore? Yeah." Charlotte sighed. "I feel bad that I do. Like I'm not supposed to."

"He has a lot of work to do to make up for what he did." Spencer gave a slight shrug. "But it seems like he's willing to try. And I want him to try. The city would be better off with him helping instead of locked up in a cell."

"I agree," Charlotte said. "I guess I'm just afraid of what the other heroes would think." She lowered her gaze. "Of what you would think."

"You should do what you think is right, Charlie. As long as you're doing that, I'm with you."

Charlotte pressed her lips together and nodded. "I don't know if I'm quite ready yet, but...thank you."

The other heroes arrived soon after, and Harper dragged herself downstairs two minutes before the clock hit nine. Julian brought eggs into the dining room, along with a plate of French toast.

"There's not much, but that bread was getting close to expiring," he said. Two of the darker pieces appeared to have been salvaged from Charlotte's initial breakfast attempt, and he took those for himself.

The heroes eagerly started putting food on their plates. Charlotte was cutting off her first piece of toast when Wendy got her attention.

"Charlotte," Wendy said. "Have you remembered anything else about Blazar?"

"Sort of," Charlotte replied. "I was reading through his journals again last night, and I had some dreams about fighting him. But I haven't seen anything that will help us, yet." She lifted her fork to her mouth. "I'll read some more this afternoon. There has to be something."

"You'll have plenty of time to read," Spencer said. "We're only going to train until lunch." He lifted an eyebrow. "And tonight, we're going out."

"Out?" Julian asked.

"Tomorrow's going to be even tougher than today," Spencer said.

Charlotte swallowed her food. "Why?"

"Because it's the day before Friday. This is our last chance to relax." Spencer shrugged.

"Don't get me wrong, I'm totally on board with this," Wendy said. "And glad I cleared my schedule like you asked. I'm just surprised you're the one suggesting it."

Charlotte was too, at first, but this was actually pretty typical for Spencer. He worked his ass off to get everything done, but once he'd done what was needed to ace his classes, he surprisingly loved parties.

"I'm still confused," Julian said. "Where are we going?"

"It's a karaoke bar and grill on Gold Street called Gerard's," Spencer said. "It's pretty far from Blazar's base. I doubt he'd be anywhere near this part of town."

"You're definitely right about that." Julian rolled his eyes. "He prefers high-end places. Mostly on the north side."

"I figured as much." Spencer glanced at Harper. "But the other reason I picked the place is that they have a costume night every other Wednesday. People who dress up get half off their meal. I figured we could use that to get Harper in without too many questions."

Harper, who'd started to look glum as Spencer described the place, lit up. "I can come?"

"Just try not to move your wings too much. If anyone asks too many questions about where you got them, you're a cosplayer." Spencer lifted an eyebrow. "But you won't be able to drink, obviously."

"Fine by me," Harper said with a smirk. "That means I get to watch Julian act like an idiot."

"I don't act like an idiot," Julian muttered.

Harper turned to Spencer. "You did say they have karaoke, didn't you?"

"Yep."

Harper grinned.

"But if we want to party, we have to earn it," Spencer added. "So, eat up, then we're headed to our training spot."

They took Jack's SUV again. The other heroes must have trained out here before, because Jack needed no instructions to drive the group to a quiet clearing about forty minutes outside of the city, even farther than where Charlotte and Julian had gone to practice.

Charlotte primarily focused on flying, though she did return to the ground now and then for quick combat matches with the others. Everyone else already had a pretty good grip on their abilities, so Spencer didn't want them to waste too much energy before the big fight.

Julian spent his time at the edge of the clearing, twirling stone blades in his hands and throwing them at trees. Charlotte tried not to let him distract her.

Finally, not long after noon rolled around, Spencer cupped his hands around his mouth and shouted, "Okay, let's wrap it up!"

Charlotte lowered herself back to the earth. "Charlotte," Julian said as she touched down at the edge of the clearing. He lifted his fists. "Quick match?"

She smirked. "Sure, if you're ready to lose." She threw the first punch, only putting a fraction of her strength into it. Julian sidestepped the attack.

The two circled each other as they dodged each other's blows. Finally, Charlotte stepped aside slowly enough for Julian's fist to graze her shoulder. The blow barely moved her, though, and as he stepped forward, she grabbed him and pushed him into the nearest tree.

"I caught up to you pretty quickly, didn't I?" she asked.

His head turned to the side, letting her see the smile on the corner of his mouth. "I think I'm just a really good teacher."

Charlotte leaned closer and lowered her voice. "So, you agree that I won?"

Julian cleared his throat. "Yeah," he said. "Yeah, you won."

They joined the others climbing back into the SUV. Julian wound up between Charlotte and Harper this time, and Charlotte's heart skipped a beat every time a sharp turn made her leg brush against his.

Back at the base, Spencer gave strict orders for everyone to "chill out until dinner." "Except you, Julian," he said.

Julian stopped at the foot of the staircase and glanced back. "Hm?"

"We're going to go add your fingerprints to the entrance scanners," Spencer said. "Mind you, they can always be deleted."

"Noted," Julian replied as he followed Spencer to the door.

As the door closed behind them, Charlotte walked to the living room to pick up where she'd left off with Storm Warning's journals.

Harper entered a few minutes later and sat at the other end of the couch. She picked up the remote and nearly turned the TV on before she paused. "Is it okay if I watch a show?" she asked, thumb hovering over the power button.

"Go ahead," Charlotte said as she turned a page. "I wouldn't mind a little background noise."

While Harper watched TV, Charlotte skimmed a dozen accounts of Storm Warning's battles. She found several on Blazar, but none ended with Blazar getting seriously injured before he ran off. When she reached the end of the notebook, she sighed in frustration and looked at the rest of the stack. There was still a lot to get through.

Julian and Spencer returned not long after she started the next journal. While Spencer headed upstairs, Julian came into the living room and sat down between her and Harper.

"Did you remember anything else?" he asked.

"Still nothing." Charlotte shook her head. "Sorry."

"It'll be okay," Julian said. "With all of us fighting Blazar, something's bound to stick. And you still have all of tomorrow to go through Storm Warning—Oliver's memories."

He was right. No need to panic. Yet. "I'll find something," Charlotte said, more to herself than him. "I know I will." She looked at him. "What are you going to do now?"

Julian stood up. "My wounds are feeling a bit achy. Spencer said they need a little more time to heal, so I'm gonna go rest until dinner."

"Good idea," Charlotte told him. "See you then."

"See you." Julian gave Harper a quick wave and left the room.

"So..." Harper said slowly, the moment he was gone.

Charlotte raised an eyebrow. "So?"

"Thanks for not, like, murdering him." Harper picked up the remote and turned the TV volume down. "And for helping him rescue me. And—" She hesitated. "You know, if it weren't for you, both of us would still be stuck with Blazar."

"You're welcome." Charlotte gave her a small smile. "I guess Julian's not so bad, when he's not robbing banks."

"Yeah. Kind of a dumbass, though," Harper said. "I had to tell him to be less weird when he texted you."

Charlotte laughed. "Oh, that was you? I was wondering what made him stop sounding so... formal."

"He picked up 'War Cry Ultimate: Apocalypse' pretty quickly, so maybe he's not a total lost cause."

"The video game?" Charlotte asked. She recognized the name from commercials that were mostly gunfire and explosions.

"Yep." Harper's face lit up. "Oh, finally," she said as she brought the TV volume back up. "I've been waiting for this guy to tell his fiancée he doesn't like the color scheme for twenty minutes!"

Still smiling, Charlotte went back to reading the journals.

At five o'clock, the others began to gather in the living room. Spencer was the first to arrive, followed by Cassidy and Wendy, then Jack, and finally, Julian. Wendy brought a bag from a party store with stuff Harper could use to throw together an insect costume, including a headband with antennae and a baggy, shimmery blue dress that looked to be mostly made of sequins.

On the walk to Gerard's, Charlotte told Spencer about the assignments she still had to do for her classes to make up for not being there, though she kept part of her attention on Julian and Harper as they walked a few feet ahead.

"You look anxious," Spencer finally said as they entered Gerard's. "Is it the school stuff?"

Charlotte sighed. "No, not really. I guess it's just—" Her voice lowered. "Blazar."

"Hey, that's something to worry about tomorrow, okay? There's literally nothing we can do about it right now."

A waiter approached them and eyed their group. "Seven? You're in luck, I just cleared a large table, if you don't mind being near the karaoke stage."

"That's perfect," Spencer said. "Thank you."

They were escorted to a large corner booth. Charlotte found herself between the edge of the bench and Spencer, while Julian was seated directly across from her. As the group settled in and took menus from the waiter, Charlotte's mind still continued to jump between Blazar and the journals and her frustration.

"Can I get you all started with drinks?" the waiter asked.

Wendy, Jack, and Cassidy placed their orders first. Julian lifted his hand and held up two fingers. "Bring me a couple of margaritas."

"Something to eat, first," Spencer said sternly.

Julian raised an eyebrow. "You said we were here to have fun."

"Yeah, to have fun, not get sick."

"Fine, make that one," Julian told the waiter. "For now."

"I'll have one, too," Harper said sarcastically.

"She'll have a soda," Julian said.

"Orange soda," Harper added, setting down her menu.

"Could you bring everyone a water, too?" Jack asked after Charlotte and Spencer ordered their drinks. The waiter nodded and walked away.

They ordered their food when the waiter returned, and before long, the table was littered with plates of fries and burgers and sandwiches and nachos and even more drinks. Slowly but surely, Charlotte's worries faded from her mind.

Charlotte leaned forward, resting her elbows on the table. "Julian, I'll trade you the rest of my piña colada for a couple of those garlic fries."

He slid the plate toward her with a grin. "Take as many as you'd like."

Five minutes later, they lost Julian, Harper, Jack, and Cassidy to the karaoke machine.

"Please record this," Harper said to Charlotte as she walked away. "At the very least, we can use it as blackmail."

"On it," Charlotte said, pulling out her phone.

Julian was talking animatedly to the employee by the machine, waving around the microphone in his hand. "No, no, the other ABBA song," he said.

The employee gestured to the screen in front of her. "Maybe seeing their names would help?"

Julian leaned forward and squinted at the screen for a long moment. "Yeah, yeah, yeah, that one," he finally said, pointing.

The first notes of "Gimme! Gimme! Gimme!" started playing.

"Boo!" Charlotte called jokingly. "'Lay All Your Love On Me' is the best ABBA song."

Julian pointed his microphone at her and flashed a grin. "Then come sing it when we're done."

"I'll pass, thanks. But you have fun."

Charlotte opened her phone's camera, tapped the record button, and slowly pointed it at the group. They all seemed to be too drunk to notice. Well, except Harper, who winked at Charlotte as she lifted the microphone to her mouth.

Spencer chuckled as the group started singing. "I think my new plan is to round up all the city's supervillains and stick them in therapy," he said. "It probably won't work on all of them, but I bet at least a few will get something out of it."

"I mean, the more people with superpowers on our side, the better," Charlotte replied. Though, she expected most villains would need something above your standard therapist.

Wendy nodded. Momentarily looking away from the others, she said, "It would be more useful if we convinced them to use their powers for good, instead of letting them rot away in prison. Hell, it's a better way to make up for what they've done." She sighed. "Unfortunately, some of them are just too dangerous to set free."

The song was ending. Harper waved her hand and called out to Charlotte. "Come join us, we're doing another!"

"Oh, I don't know—" Charlotte started.

Julian held up a hand and waved, a grin spread wide across his face. The sight sent Charlotte's heart racing.

Spencer shoved her out of the booth and laughed. "Just go already."

Charlotte walked up to join the group and accepted a microphone from the employee.

"Okay, fine," she said, turning to face Julian. "One song."

CHAPTER FORTY-ONE

Julian couldn't remember much leading up to the moment they left Gerard's. They definitely sang at least two or five more songs. Then, he'd been sitting back in the booth, laughing at a story Jack was telling.

The next thing he knew, Charlotte had her arm around him as they stepped out of the building.

The rest of the group was nearby. He could hear their voices. But they may as well have been speaking another language, for all he understood.

"Is my cape stupid?" Julian asked Charlotte. "Blazar thinks my cape is stupid."

Charlotte adjusted the arm she had around him. "No, no, not at all." Her other hand moved to his chest to help support him.

He wasn't sure if he believed her. "You said you didn't like capes."

She considered for a moment. "Honestly, I'd like it a lot more if it were a different color," she said. "The gold's a bit much."

Julian laughed. And then Charlotte was laughing, too.

"I could do black," he said.

"Everyone does black," Charlotte replied. "Maybe dark purple?" She laughed again. "But then you might want to change the rest of your suit, too."

"Hang on," Julian mumbled. "I need a piece of paper. I have to redesign my whole costume." He looked around and realized they were still walking outside.

"How about we save that for tomorrow?"

A minute—or ten?—later, they were walking into the base. Someone put a glass of water in Julian's hand before he and Charlotte went up the stairs. They entered Julian's room.

Charlotte pulled her arms away from him as he sat down on his bed. "Drink all that water Jack gave you, okay?"

"Okay." Julian looked up at her, at the curls framing her face, at her lips. The bedroom light was still off, leaving only the light from the hallway to spill in and illuminate her. It was the most beautiful sight he'd ever seen.

Charlotte held a hand to the side of his face and leaned down to kiss his cheek. Her lips still hovered inches away as she murmured, "Good night, Julian."

He lifted his own hand to the spot as she left, closing his door behind her, leaving him in darkness.

He smiled.

A few hours later, Julian woke up in the early morning from a nightmare. The world collapsing around him, then the sensation of being trapped in endless black. The home he'd grown up in gone.

He sat up and took in the gray light bathing his bedroom. The empty glass next to his bed. His flowering succulent.

They had one day left. Julian climbed out of bed and moved to stare out the window at the waking city. He rested his hands on the windowsill. By the time the dust settled on Friday, would he still have Charlotte? Would he still have his own life?

He had something he needed to do. Something he needed to ask someone. But if he told Charlotte, she might think it was a bad idea.

He'd have to go alone.

Julian didn't see anyone else on his way out of the base. The subway ride was just as uneventful as it had been the first time, and he arrived at Skyline High School as the first students were trickling in.

He walked directly to Ray's office and knocked on the door. It took all of his effort to steady his heart, to keep his emotions off his face.

"Come in," Ray's voice called.

Julian turned the handle. Stepped in. "Hi, Ray."

"Julian!" Ray greeted him with a smile that surprised Julian with its warmth. "Good to see you. Is Charlotte here, too?"

"Oh, uh, no. Just me." Julian eased the door shut and settled into one of the chairs.

"Well, I'm glad to see you're doing better."

"Yeah, I had, uh—" Julian cleared his throat. "I'm not sure exactly, but I'm fine now."

"Panic attack?" Ray suggested.

"I—I don't know." He wasn't sure he wanted to give a name to the feeling that had squeezed his heart and lungs. The feeling that had stirred up nausea and choked him from the inside.

Ray grabbed a sticky note off his desk. "Maybe it's a one-off thing, but I used to get them all the time. Found a great doctor." He grabbed a pen and scribbled down a name and number. "If you keep having problems, maybe give her a try?" He held the note out to Julian.

Julian stared at the paper. At the name. "Thank you," he said weakly. He couldn't deny he felt genuine gratitude.

Toward the man who'd killed his parents.

"Sorry to derail the conversation so quickly," Ray said. "What did you want to talk to me about?"

Julian stuck the note in his pocket and cleared his throat. "Oh, I was just in the area," he lied. "Figured I'd drop by and see if you'd been able to contact any other heroes."

"Oh, right." Ray sighed. "I can't say for sure how much backup you'll have. Everyone I called said they would try to make it here in time, but no one could guarantee it. I wish I had better news for you."

"Well, thank you for trying," Julian said. He hesitated. "There was something else I wanted to ask you, too."

Ray nodded. "Of course."

"I've decided to become a hero. I guess." He lowered his gaze. "But I'm terrified. Not for my own life, but... I made a lot of mistakes in the past. I don't know if the city will be able to look past them."

"I think I understand. I made mistakes too, you know. No hero is perfect."

Julian glanced up. Ray gave him a sympathetic smile. "There were times when I thought I'd turned the world against me," he continued. "No matter how hard I tried, there was collateral damage. I had to make choices to stop villains and it didn't always work out the way I hoped."

A lump formed in Julian's throat. He blinked away the sting in his eyes.

Ray's head turned so that he could stare at the wall. "It still tears me up inside, all these years later. People got killed because of things I did. And it doesn't matter to them how many I saved."

"Have you ever met any of them?" Julian asked quietly. "People you hurt?"

Ray shook his head. "I stayed away from civilians as much as possible while I was in costume. Maybe I'm a coward, deep down. I'm still terrified they'll find me, sometimes. The people I left behind."

His gaze met Julian's again before he continued. "Sorry, you were looking for encouragement, weren't you?" He managed a small smile. "Despite everything, I don't regret being Sunbeam. I can't tell you if the world would be better if I'd made different choices, but I did my best to save as many people as possible. That's all any of us can do."

Julian rose to his feet. "Thank you, Ray," he said, barely keeping his voice from breaking. "For everything."

"Of course. And good luck tomorrow," Ray said. "I'll be rooting for you."

Tomorrow. Right. Julian nodded.

He paused at the door to Ray's office. "Sorry to be a bother," he said. "But I have one last question for you. Unrelated to hero stuff."

After Ray offered some advice about getting into Skyline High School with a sizeable educational gap, Julian left the building. He wasn't sure he felt better, but he did feel different. Maybe, in time, he could find closure in what Ray had said.

There was no point telling Ray the truth, Julian decided. No point forcing him to look at the kid whose parents he'd killed. It wouldn't undo what Ray had done. And it wouldn't undo what Julian had done, either.

When he returned the base, Charlotte was awake, sitting at the dining table. "Where were you?" she asked.

"Just out for a short walk." Julian walked to the table and stood next to her. "Sorry. Were you worried?"

"A little," Charlotte said. "Just, you know, with everything going on."

Worried I was hurt, or worried I wouldn't come back? Julian decided against asking. He sat down at the table next to Charlotte. His knees brushed against hers.

"I think I'm getting close with the Blazar thing," Charlotte said. "I had more dreams about fighting him last night. But it's all a blur." She shook her head. "I felt like I was so close to figuring something out. I could feel Storm Warning putting the pieces together."

"It sounds like you're almost there," Julian said. He rested a hand on top of one of hers. "You'll get it."

She nodded.

"The memories," Julian said slowly. "You said you think some of them were triggered by you experiencing a similar event, right? Maybe, worst case, you'll remember how to hurt Blazar when you go to fight him."

"Maybe," Charlotte said. "But flashing back in the middle of a battle sounds like a great way to get killed."

"Good point." Julian sighed.

"But hey, I can fly, and he can't. So, I can probably make it work."

"Sure," Julian said. After a moment, he said, "I have a question. About Shadowmaster and Red Tempest."

Charlotte nodded.

"Why did Red Tempest give up the Eye?" Julian asked.

Charlotte blew out a deep breath. "Because he loved Shadowmaster."

Julian blinked. "Oh."

"You know, those flashbacks I had of the two of them while we were at Dove Park—I think that was before Red Tempest became a villain," Charlotte said. "They knew each other for a long time before their public rivalry started."

"And you remembered that because—" Julian started.

"Red Tempest felt the same way about Shadowmaster that I felt about you. At the park, I mean. But he fell into villainy and Shadowmaster was a hero and, well, you know the rest of the story."

Julian was still processing all that when the door opened, making him glance up in surprise. Wendy entered the base, with Jack and Cassidy behind her. "You two ready for training?" she asked.

Julian pulled his hand away from Charlotte's and stood up. "Yeah. We're ready."

CHAPTER FORTY-TWO

Training was pushed to after lunch, though Spencer was adamant that the group be done by five so that they could rest.

Julian didn't want to waste energy generating stone that he would need tomorrow, so he focused on working with Harper on her combat skills. Charlotte, meanwhile, drifted around the clearing with a notebook in her hand, still searching for something that would help them in the fight against Blazar. Cassidy used nearby trees as target practice to launch spines at, while Wendy, Jack, and Spencer took turns in practice fights.

There was one last thing they needed to sort out, but Julian already had an idea in mind when Spencer brought it up.

"We need to make sure everyone will be able to destroy the generators tomorrow," Spencer said as the heroes wrapped up their training. "I think I'll be able to handle one on my own with my power, but—"

Julian held up a hand to stop him. "If Saturn built them, it's not going to be easy to smash them up," he said. "In fact, the only thing I'd be confident using against them—besides you, Spencer—is her own tech."

Spencer raised an eyebrow.

"The bombs we stole from her at Dove Park?" Wendy asked.

Julian nodded. "I can show you all how to activate them. And we definitely have enough to blow up the generators with. It's the safest bet." He turned to Spencer. "If that fails, we'll have to hit them with everything we've got, but the moons should work."

Spencer nodded. "And that just leaves Blazar."

Charlotte, who was still hovering in the air above them, yelped in surprise. "I've got it!"

Julian looked up at her. "What—?"

As Charlotte started to wave around the notebook she was holding, her expression fell. A white glow took over her eyes. She was remembering something.

And falling.

Julian rushed forward to catch her before she hit the ground. "Charlotte?" He adjusted his hold on her. Her eyes were still open. Glowing. "Charlotte, can you hear me?"

"Blazar," she gasped. "I—I've got him. I'm so close to figuring it out—"

Her eyes closed. Electricity sparked on her fingertips, sending a shock through Julian. He grimaced but didn't let go of her. Not until her eyes opened again and they were back to their usual brown and she was looking at him and actually seeing *him*.

"I've got it," Charlotte repeated as she slid out of Julian's arms. Her feet hit the ground with a solid thud. "I know how to hurt him."

The other heroes gathered around.

"Blazar always slows down to fight, right?" Charlotte asked.

Julian nodded. It was still dizzying when Blazar appeared out of nowhere to throw a punch, but he delivered the blows themselves at normal speed. It wasn't something Julian had ever given much thought, since up until Dove Park, he'd only ever fought Blazar as part of his training.

"That is weird," Julian realized. "If he punched at super speed, he would do way more damage, wouldn't he?"

Charlotte nodded. "Storm Warning thought so, too," she said. "I remembered a fight where Storm Warning hit Blazar with lightning while he was running. Usually, he moved too fast for Storm to strike him unless they were fighting, but he got a lucky hit in."

Julian's eyes widened. "That night he came back to the Complex injured—"

"Storm Warning almost had him. Blazar was lucky he got away."

"And it's because Storm Warning hit him while he was running?" Harper asked.

"Yep," Charlotte said. "Blazar's nearly invincible ordinarily, but however his super speed works, it weakens him. When he's moving fast, it's easy to injure him."

"Okay, slight problem." Julian folded his arms. "Hitting him while he's running is going to be difficult."

"Storm Warning did it once," Charlotte pointed out. "And he didn't get many chances to try again after that." She lifted her chin. "I'll get him. I know I can."

Julian hoped she was right. This was going to be harder than simply controlling her powers. Harder than flying, even.

Spencer was the first to turn and walk toward the SUV. "Great. I'm starving. Julian, you up for making dinner?"

Julian smirked as he followed. "You know, I could also teach you all how to cook."

"Ah, but you gotta make yourself useful somehow, right." Spencer looked back at him and grinned. "I wouldn't mind getting that risotto recipe Charlotte was raving about, though."

Julian glanced at Charlotte. She folded her arms and pretended to look at something off in the trees, but he caught a hint of a smile on her lips.

"Well then," Julian said, looking forward again. "Once it's safe for me to go back to my apartment, I'll track it down for you."

The light mood of the group was short-lived, though it had barely been there in the first place. The drive back to the base was quiet, and the uneasy tension still hung between them even as they gathered in the living room. They were down to hours.

"Everyone's good to sleep here tonight, right?" Spencer asked. "We should head out before the sun's up, since we have no idea when the generators will actually be ready."

The others all confirmed they'd be staying. Julian glanced toward the kitchen. "I'll start dinner," he said.

Charlotte, who'd just sat down on the couch, jumped back to her feet. "Oh, uh, Julian. One last thing," she blurted. All eyes moved to her, and she flushed. "Just, since I'm thinking about it now. After dinner, would you want to look through the costume stuff upstairs? I figured since you're...not a villain anymore, you might want to change your look before the whole city sees you tomorrow."

"Oh, yeah. Good idea." Julian had forgotten the issue of his costume, with everything else going on. It would be best if people didn't see him and automatically assume he was on Blazar's side. Especially any other heroes that showed up.

He entered the kitchen and started pulling out vegetables and white rice. Would it be enough to simply change his costume? Maybe fighting Blazar tomorrow would prove he wasn't a villain anymore, but what if people were still skeptical afterward?

He could change his identity entirely. Take a new name, a completely different look. No one would ever have to know he was Citadel. The hardest part would be selling the fact that he had the same powers as mere coincidence.

Julian weighed his options as he cooked. By the time he was putting the food on plates and the others were coming in to eat, he was still thinking.

There wasn't much dinner conversation. While Julian's eyes were mostly on his food, he occasionally glanced up to find Charlotte looking at him. He thought he'd gotten used to...her, but something in her expression was making him nervous all over again.

When the food was gone, Julian stood up and reached for his empty plate, but Harper grabbed it first.

"I'll get the dishes. Go figure out your costume thing," Harper said. After a moment, she added, "Dumbass."

Julian rolled his eyes as he smiled. "Nice try, but you already said the nice thing." He stepped away from the table and looked at Charlotte, wanting to ask if she'd join him, scared she had no interest in helping with something he could easily do himself.

Charlotte stood up and raised an eyebrow. "Based on what you said last night, I'm guessing you want my input?"

Julian vaguely recalled the conversation they'd had about his cape after leaving the bar. "A second opinion might be good."

The other heroes were heading off to their own rooms. Despite the fact that it wasn't too late in the evening, they all whispered good nights to each other. Gave each other solemn nods.

Julian wondered what Blazar was doing right now. Would he and Saturn be arguing about every little detail of tomorrow's plan? Or would they be celebrating their nearly guaranteed success?

The base fell quiet as Julian and Charlotte stepped off the stairs. They walked to the room containing the costume pieces and clothes in silence.

"I'll probably have to go rewash the dishes once Harper's done with them," Julian said as he flipped on the light. "I don't think I've seen her clean a single thing, ever."

Charlotte laughed softly. "I'm sure she'll figure it out." She watched Julian as he moved to the closest shelf and looked it over. "I know she missed a lot, but she picks things up pretty quickly."

"Yeah. She's smart." Julian knelt down and popped open a bin on the floor next to the shelf. "And Blazar just saw her as someone who could fly and break things."

"Do you think Saturn was really trying to help her by lying about the wings?" Charlotte asked, voice softening.

"The sad thing is, I think she was." Julian selected a purple cape out of the bin. He held it up for examination. It wasn't bad, but he was hoping to find something more similar to the shape of his old one. Ideally with the same collar.

"You thinking you're gonna do the same color scheme?"

"Yeah, I thought I'd just move the colors around. And maybe make a few other adjustments." Julian looked up at her. "I was actually thinking I didn't want to change too much. I want people to see that I'm still Citadel."

Charlotte walked forward and knelt next to him. "Why's that?"

Julian swallowed. "I want them to know that villains can decide to change. And that the world would be better if they used their powers for good, even if they did wrong in the past," he said. He gave her a slight smile. "Maybe I'll even persuade a few other villains to switch sides."

Charlotte stared at him for a long moment. "Yeah," she finally said, slowly mirroring his smile. "Yeah, I think that's great."

They stood up at the same time. "It does make me wonder, though," Julian began, "if there are other villains who became heroes, and we never knew because they didn't want people to know what they were before." He wouldn't blame them for wanting to hide from their past, but it would be nice to know just how many other people were out there trying to undo their mistakes. Trying to redeem themselves.

Charlotte nodded. "I mean, it's not going to be easy. Some people will probably hold Storm Warning's death against you for the rest of your life."

"I know." Julian lifted up the cape he was holding. "I want to find something a little closer to my old cape in this color. And I'll keep my gold mask." He looked at Charlotte. "Now I just have to figure everything else out."

"I'll start looking for more capes," Charlotte said. As she walked to another shelf, she added, "Maybe a black suit? I'm guessing you want a two-piece that looks like your old one, too?"

"That sounds good." Julian went back to digging through the bin he'd found the first cape in. "I guess I could switch to purple boots and gloves, then."

"Or these."

Julian glanced over. Charlotte was holding a pair of boots that were a dark shade of gold, like his mask. Almost as shiny, too. "That's a lot," he said.

"Not as much as your old cape was," Charlotte replied with a smirk.

"Touché." Julian held up his hands, and Charlotte tossed the shoes to him. Well, they were his size. Maybe it was a sign. Or maybe he should come up with a better way to pick out clothes.

Another twenty minutes of digging turned up a cape that was surprisingly close in style to his old one, in a more vibrant shade of purple. Charlotte found him some gloves in the same color. Julian, meanwhile, located some black suit pieces that felt as sturdy as his old costume had been.

"Is that everything?" Charlotte asked as she set what she'd found on top of the pile in his arms.

"I think so."

"Here, why don't you change into this and come show me?" Charlotte asked. "I'll just...wait in my room."

Right now? Julian looked down at the pile. There wouldn't be much time tomorrow, he supposed. "Sure," he said.

Charlotte left, and he quickly put everything on. It really did feel like his old costume with the colors changed around. A bit stiffer, maybe, but it shouldn't take long to break it in.

He liked it.

Heart pounding, he walked upstairs to Charlotte's room. Charlotte, who'd been sitting at the edge of her bed, jumped up when he entered.

"I like it!" she exclaimed. She immediately winced. Quieter, she said, "I think people are trying to rest." She moved past Julian to ease the door shut.

"But you like it?" Julian asked, turning to watch her.

"Yeah." Charlotte faced him. "I mean, the important thing is that you do, but—"

"I do. I think it'll work great." Julian grinned at her. "I could go grab the mask to complete the look, but—"

"Let's save it for tomorrow." Charlotte folded her arms and looked him up and down. "Yeah, it's great. Still Citadel, but different." She brought her gaze back up to his eyes and smiled.

His heart jumped. He took a step forward and, slowly, rested his hands on her shoulders. "Thank you for not giving up on me," he said quietly.

Charlotte flushed. "Yeah, well, thank you for helping us. I know it hasn't been easy."

"I brought a lot of it on myself."

"Not all of it." The corner of Charlotte's lips turned up in a smile. "But, yeah, a lot."

Julian chuckled, hoping it was enough to hide what a mess he was spiraling into underneath. He didn't want to let go, but he lowered his hands and took a step back. "I guess I'll see you in the morning, then." He started toward the door.

Charlotte grabbed his arm. "Wait, Julian," she said, her voice soft.

Confused, Julian turned. "What?"

She took another step forward, narrowing the space between them, her eyes fixed to his. She let go of his arm and, slowly, her hands moved up to his neck to unfasten his cape. It fell to the floor.

Julian tried to keep his heart under control, unable to let himself believe that even though she'd stopped blasting him with lightning, stopped reminding him that he'd lied to her and making jabs about the other things he'd done, that she was ready to go back to what they'd had before.

Her hands slid up to the sides of his face. She pulled him in, bringing his lips to hers. Muffling his small noise of surprise. But he sank into the kiss eagerly, eyes drifting shut.

After a long moment, they separated. Their eyes met.

And then their lips were back together, and they were wrapping their arms around each other, desperately pulling each other closer. Not close enough. Never close enough. One of Julian's hands moved up Charlotte's back, while hers slid up his neck. Her fingers ran through his hair.

Together, they stumbled to the bed.

Charlotte brought him down with her. On top of her. Julian moved his hands to her hips as he kissed her and realized he was still wearing his gloves. Still kissing her, still savoring the sighs of pleasure slipping from her lips, he tore them off and tossed them...somewhere. He moved his bare hand to the side of her face and pulled back. Brushed a thumb across her skin.

The hand on his shoulder pulled him closer to her.

"Wait, Charlotte," Julian stammered, suddenly unsure of himself again. He moved his hand, resting it against the bed next to her. "Are you—are you sure you want me?"

Charlotte took his face in her hands again as she looked up into his eyes. Breathing hard, she said, "That depends. Are you the guy who's gonna help me save New Atlas tomorrow?"

"Yes." He'd save New Atlas for her. He'd save the world for her. The hand he had pressed against the bed tightened, bunching up her sheets.

"Then yes, Julian. I want you," Charlotte said as she pulled him back in.

CHAPTER FORTY-THREE

In the early hours of the morning, when the only light creeping in through the gap in the curtains came from nearby buildings and streetlights below, Charlotte was the first to open her eyes.

She spent a minute watching the gentle rise and fall of Julian's chest. Studying the angles of his face. Wishing she didn't have to wake him up. She'd never seen him look this peaceful.

"Come on," she murmured as she rested a hand on his shoulder. She gently shook him. "We have to go stop Blazar."

Julian stirred. His eyes opened slowly. "Do I want to know what time it is?"

"A little after five."

Sighing, he sat up. The two exchanged an exhausted glance and, despite the day that loomed ahead, a small laugh. Julian took Charlotte's face in his hand and studied her lips for a long moment before kissing her with surprising ferocity. Ferocity that made her head spin.

"Okay," he said breathlessly. "But let's do that again when we're done with him."

Blushing, Charlotte nodded. She didn't feel the need to say what they both had to be thinking: *If we survive.*

Someone's alarm rang in one of the nearby rooms, marking the start of the frenzy. By the time Charlotte and Julian were dressed in their costumes and headed down the stairs, the other heroes were up and running around with half eaten granola bars, searching for their shoes or gloves and whispering words of encouragement to each other.

Charlotte slid her hand into Julian's.

Spencer emerged from the stairs behind them, a black bag in his hand. "Everyone ready?" he called. He wore his Collider armor, and his helmet was tucked under the arm opposite the bag.

The others made their way into the entryway. "Ready as we'll ever be," Wendy said as she pulled her wig up into its usual ponytail.

Spencer reached into the bag and pulled out one of the moons of Saturn. "We're going to split up to destroy the generators as quickly as possible. I'll take the one at the south end of the city." He tossed the bomb to Wendy. "Wendy, can you handle the baseball fields?"

"Will do," Wendy said.

Spencer tossed her a second bomb. "We got seven, so everyone else can take two to each generator. I'll make do with one." His gaze moved to Jack and Cassidy. "Can you two deal with the generator where the restaurant used to be?"

Jack gave him a thumbs up. "We'll get it," they said. Cassidy nodded.

After distributing bombs to those two, Spencer handed one to Julian and one to Harper. "You two take the bank lot."

"What about me?" Charlotte asked, squeezing Julian's hand.

"I think it'll be best if you stay up in the air, keeping an eye out for Blazar. Or anyone who needs help."

Charlotte nodded. "Got it."

"Once you activate the bombs, you'll have ten seconds until they go off," Julian told the others. "The blasts are strong, but you'll be fine as long as you get at least twenty feet away."

"And we just twist the top and bottom in opposite directions, right?" Jack asked.

"Yeah. It takes a fair amount of strength, so they can't be activated on accident."

"Any last questions?" Spencer asked.

Silence.

"Great." Spencer slid his helmet on. Voice warped, he said, "Let's go."

Julian lifted his half mask to his face as the heroes moved to the door. Before she put on her helmet, Charlotte pressed one last kiss to the side of his face.

Harper elbowed Julian in the side as she walked by. "All right, come on, dork. Let's go blow something up." She glanced back at Charlotte and grinned as she raised her helmet to her head.

Charlotte followed them all out. In the alley outside the base, the group split up. Once the heroes had all disappeared from sight, Charlotte took a deep breath and flew straight up into the air.

High above the city, she could see the first rays of sunlight breaking the horizon. The golden glow inched its way over New Atlas, bouncing off of buildings and cars, and illuminating Blazar as he stepped onto the balcony of the Complex.

CHAPTER FORTY-FOUR

The generator was ten feet tall. Boxes poking out of the sides here and there disrupted its cylindrical form, covered in blinking lights and sometimes connected with colorful wires. It had been set up right smack in the middle of the lot, crushing dozens of the flowers Julian had grown.

It was a stupid thing to be upset about, given everything else Blazar and Saturn had done, but it pissed him off all the same.

"It's hideous," Harper said, hands resting on her hips.

"Blazar clearly doesn't care about presentation." Julian walked up to the generator, his hand tightening around the moon bomb. As he neared it, he couldn't help but throw a glance back at the sky, at the distant figure of Charlotte hovering above the city.

"Julian!" Harper shouted. "Look out—!"

Something slammed into him. Someone. Julian's back hit the ground and the bomb rolled from his grasp.

Lord Saturn stood over him. "You should run before Blazar finds you."

"No." Julian rolled to the side, summoned a staff of stone, and swung at her as he jumped to his feet. Her rocket boots turned on, carrying her up and out of his reach.

"Harper, distract her!" Julian dove for the bomb lying on the ground nearby. Saturn flew toward him, but Harper crashed into her first. They flew toward the edge of the lot while Julian grabbed the bomb and ran back to the generator. He was a few feet away when it let out a low-pitched whine. More lights came on.

"Shit," he muttered. He adjusted his grip on the bomb and prepared to twist it.

A blast of energy rolled out from the generator in every direction, knocking him backward. This time, he kept his grip on the bomb. Unfortunately, it didn't do him much good. A white beam of light shot out of the top of the generator, bending in an arc toward the center of the city.

Saturn was next to Julian again, grabbing his arm. She yanked the bomb from his hands and threw him back from the machine. As he pushed himself up from the ground, he frantically searched the lot for Harper. She was nearby, rising on shaky legs.

"Harper!" he yelled.

"I'm okay." Harper's voice trembled. Her hands tightened into fists. "She took my bomb."

Julian glanced back at Saturn. She lifted a few feet into the air, fire shooting from the bottom of her boots. "I told you you'd fail." Behind her, the beam of light expanded into a semi-transparent wall of energy. As it stretched out from the lot, it grazed nearby buildings, turning entire walls to rubble in some places.

"No," Julian hissed. He stood and charged at Saturn. She shot up a few more feet. Harper flew over Julian's head and threw a fist. Saturn dodged the blow. Harper flew past her.

Julian turned and watched the forcefield. It expanded farther around the city, pushing, pushing, until—

It stopped.

As Julian turned in a slow circle, assessing the extent of the forcefield, he realized what had happened. He let out a cold laugh. The wall only formed one-fourth of the dome it was supposed to have created over New Atlas.

"They did it," he said, turning to face Saturn. "They destroyed the other generators."

Saturn dodged another attack from Harper and dropped back to the ground. "Damn it, Julian." She reached to her belt and grabbed a phone. "All you're doing is making Blazar angrier!"

Harper landed next to Julian. "What's she doing?"

Saturn tapped the screen. The phone went back to her belt. "We had about a week's worth of power," she said. "Now it's going to burn out by the end of the day."

The generator beeped.

"What did you just do?" Julian demanded.

"We only need one generator to make the full forcefield," Saturn said. "I made four to maximize energy storage."

Julian's eyes widened as the forcefield wall began to spread again, continuing its slow march around New Atlas.

CHAPTER FORTY-FIVE

The beam of light sent a spike of panic through Charlotte. What had stopped Julian and Harper from blowing up their generator?

She'd lost sight of Blazar when he went back inside the Complex, but he was bound to make an appearance at any moment. Until then, she should probably stay in place. Keep an eye out for him.

But the forcefield was spreading again, threatening to trap all of New Atlas, even with three of the generators gone.

Charlotte shot forward through the air, toward the lot. Toward the forcefield. Toward Julian.

She was halfway there when the first fire appeared.

Charlotte came to a halt in midair and looked down. All she glimpsed of Blazar was a blur of red. More flames appeared in his path, burning a line down the middle of the street. Cars screeched to sudden stops, often slamming into others. People climbed out of their vehicles and hurried into nearby buildings.

Fists clenching, Charlotte filled the air above the street with clouds and unleashed a torrent of rain to extinguish the flames. She lifted herself higher, scanning for another glimpse of Blazar. Smoke rose from behind the skyscraper to her right. When she flew around the corner, she was greeted with an even bigger fire.

She summoned more rain and went back to her search. The sound of nearby screams drew her another street over. Despite the lack of fire, the cars here had been abandoned as well.

In the middle of the road, Blazar stood perfectly still, his head tipped back. Watching her. He flashed a cold grin.

Charlotte lowered herself slowly, terrified of bringing herself into his reach. "Blazar!" she yelled.

"Stormbringer!" he replied with a laugh. "So nice to formally meet you, after you stole my children away from me."

Charlotte lifted a hand, ready to blast him, but she held back. The last thing she wanted was him running off again. "They're not your children."

"Legally, I did adopt them."

"And you threw one of them off a building!"

Blazar laughed again. "Funny, he was Julian when I let him go. You know his real identity, then." His head tipped to the side. "I can't believe you saved him! He killed Storm Warning, after all."

He didn't know she was Charlotte. The girl he'd forced Julian to reveal his identity to. "He certainly surprised me," she said.

"You and me, both." Blazar folded his arms. "It makes no sense. He had everything—"

Hoping to take Blazar by surprise, Charlotte unleashed a bolt of lightning from the clouds gathering overhead. Blazar shot away from her in a flash of red. She'd missed.

Charlotte dropped to the ground. She had to let him get closer. "Blazar!" she yelled. "Come out and fight me, if you're not a coward!"

Blazar reappeared in front of her and swung his fist into her stomach. Gritting her teeth, Charlotte grabbed his wrist and let out a pulse of electricity. He laughed as it hit him. "Was that supposed to hurt?" He pulled his arm free and disappeared.

"How did you get Julian to side with you?" Blazar asked from behind her. She whirled around. "He could have taken the stormoid from you easily." He paused. "I give him a lot of shit, but he is powerful when he focuses."

Charlotte tried to punch him, but she missed by a longshot. He raced around her in circles for a few seconds before stopping again at her right.

"Really," Blazar said. "I'm dying to know."

"You would never understand," Charlotte told him.

"Try me." Blazar went back to being a blur around her. Now was the perfect chance to hit him while he was weak. Charlotte spread her arms out to either side. Arcs of lightning jumped from her skin, racing toward Blazar.

He was out of her path before the lightning reached him.

Blazar was behind Charlotte again. She turned. His eyes narrowed.

"I know you, don't I?" he asked.

"What?"

"It shouldn't have taken me this long to recognize your voice, but I guess I never gave you much thought in the first place." A cold grin spread across Blazar's face. "I thought you were just a distraction."

"I don't know what you're talking about," Charlotte said, hoping he hadn't noticed the way her heart sank, hoping she could convince him he was wrong.

"Charlotte...Hathaway, was it?" Blazar chuckled. "So that's why Julian didn't take the stormoid from you. That idiot fell in love with you!"

Charlotte's face flushed. "We—That's not—"

It was no use.

"This is hilarious." Blazar rubbed his chin. "Pathetic, but hilarious. And Storm Warning, of all people!"

Charlotte's eyes narrowed. "First off, it's Stormbringer." She lifted a hand. "And it's not going to matter when we kill you."

"Kill me?" Blazar took a step back. "You can certainly try, but I already had the upper hand. And now I've got another advantage."

Charlotte aimed a strike of lightning at him. He shot three feet to the left, dodging easily. She screamed in frustration. She was supposed to wait for him to run before trying to hurt him, but she didn't have a prayer of hitting him. Maybe it would be better to keep blasting him in his invulnerable state and wait for it to start hurting.

Not that she was doing great at hitting him while he stood still, either.

"Let's see," Blazar said. "Last I saw Julian, he and Harper were fighting Saturn at the bank lot."

And then he was gone.

"No!" Charlotte screamed. She shot into the air and raced toward the edge of the city, faster than she'd ever pushed herself before.

But deep down, she knew it wouldn't be fast enough.

CHAPTER FORTY-SIX

Julian slammed a disk of stone against Saturn, knocking her out of the air.

As she tumbled to the ground, Harper raced forward, wings buzzing, arms outstretched. After so many minutes fighting Saturn, desperately trying to steal back the bombs so that they could destroy the generator, they were finally on the verge of winning.

Julian risked a quick glance up at the sky and frowned. Something was moving on the other side of the forcefield. Dark figures soared through the sky. Some had capes billowing behind them.

"Harper!" he exclaimed. "Harper, there are other heroes here!"

"Gee, that sure would be great, if there wasn't a giant forcefield blocking them out!" Harper reached for one of the moons on Saturn's belt. A swing of Saturn's leg sent her flying back.

Julian charged forward to help her. They had to get the barrier down. Smoke had begun to rise in the distance, and screams and blaring horns and sirens filled the air. They needed all of the heroes they could get.

Julian jumped and summoned a platform. The stone pushed him up to Saturn as she lifted higher in the air. He reached for the bombs at her side. She twisted. Julian narrowly jumped back fast enough to avoid the flames shooting out of her boots.

"Blake!" Saturn shouted.

Oh no.

Julian looked down. Blazar had appeared at the edge of the lot. He folded his arms as he glared up at the three floating in the air above him. "Get down here. All of you."

"You're not our dad!" Harper retorted, undoubtedly with an indignant sneer on her face.

"Maybe not," Blazar said. "But if you don't want me to kill you, I'd suggest coming down."

"How are you going to kill me if I don't come down there?"

"Sophia!"

"Blake, leave her out of this," Saturn said. "She's not a threat."

"No, but she is a problem." Blazar waved a hand as he spoke. "So, you deal with her, and I'm going to deal with Julian."

Julian laughed and held out his arms. "Come and get me, then!"

Blazar vanished from sight.

Even though there should have been no way for Blazar to get in the air, Julian's heart dropped. He turned in circles, searching for Blazar, for a red flash, for any sign of the man. Panic quickened his pulse.

"Where did he go?" Julian demanded.

Then he glimpsed it. A blur, moving through the window of a building next to the lot. And then one floor up, and then another, and then Blazar was on the roof. Racing toward the edge. Jumping. All too fast for Julian to react.

Blazar dropped to normal speed in time to grab Julian. They tumbled off the platform together.

Harper screamed and swooped toward them. Blazar's feet hit the ground. While the landing sent a jolt through Julian, Blazar was completely unfazed. Harper had almost reached them when Blazar moved back into super speed, carrying Julian away from the lot.

The world was nothing more than a blur of lights and buildings and the occasional flash of color. Julian's jaw clenched. He put all of his focus into stopping himself from being sick. Then again, maybe throwing up on Blazar would get him out of this. At the very least, it would be funny.

Or, Blazar could drop him at high enough speeds to break every bone in his body.

Blazar slowed. Not to a human speed, but slow enough that Julian could tell they'd entered a building. They raced up flights of stairs, burst through a door, and emerged on the roof of a skyscraper. Julian staggered away from Blazar the moment the man released his grip. The height was dizzying, but Julian was pretty sure his vertigo was entirely to blame on the journey up.

He only had a moment to catch his breath before Blazar grabbed his hair and pulled his head back. With his other hand, Blazar lifted a knife to Julian's neck.

"A knife?" Julian blurted. "Since when do you use knives?"

"Well, this is an unusual occasion, isn't it?" Blazar said. The edge of the blade met Julian's skin. "Grabbed it from one of the kitchens on the way up here. Looks expensive, doesn't it?"

Julian found the strength to roll his eyes. "You're going to slit my throat? That's boring."

Blazar snorted. "No, I'm not going to do that. Not yet. We have to wait for Charlotte to get here, first."

Julian's blood turned to ice. "Charlotte?" he gasped. "Why would you—?"

"Don't play dumb. I know she's Stormbringer. And I know you're in love with her." Blazar's hand tightened around Julian's arm. "I mean, really, falling for the person who got the stormoid? That had to be the stupidest possible thing you could have done!"

"You and I must have different definitions of stupid," Julian muttered.

Blazar responded with cold laughter. "No, really," he said. "How many times did she kick your ass before you gave up and ran to the heroes' side?"

Julian didn't answer. He forced himself to move his attention beyond the knife at the neck, beyond Blazar, to the rest of New Atlas.

Torrents of rain were scattered across the city, but there were still pillars of smoke reaching into the sky. Charlotte's power wouldn't be enough to put all of this out. They needed help. Plus, there was the destruction caused by the forcefield generation, and the chaos created by Blazar running through the streets.

"You're not going to win," Julian said. "Even if you kill me, even if you kill all of New Atlas's heroes, the forcefield won't last forever. The other heroes will come, and they'll kill you."

Blazar leaned in. "I'll win," he hissed into Julian's ear. "None of them can catch me. None of them can hurt me."

"You're not invincible," Julian spat back. "We know how to hurt you."

"And I know how to hurt you," Blazar replied. "You know, I thought I might kill you first. But I should save you for last, shouldn't I? You can watch Charlotte die. And—oh, what is it Damselfly calls herself? Heather?"

Julian's jaw clenched. "Her name is Harper."

"Yeah, whatever. I can't believe she joined you, too," Blazar said. "I gave her everything she wanted at the Complex."

"Not everything."

"Why do you care about her so much, anyway?" Blazar jerked Julian's head an inch to the left. The knife followed, still just barely touching his skin. "I thought you decided we weren't your family."

"You're not my father," Julian hissed. "And Saturn's not my mother. But Harper's my sister, and you're both going to pay for hurting her."

The blade nicked Julian's skin, drawing a drop of blood onto the metal.

"Enough talk," Blazar said. "Your girlfriend's here."

CHAPTER FORTY-SEVEN

By the time Charlotte reached the lot, Julian and Blazar were nowhere to be found. Lord Saturn was high in the air, staring out at the city. Harper was on the ground, on her knees, shoulders shaking.

Charlotte dropped to the ground in front of her. "Harper! What happened?"

Harper lifted her head, and the compound eyes on her helmet found Charlotte. "Blazar took Julian," she choked out. Her fingers sank into the dirt.

"I'll find him," Charlotte said. "I'll find him, but—" She glanced up at Lord Saturn. At the moons on her belt. "Harper, you need to get those bombs from Lord Saturn and destroy the generator."

Harper didn't respond.

They were running out of time. God knew what Blazar had planned with Julian. But New Atlas had to come first. Charlotte took a deep breath. "If we work together, I bet we could—"

Harper shook her head. "I'll get the generator." She forced herself up to her feet. "Go find Julian."

"Are you sure?"

Harper nodded. "I'm sure. Go."

While Harper flew up toward Saturn, Charlotte returned to the air and soared through the city as low as she dared, searching the ground for any sign of Blazar. Or Julian.

She found them standing on a roof. Julian was alive, but Blazar held a large kitchen knife against his throat.

He was waiting for Charlotte.

She sank into the air above the roof and glared at Blazar, waiting for him to speak first.

"Stormbringer!" Blazar greeted her with far too much enthusiasm. "Let's talk."

Charlotte's gaze flickered to Julian's face. He didn't give away much in his expression, and his mask made him even harder to read. "What do you want, Blazar?" she asked.

"How about this? You hand over the stormoid, and I'll give you Julian."

"Charlotte, don't!" Julian blurted.

"Julian—" Charlotte started.

"Don't give him the stormoid." Julian grimaced. "Please. The city needs you more than it needs me."

Blazar's eyes narrowed. He yanked Julian's head back. "You'd rather me kill you, Julian?"

"Don't act like you're not just going to kill me anyway!"

Charlotte glanced at the knife in Blazar's hand.

"What's it going to be?" Blazar asked. He was dropping his lighthearted facade, letting his anger claw its way onto his face and into his voice. "The stormoid, or Julian's life?"

This was going to hurt Julian. Especially if Charlotte missed. But it was better than him dying. She lifted a hand.

"Don't tell me you're stupid enough to try hitting me again," Blazar said. "All you'll do is hurt Julian." He smirked. "But that would be funny, so you're more than welcome to try."

Electricity jumped from Charlotte's palm, darted through the air, raced toward Blazar and Julian. She guided it, willing it to hit her target.

The lightning met the knife in Blazar's hand.

The blade shattered into pieces.

Julian yelped, stumbled backward, and pushed Blazar away from him. Charlotte dropped to the ground, putting herself in Blazar's path. If he ran directly at her, she'd only have a split second, but it was her best shot at hitting him.

The only way to beat his speed was to move first. Charlotte let lightning explode from her body, not knowing yet whether or not Blazar would take the bait.

He did. Blazar charged right into the field of electricity.

And screamed in pain.

As Blazar dropped to his knees, dropped out of super speed, Charlotte realized she'd unleashed too much power in her desperation to hurt him. The blast had hit Julian. He staggered backward toward the edge of the roof, doubled over in pain. His foot went over the edge.

Charlotte jumped into the air, momentarily forgetting Blazar. She flew toward Julian. Her arms wrapped around him as he went over the edge. They fell a few feet together before she carried him up.

"Julian," Charlotte gasped as she landed on a different roof, a building over from the one she'd left Blazar on. She stumbled forward. Julian didn't move in her arms, didn't respond. "Julian!"

As she laid him down on the ground, he finally let out a groan of pain. Charlotte sank to her knees. "Julian? Are you okay?"

"Well, I don't seem to be dead." Julian winced and pushed himself into a sitting position.

Charlotte placed a hand on his shoulder. "I'm so sorry. I didn't mean to use that much—"

"I'll be okay. Maybe not for a few hours, but Storm Warning's hit me harder than that." Julian lifted his hand and rested it on top of Charlotte's. "But considering how much pain I'm in, you must have hit Blazar pretty hard." He hesitated. "He was running when you hit him, right?"

"Yeah," Charlotte said. "Pretty sure."

"Then let's go see what the damage is." Grimacing, Julian climbed to his feet. Charlotte kept her hands out to steady him as he rose to his full height.

Something shot past them in a dark blur. Not as fast as Blazar, but still pretty fast.

"What was that?" Julian asked, turning in the direction the blur had gone.

A figure landed on a distant roof. Before they jumped and disappeared over the other side, Charlotte glimpsed a dark forcefield materializing around them.

"I think that was Wrecking Ball!" Charlotte whirled around. On the other side of the city, someone else swooped down from the sky toward a building split in half by the forcefield, a red cape billowing behind them. "More New Atlas heroes are out. Not just the ones on our team."

"Great," Julian said. He rested a hand on Charlotte's shoulder, and she realized he was leaning on her for support. "While they deal with all that, let's go deal with Blazar."

"Right." Charlotte looked Julian up and down. "Ready?"

"Yeah, I'm—"

He yelped in surprise as Charlotte scooped him into her arms and shot into the air.

A moment later, they landed on the roof where they'd left Blazar. He was still there, to Charlotte's relief, but he was back on his feet. He glared at them as they landed.

Julian chuckled as he slid out of Charlotte's arms. "You look terrible."

Her lightning blast had left tears in Blazar's suit, running up his arms and crisscrossing his chest. And though he was standing, his face was twisted in pain, and he had a hand pressed to his stomach.

"You look awful, too," Blazar snarled. He shot forward a few feet but stopped halfway to Charlotte and Julian. He doubled over.

"She really got you, didn't she?" Julian asked.

Charlotte grinned in pride. "Honestly, I think he might be weaker than the average person at full speed."

Blazar lifted his chin but didn't straighten up all the way. "You just got lucky." He stared daggers at them. "Like Julian did when he killed Storm Warning."

Julian shrugged. "Who cares if it's luck? We're winning."

Blazar made another attempt to charge at them. Charlotte lifted her hand and fired off more lightning. This time, he was smart enough to not run directly at her, and instead started to circle them. The first blast of lightning missed.

But he was moving much slower than he had before.

"Uh, Charlotte—" Julian started, his voice veering on anxious.

"I've got him." Charlotte watched Blazar move, getting a feel for how fast he was going. She lifted her hand. The first flames sprang to life around them. She had seconds to act.

For a heartbeat, she was Storm Warning, taking aim at Blazar. The hero's power surged through her.

She knew exactly where to aim.

A single arc of lightning burst from Charlotte's palm, striking Blazar as he stepped into the spot she'd been aiming for. His sprint came to an abrupt halt, and he collapsed to the ground.

Fire continued to burn around them. With one sweep of her arm, Charlotte summoned a torrent of rain that extinguished all of the flames within seconds.

"Oh, just you wait." Blazar slowly lifted himself to his feet. He certainly was stubborn, wasn't he?

The rain disappeared, leaving nothing behind of the fire but a few fleeting traces of smoke. Blazar continued, his chest heaving with ragged breaths. "The moment I'm back to full strength, I'm going to tear you to shreds with my bare hands—"

A distant explosion cut him off. Massive, glowing cracks shot up the walls of the forcefield, racing to the tip of the dome. Charlotte, Julian, and Blazar all tipped their heads back to watch the cracks meet in the center.

When they did, the forcefield tore open.

The gap widened rapidly. As the barrier retreated, the heroes hovering outside flew in. They spread out, racing off to deal with spreading fires or half-collapsed buildings where people were still trapped. The sky above New Atlas returned to a vibrant shade of blue.

Only moments after the last of the forcefield vanished, a new figure appeared in the distance. Charlotte's heart sank when she recognized the silhouette of Lord Saturn's helmet. And then, Harper emerged from behind the villain, darting forward to meet Charlotte and Julian on the roof.

"Harper!" Julian exclaimed in relief.

Harper landed and wrapped her arms around him. He grunted in pain. She quickly drew back. "Sorry!" she exclaimed. "Are you okay?"

"Mostly." Julian glanced behind her as Saturn touched down on the roof. "Looks like you blew up the generator, then."

"Well, actually—"

"Sophia!" Blazar flung out an arm in an angry gesture. "What the hell happened to the forcefield?"

"I took it down." Saturn stormed toward him. "Blake, look at you! You're going to get yourself killed!" She pulled off her helmet. Underneath, her expression was...terrified.

"I'm fine!"

Saturn lifted a hand and slapped him.

"Ow!" Blazar pressed a hand to the side of his face.

"We already had everything we needed." Saturn grabbed his shoulders. "Why did you have to do this?"

"Oh, come on!" Harper groaned. "He's not worth it!"

Blazar's jaw clenched. He drew back a fist and swung at Saturn. She dodged and threw him to the ground. He jumped back up and tried again. That blow sent Saturn staggering to the left. She retaliated with a roundhouse kick to his stomach. Blazar was still moving fast, but nowhere close to full speed.

Charlotte, Julian, and Harper watched as the two danced around each other, dodging each other's blows. Blazar was faster, but he'd been weakened dramatically, to the point that Saturn might have actually been tougher than him. Finally, Saturn grabbed him, threw him to the ground on his back, and drew a small blade hidden in her belt. She held it to his neck.

After a long moment, the blade fell from her hand and clattered against the roof.

"Pathetic," Blazar spat.

"All right." Julian took a step forward. "That's it. I'm ending this." He pushed Saturn away from Blazar and reached down to grab Blazar by the front of his suit. A stone platform formed beneath the two, and they shot up into the air.

CHAPTER FORTY-EIGHT

Even after watching Saturn land blows on Blazar that looked to be pretty painful, it was hard to be sure exactly how vulnerable he was. Julian glared into the man's eyes as he raised his platform up into the air, higher above New Atlas than he'd ever been.

The night Blazar had come back injured, it hadn't just been from Storm Warning's lightning. He'd had a broken arm, fractured ribs, bruises and scrapes that Julian had never seen him with before or since.

"What are you doing?" Blazar demanded.

Julian brought the platform to a gradual stop. He let Blazar fall back against the stone and rose to his full height. "Nowhere to run up here, Blazar."

"I might be a little weaker than usual right now, but you're still not strong enough to kill me." Blazar propped himself up on an elbow and peered down at the city below. "I've fallen from this high before and walked away."

"I don't doubt that," Julian replied coolly. "But you look scared. That lightning really weakened you, didn't it?"

"You don't know how much. I could still survive."

Julian summed a blade of stone and dropped to one knee. Blazar tried for a punch. Julian caught the arm. With his other hand, he held the blade to Blazar's chest. Pushed it in. Blazar hissed in pain as the blade passed through his suit. Through his skin. The first blood Julian had ever seen him bleed spilled from his body.

Blazar swung again, this time managing a blow to Julian's stomach. A weak blow, but it was enough to make Julian grimace. Blazar reached for the hand with the blade.

Julian yanked the hand back and swung, smashing his fist against Blazar's face. Satisfaction overwhelmed him at the sight of Blazar's head snapping to the left, at the man's grunt of pain.

He swung again.

Years of repressed anger, ignored feelings, denied resentment—they all boiled in Julian's blood. Burned their way to the surface. He drew his fist back, ready to deliver another blow. Blazar glared up at him, but there was resignation in his gaze. Blood trickled from his nose.

Julian's shoulders sagged. He leaned back. His rage wasn't enough to fend off the pain and exhaustion clinging to every inch of his body. And beating the shit out of Blazar before killing him, satisfying as it might be, wouldn't fix anything.

Time to end this.

Julian pushed the platform west. To the Complex. He brought the platform to a halt again directly above its roof.

One of Blazar's hands shot up to grab Julian's wrist. "Come on," Blazar gasped. "It doesn't have to end like this. We can work something out."

And there it was. Bargaining for his life. He knew he was as good as dead if he went over the edge.

"What could you possibly say to change my mind?" Julian asked. "How many people do you think died today, because of what you did?"

"Don't tell me you actually care about them."

Julian's eyes narrowed. He grabbed Blazar's suit again and rose to his feet, lifting the villain into the air. His muscles strained with the effort. "Have you ever felt guilt?" he asked. "Ever felt bad about a single thing you did?"

Blazar rolled his eyes. "Other people's feelings aren't my problem. And if you think I'm going to spend my last moments begging for forgiveness, think again."

"If you really wanted to earn forgiveness, I'd spare you." But that would never happen. If Blazar got away today, he'd keep hurting people. Killing them. And he'd never think twice about it.

"Like you?" Blazar laughed and shook his head. "No. I'd rather die than slave away for a city of people who mean nothing to me."

Julian took a step forward, bringing Blazar closer to the edge of the platform.

"Fine," Blazar hissed. "Kill me, like you killed Storm Warning. Have fun being a hero with more blood on your hands."

"There'd be more blood on my hands if I let you live." Julian took one final step. "You know what the sad part is, Blazar?"

Blazar stared at him.

"No one's going to miss you," Julian told him.

He let go.

CHAPTER FORTY-NINE

The sun shone behind Julian as he descended to the roof. Charlotte stepped forward to meet him, her heart pounding in her chest.

"Is it over?" she asked.

Julian stepped off his platform. "Just about." He turned.

In the middle of the roof, Saturn sat on the concrete, glaring at them. Harper hovered next to her, holding the rocket boots she'd taken. Without them, Saturn was too injured to make it far.

"You brought this all on yourself, Sophia," Julian said.

"I guess I did," she replied, her voice cold. "He's dead, isn't he?"

Julian nodded.

"And you're going to prison," Harper added. She glanced at Charlotte and Julian. "She is going to prison, right?"

"Definitely," Charlotte replied with a nod.

"How'd you convince her to destroy the last generator?" Julian asked Harper.

Harper shrugged. "I didn't. She saw Blazar get blasted with lightning and decided to do it herself."

"From that far away?" Charlotte asked, brow furrowing.

"I think the cameras in her helmet are telescopic," Julian said.

Behind Saturn, Jack shot up from the street and landed on the roof. "Did we do it?" they asked.

"We did it," Julian confirmed.

Jack yelled down at someone below the building, "We did it!" Turning, they added, "The other heroes are down there. And also a bunch of reporters. They still want to know what happened."

Spencer floated up and hovered in the air next to Jack. He grabbed their shoulder and pulled himself forward onto the roof. "I'll deal with Lord Saturn," he said. "Citadel, you wanna go tell those confused reporters why you just dropped Blazar out of the sky?"

Julian nodded. He turned to Charlotte and held out a hand. "Care to join me?"

She took his hand and grinned. "I think I'd better make sure you don't collapse."

"Because you accidentally hit me with lightning, you mean?"

"Key word 'accidentally.'"

Julian laughed and pulled her back a few steps onto his platform. They lifted off the roof. He carried them down to a spot in the air twenty feet above the sidewalk where Cassidy and Wendy were dealing with a growing crowd.

Charlotte cupped her hands around her mouth. "Airborne! The Cactus!" she yelled. "We still need to help the other heroes with one last sweep of the city."

Wendy raised a hand and nodded. "We're on it!"

The two of them ran off, and the frenzied crowd turned their attention to Charlotte and Julian. It looked like mostly civilians, with many waving cellphones in the air, but a few people had professional microphones and cameras.

"Stormbringer!" one woman yelled. "Are you and Citadel working together?"

Charlotte lifted her chin. "The other heroes and I wouldn't have been able to save New Atlas without him." She looked at him and smiled. "He's working with us now."

The crowd exploded into chatter. People shouted their questions, their voices getting lost as everyone tried to talk over each other.

"Citadel, why did you kill Blazar?"

"How did you start working with the heroes?"

"Didn't you work for Blazar?"

That last question got a response. "I never worked *for* Blazar," Julian said indignantly, folding his arms. "We were associates. But he was an asshole, so…"

"So, would you consider yourself a superhero now?"

It took a moment for Julian to answer, "Yes. I am."

A man with a microphone spoke. His question drowned out the crowd around him. "What made you decide to become a hero?"

Julian laughed and threw an arm around Charlotte's shoulder. "What can I say? The new Storm Warning's surprisingly charming."

Charlotte elbowed him in the side, but she was still smiling. "Actually, I kicked his ass a few times and he decided being a villain wasn't worth it."

"I think there was more to it than that."

"Sure."

"We barely had any real fights!"

Charlotte smirked. "The important thing is that he's devoted to helping New Atlas now."

"I mean, 'devoted' is a strong word," Julian muttered.

"You can come up with a better one later."

"Oh, I can do devoted." Voice lowering, he added. "I'll *show* you devoted once we get out of here—"

"And what about Damselfly?" someone else shouted, distracting Charlotte from the flush creeping onto her face.

"I think she's decided on an early retirement," Julian told them.

"And we're turning Lord Saturn over to the authorities," Charlotte added. "She's the one who built the forcefield generators for Blazar, and she'll answer for that."

More questions flew at them. Some people started climbing onto abandoned cars in an attempt to get closer to Julian's platform.

"Do we have to answer all their questions?" Julian asked, loud enough for the crowd to hear. "I mean, there was a forcefield, we destroyed it, Blazar's dead, end of story."

"Yeah, I think we're done here." Charlotte waved at the crowd. "If any villain tries to take Blazar's place, we'll be there to stop them."

Charlotte and Julian shot into the air. Julian carried them up to where the top of the forcefield had been. Charlotte laughed as the wind raced past them.

As they came to a stop, Charlotte glanced down. Cracks had appeared in the stone, offering glimpses of dirt materializing inside the platform. Green leaves sprouted from nothing and rapidly grew into flowers.

Julian set his hands on the sides of her helmet. "As much as I like the helmet, there is one thing that bothers me about it."

Charlotte lifted an eyebrow. "Oh yeah?"

He slid it off. "I can't kiss you while you're wearing it." He placed a hand on the back of her head and pulled her in.

Charlotte wrapped an arm around him as she kissed him back. Forehead pressed against his, she broke away and asked, "Are you feeling better, then?"

"Oh, no. I'm in so much pain right now." Julian kissed her again.

Charlotte laughed. "Okay, okay, once the blue's gone from my hair, I can try out a mask," she said. "But hey, at least my skull's not cracking anytime soon." She reached up a hand to take off his mask.

Green eyes met hers. He grinned. "You know, I'm pretty sure your super strength is going to be better at protecting you than whatever that helmet's made of."

Charlotte playfully jabbed a finger at his chest. "Hey, it's extra insulation, regardless of how strong I am underneath."

"I know you're saying words at me, but I'm mostly just hearing, 'Wow Julian, darling, thank you for killing Blazar, that was amazing, please kiss me.'"

"Fine, I have to give it to you, you did do good today."

"Good?"

"Yes. Good." Charlotte kissed him. "Morally speaking, I mean."

Julian's lips hovered an inch from hers. "Okay, on second thought, I might need some painkillers."

"Let's finish cleaning up the city and go home, then."

"Hm. And where would that be?" Julian rested a hand on the side of her face and smiled. "Now that Blazar's gone, both of our apartments should be safe."

Charlotte perked up. She'd forgotten all about that. "Oh, right!" She smiled. "Well, for now, I guess we should go back to the base with the other heroes. But maybe after that, we could go back to your apartment..."

Julian lifted an eyebrow.

"... and you could cook for us," Charlotte finished.

"Even though I'm seriously injured?"

"Okay, I'm starting to think you're milking it."

"Maybe a little."

They kissed, and flowers bloomed beneath them.

CHAPTER FIFTY

It was quiet in the hospital room. There was the faint hum of machinery, distant voices in the hallway, and the occasional beep, but the air felt heavy with unspoken words. Julian sat next to the bed, his hand resting on Harper's arm.

He'd been watching her sleep for nearly an hour now. Even though Wendy insisted the surgery had gone perfectly and that she'd be awake soon, he couldn't bring himself to leave her side. Besides, he wanted to be here when she woke up. To see her reaction.

Finally, her eyes fluttered open.

"Harper?" Julian leaned forward. "Harper, can you hear me?"

Her eyes moved to him. "Yeah, I can hear you, dumbass."

Oh good. She was back to her usual self already. "How do you feel?" Julian asked.

Harper pushed herself up and winced. "Awesome." She moved a hand to her back.

"Wendy said they might need to up the painkillers, if it still hurts—"

"Holy shit," Harper cut him off with wide eyes. "They're—they're really gone." She laughed. And...started crying.

"Are you okay?" Julian asked.

Smiling, Harper nodded. She sniffed. "Yeah." She ran a hand along her back again. "I just can't believe it."

The door eased open. Wendy peered in. "Sounds like someone's awake."

Julian lifted a hand in greeting. "Yeah. She's awake."

"I have another surgery to get to, but I'll stop by later to check in." Wendy waved to Harper before ducking back out.

"Can I get you anything?" Julian asked. "You probably shouldn't eat yet, but there's a TV."

Harper yawned. "Yeah, alright, TV it is. I wanna see if they're still talking about us."

In the days since the battle, news stations across the country had been repeating the story of how Citadel killed the supervillain Blazar, of how he and Stormbringer and other heroes saved New Atlas. A lot of debate had followed, particularly around Citadel. Around whether or not he could actually be called a hero.

Julian grabbed the remote from the small table by Harper's bed and turned it on. The local news was back to discussing the new subway routes being constructed on the east side of the city.

"Booooring." Harper leaned back against her pillow. "Switch to channel 12. Pranksorcist should be starting soon."

"What about Wedding Haunters?" Julian asked as he flipped through the channels.

"It's called Haunted Weddings, and the season finale was on Thursday," Harper said. "Now everyone's talking about this new show. This guy goes to people who think their house is haunted and says he'll perform an exorcism, but then he pranks them instead."

"Do they just let anyone on TV?" Julian muttered. He set the remote down as a man dressed as a priest appeared on screen, talking directly into the camera.

The door opened again. Charlotte stepped in.

Julian was on his feet in an instant. He wasn't sure when his heart was supposed to stop racing every time he saw her, but it hadn't happened yet.

"Oh, she's awake!" Charlotte exclaimed as Julian grabbed the remote to turn down the TV.

Harper waved her hand and grabbed the remote from Julian. "How about you two go talk outside while I watch my show?"

"Sounds like she's doing well," Charlotte said.

Julian smiled as they walked to the door. "Yeah. Wendy said she should be able to go home tonight."

They stepped out of the room. The door clicked shut.

"Speaking of," Julian continued. "Are you still okay to come over tonight? I know you said you have class in the morning—"

"Yeah, it's not until ten. I can help you take care of Harper tonight," Charlotte told him. "Seriously, Julian, you can relax now."

Julian blew out a breath of air. "Yeah, it's just—it's hard. I've never had this many good days in a row before."

Charlotte rested a hand on his shoulder. "Well, get used to it." After a moment, her face lit up. "Oh! Later tonight, I have some ideas for the library posters ready for you to look at it."

"Can't wait." Julian grinned. "And, uh, Harper's surprise is going to be ready for her, right?"

"Yep. Spencer, Cassidy, and Jack are there as we speak," Charlotte said. "I think between the three of them, they can figure out how to set up a video game console. Hopefully."

"As long as it's ready by the time my shift ends at five, I'll be happy," Julian told her. "After I leave the library, I'll grab my car and pick Harper up here."

"So, have everyone ready by, what, 5:45?"

"That should be perfect." Julian glanced back at the door. "Do you have time to watch TV with us for a bit?"

"I wish, but I have to drop off a portfolio before my next lecture." She rose up onto her tip toes and almost kissed him when a thought interrupted her. "One last thing! Did you wind up talking to the police?"

"Yeah, I talked to them," Julian told her.

The authorities had learned Blazar's true identity, of course, which led them to go knocking on the door of his legally adopted son, Julian Godfrey. Julian had explained to them that he'd moved out of Blake Sullivan's place the day he turned eighteen, and recently took in the man's other runaway daughter, Harper Reed. Of course, while he'd hated the man, he was still shocked that he'd kept a secret life of crime from his supposedly beloved children.

Now that they had Sophia Novak in custody, the police were attempting to identify Blazar's other former associates, Citadel and Damselfly. Sadly, Julian had been unable to help them with that.

"Sounds like you'll have to be careful," Charlotte said after he'd relayed his interaction with the authorities.

"When am I not?" Julian asked.

"I can think of a few incidents."

"Ouch, okay." With a sly grin, Julian said, "The officers didn't seem very interested in actually tracking Citadel and Damselfly down. That's a job for superheroes, and none of them have plans to stop me now that I'm on their side." They might not fully trust him, but they seemed willing to give him a chance.

"That's comforting." Charlotte finally kissed him. "Okay. I'll see you tonight."

Julian pulled her in for one more kiss that turned into two, three, five—

"Mm." Charlotte pulled back and laughed. "Sorry, I really have to go. Good night. I mean, I'll see you tonight—"

He chuckled. "See you then."

Julian waited for Charlotte to disappear around the corner before returning to Harper's room. He watched TV with her until he had to leave for the library, with the promise that he'd be back after five to take her home.

Harper hadn't been to Julian's apartment yet. She'd hung out at the heroes' base after the battle, insisting that she didn't want to step foot in her new home until her wings were gone. "New home, new me," she'd said. Julian didn't really understand it, but he was happy to let her stay at the base while he cleaned up his spare bedroom and got everything ready for her.

His library shift was fine, but it dragged by slower than usual. The woman working the front desk today apparently noticed him throwing frequent glances at the clock, because she caught his attention when he walked by around four.

"You waiting for something?" she asked.

Julian paused in front of her desk, holding a stack of returned books. "Sort of. I'm picking up my sister from the hospital at the end of my shift."

"You have a sister?"

"Yeah. Adopted," Julian said. "We...lost our father recently."

"Oh, I'm sorry."

"Don't be. He was terrible." Julian adjusted the books in his hands. "Anyway, she's moving into my place. But she had surgery this morning. It's a lot." He glanced at the receptionist's name tag. Lisa.

"Sounds like it," Lisa replied. "You know, I don't think I've heard you talk this much before."

Julian hadn't spoken much to his coworkers in the past. He'd never seen the point. But... "I've been through a lot, the past few days."

Lisa chuckled. "I think we all have," she said.

Right.

"Hey, your girlfriend's designing our posters for the Teller signing, right?" Lisa asked. "I think Pete said something about it."

"Yeah, she is."

"You should bring her to the employee party this weekend. We're going to a place called Gerard's."

"I'm familiar," Julian said. "I'll let her know. I'm sure she'd love to." Love to watch him embarrass himself again, that was. But his memories of singing karaoke with her, vague as they were, made him smile as he walked away.

CHAPTER FIFTY-ONE

Julian managed to survive the last hour of his shift, slow as it was. After he clocked out and waved goodbye to Lisa, he walked to the garage where his car waited and drove back to the hospital.

"Hey, nerd," Harper said when he walked back into her room. The nurse had helped her change into sweatpants and a t-shirt with a frog on it. "How are your books?"

"The books are great," Julian replied. "Are you ready to go?"

"Hell yeah. Let's get out of here." Harper swung her legs over the edge of the bed. She yelped in pain when her feet hit the ground. "Ow!"

"Do you need me to carry you?"

"No," Harper answered defensively. "Just stand there so I can lean all my body weight against you."

Rolling his eyes, he let her wrap an arm around him. Slowly but surely, they made their way to the front desk to check out—Harper refused the wheelchair they offered—and then to his car. He helped her into the passenger seat.

The drive was almost as agonizingly slow as Julian's shift at the library. And evening traffic didn't help. He could hardly contain his excitement as they pulled up to his apartment building. He squeezed into the last open street parking spot, climbed out of the car, and circled around to Harper's side.

"So, I could totally walk up all those stairs," Harper said when he opened the door. "But how about you carry me anyway? You know, to save time."

"Sure." He helped her out of the car and carried her up to the front door of his apartment.

"Hey, Julian, I think you left your lights on," Harper said. "That's kind of embarrassing. Do you know how much electricity costs?"

"Yeah, I know." Julian set her down and reached for the door handle.

"And you can't even steal stuff to pay bills anymore, so…"

The door opened, and they were greeted by the sight of Charlotte, Spencer, Wendy, Jack, and Cassidy waiting in the entryway.

"Surprise!" Cassidy and Jack exclaimed in unison. They must have found Julian's closet of cleaning supplies, because Cassidy was clutching a broom, and Jack held a duster in their hand.

Harper blinked. "They're not moving in too, are they?"

Spencer laughed. "No, we just came to bring by some gifts. Come here."

They all moved into the living room, where the massive TV monitor from the Complex had been set up. Along with…

"No way." Harper grinned. "The new Joybox? Where'd you find it?"

"This tiny video game store near Gerard's," Spencer answered as Julian helped Harper across the room. "I don't think most people realize it's there. We got a ton of games for it, too."

"And all your old stuff from the Complex," Charlotte added. "We cleaned the place out right after Julian killed Blazar, before the police could raid it."

"At least, I think all your stuff's there," Spencer added. "I wasn't totally sure what was video game consoles and what was Saturn's tech, so I just threw it all in a box."

Harper sank to the ground in front of the console and picked it up. Tears brimmed her eyes. "Oh my god."

Julian knelt down next to her and smiled. "Are you crying?"

"I'm not crying! Julian, your apartment's full of dust."

Jack glanced at the duster in their hand. "But I just…"

"Hey, about we eat?" Wendy suggested, resting a hand on her hip. "I've been on my feet all day."

"Great idea." Spencer clapped his hands together. "Come on, everyone, into the kitchen."

Everyone moved from the living room into the kitchen, somehow managing to make the spacious apartment look cramped. "Sorry, I only have four chairs," Julian told the heroes as they swarmed the dining table. He helped Harper into one of them. "Find a seat wherever you can. Or stand."

"Guess you'll have to buy some more," Jack said as they moved to stand between Cassidy and Wendy.

Julian smiled. "Guess so."

While the others finished settling into various spaces around the table, Spencer brought over boxes of pizza.

"I know you liked stealing pizza from this place," Julian said to Harper as Spencer set the boxes down. "And that you hated you couldn't order delivery because the Complex didn't have a front door."

Harper lifted the lid of the top box and grinned. Before Julian could ask if they'd gotten the right ingredients, she pulled the entire box into her lap and started on her first piece.

"Guess we'll start on this box, then," Spencer said, opening the lid of the next one.

While everyone ate, Cassidy told them all about how she'd captured Night Sword the night before, using her new lasso. Jack followed with a story of how they'd run into Wrecking Ball while chasing some bank robbers, and that the guy had said he'd reconsider joining their group.

"He did ask if we had a name," Jack said. "I told him we're still working on it."

Not long after that, the heroes said their goodbyes and headed for the door. Julian held it open for them as they filed out.

"Thank you all for your help," Julian told them as they left.

Spencer was the last one out. He paused and smiled at Julian. "I think it's about time I formally apologized for beating you up. And punching you in the face."

Julian waved his hand. "No need to apologize. I deserved it."

"Correct answer." Spencer waved as he stepped out. "Good night!"

Julian let out a sigh that was nearly a laugh. "You too." He closed the door.

He returned to the kitchen, and from there, he and Charlotte led Harper down the hallway to the room he'd set up for her. It was pretty bare at the moment. He'd mostly been concerned with getting her bedding.

"Once you're feeling better, we can go buy you new clothes and whatever else you need," Julian told Harper as she eased onto the bed.

"Okay." Harper sniffed. She had tears in her eyes again. "I didn't know people could be so nice."

"Really, it's nothing—" Julian started.

Harper punched him in the arm. "Not you, dumbass. The other heroes."

Charlotte chuckled. Julian smiled. "Yeah, they're pretty great," he said.

Harper sniffed again. "Is that what a family's supposed to be like?" she asked quietly.

Memories came rushing over Julian. His parents driving him to the hospital when he fell off the roof and broke his arm. The neighbors bringing them cookies. Family friends visiting for dinner, eating food Julian helped his parents cook. Birthday parties. Movie nights.

"Yeah," Julian said, barely holding back the sudden wave of emotion. Maybe if he hadn't spent so many years trying to forget his old life, the pain of it wouldn't feel so sharp. He straightened up. "Hey, if you're feeling better Monday, Ray said we could go down to Skyline and he'd show you around. One of the counselors can help you figure out what online courses you need to take over the summer."

"You said you'd start teaching me how to drive on Monday," Harper reminded him.

"We can do that after." Julian rubbed the back of his neck. "And don't forget you have your therapy appointment on Tuesday."

"I thought that was you."

"I'm Thursdays."

"Okay." Harper scooted further back onto the bed.

"Do you need anything?" Julian asked. "Wendy brought by painkillers, if your back still hurts."

Harper gave him a weak smile. "I'm okay. Just exhausted." She looked around. "Hey, could we put a TV in here?"

"That's not happening. But I'll grab you my laptop, if you want to watch something while you fall asleep."

Harper nodded. Julian and Charlotte walked back out to the living room, and Julian grabbed his laptop off the desk. Charlotte grabbed the backpack she'd left sitting on the couch.

"You're making enough at the library to keep this place, right?" Charlotte asked as they returned to the hallway.

"I'll manage," Julian said. "And I've got a lot in savings—"

Charlotte lifted an eyebrow.

"—that I'm mostly going to donate to the city to help pay for the damage I caused." Julian cleared his throat. "But I did set aside a lot of what I actually earned. And I was thinking I'd sell the Porsche, too."

"Really?"

"Yeah. It might be good to get something with more than two doors."

Charlotte laughed. "Good. We need more people to take turns driving us all around."

Julian handed the laptop off to Harper. She opened it and frowned. "What the hell is your desktop background?"

Julian's brow furrowed. "It's the default setting."

"Yeah. It's weird."

"It's a beach."

"Like I said. Weird." Harper rolled her eyes. "Don't worry, I'll find something cooler for you."

"Can't wait." Julian headed for the door. "Good night, Harper."

"Good night."

Julian closed Harper's door, took Charlotte's hand, and led her to his room farther down the hall.

"So," Charlotte said as they entered. She eyed the row of plants in his window. "I see you've added to your collection."

"I thought the one you gave me might want a few friends."

Charlotte laughed. She reached her free hand into her bag and pulled out her tablet. "Okay, my posters…"

They sat down on the bed. Charlotte swiped through her designs advertising the book signing event. Their hands stayed together as she talked, explaining her design process while Julian hung on to every word.

"They're all great," Julian said when she was done.

"We can't do all of them," Charlotte replied, laughing. "You have to pick one. Or maybe two."

"Three?"

"All right, we'll narrow it down to three." Charlotte looked at him and raised an eyebrow. "Which ones?"

"I need to think on it," Julian told her.

"Fine." Charlotte leaned over to set the tablet on the nightstand. "We'll choose first thing in the morning."

"Well, maybe second or third thing. How about we come to a decision after breakfast?"

"Okay, but breakfast better not get interrupted by someone committing arson downtown like it did yesterday." Charlotte leaned forward to kiss him.

"Please," Julian said slyly once they pulled apart. "That guy took us five minutes to stop. He didn't even have fire powers, just way too many lighters."

"Way too many," Charlotte agreed. "Oh, unrelated, my parents wanted to know if we would get dinner with them when they visit."

"Sounds great," Julian said. "Are you going to tell them you're Stormbringer?"

She shook her head. "God, no. They'd be worried sick. Plus, I'd have to explain the Citadel thing to them, too."

"They might be confused by the fact that you're…taller." As Julian said the words, he slid a hand up her muscled arm. "Among other things."

Charlotte blushed. "I'll think of something."

"I'm sure you will." Julian leaned in. "By the way, you're invited to come with me to the employee party at Gerard's this weekend."

"I'm in." Charlotte kissed him. When she pulled away, she lifted her hand and brushed her thumb across his lip. He wrapped his arms around her and pulled her into a deeper kiss.

Maybe Julian could have stolen the Eye of the Storm, all of New Atlas, the entire world. But he'd never have been able to steal this.

And Charlotte was worth more than the world, anyway.

Thank you for reading
VILLAIN COMPLEX

To get updates and find out how you can be the first to read
new books, find me at:

www.rorynorth.com

If you enjoyed the story, please help support this indie
author!
Tell a friend, leave reviews, request the book at your local
library, and talk about it on social media! #villaincomplex

A Drop of Haunted Blood: After a magician kills his family, Felix discovers his latent ability to bind ghosts to his soul and wield their magical abilities.

Van Terra: Cyborg thief Jasper Van Terra is after revenge. Escaped lab experiment Grace Alvarez might be just what she needs.

Plague Saint: In a frozen city in the distant future, Winter Pierce kills the hospital's Plague Saint to save her mother after discovering his corruption. When she steals his identity, she quickly finds herself tangled up in a government conspiracy.

Be the first to know about new stories and upcoming releases! Sign up for my newsletter at:

rorynorth.com/starchatter

VILLAIN
COMPLEX
Rory North